I'd KNOW You Anywhere

LAURA LIPPMAN

wm
WILLIAM MORROW
An Imprint of HarperCollins*Publishers*

This book is a work of fiction. References to real people, events, establishments, organizations, or locales are intended only to provide a sense of authenticity, and are used fictitiously. All other characters, and all incidents and dialogue, are drawn from the author's imagination and are not to be construed as real.

This book was originally published in hardcover in 2010 by William Morrow, an imprint of HarperCollins Publishers.

HarperCollins books may be purchased for educational, business, or sales promotional use. For information please write: Special Markets Department, HarperCollins Publishers, 10 East 53rd Street, New York, NY 10022.

FIRST WILLIAM MORROW PAPERBACK EDITION PUBLISHED 2011.

Designed by Jamie Lynn Kerner

Library of Congress Cataloging-in-Publication Data has been applied for.

ISBN 978-0-06-207075-3

11 12 13 14 15 OV/BVG 10 9 8 7 6 5 4 3 2 1

Praise for Laura Lippman and *I'd Know You Anywhere*

"Lippman is at the height of her powers here, smoothly alternating between the horrors of Eliza's fifteenth summer and her present, excruciating, dilemma—does she respond, hoping to quiet Walter and preserve her hard-won privacy, or ignore him and risk his wrath? Sensitively examining capital punishment from every side, Lippman delivers an emotionally complex drama that cements her reputation as one of the smartest crime writers around." —*People*

"She's one of the best novelists around, period." —*Washington Post*

"How likely is it that a suburban wife and mother who was kidnapped at age fifteen and held for almost six weeks by a rapist and murderer would let her former captor con her into visiting him on death row? The odds don't look great, but then again, a good writer, like a clever sociopath, can talk people into all kinds of improbable situations. Laura Lippman is quite a good writer, and in her creepy psychological-suspense novel, *I'd Know You Anywhere*, she sets up this bizarre scenario as a way to examine the power that comes from intimate knowledge of another person." —*New York Times Book Review*

"*I'd Know You Anywhere* ranks with her very best." —Associated Press

"This is a story that grips you not with suspense but with its acute psychological autopsy of a survivor. Lippman's knack for elucidating the horrors humans can inflict on one another through violence and manipulation—while telling a compelling story—is disarming and fascinating." —*USA Today*

"Award-winning Lippman continues to send depth charges into the sea of crime fiction, taking measure of psychic pain in the wake of violence, and the mysteries of memory. . . . Stoked by stinging dialogue and arresting evocations of the fog of fear, doubt, and guilt versus the laser-lock pursuit of survival, Lippman's taut, mesmerizing, and exceptionally smart drama of predator and prey is at once unusually sensitive and utterly compelling." —*Booklist* (starred review)

"Ex-journalist Lippman never forgets as she moves from past to present and from perspective to perspective that nothing is more important—or more elusive—than the truth." —*Kirkus Reviews*

"[An] outstanding novel of psychological suspense. . . ."
—*Publishers Weekly* (starred review)

"*I'd Know You Anywhere* continues Laura Lippman's extraordinary run of stand-alone novels. . . . From its unsettling opening to its breathtaking conclusion, *Anywhere* exemplifies Lippman's strengths: compassion, intense prose and deep empathy for the snares of ambiguous emotions." —*Seattle Times*

"Laura Lippman is one of those uncommonly talented authors whose work continues to get better in every book she writes. *I'd Know You Anywhere* is a riveting psychological suspense novel."
—*Globe and Mail* (Toronto)

"The alchemy of memory and fact, of guilt and surviving, and the relationship between predator and prey meld in the superior psychological thriller *I'd Know You Anywhere*. . . . Once again, Lippman shows she understands the human heart, the power of love and the value of self-preservation. Lippman . . . delivers thorough character studies in the superb *I'd Know You Anywhere*." —*Kansas City Star*

"*I'd Know You Anywhere* is a crime story, but it's not a whodunit. Rather, it's an exquisitely sensitive story about the psychological impact of crime on its victims. It's a story about shame, about anger, about survivor's guilt." —*Fort Worth Star-Telegram*

"*I'd Know You Anywhere* is compelling reading, its socially-conscious topic putting me in mind of Jodi Picoult's books. . . . Ms. Lippman appears to inhabit her characters with ease, switching voices—and in the case of Eliza, ages—convincingly. She channels serial-killer Walter with aplomb. . . . Ms. Lippman's writing is eminently readable. The action is unpacked slowly, suspensefully, in tightly-constructed chapters that are real page-turners. . . . *I'd Know You Anywhere* should make any lover of contemporary crime fiction happy." —*Seattle Post-Intelligencer*

I'd KNOW You Anywhere

ALSO BY LAURA LIPPMAN

The Girl in the Green Raincoat

Life Sentences

Hardly Knew Her

Another Thing to Fall

What the Dead Know

No Good Deeds

To the Power of Three

By a Spider's Thread

Every Secret Thing

The Last Place

In a Strange City

The Sugar House

In Big Trouble

Butchers Hill

Charm City

Baltimore Blues

For Dorothy and Bernie

Part I

I'D KNOW YOU ANYWHERE

1

"ISO, TIME FOR—"

Eliza Benedict paused at the foot of the stairs. Time for what, exactly? All summer long—it was now August—Eliza had been having trouble finding the right words. Not complicated ones, the things required to express strong emotions or abstract concepts, make difficult confessions to loved ones. She groped for the simplest words imaginable, everyday nouns. She was only thirty-eight. What would her mind be like at fifty, at seventy? Yet her own mother was sharp as a tack at the age of seventy-seven.

No, this was clearly a temporary, transitional problem, a consequence of the family's return to the States after six years in England. Ironic, because Eliza had scrupulously avoided Briticisms while living there;

she thought Americans who availed themselves of local slang were pretentious. Yet home again, she couldn't get such words—*lift, lorry, quid, loo*—out of her head, her mouth. The result was that she was often tongue-tied, as she was now. Not at a loss for words, as the saying would have it, but overwhelmed with words, weighed down with words, drowning in them.

She started over, projecting her voice up the stairs without actually yelling, a technique in which she took great pride. "Iso, time for football camp."

"Soccer," her daughter replied in a muffled, yet clearly scornful voice, her default tone since turning thirteen seven months ago. There was a series of slamming and banging noises, drawers and doors, and when she spoke again, Iso's voice was clearer. (Where had her head been just moments ago, in the laundry hamper, inside her jersey, *in the toilet*? Eliza had a lot of fears, so far unfounded, about eating disorders.) "Why is it that you called it soccer when everyone else said football, and now you say football when you know it's supposed to be soccer?"

At least I remembered to call you Iso.

"It's your camp and you're the one who hates to be late."

"Football is better," said Albie, hovering at Eliza's elbow. Just turned eight, he was still young enough to enjoy being by—and on—Eliza's side.

"Better as a word, or better as a sport?"

"As a word, for soccer," he said. "It's closer to being right. Because it's mainly feet, and sometimes heads. And hands, for the goalie. While American football is more hands than feet—they don't kick it so much. They throw and carry it."

"Which do you like better, as a sport?"

"Soccer for playing, American football for watching." Albie, to Eliza's knowledge, had never seen a single minute of American football. But he believed that affection should be apportioned evenly. At dinner, Albie tried to eat so that he finished all his food at about the same time, lest his peas suspect that he preferred his chicken.

Isobel—*Iso*—clattered down the stairs, defiant in her spikes, which she wasn't supposed to wear in the house. At least she was ready, in full uniform, her hair in a French braid, which she had somehow managed to do herself. Eliza couldn't help raising a hand to her own head of messy red curls, wondering anew how she had given birth to this leggy creature with her sleek hair and sleek limbs and sleek social instincts. Isobel had her father's coloring—the olive skin and dark hair—but otherwise could have been a lanky changeling.

"Are we snack family today?" she asked, imperious as a duchess.

"No—"

"Are you sure?"

"Yes —"

"It would be *horrible* to forget," Iso said.

"Horrible?" Eliza echoed, trying not to smile.

"Almost as bad as the first time we were snack family and you brought that disgusting jerky."

"Biltong from Daddy's trip to South Africa," Albie said, dreamy with remembering. "I liked it."

"You would," his sister said.

"Don't squabble," Eliza said.

"I don't." Albie was not only keen to be fair, but accurate. His sister was the instigator in almost all their disagreements. Iso rolled her eyes.

They never used to fight, even in this one-sided fashion. They had been close, if only because Albie worshipped Iso, and Iso enjoyed being worshipped. But when they left London, Iso decided she had no use for Albie's adulation. To Eliza's dismay, she appeared to have conducted a ruthless inventory of her life, jettisoning everything that threatened her newly invented self, from her little brother to the last syllable of her name, that innocuous and lovely "bel." ("Iso?" Peter had said. "People will think it's short for Isotope. Shouldn't it be Izzo?" Iso had rolled her eyes.) A freckled, redheaded little brother—prone to nightmares and odd pronouncements, not English, but not quite American again, not yet—did not fit Iso's new image. Nor did her mother, but Eliza expected no less. It was the slights against Albie that she found unbearable.

"Did you remember our chairs?" Albie asked his mother.

"They're in the—" She stopped herself from saying *boot*. "Trunk."

Iso was not appeased. "It's not a trunk. It's a luggage compartment."

Eliza hustled the children into the car, a Subaru Forester in which she already spent much of her days, and would probably spend even more hours once school started.

At 8:30 A.M., the day was already hot; Eliza wondered if the camp would cancel, after all. There was some sort of formula, involving temperature, humidity, and air quality, that mandated the suspension of outdoor activities. Other mothers probably checked the Internet, or had an alert programmed into their mobiles—*cell phones*—but Eliza had long ago accepted that she was never going to be that kind of a mother.

Besides, this was a private camp, and a very macho one, with serious aspirations and a pronounced Anglophilia. Iso's six years in London provided her great cachet, and she pretended to a much grander knowledge of UK soccer than she had acquired while living there. Eliza had marveled at how she did it: a few sessions at the computer, reading the UK newspapers and Wikipedia, and Iso could pass herself off as quite the expert, chatting about Manchester United and Arsenal, professing to be a fan of Tottenham Hotspurs, which she breezily called the Spurs. Eliza was torn between admiration and disapproval for her daughter's social ambitions, not to mention her ability to execute them. She tried to tell herself that Iso's adaptability would keep her safe in this world, yet she worried far more about calculating Iso than she did about trusting Albie. Cynics fooled themselves into thinking they had sussed out the worst-case scenarios and were invariably surprised by how life trumped them. Dreamers were often disappointed—but seldom in themselves. Eliza had installed spyware on the computer and monitored Iso's IM sessions, which appeared benign enough. Now Iso was pushing for her own phone, but Eliza wasn't sure if she could track text messages. She would have to seek the advice of other mothers—assuming she eventually made friends with any.

On the shade-deprived field, she set up the portable camp chairs, casting a covetous glance at the in-the-know mothers who had umbrellas attached to their chairs or, in the case of one super-prepared type, a portable canopy. Eliza wished she had known, back in June, that such things existed, but she probably wouldn't have availed herself of them anyway. She had felt decadent enough purchasing chairs with little mesh cup holders. She and Albie settled in under the unforgiving sun, Albie reading, with no sense of self-consciousness, *Diary of a Wimpy Kid,* Eliza pretending to follow Iso's progress through the drills. She was actually eavesdropping. Although the other mothers—and it was all mothers, with the exception of one laid-off father who inhabited his Mr. Mom role with a little too much gusto for Eliza's taste—were kind, they had quickly ascertained that Eliza's children were not attending the same schools as theirs, which apparently meant there was no reason to befriend her.

"—on the sex offenders list."

What? Eliza willed the other ambient noises to fall away and honed in on this one conversation.

"Really?"

"I signed up for telephone notification with the county. The guy lives five doors down from us."

"Child sex offender or just regular sex offender?"

"Child, third degree. I looked him up on the state's site."

"What does that mean, third degree?"

"I don't know. But any degree has to be bad news."

"And he's in Chevy Chase?"

Long pause. "Well, we do have a Chevy Chase mailing address."

Eliza smiled to herself. She knew from her family's own real estate search how people fudged certain addresses, that even within this very desirable county, one of the richest in the United States, there were hierarchies upon hierarchies. Which was worse: having a child sex offender on your block, or admitting you didn't live in Chevy Chase proper? The Benedicts lived in Bethesda, and Peter had made sure there wasn't a sex offender, child or adult, within a six-block radius, although one of their neighbors, a sixty-year-old civil service employee, had been picked up for soliciting in a bathroom at the Smithsonian.

The game done—Iso won it for her team on a penalty kick, a victory she carried lightly, gracefully—the Benedicts got back into the car and headed into the long, endless summer day. The heat was pronounced now; it would reach into the upper nineties for the third day in a row, and the lack of trees in this raw, new development made it feel even hotter. That was one thing Eliza loved unreservedly about their new house, the greenness of the neighborhood. Full of mature shade trees, it felt five to ten degrees cooler than the business district along nearby Wisconsin Avenue. It reminded Eliza of Roaring Springs, the revitalized Baltimore mill village where she had grown up, which backed up to a state park. Her family didn't even have air-conditioning, only a series of window fans, yet it was always cool enough to sleep back then. Then again, her memory might be exaggerating. Roaring Springs had taken on a slightly mythic air in the Lerner folklore. It was to them what Moscow had been to Chekhov's three sisters. No, Moscow was a place where the sisters were always intending to go, whereas Roaring Springs was the place that the Lerners were forced to leave, through no fault of their own.

Eliza stopped at Trader Joe's, which the children considered a treat in the way the "real" grocery store was not. She let them pick out one snack each while she roamed the aisles, bemused by the store's arbitrary offerings, the way things came and went without explanation. At summer's beginning, she and Albie had discovered the loveliest ginger cookies, large and soft, but they had never appeared again, and it seemed wrong, somehow, to inquire after them. "It must be a relief," the wives of Peter's new coworkers had said upon meeting her, "to have real grocery stores again." American attitudes about England seemed to have gelled circa 1974, at least among those who hadn't traveled there. The wives assumed her life abroad had been one of cold deprivation, huddling next to an inadequate space heater while being force-fed kidney pie and black puddings.

Yet the same Americans who believed that England was a land of material deprivation gave the UK too much credit for culture, assuming it was nothing but Shakespeare and the BBC. Eliza had found it even more celebrity-obsessed than the US. Germaine Greer had appeared on *Big Brother* during their time there, and it had depressed Eliza beyond reason. But then all television, the omnipresence of screens in modern life, depressed her. She hated the way her children, and even her husband, froze in their tracks, instantly hypnotized by a television or a computer.

"Some people," Albie announced from the backseat, "have DVD players in their cars." He had an eerie knack for picking up Eliza's wavelength at times, as if her brain were a radio whose dial he could spin and tune. His voice was sweet, wondering, sharing a fun fact, nothing more. Yet he had made the same point once or twice every week since they had bought the new car.

"You'd throw up," Iso said. "You get motion sick *reading*." Said as if the very act of reading was suspect.

"I don't think I will here," he said. "That was just in England." For Albie, England was synonymous with being a little boy, and he had decided that whatever troubled him there had been left behind, that it was all past. No more nightmares, he had decreed, and just like that, they were over, or else he was doing a good job of white-knuckling his way to morning. A picky eater, he also had decided to reinvent himself as an adventurous one. Today, he had chosen chili-pepper cashews as his treat. Eliza had a hunch he wouldn't like them much, but the rule was that the children could select whatever they wanted, no recriminations, even if the food went to waste. What was the point of giving children freedom to experiment and fail, if one then turned it all into a tiresome object lesson? When Albie picked a snack that was, for him, inedible, Eliza sympathized and offered to substitute something from the nearby convenience store. Iso, meanwhile, stuck to the tried-and-true, almost babyish snacks like Pirate's Booty and frogurt. Iso was a thirty-five-year-old divorcée in her head, a three-year-old in her stomach.

Yet—mirabile dictu—Albie liked the cashews. After lunch, he put them in a bowl and carried them out to the family room with his "cocktail," a mix of Hawaiian Punch and seltzer. Peter had entertained a lot in his former job, and Eliza worried that London's more liquid culture had made too vivid an impression on her son. But it was clearly the ceremony, the visuals, that excited him—the bright colors of the drinks, the tiny dishes of finger food. Eliza could stomach very little alcohol. It was one of those changes that had arrived during pregnancy and never went away. Pregnancy had also changed her body, but for the better. Bony and waistless into her twenties, she had developed a flattering lushness after Iso's birth, at once curvy and compact.

The only person who disapproved of Eliza's body was Iso, who modeled herself on, well, models. Specifically, the wannabe models on a dreadful television show, an American one that had been inexplicably popular in England. Iso's sole complaint about the relocation to the States was that the show was a year ahead here and therefore a season had been "spoiled" for her. "They give away the winner in the opening credits!" she wailed. Yet she watched the reruns, which appeared to be on virtually every day, indifferent to the fact that she knew the outcome. She was watching an episode now while Albie stealthily tried to close the distance between them, advancing inch by inch along the carpet.

"Stop breathing so loud," Iso said.

"Loudly," Eliza corrected.

The afternoon stretched before them, inert yet somehow demanding, like a guest who had shown up with a suitcase full of dirty laundry. Eliza felt they should do something constructive, but Iso refused the offer of shopping for school clothes, and Peter had asked that they hold off the annual trip to Staples until this weekend. Peter loved shopping for school supplies, if only because it allowed him to perform his own version of the commercial, the one in which the parent danced ecstatically to "The Most Wonderful Time of the Year." (Peter could get away with things that Iso would never permit Eliza to do.) The Benedicts didn't belong to the local pool, which had a cap on memberships, and it was too hot to do anything else outdoors. Eliza got out drawing supplies and asked the children to sketch ideas for their rooms, promising that they could paint the walls whatever colors they desired, pick out new furniture at Ikea. Iso pretended to be bored but eventually began using the computer to research various beds, and Eliza was impressed by her daughter's taste, which ran toward simple things. Albie produced a gorgeous jungle forest of a room, filled with dinosaurs, his current passion. Probably not reproducible, at Ikea or any other store, but it was a striking feat of the imagination. She praised them both, gave them Popsicles, indulged in a cherry one herself. Perhaps they should save the sticks for some future project? Even before Peter had taken a job at an environmentally conscious investment firm, the Benedicts had been dutiful recyclers.

Mail clattered through the slot, a jolt of excitement on this long, stifling afternoon. "I'll get it!" Albie screamed, not that he had any competition. A mere six months ago, his sister had scrapped with him over an endless list of privileges, invoking primogeniture. Fetching the mail, having first choice of muffin at breakfast, answering the phone, pushing elevator buttons. She was beyond all that now.

Albie sorted the mail on the kitchen counter. "Daddy, bill, junk, catalog. Daddy, junk. Junk. Junk. Daddy. Mommy! A real letter."

A real letter? Who would write her a real letter? Who wrote anyone real letters? Her sister, Vonnie, was given to revisiting old grudges, but those missives usually went to their parents via e-mail. Eliza studied the plain white envelope, from a PO box in Baltimore. Did she even know anyone in Baltimore anymore? The handwriting, in purple ink, was meticulous enough to be machine-created. Probably junk mail masquerading as a real letter, a sleazy trick.

But, no, this one was quite authentic, a sheaf of loose-leaf paper and a cutting from a glossy magazine, a photo of Peter and Elizabeth at a party for Peter's work earlier this summer. The handwriting was fussy and feminine, unknown to her, yet the tone was immediately, insistently intimate.

Dear Elizabeth,

I'm sure this is a shock, although that's not my intention, to shock you. Up until a few weeks ago, I never thought I would have any communication with you at all and accepted that as fair. That's how it's been for more than twenty years now. But it's hard to ignore signs when they are right there in front of your face, and there was your photo, in Washingtonian *magazine, not the usual thing I read, but you'd be surprised by my choice of reading material these days. Of course, you are older, a woman now. You've been a woman for a while, obviously. Still, I'd know you anywhere.*

"Who's it from, Mommy?" Albie asked, and even Iso seemed mildly interested in this oddity, a letter to her mother, a person whose name appeared mostly on catalogs and reminders from the dentist. Could they see her hands shaking, notice the cold sweat on her brow? Eliza wanted to crumple the letter in her fist, heave it away from her, but that would only excite their curiosity.

"Someone I knew when I was growing up."

It looks as if they'll finally get around to completing my sentence soon. I'm not trying to avoid saying the big words—death, execution, what have you—just being very specific. It is my sentence, after all. I was sentenced to die and I am at peace with that.

I thought I was at peace across the board, but then I saw your photo. And, odd as it might seem to some, I feel it's you that I owe the greatest apology, that you're the person I never made amends to, the crime I was never called into account for. I'm sure others feel differently, but they'll see me dead soon enough and then they will be happy, or so they think. I also accept that you might not be that interested in hearing from me and, in fact, I have engaged in a little subterfuge to get this letter to you, via a sympathetic third party, a person I absolutely trust. This is her handwriting, not mine, in case you care, and by sending it via her, I have avoided the problem of prying eyes, as much for your protection as for mine. But I can't help being curious about your life, which must be pretty nice, if your husband has the kind of job that leads to being photographed at the kind of parties that end up in Washingtonian, *with him in a tux and you in an evening dress. You look very different, yet the same, if that makes any sense. I'm proud of you, Elizabeth, and would love to hear from you. Sooner rather than later, ha-ha!*

Yours, Walter

And then—just in case she didn't remember the full name of the man who had kidnapped her the summer she was fifteen and held her hostage for almost six weeks, just in case she might have another acquaintance on death row, just in case she had forgotten the man who had killed at least two other girls and was suspected of killing many others, yet let her live, just in case all of this might have slipped her mind—he added helpfully:

(Walter Bowman)

2

1984

WALTER BOWMAN WAS GOOD-LOOKING. Anyone who said otherwise was contrary, or not to be trusted. He had dark hair and green eyes and skin that took a tan well, although it was a farmer's tan. He wasn't a farmer, actually, but a mechanic, working in his father's garage. Still, the result was the same, as far as his tan went. He would have liked to work with his shirt off on warm days, but his father wouldn't hear of it.

He was good-looking enough that his family teased him about it, as if to make sure he wouldn't get conceited. Yes, he was a little on the short side, but so were most movie stars. Claude, at the barbershop, had explained this to him. Not that Claude compared Walter to a movie star—Claude, like his family, like everyone else in town, seemed intent on keeping Walter in his place. But Claude mentioned one day that he had seen Chuck Norris at a casino in Las Vegas.

"He's an itty-bitty fella. But, then, all movie stars are little," Claude said, finishing up. Walter loved the feel of the brush on the back of his neck. "They have big heads, but small bodies."

"How little?" Walter had asked.

"The size of my thumb," Claude said.

"No, seriously."

"Five seven, five eight. 'Bout your size."

That was what Walter wanted to hear. If Chuck Norris was about his size, well, that was almost the same as Walter being like Chuck Norris. Still, he needed to make one small clarification for the record.

"I'm five nine. That's average height for a man, did you know that? Five nine for a man, five four for a woman."

"Is that the average," Claude asked, "or the median? There's a difference, you know."

Walter didn't know the difference. He might have asked, but he suspected Claude didn't really know either, and all he would get was Claude making fun of his ignorance.

"Average," he said.

"Well someone has to be average," said Claude, who was tall, but skinny and kind of pink all over—splotchy skin, pale, pale red hair, watery eyes that were permanently narrowed from years of staring at the hair that lay across his barber scissors. Everyone was always trying to put Walter in his place, keep him down, stop him from being what he might be. Even women, girls, seemed to be part of the conspiracy. Because, despite Walter's good looks, he could not find a woman who wanted to go with him, not even on a single date. He couldn't figure it out. Things would start out okay, he could get a conversation going. He read things, he knew things, he kept an interesting store of facts at his disposal. Claude's Chuck Norris story, for example, became one of his anecdotes, although he added his own flourish, holding his thumb and forefinger out to show just how itty-bitty Chuck Norris was. That usually got a laugh, or at least a smile.

But then something would happen, he could never put his finger on what, and the girl's face would close to him. It was a small town, and it soon seemed there wasn't a girl in it who would consider going out with Walter Bowman. And on the rare occasion when a new family moved in, one with daughters, someone must have told them something, because they didn't want to go with him either.

Then, one day, on an errand for his father, he saw a girl walking down the road just outside Martinsburg. It was hot, and she wore shorts over a lavender bathing suit, a one-piece. He liked that she wore a one-piece. Modest. He offered her a ride.

She hesitated.

"Wherever you're going," Walter added. "Door-to-door service. Truck's air-conditioning is so cold, you'll need a sweater."

It was cold. He saw what it did to her breasts when she got in. They were large for such a short girl, not that he let his eyes linger. He looked only once.

"Where you going?" he asked.

"The Rite Aid," she said. "I want to buy some makeup, but my mother says I can't. It's my money, isn't it?"

"You don't need makeup." He meant it as a compliment, yet she flushed, balled up her fists as if to fight him. "I mean, you're lucky, you look good without it, but you're right. It's your money, you should be able to do with it what you want." He couldn't quite stop himself. Maybe that was the problem, that he just couldn't stop talking soon enough. "Although you shouldn't buy anything illegal with it, drugs or whatever. Just say no."

She rolled her eyes. She was a girl, not as old as he had thought when he first picked her up. Maybe no more than fifteen, but she clearly considered herself more sophisticated than Walter. Was that it? Was that why girls like this were forever eeling away from him? There were some girls—plain, slow witted—who didn't mind his company, but Walter couldn't get interested in just anybody. He was good-looking. He should be with someone as good-looking or better-looking. Everyone knew that was how it worked. A beautiful woman could go with the ugliest man on the planet, but a man had to date above himself, or be shamed. He deserved someone special.

"I smoke pot," this girl announced.

He didn't believe her. "You like it?"

The question seemed to catch her off guard, as if that wasn't the point, liking it or not liking it. "Yeah," she said, as if it were a guess. She probably didn't know the difference between average or median either, although Walter did now. He had looked it up. He always looked things up when he didn't know them. No one had to be stupid. Stupid was a choice. He was forever learning things. He knew all the US state capitals and he was working on world capitals.

"What's it like?" he asked.

"You don't know?"

"No, it's not something I've gotten around to."

"You wanna find out? I got some in my purse."

He didn't, actually, but he wanted to stay in this girl's company a while longer.

"What's your name?" he asked.

"Kelly. With a *y*, but I'm thinking of changing it to an *i*. There are three Kellys in my class at school. What's your name?"

"Walt." He had never called himself that, but why not try it out, change his luck. Within the hour, they were in a little cove off the river, and she was trying to show him how to smoke pot. She said he was doing it wrong, but he was doing it wrong on purpose, wanting to keep his wits about him. He didn't believe in drugs or alcohol, but if he needed to pretend in order to spend time with this girl, Kelly, Kelli, whatever, he would. He found himself wishing she wore a two-piece. A one-piece, that wasn't going to come off easily, it wasn't something you could slip a girl out of, bit by bit. He knew he had to take it slow, but he couldn't, he just couldn't. She was lying on her stomach, on a long flat rock. He blew on her neck, thinking of Claude's brush. She wrinkled her nose, as if a bug had landed on her. He tried to give her a back rub, but she shrugged his hand off. "No," she said. His hand returned, not to her shoulder blades this time, but between her legs. "Hey," she said. "Don't." But she wasn't quite as bossy and superior now. He tried to be sweet, kiss her neck, stroke her hair. He knew from magazines that foreplay was important to girls. But things just didn't go the way they were supposed to. It was only later, when she was crying, that his mind began to catalog the possible outcomes—she would be his girlfriend, she would tell her parents, she would tell other girls, she might even tell the police, she was never going to stop crying—that he realized he had only one option.

"HOW'D YOU GET SCRATCHED UP, Walter?" his father asked at dinner that night.

"Stopped to relieve myself on the side of the road, walked right into one of those prickly bushes along the highway," he said. If someone had seen his truck parked out on Route 118, that would explain it.

"Sure took you a long time to find that fan belt."

"Like I said, I had to go all the way to Hagerstown, and they didn't have one either. I ordered it."

"Coulda sworn Pep Boys in Martinsburg said they had what I wanted in stock."

"Nope, wrong size. People in those places, they're just ignorant. No work ethic, no interest in customer service."

That was all his father needed, and he was off to the races about the death of the small businessman.

By the weekend, the local news was full of stories about the missing girl, Kelly Pratt. She'd never get a chance to change her name now, Walter realized. A week went by, a month, a season, a year. He thought of her as Kelly Brat. He had showed her who was boss. It could have been nice, she shouldn't have taken him down to the river to smoke pot, the pot was what screwed him up, he probably wouldn't have been her first, and her just fourteen, according to the news stories. Slut. Druggie. The very fact that they never found her, that he didn't get caught, that the police never came to speak to him, that no one came forward to say that they had seen Walter Bowman's pickup parked on the hill above the river that day, that they never even searched near that part of the river—all those things proved he had been right to do what he did.

He found himself taking long drives on his days off, looking for other girls who might need a ride.

3

"HA-HA," PETER MARVELED. "He actually wrote 'ha-ha.'

"If it were an e-mail, if he had access to a computer, he probably would have put an emoticon there, the one that uses a semicolon to wink at you."

Peter held the letter at arm's length, although he was not the least bit farsighted, not yet. He was actually a year younger than she was. He inspected the letter as if it were a painting, an abstract portrait of Walter Bowman, or one of those 3-D prints that had been popular for a time. Examined up close, it was words, in that furious, fastidious purple ink. At a distance, it melted into a lavender jumble, an impressionistic sketch of heather-colored hills.

Peter had arrived home at seven-thirty

that evening, early for him these days, but Eliza had waited until the children went upstairs to tell him about the letter. She might have been able to reference it covertly, using a familiar code: *the summer I was fifteen.* Over the years, this had been used to explain any number of things. Her need to leave a film that had taken an unexpected plot turn, her disinclination to wear her hair short, although the style suited her better than this not-long, not-short, not-anything haircut. Come to think of it, they hadn't used the code for some time, not since Peter returned to the States earlier this year and began house hunting on weekends.

"The Victorian that you like, it's near—well, one county over—from where Point of Rocks is," he had told her via Skype. "It's about an hour out of the city, but on the commuter line and it's really pretty up there. Lots of people do it. But I thought—"

"You thought it would bother me. Because of the summer I was fifteen." They were meeting each other's eyes, yet not meeting each other's eyes. She could never quite master that part of Skype.

"Yes."

"I'm not sure it would, but if you're willing to commute, what about Roaring Springs, where I grew up?"

"The trains on that line don't run late enough, hon. And we'd have to have two cars, because I'd have to drive to the station."

"Oh." She still wasn't sure why Point of Rocks was in contention but Roaring Springs was not. Wouldn't he need to drive to the train station out there, too? "Well, I'd rather you had less of a commute, so if we can afford something closer in, something near a Metro line, that would be my choice."

They could—barely—so they did, and that was that.

"That stupid party," he said now, still studying the letter. "And you didn't even want to go. It never occurred to me that we should worry about such things."

"Or me, to be fair. I didn't want to go to the party because, well, I didn't want to go to the party. I never thought—he never, all these years, made any overture to me, or even my parents or Vonnie, who are much easier to find, still being Lerners. Between taking your name and moving, first to Houston, then to London . . ."

Peter poured himself a glass of white wine and Eliza, as she sometimes did, took a sip. No, even as Peter upgraded the wines he drank, she still found the taste acidic, harsh. She preferred the Albie cocktail of fruit punch and seltzer.

"So, he's on death row, reading the party pages in *Washingtonian*—"

"It's almost funny. Almost."

"Are you going to write him back?"

They had been sitting on opposite ends of the sofa in the family room, her feet in his lap. Now she put his sweating wineglass on a coaster and curled up next to him, indifferent to how warm the room was, even with the house's various window units droning away. She thought once again of the house in Roaring Springs, cool on the hottest summer nights with nothing more than window fans. Global warming? The fallacy of memory? Both?

"I don't know. And the very fact that I don't know bothers me. I should be appalled, or angry. Which I am. But mainly, I just feel exposed. As if everyone knows now, as if tomorrow when I leave the house, people will look at me differently."

Peter glanced at the letter, now lying on the old chest they used as a coffee table. "No reference to the kids."

"No. All he knows is that I have a prominent husband and a green dress. But it came to our address, Peter, from a Baltimore PO box. Someone did that for him. Someone else knows."

"A woman, I'm guessing. A woman with a purple pen. Walter's sister?"

"I doubt it. His family essentially cut all ties after his arrest. They didn't even attend the trials."

She pressed her face into his neck. He smelled of an aftershave that seemed particularly British to Eliza, crisp and citrusy. She wasn't sure where it was made, only that Peter had started wearing it during their London years. Their growing-up years, as she thought of them, although two thirty-somethings with small children should have been much further along the road to being grown-ups. Peter's jobs had always dictated their sense of themselves. When he was a reporter at the *Houston Chronicle,* they had felt young and bohemian, and their lives had a catch-as-catch-can quality, right down to the funky little house in Montrose. His jump to the *Wall Street Journal* had dovetailed with the arrival of the children, but they remained in Montrose, although minus the wild parties for which they had been known, parties famous for benign drunkenness and unexpected couplings. At least three marriages in their circle had started at one of their parties, and two had ended. It was as if Peter, with his serious, stuffy job at the *Journal*—not to mention a wife and children—needed to prove he was still a young man.

London changed that. They were certifiable grown-ups within months of arriving there, and Eliza wasn't sure if that was because of Peter's job, as bureau chief, or the city itself. Perhaps their newfound maturity was a result of the sheer distance from everything and everyone they had known. Now, back in the States, she felt old, on the verge of dowdy. Yet her own mother didn't even have her first child until she was thirty-six and remained exuberantly youthful in her seventies. Maybe it was their old-fashioned roles—full-time mother, full-time breadwinner—that were weighing them down, making them middle-aged, out of touch.

"I know this sounds odd, but I kind of *forgot* about Walter. That is, I forgot they were going to execute him. He never thought he would die that way."

Peter shifted, redistributing her weight, moving her arm,

which had left a damp stripe across the front of his shirt. "I don't remember that in the letter."

"Then. The summer I was fifteen. I think he thought it would end in a slow-motion hail of bullets, like a movie. As opposed to a routine traffic stop at the Maryland line."

Peter kissed the top of her head. His skin was warm, but then, it always was. Energy poured out of him, even when he was still.

"I love you," he said.

"I love you, too."

"You don't know what love is."

This was a joke, their own private call-and-response, so ingrained that Eliza couldn't remember its origins, only that it always made her feel safe.

"Gross." It was Iso, standing on the threshold. "Get a room." Eliza wondered how long she had been standing there, what she had heard and whether she could make sense of any of it. *The summer I was fifteen, hail of bullets, routine traffic stop.*

"What do you need, baby?" Eliza asked.

Iso made a face. Possibly because of the word *baby,* or possibly because the mere sound of Eliza's voice irritated her. "I came down to remind you to wash my Spurs jersey, in case you forgot. I want to wear it tomorrow."

"I did. Wash it, that is. Not forget. But, Jesus, Iso, that jersey is made for damp England, not ninety-degree days in Montgomery County. Can't you wear a T-shirt like the other kids?"

"No. Did you wash my socks, too? I had to dig a pair out of the hamper this morning."

"Socks, too."

"You know," Peter put in, "if you can work an iPod and the television and the computer and TiVo, you could probably learn how to operate the washing machine, Isobel."

Iso looked at him as if he were speaking Portuguese. Peter

didn't annoy her as much as Eliza, but she refused to acknowledge he had any power over her. She stalked off without a reply.

"I don't want them to know," Eliza said to Peter. "Not yet. That's all I care about. Albie's just gotten over those awful nightmares, and even Iso is more impressionable than she lets on."

"It's your call," Peter said. "But there's always the risk of someone else telling them. Especially as the execution draws closer."

"Who? Not you, not my parents. Not even Vonnie, volatile as she can be, would go against our wishes."

Peter shrugged noncommittally, too polite to say that he considered his sister-in-law capable of just about any kind of bad behavior. It was funny how Peter and Vonnie, who had so much in common—similar intellects and interests, even some parallels in their career paths—remained oil-and-water after all these years. *You say funny,* Vonnie sneered in Eliza's head, *I say Freudian. He wanted a mommy, so he married one.* Peter was more diplomatic about Vonnie: *She's a feisty one. You always know what's on her mind.*

Eliza pressed him for agreement: "No one else knows."

"Walter knows, Eliza. Walter knows, and he found you. Walter knows, and he might tell someone else. He *has* told someone else. The person who wrote the letter. Who clearly has our address, not that addresses are hard to find these days."

"Well, there's no one—oh, *shit.* That asshole. That alleged journalist, Garrett. But I'm sure he's moved on to other lurid tales, assuming he's still alive. Is it a proper use of *irony* to say that it would be ironic if he died in some hideous, salacious crime?"

"I don't know if it would be irony, but it has a certain poetic justice."

"Walter never spoke to him, though. Not during the trial, and certainly not after that book. He probably disliked that book even more than I did."

"But his book is out there. Nothing really disappears anymore. Once, that kind of true-crime crap would be gone forever, gathering dust in a handful of secondhand bookstores, pulped by the publishers. Now, with online bookstores and eBay and POD technology, it's a computer click away for anyone who remembers your original name. For all you know, he's uploaded it to Kindle, sells it for ninety-nine cents a pop."

Eliza wasn't worried about computer clicks. But if she complained to the prison officials, that would be another set of people who knew definitively who she was and where she was. Why should she trust them? Better to ignore Walter, although she knew that Walter was most unpredictable when someone dared to ignore him. Only not where he was now, locked away. And usually not to her. The One Who Got Away, to borrow the hideous chapter heading from that nasty little book. As if she were a girl in a jazz ballad, a romantic fixation. *The One Who Got Away.* The one who was, as the book said repeatedly, "only raped, allegedly." Only. Allegedly.

Only a man who had never been raped could have written that phrase.

"Let's wait him out," she told Peter. "He'll either drop this, or he won't. As he said, he doesn't have long. And he's not being put to death for what he did to me."

THAT NIGHT, IN BED, she surprised Peter by initiating sex, quite good sex, with those little extras that long-married couples tend to forgo. It was, by necessity, silent sex, and she had to clap her hand over Peter's mouth at one point, fearful that the children would hear him. But it was important to remind herself tonight that her body belonged to her, that *this* was sex, *this* was love. She deserved her life. She had created it, through sheer will and not a little help from Peter and her family. She had every right to protect it.

But as she fell asleep, spooned by her husband, the other girls came to her as they sometimes did. Maude and Holly, followed by all the faceless girls, the ones that Walter was suspected of killing, although nothing had ever been proven. Two, four, six, eight—the estimates climbed into the teens. They were, all things considered, remarkably kind and forgiving little ghosts. Tonight, however, they were mournful in their insistence that she was not alone in this, that they must be factored into any decision she made about Walter. Holly, forever the spokeswoman, reminded Eliza that her life was theirs, in a sense. Polite even to her phantoms, Eliza did not argue.

Eventually the others slipped away one by one, but Holly lingered in Eliza's thoughts, keen on some private business. "I was the last girl," she said. "They shouldn't have called you that. I was the last girl, and he's going to die for what he did to *me*."

"Oh, Holly, what does it matter? Last or next-to-last? Ultimate or penultimate? They're just words. Who cares?"

"I do," Holly said. "And you know why, even if you always pretend that you don't. Ha-ha!"

4

1985

POINT OF ROCKS. He had always liked that name, seen it on signs for years, but somehow never managed to visit. Now that he had—well, it wasn't that much different from any of the towns along the Potomac. From his own town, in fact, back in West Virginia. Almost heaven, the license plate said, and Walter agreed. Still, he liked to drive, wished he could see more of the world.

When he was a child, no more than four or five, his father took him to a spot in Maryland, Friendsville, where it was possible to see three states—Maryland, West Virginia, Pennsylvania. He had been disappointed that the area wasn't marked, like a map or a quilt, that one state was indistinguishable from another. He told his father he wished they could go out west, stand in the four corners, which he had heard about from his older sister.

"If wishes were Mustangs," his father said. It was one of his favorite sayings. He didn't believe in vacations. Years later, Walter felt a bit betrayed when he started working at his father's repair shop and found out just how steady the business was. They could have taken trips, known a few more luxuries. Maybe not all the way west, but to that big amusement park in Ohio, the one with the tallest roller coaster in the world. Or his father could have sent Walter, his mother, and his sister on a vacation if he really felt he couldn't close up for seven days, or leave the place under the care of one of his employees. The only trip Walter ever took was to Ocean City, Maryland, after high school graduation, and it felt like he spent more time on the bus than in the town itself.

Now that Walter worked for his father, he didn't get vacations, just Sundays and Wednesdays off. What could he do with that mismatched pairing of days? Today was a Sunday, and he was thinking about turning back, going home. There was no law that a man had to do anything with his day off, no rule that said he wasn't allowed to spend the afternoon watching television, then enjoy Sunday-night supper with his family. Lately, his mother seemed to be dropping hints that he might want to get his own place, move out and on, but he was ignoring her for now. He didn't want to move out until it was to move in with someone, set up his own household. But, wait—maybe that was the problem? Maybe the reason he had trouble meeting women was because he didn't have a place to take them? There were all those jokes about men who lived with their parents, but he didn't think that applied to him. He worked in his father's business. Why shouldn't he stay at home until he could afford a proper house, not one of those cinder block motel rooms that people rented by the week, making do with hot plates and mini fridges. Living that way, in a single room, wasn't living at all. He'd wait for the real thing. Real love, real house, a partnership in his father's business. Already he had asked his father why they couldn't change Bowman's Garage to Bowman and Son's Garage. His sister, now married but living on the same street, said it didn't sound right, and his father said he didn't want to pay to change all the signs and stationery, and when Walter had said the sign would be enough—wait, was that a girl?

It was, a tall, shapely girl brushed with gold, her hair and skin almost blending with the cornfields on either side of the road. She had a funny walk, kind of a lope, but she was otherwise lovely and her body was magnificent, like a movie star's. He slowed down.

"You want a ride?"

She looked confused, on the verge of tears. "One-oh-three Apple Court, Point of Rocks. One-oh-three Apple Court, Point of Rocks."

"Sure I can take you there, just tell me—"

She shook her head, kept repeating her address. She looked to be at least eighteen, but she was acting like she was six. *Oh.*

"Calm down, calm down, I'll get you home. We'll have to find someone who can tell me the way, but I'll get you there, okay?"

She climbed into his truck. Gosh, she was pretty. Too bad she was slow, or retarded, or whatever it was called now.

"You got lost?"

She nodded, still hiccuping from her tears. Eventually she gulped out that she had been in a store with her mother and she had gotten thirsty, gone to find a water fountain in the store, but when she came back, she couldn't find her mother, so she had decided to walk home.

"You still thirsty? You want something to drink? A soda or something?"

"Home," she said. "One-oh-three Apple Court, Point of Rocks."

"I'll take you home," he said. "But I have to stop anyway, to ask directions. If you want a drink or a snack, you just let me know."

He pulled over at the next convenience store he saw, a Sheetz. His father loved to say that name, drawing out the vowel sound to the *t*. *Sheeeeeeeeeeeet*—then waiting a split second before adding the *z*. And his mother laughed every time, as if it were new. That's all Walter wanted. A wife, a world of private jokes. It shouldn't be so hard.

He parked at the far end of the parking lot, where his truck wouldn't be in view of the cash register. Inside he bought two sodas and some candy. He did not ask directions, at least not to 103 Apple Court. Instead, he asked if there were any good fishing spots nearby.

SHE LIKED IT AT FIRST, he could swear that she did. He told her it was a game, and he fed her M&M's for each step she mastered. Fact is, she might have done it before. It happens, with retarded people. They get up to all sorts of things. That was why the girl in his grade school had to be transferred, because she was doing things with the older boys. She had a woman's body and a little girl's mind. That was no way to be. He was doing this girl a kindness, if you thought about it. But, in the end, it wasn't right. He needed someone who could help a little. He wouldn't make this mistake again.

Later, when he shouldered her body and carried it deep into the woods, trusting that no one would be looking for her here, not soon, he found himself feeling very tender toward her. She wasn't happy in this life, couldn't really be. Everyone was better off now.

He was home in time for supper.

5

ELIZA'S PARENTS LIVED ONLY THIRTY minutes from the new house, another mark in its favor. (Funny, the more Eliza kept enumerating the house's various advantages in her mind—the trees, the yard, the proximity to her parents—the more she wondered if there was something about it that she actually disliked but didn't want to admit to herself.) She had assumed that their lives, maintained at a physical distance for so long, would braid together instantly, that she would see them all the time. But, so far, they met up no more than once a month, and it was typically a rushed restaurant meal in downtown Bethesda, at a place that offended no one and therefore disappointed everyone.

Perhaps they were all just out of practice

at being an extended family; Eliza had lived a minimum of 1,500 miles away since college graduation. Besides, both her parents, now in their late seventies, continued to work, although her father had cut back his practice; her mother was an academic, teaching at the University of Maryland in downtown Baltimore. They were not, nor would she want them to be, the type of settled grandparents whose lives revolved around their only grandchildren. Still, she had thought she would see more of them than she did.

This week, however, they were having dinner at her parents' house, an old farmhouse in what had been, back in 1985, a rural enclave in Western Howard County. Their road still had a country feel to it. But all around, development was encroaching. For Inez, those new houses were like battleships in a harbor, massing, readying an attack. As for the large electrical towers visible in the distance—those made her shiver with revulsion, although she did not believe in the health claims made against them. She just found them ugly. "Imagine," she often said, "what Don Quixote would have made of those."

Yet the Lerners had never thought twice about relocating here, leaving their beloved house in Roaring Springs in order to enroll Eliza in a different high school. One county over, Wilde Lake High School had been far enough so a new girl, known as Eliza, would have no resonance. There was always the slight risk that someone from the old school district would transfer and that Eliza's identity would be pierced. But as her parents explained to her repeatedly, the changes were not about shame or secrets. They moved because the old neighborhood had dark associations for all of them, because some of the things they loved most—the stream, the wooded hillsides, the sense of isolation—were tainted. They chose not to speak of what had happened in the world at large, but that was because the world at large had nothing to contribute to Eliza's healing. If she had returned to Catonsville High School with her friends—and it was her choice, they stressed—her parents didn't doubt that people would have been sensitive. *Too sensitive.* They did not want their daughter to live an eggshell existence, where others watched their words and lapsed into sudden, suspicious silences when she happened onto certain conversations. New house, new start. For all of them. A new house with an alarm system, and central air-conditioning, despite Inez's hatred of it, because that meant they didn't sleep with open windows.

Iso and Albie loved their grandparents' house, which was filled with the requisite items of fascination that grandparents' homes always harbor. But the real lure for them was the nearby Rita's custard stand. As soon as they left with their grandfather for an after-dinner treat, Eliza told her mother about Walter's letter.

"What are you going to do?" she asked.

"Nothing," Eliza said.

"Doing nothing," Inez said, "is a choice in its own way. When you do nothing, you still do something."

"I know."

"I assumed you did."

They were sitting on the screened porch that ran along the back of the house, a place where the view was still, more or less, as it had been when the Lerners purchased their home. They had bought it quickly, almost instinctively, a month after Eliza came home. It was actually larger than the eighteenth-century stone house they had known in Roaring Springs, and better appointed in almost every way—updated bathrooms, more generously proportioned rooms. Yet when Vonnie had come home for Christmas break, glum over her poor academic performance in her inaugural quarter at Northwestern, she had pitched a fit over her parents' failure to consult her on this important family matter. Vonnie had always been given to histrionics, even when she had little cause for them, and her family was more or less inured to the melodrama.

But no one, not even psychiatrist parents as well trained as the

Lerners, could have been prepared to hear their eldest daughter proclaim: "It's just that everything's going to be about Elizabeth—excuse me, *Eliza*—from now on."

The statement, delivered at the dinner table, was wrong on so many levels that no one in the family spoke for several seconds. It was factually wrong; the whole point was that the Lerners were trying to make a world in which things were neither about, nor *not* about, what had happened to Eliza. Besides, they had always been fair-minded, never favoring one daughter over the other, honoring their differences. Vonnie was their high-strung overachiever. Eliza, even when she was known as Elizabeth, was that unusual child content simply to be. Good enough grades, cheerful participation in group activities in which she neither distinguished nor embarrassed herself. Inevitably, it had been speculated—by outsiders, but also by Inez and Manny, by Vonnie, and even by Eliza—that her temperament wasn't inborn but a subconscious and preternatural decision to opt out. Let Vonnie have the prizes and the honors, the whole world if she wanted it.

From a young age, Eliza was also a willing, complacent slave to her older sister, which probably undercut whatever traditional sibling rivalry there might have been. She was simply too good-natured about the tortures her sister designed for her in their early days. Oh, when she was a baby, she cried when Vonnie pinched her, which the newly minted older sister did whenever the opportunity presented itself. But once Eliza could toddle about, she followed her sister everywhere, and not even Vonnie could hold a grudge against someone who so clearly worshipped her.

But she could—apparently, amazingly—seethe with resentment over the way her sister's misfortune had transformed the family dynamic.

"Would you rather be Eliza?" her father asked Vonnie the night of her unthinkable pronouncement.

Eliza couldn't help wanting to hear the answer. Obviously,

Vonnie had never wanted to be Eliza back when she was Elizabeth, so it would be odd to think she might want to trade places now. But what if she did? What would that signify?

"That's not what I meant," Vonnie said, her anger deflating. Imploding, really, from embarrassment. "I was just trying to say that, from now on, so much of what we do will be controlled, influenced, affected by . . . what happened."

"Well, that's true for Eliza, so I think it's fitting that it be true for our family as a whole," their father said. "This happened to all of us. Not the same thing—there is what Eliza experienced, which is unique to her, and what your mother and I experienced, which is another. And what you felt, going off to school while this was happening, was yet another unique experience."

Manny was always careful to use the most neutral words possible—*experienced,* not *suffered,* or even *endured*. Not because he was inclined to euphemisms, but because Eliza's parents didn't want to define her life for her. "You get to be the expert on yourself," her father said frequently, and Eliza found it an enormously comforting saying, an unexpected gift from two parents who had the knowledge, training, and history to be the expert on her, if they so chose. They probably did know her better than she knew herself in some ways, but they refused to claim this power. Sometimes she wished they would, or at least drop a few hints.

"I was willing to defer admission," Vonnie reminded her father. This was accurate, as far as it went. She had offered to delay entering Northwestern, but not very wholeheartedly, and there was a risk that her parents would have to forfeit part of her tuition. Besides, now that Eliza was home, her parents were still keen on making distinctions between authentic issues, as they called them—her need to know that the house was locked at night, not so much as a window open, even on the fairest spring evenings—and rationalizations, or any attempt to use her past to unfair advantage.

Yet it was Vonnie who was inclined to leverage her sister to garner attention. Oh, she didn't tell her new college friends too much. But she hinted at a terrible tragedy, an unthinkable occurrence, one that had made the national news. She was perhaps too broad in her allusions. Over the years, as Vonnie's various college friends visited, they were clearly surprised to meet a normal-seeming high school girl with all her limbs and no obvious disfigurement. At least one had believed that Eliza was a young flautist, who lost her arm after being pushed in front of a subway train.

"Remember," Eliza said to her mother now, "how Vonnie hated this house at first? Now she has a meltdown if you even suggest you might want to downsize."

"I think we're still a few years away, knock wood." Inez did just that, rapping her knuckles on a small, rustic table that held their glasses of tea mixed with lemonade. Known as Arnold Palmers to most of the world, half-and-half at the Korean carry-outs in Baltimore, this drink had always been called Sunshines in the Lerner household. At a makeshift campsite in West Virginia, Eliza-then-Elizabeth had shown Walter how to make them. First, how to prepare the tea itself, in a jar left in the sun, then how to make homemade lemonade, with nothing more than lemons, water, and sugar. Walter thought that all juice came in frozen cans of concentrate; the lemonade proved almost too genuine, too tart, for his taste. But he had liked it, mixed with tea. "What do you call this?" he'd asked Eliza, but she hadn't wanted to tell him. "No name," she'd said. "Just tea and lemonade." "We should make up a name for it," he'd said, "sell it by the roadside." Like most of Walter's plans, this was all talk.

"Where will you go when you do sell this house?" she asked her mother now.

"Downtown D.C., I think, what they call the Penn Quarter neighborhood now."

"Not Baltimore?"

Inez shook her head. "We've been gone too long. We have no real ties. Besides, in D.C., we could probably give up both cars, walk most places. Theater, restaurants. You know me, it's all or nothing, city or country, nothing in between. If I can't see deer destroying my garden, then I want to breathe big, heavenly gulps of carbon monoxide and rotting trash, know the neighborhood panhandlers by name. I'm Eva Gabor *and* Eddie Albert in *Green Acres*."

Eliza had to laugh at this image, her bohemian, unaffected mother as Eva Gabor and Eddie Albert. The children burst in, faces smeared with the residue from Rita's, their favorite custard stand, whose neon letters promised ICE * CUSTARD * HAPPINESS. She couldn't have felt any safer, even if the windows had been closed and locked.

The windows were open. That's what was different about the house tonight. She was happy for her mother, even if she couldn't imagine what it would be like to live that way.

ELIZA HEADED HOME ALONG the twisting country roads on which she had learned to drive twenty years earlier. Her driver's ed teacher had been a horse-faced woman oddly intent on letting Eliza know she had been a popular girl in her day, pointing out the former houses of various boyfriends, providing little biographies of each one. The sports played, hair color, the cars driven. Eliza knew the instructor did this only to girls she perceived to be popular, so she accepted this strange patter as a compliment. But it was irritating, too, a form of bragging, an unseemly competitive streak in a woman who should be past such things. Once, when the driving teacher directed Eliza down a section of Route 40, narrating her romantic adventures all the way, Eliza had wanted to say: "You see that Roy Rogers? That's where I was headed the day I met the first man who would ever have sex with me. He didn't play any sports, but he had dark hair and green eyes and drove a red pickup truck. And when he broke up with a girl, he usually broke her neck. Except for me. I was the only one he didn't kill. Why do you think that was?"

"Mommy?" Albie said from the backseat. "You're driving on the wrong side of the road."

"No, honey, I'm—" Oh God, she was. She pulled the steering wheel more sharply than necessary, horrified by what she had done, only to glimpse a flash of something white zipping behind the car.

"What was that?" Albie asked.

"A deer," Iso said, utterly bored by their brush with death.

"But it was white."

"That was the tail."

A deer. Eliza was relieved that her children had seen it, too. Because, like Albie, she wasn't sure what had dodged their car. For a moment, she thought it might be a girl, blond hair streaming. A girl, running for her life.

6

1985

"WANNABE," HER SISTER SAID.

"I'm not," Elizabeth said, but her voice scaled up because she didn't know what Vonnie meant, and Vonnie pounced on that little wriggle of doubt, the way their family cat, Barnacle, impaled garden snakes.

"It's a term for girls like you, who think they're Madonna."

"I don't think I'm Madonna."

But Elizabeth secretly hoped she looked like her, a little, as much as she could within the restrictions her parents had laid down. It was rare for her parents to make hard-and-fast rules. They gave Vonnie a lot of leeway—no curfew, although she had to call if she was going to stay out past midnight, and they trusted her never to get in a car with someone who had been drinking. But this summer, Elizabeth had suddenly discovered that there were all sorts of things *she* was forbidden to do. Dye her hair, even with a nonpermanent tint. Spend her days at the mall or the Roy Rogers on Route 40. ("Watch all the television you want, take long walks, go to the community pool, but no just *hanging*," her mother had clarified.) And although she wasn't actually prohibited from wearing the fingerless lace gloves she had purchased when a friend's mother took them to the mall, her mother sighed at the mere sight of them.

Elizabeth put those on as soon as Vonnie left for her job at a day camp for underprivileged kids, checking herself in the mirror. She had a piece of stretchy lace, filched from her mother's sewing basket, tied in her reddish curls, and a pink T-shirt that proclaimed WILD GIRL, which even she recognized was laughably untrue. Although it was a typical August day, hot and humid, she had layered a bouffant black skirt over a pair of leggings that stopped at her knees, and she wore black ankle boots with faux zebra inserts worked into the leather. She thought she looked wonderful. Vonnie was jealous.

Vonnie simply didn't like Elizabeth, she was sure of it. Her mother said this wasn't true, that sisters were never close at this age, but it was an essential stage through which they had to pass. Her mother sounded hopeful when she laid this out, as if saying it might make it true. Elizabeth was fifteen years old now to Vonnie's soon-to-be eighteen and all her life she had carried the distinct impression that she had spoiled a really good party, that Vonnie had been miserable from the day the Lerner trio became a quartet.

And Elizabeth couldn't figure out why. Vonnie still got most of the attention, excelling in everything she did, whereas Elizabeth was always in the middle of the pack. Vonnie was a good student, she had gone to the nationals in NFL—National Forensics

League, not National Football League—and placed in extemp, short for extemporaneous, which meant she could speak off the cuff. That was no picnic, having an already combative older sister who was trained to speak quickly and authoritatively on any topic. Vonnie was going to Northwestern in the fall to study with Charlton Heston's sister. Of course, Charlton Heston's sister was simply another teacher there, in the drama school, and she had to take whoever signed up for her classes, but Vonnie managed to make it sound like a very big deal: *I'm going to Northwestern in the fall. I'm going to study with Charlton Heston's sister.* Although barely two years older than Elizabeth, she was three years ahead in school because her September birthday had allowed her to enroll in school early, whereas Elizabeth had a January birthday. Elizabeth didn't mind. It meant Vonnie went away all that much earlier. She was looking forward to seeing what it was like, being home alone. Maybe once Vonnie was gone, Elizabeth might discover what she did well, where her own talents lay. Her parents insisted she had some, if she would just focus. So far, all focus had brought her was the uncanny ability to ferret out dirty books in the houses where she watered plants for people lucky enough to go somewhere in this long, boring summer. Erica Jong and Henry Miller and—in one house, hidden behind the *Encyclopaedia Britannica*—the complete set of Ian Fleming. *The Spy Who Loved Me*—wow, that was nothing like the movie.

She left the house, with no particular destination in mind, but then—the only places she wanted to go were the ones that were explicitly forbidden. Her parents thought their neighborhood, Roaring Springs, was a big deal, but Elizabeth thought it was boring, boring, boring. Roaring Springs was nothing more than a bunch of old stone houses, remnants of a nineteenth-century mill village not even a mile from busy Frederick Road. But because their house backed up to a state park, thick with trees, no one could ever build near them. The isolation suited her parents, and even Vonnie never complained about living in this quirky stone house among other quirky stone houses, filled mostly with people like their parents, only childless. Everyone in Roaring Springs was proudly, determinedly eccentric, indifferent to trends and what was popular. They all professed to hate television, too. They might as well hate television: The county had yet to extend the cable system out here, which meant that Elizabeth saw MTV and VH-1 only when she went to friends' houses after school. She wondered, in fact, how her mother even knew enough about Madonna to find her objectionable. Her father had glossy magazines in his office, for the parents who waited while he consulted with their children, but she didn't imagine there were magazines in her mother's office. Of course, she had never been allowed to visit there, given that it was in the state prison.

There was a small, old-fashioned family bakery on Frederick Road, and she stopped there, inspecting the various treats on display. Vonnie had said the other day that Elizabeth may be straight-up-and-down skinny, but she was prone to having a potbelly and she better watch it. The problem with Vonnie was that she said some things merely to be mean, but she said other things that were mean and true, and it was hard to sort them out. Elizabeth turned sideways, smoothing down her T-shirt, trying to assess her stomach. It looked okay to her. It would look better if she had boobs, real boobs instead of these A-cup nothings. Real boobs would balance her out. But she was okay with how she looked, today. Gazing in the bakery window, she thought about going in, but the problem was that she wanted *everything*: the lacy pizelles, the cunning pink-and-green cookies, the cannolis, the éclairs. Lately, she never felt satisfied, no matter what she ate. Theoretically, she could buy one of each, eat them all, then throw them up, but she had failed repeatedly at the throwing-up part, no matter how her girlfriends coached and encouraged her.

She continued up Frederick Road, trying to catch her reflection in the windows she passed along the way. Elizabeth wanted to know what she looked like when no one was looking. She wanted to stumble on herself unawares, sneak up on her image, but she had yet to master that trick. She was always a split second ahead, and the face she saw was too composed—mouth clamped in what she hoped was a shy, and therefore alluring, smile, chin tilted down to compensate for her nose, her nostrils, which she found truly horrifying. "Pig snout," Vonnie had said, and that one had stuck, although her mother said it was a "ski jump" nose. Elizabeth had asked her mother if she could have a nose job for her sixteenth birthday, and her mother had been unable to speak for several seconds, a notable thing unto itself. She was a psychiatrist, but a really interesting one, who worked with criminals at the special prison for the insane. She could never talk about her work, though, much to Elizabeth's disappointment. She would love to know about the men her mother met, the things they had done. Right now, she was pretty sure that her mother was working with a boy who had killed his parents, his adoptive parents, just because they asked him how he did on a test. He was actually kind of handsome; Elizabeth had seen his picture in the newspaper. But her mother was careful never to speak of her work. Her father, also a psychiatrist, didn't speak of his work, either, but all he did was sit in an office and listen to teenagers. Elizabeth was pretty sure she already knew everything her father knew, probably more.

Elizabeth's friends thought it was weird and creepy, what her parents did. They thought the Lerners could read minds, which was silly, or see through lies more easily than "normal" parents. "They're not witches," she told her friends.

In some ways, her parents were easier to fool than others. This was because Elizabeth told them so much that it didn't occur to them that she ever withheld anything. Of course, what she mainly told them about was her friends—Claudia's decision to have sex with her boyfriend while her parents were away one weekend, Debbie trying beer and pot, Lydia getting caught shoplifting. Each time she shared one of these stories, her parents would ask, gently, if Elizabeth had been involved, and she could always say "No!" with a clear and sunny conscience. This made it easier to keep what she needed to keep to herself. Trying to make herself throw up after eating too much, for example. She knew it was bad, but she also knew it was a problem only if you couldn't *stop*. Given that she never got to the point where she actually threw up, she couldn't see how there was anything wrong with trying. Claudia said she should use a feather or a broom straw if she couldn't force her finger far enough down, but—*gross*. The idea of a feather made her want to throw up, yet the *fact* of a feather didn't. Was that weird? It was probably weird. Elizabeth worried a lot about being weird. Unlike Vonnie, she didn't want to stand out, didn't want to attract too much attention. She wanted to be normal. She wanted just one boy to look at her like, like—like that way Bruce Springsteen looked in that video, when he rolled out from under the car and he knew he shouldn't want the woman who was standing there in front of him, but he just couldn't help himself.

None of her friends lived close by. They lived on the other side of Frederick Road, in the kind of houses where Elizabeth's mother would not be caught dead, to use one of her favorite expressions. *I would not be caught dead living there, I would not be caught dead shopping there, I would not be caught dead going on vacation there.* Finally, Vonnie had said: "Do you get much choice, about where you're caught dead?" and it had become a family joke. They had started naming the places where they *would* be caught dead. Still, their mother was pretty serious in her dislike of modern things. She had wanted to stay in the city, in their town house, which was almost right downtown, on a pretty green square built around the Washington Monument. But, about the time Vonnie turned fourteen, Elizabeth's father had seen a chance to build a practice in the suburbs, where more parents were inclined to seek help for their children. And could pay for it, too, no small consideration. Roaring Springs was a compromise, thirty minutes from her mother's job at Patuxent Institute, not even ten minutes to her father's office in Ellicott City. It was his daytime proximity that gave Elizabeth her freedom on these summer days. But it wasn't much of a freedom, when one was alone, with all these rules.

She tracked back to the park and began walking along the stream known as the Sucker Branch. If she followed its banks, she would come out at Route 40, not that far from Roy Rogers, maybe a mile or so. At least, she thought she might come out there. She wasn't allowed to walk to the Roy Rogers because it was a hangout, and her parents believed that being idle was what got most kids in trouble. But they liked the idea of her being outdoors on summer days, so if she explained that she was simply following the stream and found herself there by accident and she was terribly thirsty after the walk, that would be okay. If they asked, and they might not even ask. She would go to Roy Rogers, see if anyone was there. If no one was around, she could still get a mocha shake, maybe some fries. Then—she was resolved—she was going to throw it up, she would learn how to throw up today. Her worries over her body were secondary; she didn't need to lose weight, only the potbelly, if she really did have one, and she still wasn't sure. What she needed was something to tell her friends when they were reunited as high school sophomores in two weeks. She wanted to have *something* to show for her summer. Unlike Claudia, she didn't have a boyfriend. Unlike Debbie and Lydia, she wasn't daring enough to shoplift, and she had no interest in her parents' booze. She had to do something in these final weeks of summer that counted as an achievement, and learning how to throw up was her best bet.

Following the stream, high in its banks after the weekend's heavy rains, turned out to be much harder than she expected.

Mud sucked at her boots, and when she came to the spot where she needed to cross, she couldn't. The unusually deep water covered the rocks she had planned to hop across, and it was moving quickly. She paused, uncertain. It seemed a shame to turn back, after making it this far. She thought she could hear the traffic swooshing by on Route 40. She was close, very close.

Then she saw a man on the other side, leaning on a shovel.

"It's not so swift you can't wade through," he said. "I done it." He looked to be college age, although something told Elizabeth that he wasn't in college. Not just his grammar, but his clothes, the trucker's hat pulled low on his forehead. "Just go up there, to where that fallen tree is. The water won't go above your shins, I swear."

Elizabeth did, taking off her boots and tucking them beneath her armpits, so they were like two little wings sticking out of her back. Zebra-patterned wings with stilettos. He was right, the current was nothing to fear, although she worried that the water itself was dangerous, filled with bacteria. Luckily she'd had a tetanus shot just two years ago, when she stepped on a rusty nail. And the man was nice, waiting to help her scramble up the banks on the other side, taking hold of her wrists. He wasn't that much taller than she was, maybe five seven to her five three, and his build, while muscled, was slight. He was almost handsome, really. He had green eyes and even features. The only real flaw was his nose, narrow and pinched. He looked as if the world smelled bad to him, although he was the one who smelled a little. B.O., probably from shoveling on such a hot day. His T-shirt showed sweat stains at the armpits and the neckline, a drop of perspiration dangled from his nose.

"Thank you," she said.

He didn't let go.

"Thank you. I'm fine now. I can stand just fine."

He tightened his grip on her wrists. She tried to pull away, and her boots fell, one rolling dangerously close to the water. She began to struggle in earnest and he held her there, his face impassive, as if he were watching all of this from a great distance, as if he had no part in holding her.

"Mister, *please.*"

"I'll take you where you're going," he said.

7

ELIZA HAD NEVER GOOGLED HERSELF. What would have been the point? Eliza Benedict was not the kind of person who ended up on the Internet, and the story of Elizabeth Lerner was finite, the ending written years ago. Peter was all over the Internet—most of his work behind a pay wall, but nevertheless *there*—represented by almost a decade's worth of his own words, probably more than a million when one included his *Houston Chronicle* days. And since taking his new job with the venture capital firm, he was even more omnipresent in this shadow world: a source, a personage, someone to be consulted and quoted on these new financial products, which Eliza didn't understand. She didn't even understand the term "financial product." A product should be real, concrete, tangible, something that could be bagged or boxed.

However, Eliza knew, even before Walter had written her, that she showed up at Peter's elbow in the occasional image, especially now that Peter had crossed over to the dark side—his term—and they had to go to functions. That was *her* term, but it made Peter laugh. "You couldn't call that a party," she said after her first foray into his new world. "And they didn't serve dinner, only finger food, all of it impossible to eat without dribbling. No, that was truly a function."

Sitting on their bed, Peter had laughed, but his mind wasn't on the party, or on what to call it. "Leave your dress on," he said. "And those shoes." She did. But even Peter's admiration for her that night hadn't been enough to send her searching for her own image, despite the knowledge that they had been photographed repeatedly. She hated, truly hated, seeing photographs of herself. A tiresome thing to say, banal and clichéd, but more true of her than it was of others who professed to feel the same way. Her photographic image always came as a shock. She was taller in her head, her hair less of a disordered mess. She and Peter looked terribly mismatched, like an otter and a . . . hedgehog. Peter was the otter, with his compact, still hard-muscled body and thick, shiny hair, while she was the hedgehog. And not just any hedgehog, but Beatrix Potter's Mrs. Tiggy-Winkle. Even dressed up in expensive clothes, she gave the impression that she had just been divested of an apron and a bonnet, a happy little hausfrau who couldn't wait to get home and put the kettle on.

Which, in a way, was pretty close to the truth.

The dress that had excited Peter wasn't a sexy dress, not really, but it wasn't the sort of thing she normally wore, and that was novelty enough. The shoes had been a London splurge, a ridiculous thing to buy there, given the exchange rate at the time. Vonnie could have picked up the same shoes in New York for almost half the price and brought them to Eliza on one of her business trips. Eliza had purchased them to save face when she was snubbed in a Knightsbridge boutique, the kind of shop where the clothes appeared to have been tailored in defiance of the female body. The shoes were not visible in the photograph in *Washingtonian* magazine, but the dress—emerald green, with a bateau neck—was. She studied it now. This was what Walter had seen, this was how he had found her. Did she really look that similar to her teen self? She had been almost eighteen the last time she saw him, and although she had filled out since the summer he had kidnapped her, she still looked younger than her age. Even now, ten pounds over her ideal weight, her face remained thin, her jawline sharp. Maybe that was all he needed to spot her. That, and the shortened first name, which wasn't much of a mask when someone knew the real one.

"Mom?" Albie's voice seemed to be coming from the kitchen. "Are we going to have lunch?"

"Soon," she called back from the desk in the family room, still looking at her photo, trying, and not for the first time, to see herself as Walter had seen her. She looked nothing like his two known victims, tall blondes. She understood why he had taken her, but why had he let her live? He claimed he had been planning to let her go when he started driving toward Point of Rocks, but was that just a story he told after the fact? It didn't matter. They had found Holly's body at the bottom of a ravine; they had already dug up Maude, the Maryland girl he had attempted to bury in Patapsco State Park.

It occurred to Eliza, truly for the first time, to try her old name in an Internet search. *Paging Dr. Freud,* Vonnie would have said with a snort. But Eliza's identity had been so entrenched as Eliza Benedict by the time the Internet became a part of daily life that she had never stopped to think about Elizabeth Lerner.

It was a common enough name that multiple Elizabeths popped up, in family trees and press releases and blogs. The first reference she found to herself was taken from *that* book. Ugh. *Murder on the Mountain* was a disgusting quickie churned out by Jared Garrett, a bizarre cop groupie who had followed Walter's story with what even a teenager could see was an inappropriate fascination. There was an excerpt on Google, and her name leaped out from the leaden prose.

A boyish girl who looked younger than she was, Elizabeth testified that Walter did not attempt sexual congress with her for several weeks, but that she was, ultimately, subjected to his advances. Curiously, he left her alive. Walter clearly considered Elizabeth different from his other victims, although he himself has refused to explain the relationship, other than to remark once, in an interview with state police: "She was good company." Asked if she was a hostage, Bowman said: "I didn't demand ransom, did I?" His answers did little to deflect curiosity about the true nature of the relationship between the two.

"WHAT ARE YOU DOING, MOM?" Albie leaned against the doorjamb, hands in pockets. He didn't seem particularly interested in his mother's activities, merely bored enough with his own life to try to engage her.

"Nothing," she said, erasing the cached history and closing the window. She wouldn't want Iso's prying fingers to wander into any of these Web sites. "Are you hungry? What do you want for lunch?"

"Those sandwiches that Grandmother makes?" he asked hopefully. Peter's mother made elaborate sandwiches from deli roast beef and dark bread, chopping cornichons and putting them in brown mustard, then adding horseradish and a judicious sprinkling of salt and pepper.

"I might not have everything Nonnie has, but I think I could make a fair approximation," she said, taking a quick mental inventory of the refrigerator's contents, calculating that butter pickles would approximate the experience Albie craved, which was more about the chopping and mixing, making an exciting ritual out of something mundane. Albie loved productions, and with a child as easily pleased as Albie, it seemed a shame not to try to meet his expectations. Especially now, when everything and anything she did antagonized Iso. "Mom, you're breathing too loud," she had said the other day in Trader Joe's. "Loudly," Eliza had corrected, then felt awful for using grammar to one-up her daughter. Not that it had worked.

Albie put his hand in hers, as if the walk to the kitchen were a journey of miles. She wished it were, that he would stay this age for three, four years, then be nine for a decade or so, then spend another ten years being ten. But onetime graduate student of children's literature that she was, she knew there was no spell, no magic, that could keep a child a child, or shield a child from the world at large. In fact, that was where the trouble almost always began, with a parent trying to outthink fate. *Stay on the path. Don't touch the spindle. Don't speak to strangers. Don't pick the rose.*

8

1985

HE HAD GONE TOO FAR this time. Literally, too far. He had headed out Wednesday morning, telling himself he had no plans, then driven and driven until the landscape had changed, civilization coming at him all of a sudden. He would never get back in time for dinner now. And, although there were girls everywhere, they were never alone, but traveling in groups, gaggles. He stopped at a mall and almost became dizzy at the sight of all the girls there, girls with bare midriffs and short shorts. He leaned on the railing on the second floor, watching them move in lazy circles below, flit in and out of the food court, where they would briefly interact with the boys, then plunge back into the mall proper. The boys looked baffled by these quicksilver girls. They were too immature, they couldn't give these girls what they wanted.

But neither could he, unless he got one alone, had a chance to sweet-talk her. He would go slow this time, real slow.

He drove past a fenced swimming pool—that was a kind of water, wasn't it?—stationed himself in the parking lot, stealing glances through the chain-link fence. The girls here seemed intertwined. Not actually touching but strung together by invisible threads, their limbs moving in lazy unison. They would flip on cue, sit up on cue, run combs through their hair at the same moment. Boys circled these girls, too, silly and deferential. They didn't have a chance.

He caught an older woman, a leathery mom, frowning at him, decided to move on.

He had almost given up, was wondering how he would explain all the miles on the truck—he could fill the gas tank, but he couldn't erase seventy, eighty, ninety miles from an odometer—when he saw the right girl. Tall, filled out, but walking as if her body was still new to her, as if she had borrowed it from someone else and had to give it back at day's end, in good condition. She was on a sidewalk in a ghost town of a neighborhood, a place so empty and quiet that it felt like they were the last two people on earth. He stopped and—sudden inspiration—asked her for directions to the mall, although he knew his way back there. Her face wasn't quite as pretty as he had hoped—Earl, the other mechanic back at his father's place called this kind of girl a Butterface—but she had a serious expression that was very touching, as if she wanted to make sure she gave precise directions. Only she kept getting a little mixed up over the street names, trying to give him directions according to landmarks he couldn't know—the Baileys' house, the nursery school where her little sister went, the High's store.

"I admit, I just can't follow all these directions," he said with an aw-shucks grin. "Are you going that way? Maybe you could show me."

Oh, no, she wasn't going that far. She just had to catch a bus to Route 40.

Maybe he could take her as far as she was going?

The sun was strong, so powerful that everything looked white, unreal. This was a pale girl, one who didn't get to spend her afternoons at the pool. She was heading to work. He could take her to work, Walter said, and then she could draw him a map on—where did she work?

"An ice-cream parlor."

"Friendly's? Swensen's? Baskin-Robbins?"

"Just a local place. It's kind of old-fashioned."

She could draw him a map on a napkin, then, once he dropped her off. How would that be?

He waited until she was in the cab of the truck and they had driven a little ways before pointing out that she would be early for her shift. Right? She had been walking to a bus stop, and the bus would take so much longer than a direct shot in the truck. He was hungry. Was she hungry? Would she like to stop for something?

She got to eat free at work, she said.

Well, gosh, that was great, but he sure didn't expect her to give him the same deal.

"No," she said. "The manager is really strict, always looking out for girls who gave freebies to their . . . friends."

"Boyfriends?" he asked, and she blushed. "Do you have a boyfriend?"

She considered the question, which struck him as odd. Seemed a clear yes-or-no proposition to him. Maybe she had a boyfriend who didn't satisfy her. Maybe she was thinking about breaking up with him but was tenderhearted, didn't want to hurt his feelings. What a nice girl she was.

"Anyway," she said, not answering him either way, "it's only ice cream, no burgers or hot dogs or even pizza. We had hot pretzels for a while, but no one wanted them and—"

Then maybe they could stop at this little place he knew, by a stream? There was a metal stand, kind of like an old-fashioned trailer, and it made the best steak sandwiches. There was no such place, not nearby, but Walter had heard a gentleman at the shop describe the steak sandwiches he had eaten in his youth, back in Wisconsin.

Walter got lost, looking for the steak shack that wasn't, driving deeper and deeper into what turned out to be a state park. He made conversation, asked again if she had a boyfriend. She hemmed and hawed but finally said no. Good, he wouldn't like a girl who would cheat on her boyfriend. She was getting nervous, her eyes skating back and forth, but he promised her that she would be on time for work. He told her he was surprised that a girl as pretty as she was didn't have a boyfriend. He could tell she liked hearing that, yet she continued to hug the door a little. The road ran out and he parked, told her that he had screwed up, the steak place was on the other side of the creek, but they could cross it and be there in five minutes, if she would just take his hand. Once he had his hand in hers, he tickled the palm with his middle finger, a trick he had heard from Earl, before Earl ran off and joined the Marines. It was a signal and, if the girl liked you, she tickled back. Or maybe if she just didn't jerk her hand away, he decided, that was proof enough that she was up for things.

He tried to take it slow, but she kept talking about work, fretting about being late, and then she started to cry. She cried harder when he kissed her, and he was pretty sure he was a good kisser. She cried so hard that snot ran out of her nose, which was gross, and he stopped kissing her.

"I guess you don't want to be my girlfriend, then," he said. She kept crying. Why were girls so contrary? Of course, he lived pretty far away. They wouldn't be able to see each other except on his days off. But she should be flattered, this girl who no one else had claimed, that a man, a nice-looking man, wanted her. A man who would please her, if she would allow herself to be pleased.

"Are you going to tell?" he asked.

She said she wouldn't, and he wished he could believe her. He didn't, though. So he did what he had to do. He was tamping down the hole he dug when he saw the other girl coming. How much had she seen? Anything, everything? He thought fast, told her how to cross the stream. He held his hands out to her, and she didn't hesitate. Her hands felt cool and smooth against his, which were burning with new calluses from the digging. If anyone should have wanted to let go, it should have been him. It hurt, holding her hands. He studied her face. He wished women didn't lie so much, that there was a way to ask if she had seen anything without giving away that there had been something to see. It was like that old riddle, the one about the island with just two Indians, one who always lies and one who always tells the truth, but there's one question that will set things straight. Only he could never remember what the question was. Something like: If I ask your brother, will he tell me the truth? No, that wasn't it, because both would say no. What should he ask her? But he had taken too long, held her hands too roughly, and given himself away.

"You're with me now," he said, buckling her into the seat next to his, then tying her hands at the wrists with a rope from the bed of the pickup.

Then, as an afterthought: "What's your name?"

9

SHE DECIDED TO WRITE WALTER a letter, nothing more. That's the way she characterized her decision, when she spoke of it to Peter and her parents. "I'm going to write him a letter," she said, "nothing more." A letter would be private, final. (Although she supposed his mail was read by prison officials. Again, there was the worrying detail of his confidante, the person who had written the letter on his behalf, but she didn't want to write him in care of that PO box in Baltimore.) A letter seemed the best way to go if she wanted to keep this matter contained.

Yet whenever she sat down at Peter's home computer, trying to use those oddments of minutes at a mother's disposal, she ended up second-guessing herself. A letter wasn't a small thing, not these days.

Even when she lived in London, she hadn't written letters. Trans-Atlantic calls weren't that expensive, and e-mails were always handy for rushed bulletins, or sharing the details of their visits home. Eliza couldn't remember the last time she had written a letter, and Walter's was the first real one she had received in years, probably since Vonnie switched to computers for those furious missives about how everyone in the family had disappointed her, a brief mania during her early thirties, when she was under the sway of a disreputable therapist, possibly her lover. But how else did one communicate with a man in prison?

Eliza smiled in spite of herself, thinking how this question would fit nicely on the running list she and Peter kept, "Things We Never Expected to Say." They had been keeping this since their college days, almost since the day they met, and it was actually a list of things they had overheard: *The bouillabaisse is dank. I left my poncho at the Ritz-Carlton. I have a fetish for fried chicken.*

Except—*How does one communicate with a man in prison* was not quite that bizarre, much less unique. Not in the world at large, and certainly not in Eliza's world in particular, given her mother's work at the Patuxent Institute and Eliza's peculiar history. One could even argue that it was an inevitable question, that if she had allowed herself to think about such things, she would have known that Walter would not leave this world without sending out some sort of manifesto. Not to her, necessarily. She really had come to be almost smug about how she had hidden herself in plain sight. She may not have deliberately chosen to hide herself from Walter, but between Peter's surname and the move to London, she had felt relatively invisible.

Walter always had a grandiose streak, a concept of himself as someone much larger than he was, in every sense of the word. He had insisted he was five nine, when he was clearly no more than five six or five seven. He became about as angry as Eliza ever saw him, talking about his height, claiming those inches he didn't have. It was one of the rare times she felt she had the upper hand with him, which had been terrifying and pleasing in equal measure. She couldn't afford the upper hand with Walter, or so she thought. Later, when people used terms like "Stockholm syndrome"—not her parents, but people far removed from her, prosecutors, journalists, and that odious Jared Garrett—she had found it offensively glib. That experience of being labeled had left her with a lifelong distaste for gossip, a reticence so pronounced that many people thought her incurious, when her real problem was an almost pathological politeness. She hated Iso's fascination with celebrities, the way she pored over magazine and Internet photos, passing judgment on dresses and hairdos and habits of people she had never met. But Eliza could never explain the virulence of her revulsion to her daughter, not unless she was willing to tell her everything. She would, one day, not today.

As she dawdled at the computer—it was late, after ten, but Peter had yet another function, one from which she was spared because the babysitter had fallen through—an icon glowed in the lower corner of her screen, announcing her sister's arrival into this netherworld.

Hi, Vonnie, she typed.

Eliza! The exclamation mark signaled surprise, if not necessarily delight. Eliza had never before initiated an IM conversation with her sister, and had been famously taciturn when her sister tried to engage her via this mode. **What's up?**

Nothing. Just trying to write something.

WHAT? Vonnie might as well have typed: *Peter is a writer. I am a writer. You are not a writer.* She had always been territorial that way. The funny thing was—neither one was a writer, not anymore. Peter had left journalism for the world of finance, and Vonnie was an editor at a publication so small and arcane that it was essentially unaffected by the Internet-related problems roiling the mainstream media. Something that had never made significant money could not lose significant money. Vonnie edited a foreign policy journal that charged $150 a year and was even stodgier than its subscriber list, whose average age was sixty-five. The subscribers were actually beginning to petition for some limited Web-based content, but Vonnie was fighting the change. "Life is not a timed event," she liked to say. "I want to run a magazine that has the luxury of thought, with no shot clock on responses."

A letter, Eliza wrote, reflexively honest with her family. But she thought before adding: **To Walter Bowman.**

WHAT??

It was funny, provoking that kind of adolescent response from Vonnie. Her sister might as well have typed back: **For reals?** Or: **R U Serious?**

He wrote me.

The phone rang within seconds.

"Are you out of your fucking mind?" Vonnie asked.

"You know, Iso might have been the one to pick up. It's not that late."

"However, she didn't. I promise I'll be more careful in the future. Meanwhile, let me repeat: Are you out of your fucking mind?"

"No, this is something I've been thinking about for a while. His letter came"—she did a quick calculation—"about ten days ago."

"And I'm just hearing about it now? I bet you told Mom and Dad."

Eliza had fumbled that, and badly. But Vonnie was so exhausting, ceaselessly demanding, always pulling focus. She hadn't told her precisely because she wanted to avoid this conversation. She decided to try and glide by that detail.

"He recognized me, in one of those society photos taken for a local magazine. Apparently, we're pretty easy to find, once you know we're in Bethesda. I think he used property records." She was hedging her bets again, not telling Vonnie that Walter clearly had an accomplice in this. Jared Garrett? She couldn't see him as the owner of that perfect purple penmanship.

"But why would you write him back?"

"Because"—she made up an answer on the spot, then realized it had the virtue of being true—"because he'll write again, and again, until I do. I know him, Vonnie."

"He's a sociopath. No one *knows* a sociopath. He's bored, in prison. He has every reason to reach out and poke you, see if he can get a response. That's his problem, not yours. Ignore him."

Vonnie had never suffered from uncertainty, about anything.

"They've scheduled his execution date."

"Ah, there's your smoking gun. He's using the cultural mania for closure to reach out to you. The man's a sadist. If I were you, I'd write back and ask if he's trying to get in touch with his victims. Particularly the Tacketts."

"Why 'particularly'?" she asked, more sharply than she intended. Eliza had always been sensitive to this sense of hierarchy among Walter's victims, in part because she had always been at the bottom *and* the top, if such a thing were possible. She was the most interesting because she lived; she was the least interesting because she lived. Holly was the prettiest, the golden girl. Holly's death had been particularly violent.

"Well, hers is the death that will result in his death, right? That's the one he's going to die for."

"Right." Maude had been killed in Maryland, which kept capital punishment on the books but was increasingly disinclined to use it. Holly Tackett had been killed in Virginia, which apparently suffered from no such qualms. "But why would he write the Tacketts, what would he say?"

"He might confess, for once. That's not so much to ask for, is it?"

Eliza thought, but did not say: *For Walter, that's huge.* Walter never said anything that he didn't want to say. He hated, more than anything, to be forced into saying he was wrong, no matter how small the matter. The first time he had hit Eliza was when she had corrected him on the facts of the War of 1812. It had been a strange hit—a punch, direct to the stomach, something a boy might have done to another boy, and it had knocked the wind out of her. But she never corrected him again, no matter how wrong he was, and he was often wrong. On history, on math, on picayune matters of grammar and usage. And, frequently, about people. Eliza had never known anyone who was more wrong about people, women in particular.

"Look, Eliza." Vonnie had softened her tone. "You're too nice for your own good. Forget Walter. Not *forget*—I know that's impossible—"

"You'd be surprised. I'd barely thought of him, particularly in the past few months."

"Hmmphf."

Eliza knew how to change the subject with her sister. "What's new with you?"

"Nothing. Everything. I was online at this godforsaken hour because I want to check on events in the Middle East in real time. I can't wait for the morning paper anymore, or even CNN. I hate how swiftly the world moves now, how glib everyone has become. We need to think more, not more quickly. Someone—the secretary of state, administration officials—will be on all the news programs tomorrow, delivering up these great gobs of sound bites, and people will be blogging like mad. It's not productive. Foreign policy is too nuanced, too steeped in centuries of history to be reduced to banal homilies. This isn't a partisan position," she said, almost as if rehearsing her own talking points. "It's an intellectual one. These issues must be addressed with gravitas."

Eliza didn't disagree. She felt the same way, only her concerns were domestic. The world was moving too swiftly, although it was strange to hear that complaint from caffeinated Vonnie. Iso and Albie were growing up too fast, Peter's new job gobbled up twelve, fourteen hours a day, in exchange for promises that they might be rich, truly rich, within a year or two.

Her own days, however, were molasses slow. They were full, with places to go and things to do, and she was exhausted at the end of them. But they trundled along like dinosaurs. The sauropod or the stegosaurus, which, according to Albie, were the slowest of the dinosaurs.

After listening sympathetically to her sister for another fifteen minutes, agreeing with virtually everything she said, Eliza begged off, saying she was tired. Yet she remained at the computer, writing. She was self-aware enough to realize that it was not incidental that she suddenly found the words she wanted to write to Walter. She was still at the computer when Peter returned an hour later, although she quickly closed the file, reluctant to discuss the matter again this evening, even with his sympathetic ear. She was, she decided, Waltered-out.

10

1985

SHE HAD NEVER GONE to the bathroom outside before. She knew it was an odd point on which to fixate, given what was happening to her, but it was embarrassing. She tried to persuade the man that she would behave if he would allow her to use a restroom at a gas station or fast-food place, but he wouldn't hear of it. He wasn't harsh or cruel. He simply shook his head and said, "No, that won't work."

They had been in the truck about three hours at this point. He had stopped and gassed up, but he had pumped his own gas and told her beforehand that it would be a bad idea for her to try to get out. "I don't want to hurt you," he said, as if she were in control, as if her behavior would determine what he did. He pulled the passenger side of the truck very close to the pump; if she opened the door, there would barely be room for her to squeeze out, and even then, she would be between the door and the hose. Of course, she could go out the other way, the driver's side. As the gas pump clicked away—it was an older pump, at a dusty, no-name place, and the dollars mounted slowly, cent by cent—she tested his reactions, leaning slowly toward the left. He was at the driver's-side door faster than she would have thought possible.

"You need something?"

"I was going to change the radio station."

"It isn't on," he pointed out. "I don't leave the key in the ignition when I pump gas. I knew a guy, once, he left his key in the ignition and the car blew up. He was a fireball, running in circles."

"I was going to change it for later," she said, almost apologetically. Why did she feel guilty about switching a radio station? He had kidnapped her. But the odd thing about this man was that he didn't act as if he were doing anything wrong. He reminded her a little of Vonnie in that way, especially when they were younger. Vonnie would do something cruel, then profess amazement at Elizabeth's reaction, focusing on some small misdeed by Elizabeth to excuse her behavior. When Elizabeth was three, Vonnie had tied her to a tree in the backyard and left her there all afternoon. Admonished by their parents, Vonnie had said: "She was playing with my Spirograph and she wouldn't stop putting pieces in her mouth. I just wanted to keep her from choking." One April Fools' Day, she had volunteered to fix Elizabeth milk with Ovaltine, then given her a vile concoction with cough syrup and cayenne pepper hidden beneath the pale brown milk. As Elizabeth had coughed and retched, Vonnie had said: "You spilled a little." As if the stains from the drink were more damning than the devious imagination of the person who had prepared it.

"You don't like my music?"

She weighed her answer. They had been listening to country music, which was uncool according to most people she knew. "It's okay," she said. "But I like other stuff, too."

"What do you listen to?"

"C-c-c-current stuff."

"Madonna," he said, looking at her fingerless lace mitts. "I'm guessing Madonna."

"Well, yeah," she said. "But also—" She racked her mind for the music she liked. "Whitney Houston. Scritti Politti. Kate Bush."

Except for the first name, these were Vonnie's musical choices, and Elizabeth wasn't sure why she was appropriating them. Because they made her seem older, wiser? Or because she sensed that the man wouldn't know most of them and that would give her some sort of power?

"She's a bad girl," he said.

"Kate Bush?"

"Whitney Houston. 'Saving all my love for you,' right? She's having an affair with a married man. That's wrong."

"But she loves him. And isn't what he's doing more wrong?"

"Women are better than men. Most, anyway. Men are weak, so women need to be strong." He reached in and punched a button on the radio, returning it to his station, although she had never touched it. The gas pump clicked off, and she hoped he might have to go inside to pay the attendant and then she would—she looked around. What would she do? It was surprising how quickly the landscape had turned into out-and-out country, real hicksville. If she had the chance to jump from the truck, where would she go? Later, when he pulled into a drive-through to buy her a hamburger, she had tried to announce to the attendant that she had been kidnapped, but he had placed his hand over hers, squeezing hard, and said: "Don't make jokes about things like that, Elizabeth." (She had given him her name at his insistence, but he had yet to share his.) The cashier, a teenager not much older than Elizabeth, had looked bored, as if she saw such things every day. She even seemed a little resentful, tired of couples playing out their dramas and private jokes in front of her. The girl had bad acne and frizzy hair, and her uniform pulled tightly across her broad torso. Elizabeth wanted to say: "He's not my boyfriend! I've never had a boyfriend! I'm more like you than you think, except I'm not old enough to work or drive a car."

He had kept squeezing her hand. It seemed to her at the time that he managed to exert just enough pressure to let her know that, in the next squeeze, he would crush every bone in her hand if she disobeyed him. Then he stroked her arm, along the inside. She remembered a game she played with her friends, where you closed your eyes and tried to guess when a trailing finger landed in the crook of your elbow. Depending on where it stopped, you were oversexed or undersexed. Everyone screamed in protest if they got oversexed, but, of course, that was the thing to be.

Elizabeth always ended up being undersexed, begging for the finger to stop well short of the elbow hollow.

The gas tank full, they drove on. An hour later, she asked if she could go to the bathroom. She expected him to scold her, as her father might have, for not asking when they were at the gas station. But he just sighed and said: "Okay, I'll find a place where you can have some privacy."

It took her a second to get it.

"Why can't I just go to a gas station or a fast-food place? Or even a restaurant."

"No," he said. "I don't think so." This was his way, she was learning. He said no, but, unlike her parents, he never explained his reasons, didn't provide enough information to allow argument.

"I'll be good," she said. "I don't want to go to the bathroom outside."

"Number one or number two?" he asked.

She thought about lying, but she didn't think the answer would change his mind. "Number one."

"If I were you," he said, "I'd take my panties off. Some girls leave 'em on one leg, but if you want to stay clean, it's better to take them all the way off, then squat. Keep your feet wide, too."

It made her sick, hearing him say the word *panties*. She thought about the things he was going to do to her, later. She thought about her parents, sitting down to dinner with Vonnie, wondering where she was. They wouldn't be worried, not just yet. They were calm people, unexcitable compared to most parents she knew. They trusted her. They would be irritated that she hadn't called, they would be readying a lecture on consideration, how the freedom they gave her came with responsibility. But they wouldn't worry about her until the sun set, which was still late this time of August, about eight or so.

Squatting in the dirt, her panties placed carefully on a nearby rock, she cried as she peed, then did a little dance, hoping to shake free whatever drops remained. She wasn't going to use leaves to blot herself, despite his advice. What if she picked poison ivy by mistake?

"Why are you crying?" he asked in the truck. He didn't retie her, though.

As darkness fell, he considered a few small motor inns, finally settling on one in a U-shaped court. "We won't do this often," he said. "This is a treat because we've both had a long day and need a real mattress. Tomorrow, we'll get a tent, some sleeping bags." Once in the room, after testing the bed and finding out it was bolted to the floor, he bound her hands and feet, then gagged her. She began crying again, the tears falling down into the corners of her mouth.

"Shush," he said. "With time, when I can trust you, it won't have to be like this. But you have to earn my trust, okay? You earn my trust and you can have all sorts of freedoms. But if you wrong me, I'll kill you and your whole family. I'll kill your family while you watch, then kill you. Don't think I won't."

Her parents had given her similar instructions about trust—except for the killing part. She cried harder, wondering how awful it was going to be. She had read stories about rape, of course. Quite a few, given her taste in reading. And four years ago, she had watched, along with millions of others, an episode of a soap opera where a rape victim married her rapist. Of course, they had come a long way by then, Luke and Laura. They had been on the run together, evaded death, grown close. They were in love, and she had forgiven him. Vonnie had insisted, loudly and at great length, that it was all crap. But when the afternoon of the wedding came, Vonnie was there, watching as raptly as Elizabeth and her friends. They did not find the groom particularly handsome, but they understood that he was desirable because he loved his bride so much, that his love for her had driven him to commit crimes and take enormous risks. That one of those crimes had been an assault on his alleged beloved was tricky, but they understood. To be loved that way, to be desired to the point where you drove a man mad—what more could any girl want?

"Look," the man said, "can you be brave? Can you be good?"

She nodded, although she was sure she could not.

"Okay," he said. "I'll take the gag out. But you have to be good. You know what I mean, by good? No screaming or crying. If you make a sound, I'll put the gag in and show you the ways I know how to hurt people. I'm not a man to be messed with. Just go to sleep, and we'll talk things out in the morning."

Her mouth freed, she thought for a moment about screaming her head off but found she could not make the sounds come. She was too frightened, too scared. His hands lingered near her throat. She thought about the mound of dirt where she had first seen the man, working with his shovel. He had not said, explicitly, what he had done, but she knew. He was capable of killing someone. He had done it. Elizabeth decided in that moment that she would do whatever was necessary to survive. She would endure whatever plans he had for her, as long as she was allowed to live.

"What's your name?" she whispered.

"Walter," he said. "I think sometimes I should shorten it to Walt. What do you think?"

She was terrified that there was a right answer, and she wouldn't give it. "Both are nice."

He watched her for a while, hands at the ready to clamp over her mouth. His gaze was detached, curious. She snuffled and gagged a little on her tears, but was otherwise quiet as commanded. He took his hand away—and went to sleep.

Eventually, she slept, too, and they stayed that way, side by side, on top of the bedspread. He touched her only once, turning her on her side and complaining: "You snore."

11

FOR A FEW DAYS, the letter to Walter was like a pink elephant, the one in the mental exercise that instructs a person to think about anything they desired—with the exception of pink elephants. *Had he gotten it? Was it enough? Would he be disappointed?*

She had written him with what she hoped was polite finality. Yes, she was married and living in the area. (Funny to be vague, when he knew her exact address.) She omitted any reference, any hint, to Iso and Albie. Walter was not a pedophile, although there had always been some confusion about that, given the age of his victims, and she doubted he would escape, much less head toward Bethesda if he should. But the fact of motherhood was too intimate to share with him. She wrote that it was *inter-*

esting to hear from him, yet *not completely unexpected*. How she had struggled over those words, weighed each one. What would Walter read into "not completely unexpected"? He had an uncanny ability to hear what he wanted, to glean meanings that no one else could see. Later, in college, when she took a course in semiotics, she couldn't help thinking that Walter could give Derrida a run for his money. Walter took everything down to the word, then made words signify what he wanted them to, justify whatever he wanted to do. He was like a character from *Alice in Wonderland,* or one of the later *Oz* books, the one with the town where everyone spoke nonsense. Rigamarole, that was it.

Still, she also was careful not to write anything that would cause him trouble, although the letter would not be scrutinized by some official. Walter was most unpredictable, most likely to lash out, when he thought someone was trying to hurt him. She chose to send her letter via the same PO box that had been used as the return address on the letter to her, not the prison's address. She knew this meant that Walter's coconspirator, whoever it was—please, not Jared Garrett—might read the letter first, although she put it in a sealed envelope within the stamped and addressed one. But whoever was helping Walter already knew who and where she was. If she sent the letter in care of the prison, it would take only one gossipy correctional officer to send her life careering out of control.

Besides, she understood now why he had written via an intermediary. As an inmate, he was not allowed to write just anyone, a fact she had been able to establish by a cursory search of the official Web page maintained by Virginia's prison system. *Correctional* facilities, as the official jargon had it. The word struck her as sweetly naive and utterly false. While she realized that prisons did attempt to rehabilitate inmates, she was not sure how anyone on death row could be said to be in a correctional facility, unless one considered death a correction.

She struggled most over the ending. *Sincerely*? Insincere. *All the best*? More like, *All my worst*. She chose to sign her name, assigning no emotion at all.

TIME, HER OLD FRIEND, exercised its subtle power. The letter dropped to the back of her mind, like a sock lost behind the dryer. Or, perhaps more accurately, a bit of perishable food behind the refrigerator, something that would eventually stink or bring pests into the house but that enjoyed a brief, carefree amnesty in the short term. Meanwhile, there had been too much to do to prepare for the beginning of school. The children would be attending two different schools, with Iso riding a bus to middle school and Albie attending the elementary school within walking distance. It would be Eliza's responsibility to get them both off in the morning, which didn't bother her at all. This was her job, it was what she did, and she was—she admitted privately—superb at it. Privately because it was the kind of sentiment that did not land gently, anywhere. Vonnie became almost enraged at the idea that Eliza considered being a mother a full-time job, and a satisfying one at that. Even their mother couldn't help wondering where Eliza would find fulfillment as the children grew. Inez was forever suggesting that Eliza would want to return to school eventually, finish the graduate degree she had abandoned at Rice. The women in Peter's world, the ones she met at those endless functions, tried hard to remember to add "outside the home" when they asked if Eliza worked, or had ever worked, but their politeness could not mask their belief that what she did was *not* work. Hard, perhaps, tedious without a doubt. But not work.

That was okay. Eliza didn't consider it work, either, because she enjoyed it too much. It was the thing at which she excelled. She wasn't one of the smarmily perfect mothers, packing ambitious lunches, never falling back on prepared treats for classroom parties. But she was more or less unflappable, rolling with things. In fact, she liked a bit of a crisis now and then—the science project left until the last minute, lost homework, lost anything. Nothing remained missing when Eliza began searching for it. She knew her children so well that it was easy for her to re-create those absentminded moments when things were put down in the wrong place. She was aware, for example, that Iso took out her retainer while watching television, so it was often found balanced on the arm of the sofa. She understood that dreamy Albie lived so far inside his own imagination that anything could become part of that world. His knapsack might be found perched on the head of the enormous stuffed dog his aunt Vonnie had given him, creating a reasonable facsimile of an archbishop, although Albie was probably aiming for a wizard.

She was on her hands and knees, looking under the bed for Albie's missing trainer—*sneaker*—when the phone rang. Albie had been forced to wear his sandals to school, which he didn't mind until Iso teased him about it, and he had walked the five blocks to school as if heading to the guillotine, sniffling and wailing the whole way. Eliza had promised she would find his shoes before day's end, perhaps even bring them at lunchtime. She snagged the shoe, marveling at how far it had traveled from its mate, which had been discovered in the first-floor powder room, then dashed for the phone, a habit she couldn't quite break. Even when the children were in the house, present and accounted for, the ringing phone taunted her with the possibility of an emergency. Strange, because if there were an emergency, it would be much more likely to arrive via the chirpy ringtone of her cell phone. *Got that one right,* she congratulated herself, picking up the phone in her bedroom.

"Is this Elizabeth?" a woman's voice asked.

Reflexively, she almost said no.

"Elizabeth Benedict?" the woman clarified. But those two

names were never paired, ever. It must be a telephone solicitor, working off some official list, perhaps one gleaned from the county property records? But, no, she used Eliza on all official documents except her driver's license and passport, had since her registration at Wilde Lake High School in 1986. Did call centers have access to MVA records?

"Yes, but please put me on your do-not-call list. I don't buy things over the phone, ever."

"I'm not selling anything." The woman's voice was husky, her laugh a throaty rasp. "I'm the go-between."

"Go-between?"

"The person who passed that letter to you, from Walter. He wants to add you to his call list." Again, that raspy laugh. "Not to be confused with the federal do-not-call registry."

"Excuse me?"

"He's allowed to make collect calls to up to fifteen people. Of course, he doesn't have anywhere near that many. Just his lawyer and me, as far as I know. He can add you without his lawyer's knowledge. But you have to say it's okay. Is it?"

"Is it—"

"Okay." The woman was clearly getting impatient. "And telling me isn't enough. You'll have to make an official request, via the prison. Then there's paperwork. There's *always* paperwork."

"I don't . . . no, I don't think so. No."

"It's your decision," the woman said, and then promptly negated that obvious fact. "But I think you should."

"Excuse me, but who are you?"

"A friend of Walter's." She rushed on, as if forestalling a question she was asked all the time. "I'm not one of those women who moons over an inmate, one of those wackos. I'm opposed to the death penalty. In general, but Virginia is where I've decided to focus my interest, especially since Maryland has a de facto moratorium. I'm a compassionate friend to several inmates. But Walter's my favorite. Do you know that Virginia is second, nationwide, in terms of the raw numbers of people executed? Texas is first, of course, but it has a much larger population. And if you knew how the appeals process was structured here—" That laugh again. She was one of those people who used laughter as punctuation, no matter how inappropriate.

"If you really know Walter—"

"I do," she shot back, apparently offended at Eliza's use of the conditional.

"I mean, I assume you know his story and mine. Which means you know he's not someone I've been in contact with, ever."

"Do you think he deserves to die for what he did?"

"It doesn't matter what I think. He was sentenced to die for the murder of Holly Tackett, and her parents made it clear that they approved of the death penalty. I wasn't consulted."

"Wasn't your mom a Quaker?"

"Grandmother," she said, unnerved by this piece of information. Was it something she had told Walter? They talked a lot, during the weeks they'd spent together, but she had been careful not to reveal much. Even at the age of fifteen, she had been shrewd enough not to encourage Walter's envy and resentment, and she had recognized, if only in the wake of her capture, that her family was eminently enviable. She had avoided telling him that her parents were psychiatrists, for example, much less that her mother worked with the criminally insane. She described her home as average, an aging split-level on the south side of Frederick Road, the better to throw him off the track if he ever made good on his threats. She had no memory of discussing her gentle grandmother, who attended the Quaker meetinghouse in North Baltimore and thought the girls should attend the Friends School, despite the distance from their house. She had even offered to pay their tuition.

Later—*after*—that option had been raised again, sending

Elizabeth-now-Eliza to Friends, perhaps having her live with her grandmother during the week. But Eliza was the one who vetoed it. She wanted to go to a larger school, not a smaller one. She needed to be someplace where being new wouldn't attract as much attention.

"I bet your grandmother wouldn't want Walter to be executed."

"This conversation is . . . unsettling to me," Eliza said. "I'm sure you can understand that. I'm going to need to let you go."

It occurred to her that she was being kinder to this woman—why hadn't she offered *her* name—than she would have been to a telephone solicitor.

"I'm sorry," the woman said, with a sincerity that robbed Eliza of any self-righteousness she might have felt. "I get carried away. Walter would be the first person to tell you that. He'd be mad, if he knew that I had upset you. It's just—there's so little I can do. For him. Putting him in touch with you, it's one of the rare times I could do him a solid."

Do him a solid. Eliza couldn't remember the last time she had heard that phrase.

"He would be angry at me, for pressing you. That's not his way. He would love to talk to you. But he would be the first one to say that he doesn't want to bother you."

"Does he want to talk to me about something in particular?"

"No," the woman said. "He feels bad. He knows he's going to die. He accepts that. He's been on death row longer than anyone in Virginia. Did you know that? He's seen other men come and . . . go. I think he started to believe his turn would never come, but his case was so unusual. As you know."

Eliza wasn't sure that she did know the ways in which Walter's case was unusual, but she refused to be drawn into this conversation.

"Could I have your name?" she asked the woman.

"Why?" Suspicious, skeptical. Eliza wanted to laugh. *You call me, on Walter's behalf, you make it possible for him to write to me, and you question* my *motives?*

"Because I'm going to think about this and call you back."

"You better not be up to anything," the woman warned. "Don't make trouble for us. We haven't done anything wrong."

This is silly, Eliza thought, thinking for the first time to look at the caller ID feature on her phone. Blocked. "This is silly," she said. "You called me. You have asked for, well, an enormous favor and demanded an immediate reply. All I want is time to think about it."

"I'll get back to you," the woman said. "Early next week. We don't have much time, you know."

12

1985

THE HAIR RIBBON, WALTER THOUGHT when he read the Baltimore papers two mornings later. *That goddamn Madonna-inspired hair ribbon.* When had it fallen off? Had she been sly enough to drop it on purpose when he pulled her into the truck? He had remembered to grab her boots, thinking she would need shoes, and those would have to do until he could get her more practical ones. No matter. Searchers had found the ribbon, and then they had found the grave. The paper, running a day behind events, said the body had not yet been exhumed, but as soon as it was uncovered, they would know it wasn't her. The body had probably already been unearthed and identified, while he sat here with scorched coffee and runny eggs.

He was in a truck stop in western Maryland, near the fork where one had to choose whether to keep going west, toward Cumberland, or head north into Pennsylvania. East, toward Baltimore, was out of the question. *Head north, head north, head north,* his brain told him, *then west.* But his truck had West Virginia plates, and it was a funny thing, one didn't see them much on the open road, away from his home state. And he had been looking for those blue-and-gold plates, he realized. True, they probably weren't quite as rare on the Ohio Turnpike, but he was still reluctant to go that way, in part because he had never been that way. He wasn't adventurous, he realized now. He thought he had yearned to travel, to see places far beyond where he grew up, but now all he wanted was to go home. Only he couldn't. Not with her, and maybe not at all, ever again. What would he tell his parents about the time he went missing? Whatever he did with her, he would have to answer a lot of questions.

Elizabeth was flipping through the selections on the mini-jukebox set up on the table. Just thirty-six hours into their acquaintance, as he thought of it, she had already learned to speak when spoken to, not to yammer away about every little thing in her head. She had good manners, actually. This morning, she had ordered scrambled eggs and an English muffin, but accepted without complaint the fried eggs and wheat toast that came in their place. The waitress was a knockout in training, with flame-colored hair and a terrific figure, and Walter could tell she was used to not getting things right and facing no consequences. He had wanted to call her back, dress her down, but Elizabeth had said, "No, I'm fine." It was clear from how she nibbled only the whites around the yolk that she wasn't fine, but he admired her niceness. The waitress, all of nineteen or twenty, looked through him. Did she think Elizabeth was his girlfriend? Or that he was her father? Brother and sister, he decided. That would be the most believable play, the simplest.

The smarter move, he knew, would be to kill her. Kill her, get rid of the body—don't even bother to dig a grave this time, just leave her somewhere inaccessible, there was still plenty of wilderness out here—and go home. Tell his folks he'd been on a fishing trip, had some car trouble, had to wait for a part, didn't want to call collect and couldn't afford to dial long-distance because he was saving every penny to pay the mechanic in cash. There was nothing to connect the girl back in Patapsco State Park to him, or any other girl. This girl was the only one who could hurt him.

Yet there was something about her, struggling to choke down her eggs, that reminded him of someone. *She's like me,* he thought. She's polite and nice, she does her best, and people don't hear her, don't pay attention.

"Do you have a boyfriend?" he asked.

She was in the habit of thinking before she answered him. He realized this was partly because she was weighing everything she said, intent on pleasing him. That was good.

"No," she said. "Not yet."

"Well, how old are you?"

"Fifteen."

"That's too young for a boyfriend." He knew that he had attempted to go with girls her age, or not much older, but there was fifteen and then there was fifteen. She was the first kind.

"There was a boy, at this camp I went to last summer, and we were kind of boyfriend and girlfriend, but it doesn't really count at camp because you don't make plans."

"What do you mean?" He honestly didn't have a clue what she meant, and he hoped her answer might shed some light on one of the many things that baffled him when it came to women.

"Well, at camp, there's a schedule. No one can invite you to go anywhere—to a movie, or the mall, or even a McDonald's. So you sit on the bus together, or swim together, and you hold hands"—she blushed at this. Maybe he was wrong, maybe she had done more than he realized. "It's not a date, and it ends when camp ends. He called me, once, but we didn't really have anything to talk about. I wrote him letters, and he never wrote back."

"Yeah, I see your point." He didn't, not really, but he didn't have anything to contribute, so he wanted to move on. "Look, what would you do, if I just got up right now, paid the check, went out to my truck, and started driving?"

Again, she did not answer right away.

"Elizabeth?"

"I guess I'd ask the people if I could use their phone, make a collect call, and I'd call my parents, tell them where I was."

"Do you know where you are?"

"Sort of. Not exactly. But the people here, they would tell me, right?"

He looked around. "Lower your voice," he said. "I'm serious."

She flinched. It was amazing how easily he could control her. He liked it.

"I'd call my parents collect," she whispered, "and then I'd wait for them to come get me."

"What's my truck look like?"

"Red."

"Make? Model?"

She needed a second to understand that question, then shook her head. "I haven't noticed."

"License plate?"

"I haven't paid attention."

She was a shitty liar. *"Elizabeth."*

She hung her head, whispered the plate numbers.

"Look," he said, "I have to keep you with me."

"I wouldn't tell," she said. "If that's what you need me to do, I'll do it."

"No, you would tell. Because you think it's the right thing, and I can see that you're the kind of person who tries to do the right thing. Like me. The thing is— I didn't really do anything. It's just that, no one's going to believe that. This girl, she tried to get out of my truck while it was moving, she fell and hit her head."

It sounded plausible to him, now that he had said it. It absolutely could have happened just as he said, and who would believe him? It was so unfair.

"But no one's going to believe that, right?" He saw that Elizabeth didn't believe it. Her face was interesting that way. Some people would call her an open book, but Walter didn't think that expression was quite apt. An open book, glimpsed, was only words on a page, and you couldn't make out the whole story. Her face was like . . . fish in an aquarium, all her thoughts and feelings on display, but moving kind of lazily, not in a rush to get anywhere.

"I didn't mean any harm," he tried, and this had the virtue of truth, or was at least more in the neighborhood of truth, but he could see she was still dubious. "I've made some mistakes, but everyone makes mistakes. People just don't listen, you know? Girls. They don't listen. They're in too much of a hurry, all the time."

"We read this book, *Of Mice and Men,* in seventh-grade G-and-T English," she began.

"G and T?"

"Oh, um, gifted and talented. But it's my only G-and-T class." She was embarrassed to be caught bragging. She hadn't realized she was bragging at first, but now she was owning up to it. That was important. "Anyway, there's a man in it, he doesn't mean any harm, but he's really strong, and when his hand gets tangled in this girl's hair, he's just trying to calm her down, but he breaks her neck."

"And what happened to this guy?"

A long pause. "Well, he was simple. What people call retarded, sometimes, although my parents don't like that word."

"It's just a word."

She shot him a look, as if on the verge of contradicting him, then changed her mind. "That's true. It's just a word." He liked that, the way she repeated after him. "He couldn't understand the things he did. He never meant to harm anyone or anything. Once, he petted a puppy to death."

"People who hurt dogs are the lowest of the low."

"But he wasn't *trying* to hurt the dog. He was just petting it. He didn't know how strong he was. That was his problem."

"What happened to him?"

He could see her considering a lie, then rejecting it. "His friend killed him. He was too pure for this world. That's what my teacher said. He was forever a child, but in a man's body, and he couldn't live in this world."

He was taken with that phrase. Forever a child, in a man's body. It touched on something he felt about himself. Not being a child, of course. He was the opposite of simple. He was complicated. That was his problem, most likely. He was too complicated, too thoughtful, too full of ideas to have the life that people expected him to have. He should have been born somewhere intense, interesting, not in a little town where people didn't have get-up-and-get. Dallas, for example, which struck him as a place that rewarded ambition and masculinity. All the men on that television show, even the wimpy ones, were men's men, big and strong. Maybe they should go to Dallas.

And it would have to be "they," at least for a while. He couldn't let her go, but he also couldn't do anything more definitive, not yet. That was the downside of spending too much time with someone, especially someone whose fears and dreams swam across her face. It was like naming the Thanksgiving turkey. Not that a name had ever kept him from petitioning for the drumstick, come the day.

"Do you know more stories?" he asked her. "Like the one you just told, only maybe happier?"

"Well, the same guy who wrote that, he drove around the country with his poodle, Charley. I mean, for real."

"And what happened?"

"Lots of things."

"You can tell me while I'm driving."

He let her use the bathroom, having checked ahead of time that it was a one-seater without a window to the outside, and there was a cigarette machine in the hallway, so he didn't look odd, waiting there, pulling on the various handles, fishing for change. Once, when he was thirteen, he had found seventy-five cents in the pay phone at his father's gas station, and that had seemed miraculous to him. A waitress—not the redhead, but an older woman—glanced back at him, curious, and he said, just thought of it out of the blue: "Her first, um, time, you know? With her ladies' issues? And our mama's dead and she's freaking out."

"Poor thing. Should I ask her if she needs help?"

"Oh, no, ma'am. She's shy. That would just make it worse." The woman smiled, pleased with him. Maybe having a little sister would make him seem less threatening to women. Of course, this waitress was old, dried up, but maybe other women, women his age, would be charmed by a man taking care of his sister.

The pay phone gave him an idea, and he asked the waitress if she could change five dollars for him. He called his father's shop and spoke to C.J., the woman who kept the books and answered the phones. He had joined the Marines, he told her. Sold the truck to a friend, cashed out his bank account, what little there was of it. (Later that day, he would hit an ATM—take whatever it would give him—or find a branch that might cash his check.) No, please don't call his father to the phone. He would only yell. About his truck, not about his only son and coworker going off to join the Marines.

He hung up and listened to the various plumbing sounds, asking when she came out: "Did you wash your hands?" She shook her head, and he sent her back. She was a good girl. She would do whatever he told her to.

13

"THAT'S ENOUGH," PETER SAID, when Eliza told him about the phone call the next morning as he prepared coffee for the enormous travel mug he toted to work each day. (She had been asleep when he arrived home, and although she roused when he slid into bed next to her, she hadn't wanted to attempt a serious conversation so late. Besides, they had fallen in the habit of using Peter's breakfast, that quiet lull after the children had left for school, to catch up.) "Who's his lawyer? That should be easy enough to find out."

"You'll be late," she said.

"This is worth being late for."

Within five minutes on the computer and another five on the telephone, Peter was demanding to speak to Jefferson D.

Blanding, an attorney with a nonprofit in Charlottesville. Eliza couldn't help being thrilled by the way her husband came to her defense. It was one of the qualities she had admired in him, even when they were nothing more than friends. Peter took charge of everything and everyone, not just her. He didn't have to be the boss, but when certain situations came to a head—a disagreement with someone over a bill, a contractor who refused to do what he had promised, a mix-up at an airline ticket counter—Peter took over. He was forceful without being rude, intent on finding solutions, as opposed to venting his anger in a bullying way. In England, this part of him had become a little muted, so it was particularly exciting to see it engaged again, and on her behalf.

"He was actually very nice, once he understood why I was calling," Peter said. "I got the sense that he was even a little horrified, although he put it on the woman. He said she's well meaning, but in over her head."

"Who is she?"

"Barbara LaFortuny."

"No."

Peter laughed. "Yeah, and he swears it's her real name. Sounds like a stage name for some exotic dancer."

Eliza thought about the voice on the phone, the vinegary rasp. "How old a woman?"

"I didn't ask, but I had the sense she's in her forties or fifties. She was a schoolteacher in Baltimore city and she was attacked on the job several years ago, by a student with a knife. She won an undisclosed settlement from the system because the school had refused to remove the kid from her classroom despite repeated warnings. You think that would tilt her toward victims' rights, but instead she became an advocate for prisoners. Got interested in conditions in state prisons, then began looking at the death penalty. Somehow came to befriend Walter."

"She made a point of telling me she wasn't one of *those* women. You know, the kind that fall in love with an inmate."

"No, she's not in love with him. But she's grown obsessed with trying to get his execution stayed. More so than Walter, according to his lawyer. He said it's possible she's acting alone, without Walter's knowledge."

Eliza shook her head. The letter's style, its cadences—those had been pure Walter.

"She wouldn't have known me, by a photo. And I don't see how she could have learned my married name. Walter wrote that he saw the photo, that he recognized me." *I'd know you anywhere.* "Is this woman, Barbara, black?"

"It didn't occur to me to ask. Why?"

"She didn't sound black. But a Baltimore city schoolteacher and . . ." Her voice trailed off from embarrassment.

Peter smiled, shook a playful finger at her. "Are you racial profiling now, Eliza? Assuming a woman with an unusual name has to be black?"

"No, no," she protested. "It was the detail about teaching in city schools—"

Peter started laughing.

"—teaching in the schools and being swayed to the issue of prisoners' rights, despite being attacked." But she was laughing now, too, unafraid of being exposed. She had never really understood the old saying "safe as houses," but it described how she felt with Peter. Safe, solid, loved unconditionally. They had been a couple, an official couple, for six months before she told him about Walter. It had started with an argument about sleeping with the windows open. A reasonable request, on Peter's part—the New England spring, late as ever, had finally delivered its first perfect night, and they lived on the third floor of a ramshackle apartment building favored by students. But she had been adamant, oddly adamant, growing angry and tearful. Awed by this obstinacy in the otherwise pliant, easygoing Eliza, Peter had yielded. The next morning, over waffles at O'Rourke's, she had apologized. It had not been her intent to explain herself further, but she couldn't stop. The story tumbled out, as if she had never told it before. And, in some ways, she hadn't. Yes, she had testified. Yes, she had been deposed, interviewed repeatedly by various official sorts. Debriefed, in a sense, by her own parents, who also sent her to a gentle therapist.

But Eliza had never told the story of her own volition, and to use the parlance of Peter's future career, she buried the lead: "When I was fifteen, a man kind of abducted me," she began. "He thought I had seen something he had done, that I could identify him. Which was funny because when I was fifteen, all grown-ups looked alike to me, you know? I didn't notice him, and I never could have described him. But he took me."

Peter had not rushed in with questions. This would be his trademark as a reporter, in the years to come. Peter, Eliza had heard his colleagues say, was the master of the pause, silences that seemed designed to be filled with confidences.

"I was with him five weeks. Actually, thirty-nine days. Five weeks, four days. One day shy of the flood in the Bible. I never thought forty days and forty nights was that long, when I was in Sunday school. I'd think, 'It's only a little more than a month.' But it can be a really long time."

The waffles had a rich blueberry sauce on top. Eliza, who normally cleaned her plate, began mashing the tines of her fork into them, flattening them, eliminating their grids.

"Toward the end, he took another girl. But that sparked a huge manhunt, and the police found us. But not before she died."

"She died," Peter echoed. "You mean—he killed her?"

Eliza nodded. "It wasn't the first time, although no one knows how many girls he killed. He was burying a girl when I stumbled on him, in the park that ran near our old house. Some people say he may have killed as many as a dozen girls in the years before he was caught."

Eliza waited, almost holding her breath. Peter did not ask: "Why didn't he kill you?" Instead, he asked: "How were you rescued?"

She almost said: "I'm not sure I was." But she was not melodramatic that way and she had no doubt that she had, in fact, been rescued. "It was pretty anticlimactic. He ran a red light and just started babbling to the police officer. It turned out that a clerk in Piggly Wiggly had seen us in the store that morning, thought we looked odd, and called the police."

"What did she notice that no one else had seen all that time? Were you never in public?"

She did not want to lie to Peter, or mislead him, but nor could she tell him everything. "It's funny, what people don't see. He had cut my hair—god, he had given me this horrible haircut, it made me cry—and while I didn't look like a boy, which was what he intended, I certainly didn't look like the photo of me that was circulating. And I was scared of him, I didn't mouth off or try to do anything to draw attention to us."

"You know what?" Peter had said.

"What?" she had asked, fearful. She honestly could not imagine what would happen next, given that she had confided in only one other person, back in high school, and that had ended badly.

"I think you need more coffee." He didn't signal the waitress, who was busy with another table, but got up and grabbed the thermal carafe from behind the counter, filled Eliza's mug. She knew, at that moment, that Peter would always take care of her, if only she would let him.

That had been their pattern for almost twenty years now; they were solicitous of each other, dividing their duties between the world at large and their home. Peter fought the battles beyond the house, while Eliza tried to make sure that the windows were always closed and locked, their alarm system in working order. They were a team.

Over time, of course, she had told him more, in greater detail. Peter never wondered why she was the lucky one. He took it for granted that she was, and he was glad for it. "We don't ponder why lightning strikes where it does," he said once. Later, after a London-based magazine had asked him to file dispatches from New Orleans on the first anniversary of Katrina, he had written beautiful passages about the levees, human-designed and maintained systems that had failed spectacularly. He described how arbitrary water was, destroying one neighborhood while leaving another relatively intact. He never said as much, but Eliza believed he had written those words for her, that it was a sonnet of sorts, more proof that Peter understood. Walter was a natural disaster made catastrophic by human failures. She had been on one side of the levee, Holly on the other. Don't ask why.

Now, packing up his briefcase, getting ready to go, Peter said: "The lawyer, Blanding, told me that Walter's phone list is up to him, but his visiting list is another matter. It would be almost impossible for you to visit him. But Walter might ask for that, eventually. And if you were interested, it could happen because of who you are, your status."

She didn't think she was interested, she was pretty sure she wasn't interested, but she couldn't help wondering what Peter had said on her behalf. "What did you tell him?"

He looked surprised. "That it was up to you, of course. It is. I assume you don't want to see him, but maybe you do. I'll tell you this much: I'd be more comfortable with you going to see Walter, with security all around, than with you meeting up with this Barbara LaFortuny person. She's the one who scares me."

He kissed her temple, said, "Off to make the doughnuts," and headed out to another one of his twelve-hour days. Eliza no longer really understood what Peter did for a living. She knew what venture capital was, and she knew that Peter had been recruited, in part, for the lucidity of his prose and his ability to explain complicated investment tools to the most unsophisticated investors. But she didn't really know what he did, much less why it paid so well, and that was a little terrifying. Their old friends, almost all in the newspaper world, were taking buy-outs or pay cuts, getting laid off, and her family was thriving. Again: Don't ask why.

She drifted over to the computer, entered the name "Barbara LaFortuny." For an activist, she was suspiciously inactive, leaving few traces of herself in the public sphere, although there was a Baltimore *Beacon-Light* profile available only in abstract; she would have to pay to read the entire article. She wasn't that interested, and it was a relief to discover how low her threshold was: She wouldn't pay $3.95 to find out more about Barbara LaFortuny. But her fingers continued to wander, plugging the name into the images file and recoiling at the one photo that showed up: a woman with three-quarters of her face swathed in bandages. Amazing, the power of an image compared with words. Peter had stood here not five minutes ago and explained that this woman, Walter's champion, had been a victim of a knife attack. But the horror hadn't truly registered.

This was why Eliza seldom spoke of the rape. Words could not convey what Walter had done to her, the depth of the betrayal, more brutal than the act itself. And there was no photo, no image, to show the damage he had inflicted. Eliza was not inclined to be competitive about suffering; after all, there were at least two dead girls always at the ready, eager to inform her that she was, in fact, the lucky one, and a whole cadre of possible victims behind them. But she couldn't help feeling a little superior to Barbara LaFortuny. Just a little. A line from a poem came to her, something about the people who never got suffering wrong. Yet in Eliza's experience, everyone, even most victims, got suffering wrong. That's why it was better never to speak of it.

14

1985

THEY DROVE. IF THERE WAS a purpose, a destination, Elizabeth could not pinpoint it. They had dipped down into Virginia, this much was clear from the highway signs, and they sometimes crossed the Shenandoahs into West Virginia. Walter found odd jobs to make cash—chopping wood, for example, to help people with vacation homes prepare for the winter ahead, which Walter said would be a bad one, as bad as last winter, which had seen one of the worst snowstorms in the area's history. "I feel it in my bones," he said, and he was being literal. He chopped wood, he did yard work, he fixed things. Elizabeth was surprised by the ease with which he found work, how people looked past her, never questioning why she was with Walter and, after Labor Day passed, not in school. Perhaps they thought she was simpleminded, as simple as Lennie in *Of Mice and Men*. She seldom spoke. Walter had made it clear that she should answer only direct questions with as few words as possible. And although Walter had purchased clothing for her—two pairs of jeans, some T-shirts, a sweater, all from JCPenney—she always looked a little dingy because she had to wear each outfit three to four times before they could go to a coin laundry. It was one of the few times he left her alone. He would have her strip down behind a sheet, whether at a motor court or a campsite, then hand him her clothes. He tied her hands, but not her feet, and although he gagged her the first few times, he didn't even bother with that after a while.

She could, of course, have left the room or the tent, wrapped in nothing but a sheet. Her feet were free. She could have called for help when he stopped gagging her. But it was too embarrassing. She could not get past imagining those first few minutes, when she would be the girl in the sheet, when people would point and laugh and maybe worse. There was the very fact of the . . . unloveliness of her body, the potbelly, which was more pronounced from their fast-food, on-the-go diet. She could not imagine walking around in a sheet, worrying about what might be glimpsed, or how it might come untied.

The real problem was that she couldn't imagine escaping at all. He would kill her. Kill her family. She dreamed of rescue, hoped for it, prayed, but she believed it would have to be something that happened to her, not because of her.

SOMETIMES SHE WOULD TRY to pinpoint where she would be, back home, at a particular time of day. At, say, 10:15 A.M., she would picture the mind-numbing lull of late morning in school, those early periods when the day's promise has already burned off, but the end still seems impossibly distant. At 4 P.M., she would see herself lying on the sofa, watching television while doing her homework, the height of her rebelliousness. Her parents always said they didn't mind if she watched television before or after homework, only never during. But there would be no one to rat her out, since Vonnie had gone to college. Only—had Vonnie left for college, after Elizabeth disappeared? Probably. Elizabeth hoped she had. A disappointed Vonnie was a terrible, terrible thing. Vonnie seemed to believe that she should always get what she wanted, more so than other people. The drama around her college applications had been intense, affecting the entire household. They all knew better than to fetch the mail during those weeks when acceptances—and, in one memorable case, an actual rejection, from Duke—started arriving, but Elizabeth might sneak a peek into the mailbox if she got home before Vonnie. She examined the envelopes, knowing that it was all about fat versus thin, daydreamed about the day when her own letters would be waiting for her. But she didn't dare take the mail in, and even her parents ceded that privilege to Vonnie.

In the truck, driving the mind-numbingly familiar roads, Walter said: "Tell me a story. Tell me about that man and his dog."

She did. The problem was—she hadn't actually read *Travels with Charley*. She had started it but found it dull, not at all the work she was expecting after reading *Of Mice and Men* and *Cannery Row*. But she was scared to admit that she had lied—Walter prized honesty above all other values and had made it clear that she must always tell him the truth—so she made it up as she went along, trying to figure out what kind of stories Steinbeck and his poodle would have lived on the road. She borrowed heavily from a book her father had read the summer before last, *Blue Highways,* which had inspired her parents to take them on back-road drives in Maryland, Pennsylvania, and Virginia. God, it had been boring.

Sometimes, roaming with Walter, she would glimpse a place, a town, a gas station that she thought she recognized from those day trips, but she could never be sure.

"Tell me another story," Walter repeated. It was a gray, indeterminate day, out of season. Too cool to be summer, which it still was on the calendar, but lacking the crispness of autumn. The air was muggy, as damp and unrewarding as a sponge bath.

"Well, there's a time when they went to . . . Tulsa."

"Tulsa? After Milwaukee?"

"I'm not telling it in order, just as I remember it."

"Where did they start again?"

"New York."

"And where do they end up?"

"I can't tell you that. It gives too much away." She couldn't tell him, in part, because she was making it up as she went along, but also because she was scared to find out what happened should Mr. Steinbeck and his poodle ever stop moving. If they didn't reach the end, Walter wouldn't tire of her, dig a hole in some forest and leave her there.

"Okay. What happened in Tulsa?"

"They found a necklace, lying on the sidewalk. That is, Charley found it, while they were out on their walk. It had purple stones—"

"They call those amethysts."

"Yes, I know." She did know, but she hadn't thought Walter would. He surprised her, sometimes, with the facts he had at his disposal. More surprising, though, were the things he didn't know, common bits of everyday living that even little kids understood. "Amethysts, in an old-fashioned setting, big square gold frames, clearly an antique. But there was no one around and it was a block of funny old houses. It was hard to imagine that anyone living in those houses owned such a necklace. Charley lifted it from the sidewalk with his nose—"

"Aw, he made that part up. A dog couldn't do that."

She felt a need to defend Steinbeck and Charley, although the story was hers. "He has poetic license."

"What's that?"

She wasn't sure she could define it. "If you're a poet—or a writer—you're entitled to certain details, even if they're not exactly real. Like you could say there was an eclipse of the sun on a day there wasn't, if you needed to. I think."

"And do they charge you for that?"

"What?"

"I mean, like a driver's license or a hunting license. Is it something you go down and buy?"

She yearned to lie to him. That was the kind of thing Vonnie would do, set someone up, usually Elizabeth, to look like an idiot later. But he would punish her. "No, it's not a license-license. It's just a, like, way of talking." She groped for the vocabulary of school. "A figure of speech."

"So the license to make stuff up is made up?"

"Yes. Sort of. I guess. But that's not the point. The point is, Charley found this necklace. And it was valuable, and they wanted to find the real owner. But how would they do that? I mean, if you go door-to-door, and show it to people, there will always be a dishonest person who says, 'Yes, that's mine.' "

"What you do," Walter said, "is ask if anyone has lost a necklace, then get them to describe it. Or, better yet, they could have gone to the police station and asked if there had been a burglary in the neighborhood, then worked backward, right?"

"That's sort of what they did. They walked a few more blocks, then found a little business district and there was an antique store. It was run by a Holocaust victim."

"One of those people the Nazis tried to kill."

"Yes." Again she was surprised that he didn't need to have the Holocaust defined. Walter had been skeptical when she told him she needed sanitary napkins, not because he didn't know about menstruation, but because he didn't think she was old enough. "I thought you got breasts when that happened," he said, and even he could tell he had hurt her feelings. Later he explained that although he had a sister, she was thirteen years older and he didn't know much about what he called girl secrets.

"The jeweler was very old, and stooped, and he wore one of those things that jewelers use to look at things closely." She waited a beat to see if this was one of the odd things that Walter might know, but he didn't supply the word and she didn't have a clue what it was. "Mr. Steinbeck asked if any of his customers had recently had a necklace repaired there."

"But the customer might have been on the way in," Walter said. He had a real argumentative side. "And the jeweler couldn't know that."

"Only the necklace wasn't broken, and it was shiny, polished up. He was pretty sure someone had dropped it on the way home. And he was right. A teenage girl had brought her mother's necklace in to get it cleaned and repaired as a surprise to her, then it had fallen out of her purse on the walk home and she was terrified to tell her mother what had happened because it was an antique, a family heirloom."

"How did the jeweler know all that? It happened after she left."

"He didn't, but he told Mr. Steinbeck how to find the girl, and he learned the rest of the story."

"Did she offer him a reward?"

"Yes, but he said he didn't need one, that people shouldn't get rewards for doing the right thing."

Almost all her stories about Mr. Steinbeck and Charley ended this way. They did a good deed, then declined any reward for it. She hoped that Walter would eventually decide that doing the right thing—letting her go, turning himself in—would be a reward in and of itself. But so far the man-and-dog duo had traveled to Boston, Atlanta, Milwaukee, Crater Lake, Yellowstone Park—thank goodness her family had taken that cross-country trip when she was eight, she had lots of material on which to draw—and now Tulsa, always doing good deeds, and it didn't seem to make any impression at all on Walter.

THAT NIGHT, IN ONE of the motor courts that Walter preferred, places where cash and men with young girls didn't seem to excite anyone's curiosity, he asked if her period was finished.

"Yes," she said, her stomach suddenly queasy, drawing her knees to her chest. So far, he had not touched her, not in that way. So far. But maybe that was because he had thought she wasn't a woman yet, and therefore off-limits.

"So I can put these back in the truck for a while?" He held up the box of sanitary pads.

"Yes."

"For how long?"

"A month." She paused, not wanting to admit the next part. "Sometimes more."

A month. Would he really keep her for another month? Did she have a month's worth of stories about Charley and Mr. Steinbeck? She hoped so.

15

I CAN READ YOU LIKE *a book* is not generally a generous expression. It is a criticism, an accusation of naïveté, a suggestion that someone is trying to manipulate another person, but failing. Similarly, *I can see right through you* has a sinister feel to it. Or, even: *I'd know you anywhere.*

Yet in a long and happy relationship, that kind of transparency and instant recognition has an endearing comfort. So when Peter arrived home one evening, actually in time for supper with the children, and announced he was ready for the family to get a dog, Eliza had no problem discerning his motives. Peter had always opposed having a dog for any number of reasons—dirt, hair, the possibility that Albie would prove to be allergic. But his primary objection had been that Eliza would become the dog's caretaker, although she had insisted she wouldn't care. Now, he announced at dinner, in front of the children, that he had changed his mind, which left Eliza feeling a little sandbagged. What if *she* no longer wanted a dog? If Peter could change his vote from no to yes, why wouldn't he check first to see if she had changed hers?

"A *real* dog," Peter said.

"What do you mean by 'real'?" asked Iso, the young lawyer. She was waiting, Eliza realized, for the penny to drop, one of the few Briticisms she allowed herself. She preferred it to the idea of the other shoe dropping.

"Not one of those toy things, that you carry around in your arms. And not a terrier of any kind. They're too high-strung. A Lab, or . . . a German shepherd."

"I don't like the idea of purebred dogs, when there are so many dogs in kennels waiting to be adopted," Eliza said, even as Iso cried "German shepherd" and Albie countered with "Black Lab!"

"No, the shelter is fine, that's a good idea," Peter decreed. "Mixed breeds are healthier and smarter. Just as long as it's a *real* dog. We'll go Saturday."

That was three days away, and intrepid Iso quickly learned that they could search the local kennel's inventory online, which was providential, as Albie noted, "Because we can talk about the dogs without hurting their feelings." As Peter pored over the children's choices in the evening, eliminating some, approving others, Eliza began to realize what he meant by a real dog. Big. Peter wanted them to have a big dog. And she began to wonder: Had the lawyer, Blanding, told Peter something more about Walter or Barbara LaFortuny? Was that the penny that had yet to drop?

IN THE END, FOR ALL their careful study and rational discussion, they allowed a dog to choose them. Reba, a shaggy, sad-eyed mix of terrier and shepherd, had studied them with the resignation of a dog who never gets picked. She had been in the kennel, a no-kill one, for a record eighteen months. Peter demurred—she wasn't small, but she wasn't big or intimidating—and Iso was casually cruel about the dog's lack of charisma. But Eliza and Albie became passionate, intense champions and—after a surprising amount of paperwork and references—Reba came to live with them a week later.

"Can we at least rename her?" Iso asked. "Everyone will think we named her after that actress on that silly sitcom."

It took Eliza a second to sort out that Reba McEntire, forever in her head as a country singer, was apparently on a sitcom these days. Eliza wondered if Iso had any memory of the fact that, back when she was a baby in Texas, Eliza had developed a bizarre fondness for CMT, the station that played country music videos, and she had liked Reba quite a bit. There had been a whole series of videos that seemed to tell a little story, about a man and a woman who circled each other in some romance novel setting, possibly one of those islands off the coast of South Carolina. And she had been a doctor, or some such, who met the love of her life in Guatemala, or someplace, but they didn't end up together, and somehow that was okay. Madonna in the 1980s, Reba in the 1990s—who was her musical role model now, as the first decade of the new century drew to an end? Eliza wasn't sure she could even name a current pop star. Not on the basis of her work, at any rate. She knew, in spite of herself, which one had been beaten by her boyfriend, and the one who had been arrested for kleptomania, and the one who kept going to rehab. But don't ask her what they sang.

"No," Eliza told Iso, with a vehemence that caught them both off guard. "You don't just go around changing people's names."

"I did," Iso pointed out. "*You* did."

"What do you mean?"

"You were Elizabeth, when you were younger, and then you decided you wanted to be Eliza."

They were in the backyard with Albie, watching Reba adjust to her new life. She didn't seem to trust it. She would walk a few feet away from them, then turn her head back toward them as if to ask: *Is this allowed?* Even her sniffs seemed tentative, halfhearted.

Eliza caught herself before blurting out: "How do you know that?" After all, there was no reason to be defensive about shortening her name. Instead she said: "I've been Eliza so long, I sometimes forget I was ever Elizabeth."

"It's right there, on your driver's license."

True enough. Only—"What were you doing with my driver's license?"

Iso blushed. "I wanted a breath mint the other day, so I looked in your purse."

"I don't keep breath mints in my billfold, Iso." Waiting her out, not accusing her, but not letting her think that she was getting away with anything, either.

"And I needed a dollar. A girl in my class is having a birthday and we're all going to pitch in a dollar to buy her a gift."

"A dollar?" *Come on, Iso. Lie big or go home.*

"There are twenty-five kids in my class. We're getting her an iTunes gift certificate."

"And will this happen every time someone has a birthday?"

Iso was caught. Her daughter, too, could be read like a book, at least for now. Eliza thought about her own parents, how much they must have known about the little secrets she carved out for herself, how indulgent they had been. They had probably thought: *What's the harm, in her dressing up like Madonna when we're not around? What does it matter if she likes to cut through the woods to go to the fast-food places along Route 40? At least she's getting plenty of fresh air and exercise.* They had been right, yet they had been wrong, too. There was harm, everywhere.

"Oh—no. But this girl is special. She—"

It was funny, watching her daughter lie. Or would be funny, if it weren't also terrifying.

"She has a special disease. In her nervous system. You can't really see it."

At least it was a smart lie. This way, Iso didn't have to produce a classmate in a wheelchair or a leg brace. But Eliza had grown tired of their game.

"Iso, don't take money from my purse without asking, okay? Even a dollar. You really shouldn't go in it, ever, not without my permission. Just because I'm your mother doesn't mean I don't have some expectation of privacy."

"You go in my room," Iso said. "You've gone in my purse."

"Looking for lost things. Not spying. Not"—she lowered her voice so that Albie, who was walking alongside Reba as she continued to test her new backyard—"stealing."

"I didn't steal!" Vehement, defiant. "I don't steal. I needed a dollar. You wouldn't want me to be the only one who didn't contribute, would you?"

Her anger was so self-righteous that Eliza had to fight back a smile. That quickly, Iso had bought into her own story. But at least she had been distracted from the source of their original argument.

Except she hadn't. "I don't want a dog named *Reba,*" Iso said suddenly.

The dog lifted up her head, looking back at them with a puzzled expression. You couldn't call it a smile, probably shouldn't call it a smile. Anthropomorphism and all that. But Eliza saw the trace of a tentative, provisional happiness that she understood. *Please love me. Don't hurt me.*

"She knows her name," Albie crowed with pleasure.

TWO DAYS LATER, ELIZA and Reba were returning from walking Albie to school when she became aware of a green car following her. It was one of those odd cars that Albie loved, the one with the high, round shape that made Eliza think vaguely of the 1930s, gangsters and speakeasies, although there was nothing sinister about this type of car, quite the opposite. It was almost cuddly, if a car could be cuddly, attractive in its unabashed nerdiness. Kind of like Albie.

"Elizabeth," a woman's voice called from the car.

Eliza willed herself not to turn around, to keep walking.

"Elizabeth," the voice persisted.

Reba had stopped to inspect something on the ground, and Eliza didn't have the heart to deny the dog any pleasure, no matter how small. She was much too easily cowed. Eliza wanted Reba to enjoy life a little more, to stop acting so darn grateful all the time.

"Eliza, then." Exasperated, put upon, as if Eliza were a recalcitrant child.

"Yes?" she said, turning only slightly. The woman had lowered the passenger-side window, but she was hard to see from this angle.

"Why didn't you turn around before?" Her voice had the very tone that Eliza tried to avoid with Iso. Quarrelsome, demanding. You couldn't help arguing with a voice like this.

"I didn't know whom you were addressing."

The woman in the car wore enormous sunglasses. Eliza wondered if she realized how disconcerting the effect was, if she had chosen to look intimidating or simply wasn't thinking about how she presented herself. She had hair the color of spun sugar, and quite a lot of it, worn in what appeared to be a series of hairdos, as if she had sectioned this amazing mass of hair into six or eight discrete pieces and created a different style for each. There were curls and waves, even two kinds of bangs: a fringe across the forehead, then swooping wings to the side.

"But that's your name, isn't it?" It had to be Barbara LaFortuny. *Please,* Eliza thought, *let it be Barbara LaFortuny.* She didn't want to think about the implications of a world in which more and more people began showing up, calling her by her childhood name. She imagined a phalanx of women, all in Walter's employ, doing his bidding. That image made her mind leap to an artist she loved, Henry Darger, and his disturbing portraits of those 1950s-perfect, perky, pervy Vivian girls. The Walter girls, his own private army.

But Walter had no interest in armies. He had always been, in his own bizarre way, a one-woman man. Or, more correctly, aspired to be. He would even say that at times. *I am a one-woman man. I'm just looking for that one woman.*

"My name is Eliza."

"Your legal name," the woman said.

"My name," she repeated, "is Eliza. Perhaps I have you confused with someone else." She stopped, corrected her slip. "Perhaps you have me confused with someone else."

"Perhaps," the woman said with a chuckle, "I just have you confused."

She took off her dark glasses then, and although this revealed the scar that started at the corner of one eye and ran southward, she looked less menacing without the Gucci glasses. Eliza remembered what Peter had told her. A teacher, attacked in her classroom, now an advocate for inmates. Put that on paper, and it sounded like someone Eliza would like.

"He needs you, Elizabeth."

She shook her head.

"Eliza, then."

"This isn't about my name," she said. "He doesn't *need* me."

"But he does."

She tried again. "He doesn't have a right to need me."

The woman leaned across the front seat of her car, as if to motion Eliza to climb inside. Reba growled, and the sound seemed to surprise the dog, then please her. She growled again with more conviction. Barbara LaFortuny—who else could it be—pulled back, reached down, then held up a folded piece of paper.

"He asked me to hand deliver this one. He wanted to know, without a doubt, when you got it. Time is important to him. The clock is ticking. A date has been set."

Eliza studied the white piece of paper in must-be-Barbara's hand—only one sheaf, how much could it contain, how much damage could it do—and reluctantly accepted it. Evidence, she decided. She would memorize the license plate, too, when the woman drove away. She would memorize everything about this encounter. She wasn't sure what she would do with her memories, but she would have them.

Barbara LaFortuny's hands were beautiful—manicured, flashing with interesting, important rings—and, based on the impression of the quick moment in which their fingers touched, quite soft. The eccentricity of her hairstyle aside, this was a woman who had the time and means to tend to herself. Eliza folded the already folded piece of paper in half, then shoved it in the pocket of the fleece vest she had thrown over her T-shirt. It was the first cool morning of the fall. On the walk to Albie's school, she had been joyous, carrying his book bag while he took Reba's leash.

"Let's go"—she stopped herself from saying the dog's name. She didn't want Barbara LaFortuny to know anything about her family. She already knew too much. Had that green little playgangster car tracked Eliza and Albie to school that day? She considered pulling her cell phone from her pocket, snapping LaFortuny's photo then and there, so she could show it to Albie's school, and Iso's, yet the car was already moving on. Chesapeake Bay plates. SAVE THE BAY. Save Walter. Barbara LaFortuny didn't lack for causes.

Home, Eliza put on the teakettle, but then the phone rang, and in the middle of the call something arrived via FedEx, and the teakettle whistled, and the dauntingly high-tech washing machine began beeping an error code, which required getting out the manual, which required finding the manual, and before Eliza knew it, it was 3:30 P.M., time to pick up Albie and much too warm for the fleece jacket, and she was back in the maelstrom of family life. It was ten o'clock before she had the time and privacy to read the letter, eleven o'clock before she remembered that she had stashed it in her pocket.

It wasn't there.

16

1985

ALTHOUGH HE HAD GROWN UP nearby—perhaps *because* he had grown up nearby—Walter had never visited Luray Caverns, and he took a notion that he and Elizabeth should spend a day there. It seemed a foolish thing to do, given that money was always tight, yet the various highway signs called to him. He really wanted to see those caverns, not to mention the classic cars, although he didn't understand why there was a collection of classic cars at Luray Caverns. He talked himself into thinking it would be a nice treat for Elizabeth.

But Elizabeth, to his surprise, argued on the grounds that it was an extravagance. He had been picking up fewer jobs of late and they had been sleeping out more often, even as the nights got cooler here in the mountains.

"Hey, I'm just thinking of trying to do something fun for *you*." Besides, who was she to argue with him over money? Who was she to argue with him about anything? She seldom talked back, and he didn't like the fact that she was starting. This was a troubling development. She needed more discipline.

"*I've* been," she said. "Just two years ago."

"What was it like?"

"Okay. All I learned was how to remember the difference between a stalagmite and a stalactite."

He didn't want to ask, but she clearly wasn't going to volunteer the information: "And how do you remember?"

"Stalactites, which have a *c*, hang from the *ceiling*. Stalagmites come up from the ground."

"Well, then, you could just as well remember *g* for *ground*, couldn't you?"

That cowed her.

"Sure, I suppose you could."

"And you may have gone, but I've never been. Is that fair?"

"You said it was something you wanted to do for me," she said, correctly and infuriatingly. "If it's my choice, I'd rather use the money we'd spend on that for something else."

"Like what?"

"I don't know. A meal in a restaurant, one night, instead of fast food or making do with cold things from grocery stores. Something to wear."

"I've got even fewer things to wear 'n you."

She started to say something, thought better of it, slumped back in the front seat of the car with a sigh so heavy that the exhaled breath stirred the bangs hanging in her eyes. Walter saw, in that moment, what it would be like to have a teenage daughter one day, how exasperating and tender and terrifying.

In the next instant, he realized that he would never have a daughter, or a son, or a wife. Something was coming for him, something big. Yes, because of what he had done, but also because that was his destiny. His death would be heroic, at least. A chase, a battle. He would die large, and that pleased him.

Yet what had he really done except try to have the things that others have and take for granted, things that came so easily. All around him, he saw people, couples, holding hands and enjoying each other. He saw men much less good-looking than himself, and probably less capable, with knockouts, and he could not understand how that happened. He had started out wanting nothing more than a girlfriend, and he had wanted a girlfriend because, one day, he wanted to have a wife, then kids. True, he had rushed things, he had made poor choices. But it was hard, making good choices, when you had to settle for meeting people on the fly. And once you were out of school, how did you meet people at all? Working in his father's shop wasn't any way to meet women. The few that came in, he never got to talk to them, and the coveralls made him look shorter than he was. Even if they could see past the coveralls, to his nice face and his green eyes, they probably thought, *Oh, a grease monkey.* A grease monkey! Did people know how smart you had to be to work on cars? Hell, doctors weren't any smarter than mechanics. Doctors got to specialize. One did the heart, one did the brain, one did bones. He and his father were the kind of mechanics who did everything, domestic and foreign, and they were *honest*. No one who knew them had ever called them out on a single charge. One time, a stranger had been passing through and had a breakdown, and it was a newer car with an electrical ignition, always tricky, but they had gotten that guy back on the road the same day, which meant they saved him the cost of a motel, and all he wanted to do was ask why they had gone ahead and replaced his brake pads, which were thin as handed-down baby pajamas. He had been a tall man, probably only six or seven years older than Walter, who was seventeen at the time, but he carried himself as if he was important. The inside of his car smelled of cigars, and when, the repairs finally done, they had switched the car back on to check everything, the music that poured out of the radio was classical, opera. Walter didn't believe for a minute that the man really enjoyed that music. He was on the lookout to impress someone. But Walter also realized that it probably worked, and girls were impressed. God, women were shallow.

"We're going to the caverns," he said to Elizabeth. "It's educational."

She sighed harder, went beyond sighing, stuck out her bottom lip and made a noise that was downright rude. His palm itched to slap her. He flicked her cheek, not hard, and was pleased to see her eyes go fearful.

SHE WAS ENJOYING THE TOUR, he could tell, even though they weren't dressed quite warmly enough for the caverns. Soon they would require more clothes. Coats and sweaters and boots. He needed to figure things out, find more permanent work. But he couldn't land a mechanic's job if he couldn't provide references, and opening his own shop would involve way too much capital and overhead. Besides, what he would really like to do is run his own general fix-it shop, a place that promised: "If you can break it, I can fix it." Or: "I can fix anything from a screen door to a broken heart." He had stolen that line from Earl, the one who had gone off to the Marines. He had been younger than Walter, but nice, one of the few people who didn't seem to think he was a moron. Could Walter enlist? No, it wasn't like those old movies where people joined the French foreign legion and disappeared. Or that movie that had come out just a few years earlier, about a guy who parachuted out of a plane with $200,000 in ransom. Boy, the woman in that movie had been pretty, just his type. Thin, but with really big breasts and one of those curly smiles. Could he get a ransom for Elizabeth? Not much, based on what he knew about her parents. She was always talking about how they didn't have a lot of money. Computers could find anybody, no matter where they went. He had seen that movie *War Games*. *What was he going to do?* His mind was so busy running through his options, or lack of options, that he could barely pay attention to the tour guide.

There weren't many people on this tour, only one school group. Younger kids, no more than ten or eleven, and loud, loving the way their voices boomed and echoed. Elizabeth looked at them curiously, as if she couldn't remember being that young. Then he realized—it wasn't age that made her distant. It was him, the life he had created for her. She wasn't part of their world anymore, a world with parents and television and dinner and school. She had accepted this so readily that he found himself losing a little respect for her. True, he had made sure to scare the shit out of her at first, and showed her that he could hurt her—swiftly, searingly, with not much effort. But he had not raised a hand to her since those first few days, and still she stayed. He didn't count today, that was just a tap, a warning. He was stuck with her, in a way. Why this one, the one who had just stumbled on him? Why couldn't he have a girl he chose? Nothing was ever fair.

He could free her, right now. He could tap her shoulder, tell her he was going to use the restroom and she wasn't to move, and she would do just that. Or, he could wait until *she* asked to use the restroom, go through his usual rules and admonitions, about how much time she could have and how she must not speak to anyone, even if spoken to, how she would come to regret it, and don't think she wouldn't. Then, when she came out, he would be gone. How long would she wait? He'd almost want to hide himself somewhere to watch, to see how much time elapsed before she thought to speak to anyone. She would probably sit there all day until a security guard told her it was closing time.

Or, he could slowly back away, right now, eyes fixed on those narrow shoulders in the sweatshirt she claimed to detest, quietly retreating until he was out in the sunlight, then breaking into a run, getting into his truck, and driving away, seizing a head start.

What did she know, what could she tell the police? They had already found the one body, Maude's, but she didn't know where the other girls were, didn't even know there were other girls, although he had dropped hints about how far he would go when angered or challenged. Elizabeth could tell them about his truck, however. She could tell them his name, that he was from West Virginia. He had told her other things, too, the kind of things you tell people when you spend hours with them, although they weren't the kind of details that made a man findable. Favorite foods, television shows, his one and only trip to the ocean and how disappointing it had been, particularly saltwater taffy, which wasn't anywhere near as special as people had made it out to be.

He could let her go, let the screaming, singing ten-year-olds slowly close around her, gather her up, carry her forward before she noticed. She wasn't that far away from being their age, no matter what she thought. She was still a pretty innocent girl, with her stories about that dog. And her tears, the ones late at night in the bathroom, when she thought he couldn't hear her, or the ones right before sleep, which she tried to muffle with her pillow or her fist. *You're just a kid,* he wanted to tell her. *Go back, be like them.* It's not too late. He could—

She turned around, caught his eye, and the moment, the impulse, was gone. Who was he kidding? They were stuck with each other.

17

IT WAS TWO DAYS BEFORE Eliza found the piece of paper, tucked into the recycling bin, a drawing by Albie on the blank side. It was a sketch of Albie and Reba riding a bicycle built for two.

"Albie, why did you draw on"—she paused to think about what she wanted to call it—"Mommy's letter?"

"I was in the TV room and I just had an idea and I didn't want to go upstairs to get my paper and Daddy always says not to pull paper out of the tray in the computer that we should use scrap paper and I found this in his trash can—where it shouldn't have been, anyway—and I thought it would be okay to draw on the back and then I put it in the recycling because I didn't like it very much, the bicycle didn't look right."

The words came out in a rush, as if he

might be punished. But, unlike Iso, there was no guile in Albie. Not yet.

"No, no, that's okay." She tried to think of a way to ask if he had read it, without suggesting he might have wanted to read it. "It must have seemed pretty unimportant, anyway. Just a lot of dull stuff."

"It was in the trash," Albie reminded her. "I thought it was a format letter."

"A format—oh, a form letter. Yes, it is. Do you have any homework?"

"No," Albie said with a sigh, genuinely disappointed. He wanted to be like Iso, loaded down with work in middle school, but he came home with only a few, easy assignments. "We're working on multiplication tables and I already know my twelve times."

"You can put a video in, then. If you like."

Albie considered his mother's offer, which was slightly out of the ordinary. Though Eliza didn't limit the children's television, she also didn't propose it as a way to spend time. "I think I'll play a game with Reba," he said. He went into the long, rambling backyard. Almost too long, Eliza decided now, although the yard had been her favorite feature of the house. There were places along the back fence where Albie disappeared from her sight line. But he was with Reba, she reminded herself, and Reba was growing more confident every day, first growling at Barbara LaFortuny, now barking at the postman on his daily rounds. She had mentioned this to Peter, wondered at this clichéd verity. Why do dogs bark at postmen? "Because it works," Peter said. "Every day, they bark, and every day, the postman retreats."

She sat at the desk in the television room, positioning herself so she could see the yard. This letter was typed in a small, fussy font that had allowed Barbara LaFortuny to squeeze a lot of text onto the page. A form letter, Albie had thought, and he was right in a way. The writing was stilted, almost as if it had been translated from another language. Maybe Barbara LaFortuny was doing this without Walter's knowledge. At any rate, Walter's second letter seemed dry, airless, reminiscent of his droning recitations of what he would do to—for—certain women if they would just let him. Not sexual things, but nice things—holding open doors, sending flowers on ordinary days, remembering key anniversaries.

It would be nice to see you. Nice for me, of course, but also, I think, nice for you. I always liked you. I never hurt you, not on purpose.

Hurt, in Walter's world, must be a euphemism for *killed*. He couldn't honestly believe he hadn't harmed her. He had said in his first letter that he wanted to make amends to her.

I think I am a different man from the one you knew. More educated. I have read quite a bit. I have thought about the person I was and I am no longer that person. I am genuinely remorseful for the pain I inflicted—on the girls, on their families. I have been here longer than anyone, by quite a bit. In fact, I am considered quite exceptional in that way. I don't know if you kept up with me.

As if they were old friends, as if she might have searched for him on Facebook, or asked a mutual acquaintance for news of him. As if there were anything to keep up with. Getting a letter from Walter was like some exiled citizen of New Orleans getting a telegram signed "Katrina." Hey, how are you? Do you ever think of me? Those were some crazy times, huh?

I don't know if you have kept up with me, but there were some unusual circumstances in my trial. A juror came forward and admitted that they had discussions in the jury room that were strictly forbidden. One of the jurors was married to a lawyer, and she told everyone that I would never get the death penalty in Maryland—and I didn't, but she couldn't know that and shouldn't have discussed it—so Virginia was the only place where I might reasonably be expected to be put to death. I won't bore you with all the ins and outs of the law, but Virginia has formidable laws, and it is very hard to appeal here.

Remorseful, formidable. Walter was one of those people who believed that using big words would make him sound educated. She could imagine him poring over *Reader's Digest*'s "It Pays to Increase Your Word Power." Did they have *Reader's Digest* in prison? Hey, they had *Washingtonian.*

Anyway, as a result of that and some other things, my appeals have dragged on much longer, with lots of ups and downs and ins and outs. I have been here twenty-two years. The next closest has been here only ten. I guess that makes me the Dean of Death Row.

Okay, she had to give Walter that: Dean of Death Row was kind of funny, and the one thing Walter had never shown any talent for was laughing at himself. He had changed a little if he could write a line like that.

Over the years, I admit I have thought about you often. When I saw your photo in the magazine, I was excited for you, but not surprised. I expected you to have the kind of life where you went to parties and got photographed. There was always a spark to you.

A spark, but not a shine. She remembered his truck slowing down as he drank in the eyeful that was Holly. "Look at the shine on that girl."

> *But at the risk of giving offense, I have to say, I was surprised to hear from Barbara—she's very good at research—that you have chosen not to have a career. Of course, I hold motherhood in the highest esteem and, if things had been different for me, I probably would be grateful if my own wife chose to put family first. But it's not the future I envisioned for you.*

With those words, that paragraph, Walter had given something far greater than offense. Hands shaking, Eliza fed the sheaf of paper into the shredder by Peter's desk, facedown, so the image she saw sliding into the machine's teeth was Albie and Reba on their bicycle built for two. Walter never touched this piece of paper, she reminded herself. He had dictated these words to Barbara. *Perhaps these weren't even his words,* she thought. For all she knew, Barbara LaFortuny had created this entire drama. But, no, that was Walter's voice, odd as it sounded this time.

Her paranoia far from abated, she emptied the shredder's canister directly into the trash and then took the trash out to the garage, although shredded paper could go into the single-stream recycling bins provided by the county. If she could, she would have driven the garbage to the local dump, or burned it in a bonfire on her lawn, although bonfires were illegal.

But even if she could have watched Walter's words blacken and disappear in leaping flames, she could not erase the knowledge that she should have sussed out the moment she saw Barbara LaFortuny's sinister little car following her down the street. Walter not only had learned where she lived, and what her husband did, and what she looked like. He knew she had children. He knew she had children and—far more crucial—he wanted her to be aware that he had that knowledge.

He wanted something from her. A visit, a call. He wanted something, and if she didn't submit, he would find a way to use Iso and Albie to get it.

18

1985

AS SEPTEMBER DRAGGED ON, Elizabeth began to petition Walter to let her attend school. He said he would take her request under advisement. That was his preferred term for anything she sought but obviously could not have—more clothes, dinners in restaurants, a call home, a friend. "I'll take that under advisement," he would say, and nothing would change.

"I won't misbehave," she said, knowing how doomed her request was, yet incapable of not trying. "I just want to go to school, study. Education matters to me. And you always say you think it's important."

"That's good," he said. "But I don't see it working out. We'd have to settle down somewhere."

"I'd like that," she said, amending quickly, "I think you would like that."

"Not in the cards, not right now. We've got to keep moving."

"It's illegal," she said, "not to attend school if you're under sixteen. So if someone sees you with me, they might stop, ask questions. It didn't matter, at first, when it was summer. But now it's fall."

"Not quite, not by the calendar."

But the weather was fall-like. Autumn had once been her favorite time of the year, the days full of promise, the nights cool and crisp. She always felt anything could happen in autumn. She liked the very word: *autumn*. She would head back to school with her new clothes—Vonnie was so hard on what she wore that Elizabeth had seldom been forced to endure hand-me-downs—her plastic pencil pouch full of reinforcements, her binder unsullied. She would be neater this year, better prepared. She would work for As instead of settling for Bs. Those dreams were usually worn down by Thanksgiving, but September and October were golden days.

"There are all sorts of reasons a fifteen-year-old girl might not be in school," he said. "I can't imagine anyone noticing. No one ever has."

He was right. People didn't seem to see them, *her*. Their eyes swept over her, by her, around her, but never made contact with her gaze, even as she silently screamed for them to see her, take note of her. Was it because he had cut her hair short and dyed it brown, meticulously keeping up with the roots, if not the cut. ("Nice'n Easy," Walter had scoffed. "Maybe for some faggot beautician.")

Sometimes, though, she saw women noticing Walter with tentative approval. But it was very brief. A waitress, a store clerk, would rake her eyes up and down him, draw him into conversation. Then, just as quickly, they would pull back, retreat. Elizabeth, who had read reams about the mistakes girls make with boys, wondered what kind of mistakes boys made. Walter was too . . . eager. No, that wasn't the right word. He was polite, interested. He tried to draw them out. But women, grown-up women, moved away from him as if he smelled.

Elizabeth's request to go to school put a strange bug in Walter's ear, and he decided that they would spend their evenings at various libraries, reading. He insisted on approving her choices, sometimes making her put back a novel and read a nonfiction book, although he never seemed to notice that the texts on history, science, and mathematics were much too simple for her. Walter usually read history or magazines about cars, but one day—Fredericksburg, Virginia, Elizabeth believed, although the places kept getting jumbled in her head—he found a pale green book called *When the Beast Tames the Beauty: What Women Really Want* and he began reading it with great interest.

Walter, it turned out, was not a particularly fast reader, and although they stayed in Fredericksburg for several days—he had found work with a private moving company, whose owner didn't mind if Walter's "little sister" tagged along—he managed to read only the first third of the book in the hours he had available.

But when they moved on at week's end, Walter was dismayed to find that the next library didn't have the book. And the library in the next town over had it on the noncirculating shelf, which required library patrons to sign for the book at the front desk, because it was a best seller. He made Elizabeth ask for it.

Say it's for your mother, Walter said, and she did, only to find herself almost choking with tears. Her mother would never read such a book. Her mother would laugh at such a book.

The librarian didn't seem to notice how emotional Elizabeth was. She gave her the book, saying only: "We've got a waiting list for the circulating copies. More than fifty names."

Walter stole that copy of the book, an action he later justified at length to Elizabeth. "Taxpayers pay for those books," he said. "And I'm a taxpayer, and I hardly ever use the library, so why shouldn't I take just this one book?"

"But you're not paying taxes now," Elizabeth said. "Everyone you do jobs for pays you in cash. And you never paid tax in Virginia."

"Sales tax," Walter said. "Gasoline tax. I pay my share, and I'm not getting any services back. I'm not like that lady who drives her Cadillac to pick up her food stamps."

"That's a myth," said Elizabeth, who remembered her father discussing the matter heatedly at the dinner table, just last year. Had it really been only a year ago? Now 1984 seemed impossibly distant. Her parents had been Mondale supporters, of course, and Elizabeth had gone to a rally in hopes of catching a glimpse of Geraldine Ferraro. Later, at school, some of the cooler boys had ridiculed her, and she had backpedaled, saying she didn't like the Democrats, that her parents were for Mondale, but she wasn't. She felt guilty for that now, and for all the dozens of small betrayals against them, the endless denial of their existence. True, her mom didn't dress like the other moms and she wore her hair too long, loose, and unstyled. She hadn't understood when Elizabeth wanted a bubble skirt. She never understood why Elizabeth wanted anything. She said she did; she was a psychiatrist, after all. But Elizabeth could see that her mother was puzzled by her, that she didn't understand why, in a family of cheerfully loud, opinionated nonconformists, Elizabeth was determined to be like everyone else, never standing out from the crowd.

She had thought it was safer to be that way.

Walter read aloud from the stolen book to Elizabeth at night. He appeared to think it was wonderful, wise, and profound, and some of it was interesting to Elizabeth. The book counseled women to return to a more "natural" relationship with men, to celebrate their "inherent softness" while accepting that men were rough, a little wild. Meanwhile, women should realize that the best men were those who would care for them—not financially, but emotionally. They should not judge men by external things, such as clothes and looks, but learn to find men who were kind and supportive.

"This is the problem," Walter said. "I do these very exact things and it doesn't help at all. Not at all."

Elizabeth was thinking about what it meant to be "natural." Wouldn't that mean not shaving your legs, not blow-drying your hair? Her mother might wear her hair long and loose, but she still shaved her legs. Elizabeth had not been able to shave her legs since the day that Walter took her, and they were now covered with soft fuzz. She wouldn't want anyone to see it, but she liked the feel of it. At night, alone in her bed or sleeping bag, she stroked her legs, felt under her arms. Perhaps she was transforming into something new and formidable, an animal who could fight Walter or run away from him, swift and fleet.

Only she could never get away. Never.

Walter began to prefer his book to the stories that Elizabeth told and sometimes asked her to read from it as he drove. His favorite chapter was about a cold, driven businesswoman who thought she wanted someone exactly like herself.

"'Maureen, twenty-nine, appears to have it all,'" Elizabeth read. "'A willowy brunette, she works for a large department-store chain in Texas, part of the team that oversees its expansion plans. By day, she wears tailored suits, her sleek brown hair pulled back in a chignon—'"

"What is that?" Walter asked. "A shin-yon?"

"Like a bun, but fancier," Elizabeth said. She pushed back her own short curls, which could no longer be arranged into anything. "You spell it *c-h-i-g-n-o-n*." She knew that later, when Walter reread this section—and he always reread the sections she had covered during the day—he might challenge her, ask her why she had given him the incorrect word.

"Okay. Go on."

She had lost her place in the text, needed a moment to locate it. "'But at night, she lets it fall loose to her shoulders, as she prowls the clubs and nightspots of Dallas, looking for a man. She thinks she knows exactly what she wants—a professional, at her level or above—and she can tick her "no-nos" off on her fingers. "No mama's boys, still living at home."'"

"Living at home doesn't make you a mama's boy," Walter put in.

"'"No mama's boys, still living at home. No fatties. Bald is okay, if he's really cute and fit. In short—no losers." Yet Maureen, for all her calculation and precise ideas about what she wants, never seems to find the right man. Oh, she finds professional men with good salaries and chiseled physiques, but they always disappoint her because Maureen has broken faith with her own femininity. She is trying to be a huntress. She has violated the natural order of things and will never find the right man until she learns to sit back, relax, and wait for him to find her.'"

Elizabeth pondered this. Her hero, Madonna, wore a belt that said BOY TOY, but it was clear that she was the one who toyed with the boys, who used them and moved on. Elizabeth had seen the movie *Desperately Seeking Susan* four times since it appeared last winter and yet never felt thoroughly satisfied by the ending. There was Rosanna Arquette, cute enough—cute enough that her rock star boyfriend had once even written a song about her—but it seemed strange that she was paired up with the really handsome guy, while Madonna was with the less desirable one, the one with the spiky hair. And, at the very beginning of the movie, Madonna had been in bed with someone else, so it wasn't true-true love for her and the spiky hair guy, no matter how passionately they kissed. At the movie's end, they seemed more companionable than lovestruck, chomping popcorn and laughing. Just last month, Madonna had gotten married to Sean Penn as helicopters circled. She was thinner now, not that she had ever been plump, her hair short and sleek. Elizabeth remembered reading about the couple's decision to wed, how she had proposed to him because she knew it was what he wanted. She wondered what it would be like to know that a man wanted to marry you, to have the confidence to ask first. The author of this book clearly would not approve of Madonna.

"I wonder," Walter said, "if Maureen ever found anyone?"

Elizabeth looked up, startled. "I don't think she's a real person."

"Of course she is. It's nonfiction. Says so right on the spine." He pointed to the library label. Elizabeth wondered if they should scrape that off, if they would get in trouble if someone glimpsed it, so obviously far from home. But maybe if someone reported them for the stolen library book, the police would finally find her.

"I mean, she's real, but they probably changed her name and some details."

"Why would they do that?"

"I don't know why, I only know that they do. My mom explained it to me once. She has a friend who works for one of the women's magazines and they create these—I can't remember the word. They find real stories, only the people are kind of fake."

"Oh, no. Maureen is real," Walter said. "Real as Mr. Steinbeck and Charley and the people they met."

Elizabeth felt a small flush of panic. What would happen if Walter found out that she had been making up adventures for John Steinbeck and his poodle? What if Walter figured out *Travels with Charley* was in the library, decided to read it? He didn't like deception of any kind. Yet he was allowing himself to be deceived by this book. It's true, Elizabeth hadn't always understood the license that such writers employed, she had once read *Seventeen* and *Mademoiselle* and believed that every word was gospel. But she was glad when her mother explained to her that the stories were not quite true, that the writers shaped real people's stories and matched them to these glamorous, made-up people because that's what people wanted to read about. Walter, however, would not be pleased by this information.

"I'd like to meet this Maureen," Walter said. "I bet she's still single. Of course, she's older than me, and that's probably one of her rules, too. Women are funny that way. They ought to be grateful that a younger man finds them attractive. One day they will, but then it will be too late and no one will want them. I never understood that, in high school, how the freshman girls all wanted to go out with juniors and seniors, instead of freshmen."

Elizabeth, who was missing her sophomore year of high school, thought about the boys her age. They were so small, most of them. Not just short, but small. Even Elizabeth, who was not particularly tall or filled out, felt huge among them.

"I could show that Maureen a good time," Walter said. "She'd be begging for it."

If the book hadn't been open on her lap, Elizabeth might have brought her knees to her chest, hugged herself. Walter had never touched her. Well, never touched her in that way. Sometimes, he tugged the neck of her jacket, if he thought she was walking too fast, or yanked her arm to change direction. She had lain in bed, those first nights, wrists and ankles tied, expecting he would force himself on her. He had raped the other girl, the one he buried. He must have. He never said as much, but she was sure of that. She thought about that girl often, although all she knew of her was her first name. Maude. Such an old-fashioned name. The kids at school had probably teased her, called her—Maude the Odd. Unless she was really, really, really pretty and popular. Pretty girls could survive anything. But a pretty, popular girl would never have gotten into Walter's truck. Elizabeth wouldn't have, given the choice, and she wasn't that pretty or popular. Still, she knew better than to get in some strange man's truck.

Then again, what if Walter had been driving along Route 40

and a sudden rain had come up and he had stopped and offered her a ride? She had taken a ride from a man under those circumstances, just once. He had asked her where she wanted to go and she was scared to give her home address, scared to let her parents know she had hitched a ride, so she told him she was headed to the bowling alley, the Normandy Lanes, only a mile or so away. He nodded thoughtfully, started in that direction, but then announced: "The rain's too heavy. I'm going to wait it out. Better safe than sorry." He had pulled into a parking lot, then reached across to where she was—and opened the glove compartment, bringing out a little cut-glass bottle of amber liquid, from which he took a long swallow.

"You shouldn't drink and drive," Elizabeth had said.

"And you probably shouldn't hitchhike," he'd said. There was surprisingly little menace in his words. He took another swallow, sat there with the motor running, listening to a radio station that played oldies. When the rain slackened, he took her to the bowling alley.

So, yes, Elizabeth had gotten into a strange man's car, once. But would she have allowed Walter to give her a ride on a bright, warm August day? She thought not. Why had Maude agreed? Had she agreed, or had Walter grabbed her by the arm, as he had seized Elizabeth, and forced her into the cab of the truck?

Walter seldom spoke of Maude, except in passing, as a warning. He liked to talk about the girls he saw, though. "I could show her a good time," he would say when he glimpsed a girl with a good figure. "I know what I'm doing. These girls, they sell themselves cheap, don't realize what's out there, waiting for them. They're too busy thinking about movie stars."

And now he was speaking about Maureen that way in great, horrible detail, yet so matter-of-factly that one might think he was talking about a trip to the grocery store. What he would put where first—his mouth on the hollow of her throat, his tongue in her ear, then his fingers—*Oh, please stop,* Elizabeth thought, desperate to block out his voice, but Walter continued his play-by-play. Not even he seemed to find it sexy. He might have been reciting a set of instructions he had memorized. It was like listening to a seduction scene from a romance novel, but one read by a robot, so it was reduced to a road map, where he would go when.

"She'd be begging, begging for it," he said. "But still, I would make her wait. A woman like Maureen, she needs to be broken down. That's what the book is trying to explain. Women have to wait. Their anatomy dictates that. They wait, they receive. Men pursue, men give."

Elizabeth, who had read the book almost as many times as Walter—it was, after all, the only reading material available when they were in the car or in a motel room, except for a copy of *The Godfather* he had allowed her to purchase at a yard sale—did not think the book, awful as it was, meant to say all that. But she knew better than to argue.

"Look at that girl," Walter said suddenly, slowing the truck. "Look at the shine on her."

19

THAT EVENING, ONCE THE CHILDREN were asleep—well, Albie was asleep, Iso was probably under the covers, sending texts on the unsatisfactory cell phone they had given her—Eliza told Peter about the second letter. She wished now that she hadn't shredded it, that he could read it himself, if only so she wouldn't have to relive it. He listened without comment, although he raised an eyebrow at the peculiar turns of phrase she was able to re-create. *Dean of Death Row. The appeals process is formidable. I won't bore you with it.* Eliza realized she had practically memorized the letter word for word.

"What do you want to do?"

"I don't know," Eliza said. "I feel as if this is out of my control, all of a sudden.

This woman—or Walter—could go to the media anytime, tell them who I am and where I am."

"I can't imagine a responsible news organization that would write about you, if you weren't interested in cooperating," said Peter. He wasn't arguing with her, only puzzling things out, trying to imagine every angle.

"Unfortunately, the world is full of irresponsible news organizations. What if she found Jared Garrett? Do you realize how exposed we are, how exposed everyone is?"

She showed him what happened when she plugged their address into Google maps, then clicked through to street view. There was their house. Of course, this was no revelation to Peter, whose career as a journalist had taken off, in part, because of his expertise with computer-assisted research. Still, she could tell that he found this image as arresting as she did. Looking at the photo of the white brick house—complete with the clichéd picket fence—Eliza could not help imagining the score of a scary film pulsing beneath the placid image. Barbara LaFortuny had seen this house, had driven by it, then reported back to Walter—what, exactly? Anything was too much. The woman was probably gathering a dossier on Peter, the easiest household member to track, the one who had left the largest public trail. But would she stop there? What if she showed up on the sidelines at one of Iso's soccer games? Or followed Eliza en route to school with Albie, exciting his imagination, keying him up to ask all sorts of questions. *Who is that lady? Why does she want to talk to you? Why does she have a scar on her face?* What if Barbara LaFortuny tried to befriend Reba, sneaking scraps through the fence? What if she poisoned Reba, who had growled at her? Would she—

A child's all-too-familiar scream tore through the night.

"Albie," Eliza shouted, letting him know that she was coming.

"Albie," Peter repeated. "I hoped this was behind us."

I hoped a lot of things were behind us, Eliza thought as she took the stairs, two at a time.

ALBIE'S NIGHTMARES HAD STARTED shortly after they moved to London. Every pediatrician and book that Eliza consulted said it was normal for a child to have bad dreams in the wake of an enormous change, but Albie's nightmares seemed unusual to Eliza. They were incredibly detailed, for one thing, with such intense imagery and plot twists that she almost itched to write them down. It was interesting, too, to see how his unconscious reshaped the innocent stuff of the daylight hours. A book such as, say, *In the Night Kitchen,* which Eliza found wildly creepy, did not affect Albie at all. But other, almost bland icons popped up. The Poky Little Puppy foamed at the mouth. (She blamed Peter for this, because he had shown the children *To Kill a Mockingbird.*) Madeline, the usually admirable Parisian girl, turned out to be a witch, the kind of person who pinched people and then lied about it. Peter Rabbit seldom escaped Farmer McGregor's pitchfork. That particular dream had started after Eliza had eaten a rabbit dish in front of Albie at a London restaurant they particularly liked.

But the more striking aspect of Albie's nightmares was that Iso usually appeared, and always in peril. Tonight, between heaving sobs and sips of water, he told a chilling story. The family had gone to a new bakery and Iso had refused to wear her glasses, not that Iso wore glasses in real life. (Eliza and Peter glanced at each other over Albie's head; they recognized this detail from *The Brady Bunch,* the movie, which Albie loved beyond reason. He did not experience it as a hip, winking joke, but as an honest exhortation to live exuberantly, indifferent to what others thought was cool. Burst into song, chat up carjackers, be nice to everyone, and you will prevail.) The family could not enjoy the new bakery with Iso gone, and they searched for her frantically. They found her in a storeroom filled with bags of flour and she was flat, as if someone had rolled her into a gingerbread girl—and taken her legs.

"She had no legs?"

Albie nodded guiltily, as if he knew the dream could be interpreted as evidence of conflicted feelings toward his accomplished sister, whose strong, fleet limbs had granted her effortless entrée into a new peer group, while he was still struggling to make friends here. But Eliza believed Albie wasn't the least bit conflicted about Iso. He loved her, he wanted to be her. He would never hurt her, even in his imagination. He was genuinely worried that she might be harmed. What did Albie know, or suspect, about his sister? Did he have insights that Eliza lacked? Or was he simply mirroring the anxiety she felt?

"Are you concerned about Iso? In life, not in your dreams."

Albie thought about this. "No, I never worry about Iso. And she doesn't seem to worry about me. I wish she did, sometimes."

That was interesting. "In what way?"

"I wish she would ask me about school, how my day went."

"Do you ask her?" Eliza asked.

"I do. We all do. Except Iso. You ask Daddy, and Daddy asks you, and you both ask me, and you both ask Iso, but Iso never asks anyone anything anymore."

"She's a—" Peter began.

"A teenager," Albie finished for him. "You say that all the time, but what does that mean???"

"That's a big question for the middle of the night," Peter said.

"It's not even midnight," Albie pointed out. Their little dreamer could be quite literal.

"Okay, I'll tell you this much," Peter said. "When you're a teenager, there is so much going on in your body that it makes you a little different, for a while."

Albie thought about this. "Like a Transformer?"

"Sort of, but it's all on the inside. It wears you out, growing so much so fast. That's why Iso is cranky sometimes."

"She's cranky all the time."

Eliza wanted to defend Iso, but Albie was right. She was cranky all the time. It was sad, hearing this spoken aloud, and having to admit that Iso wasn't merely moody. She had one mood, at least at home, a snarling grouchiness.

"Do you want to sleep in our bed tonight?" she asked instead, knowing it would make for a cramped, sleepless night for the two adults. Plus, Reba had started sneaking into their bed.

"No, I'm too big," Albie said. "But may I leave the real light on?" The real light meaning his bedside lamp, not the night-light that guided his way to the hallway bathroom he shared with Iso. They left him there in the glow of the real light. He was asleep by the time they crossed the threshold, but Eliza did not backtrack to turn out the light. If he awoke again, it would be important to him that the light was still on, that the promise had been kept.

"It's my fault," Eliza said when they were back downstairs. "He's so sensitive he can tell that I'm jumping out of my skin these days."

"Maybe. But it could also be a coincidence."

"He might have read the letter," she said guiltily, as if her carelessness with the document indicated some subconscious agenda of her own.

"What?"

She explained how she had come to lose track of it, Albie's drawing on the back. "Truthfully, I'm fearful that Iso is the one who threw it in the trash can by the desk, although I suppose I could have thrown it out by accident, forgotten what I had in that pocket. She's a terrible snoop. She's been going through my purse lately, and lord knows what else."

"Okay, but here's the thing," Peter said, pouring himself a

glass of wine and putting on the teakettle for her, rummaging behind the pots and pans for a brand of high-end cookies that Eliza hoarded, one of the few things she refused to share with her children because they ate them too carelessly, too quickly. "If either one of them had read the letter, they wouldn't be able to hide that fact from you for long. Even if they were worried about getting into trouble for snooping. Albie, especially. So put that out of your mind for now. What's the real issue here?"

She shook her head. She couldn't put her worries out of her mind just by drinking a cup of tea, eating one of her beloved biscuits. She wasn't Albie.

"This is how I see it," Peter said. "Walter wants to make actual contact with you. He's not entitled to that wish, which he realizes. He says as much. Yet what he's doing is threatening you, implicitly. He keeps circling closer, letting you know how much he's learned about you, that he can get to our family via this LaFortuny person. If he made a direct threat, or even a demand, you could go to the prison authorities and complain. You could get him in trouble for what he's done to date, but you haven't because you believe that every person who knows about your past exponentially increases the possibility of the story getting out, which bothers you because you don't want the kids to know."

"Or anyone, really. People change, when they find out." She thought of the one girl from high school she had taken into her confidence just partway, and how badly that had ended when they decided they liked the same boy. The other girl, who knew Eliza had been raped, started a whisper campaign that she was a slut, a girl who would do it with anyone, and that's why the boy had chosen her.

"Walter wants to see you," Peter repeated. "And the point of all this—the letters, the phone calls, his accomplice—is to let you know that if you don't come see him, then maybe he will go public. Grant an interview. Start dropping hints again that he'll reveal at last how many girls he's killed. Yes, I think the Washington and Baltimore papers will protect your privacy if you decline to be interviewed on the record. But, as you said, all sorts of unsavory types won't. I think Walter is suggesting that if you go see him, he'll spare you that."

"That's so unfair," Eliza said.

"It is. But you have to focus on what *you* want, not what's right or principled. You don't want to tell the kids yet what happened to you, but you don't want the kids to find out from someone else. How do you best achieve that goal?"

"Maybe Walter wants money, cash to purchase some privilege or item he can't afford on his own."

"Maybe. But his friend Miss LaFortuny is well fixed, right? I think Walter would be offended if you offered him money."

"Walter has no right to be offended by anything I do."

"Agreed. Walter has no right to anything. And if you're prepared to weather the consequences of ignoring him, I say go for it. If you're ready to bring the kids down here and give them the PG-13 version of what happened to you when you were fifteen, I'll back you up. We can even ask your parents to point us to some experts in the field, get their advice on how to talk about it. We always knew this day was going to come. We just didn't expect Walter to be the one who forced the issue."

"No," Eliza said, nibbling at her biscuit, trying to make it last. "Albie can't handle it, and Iso won't be able to keep the secret if we tell just her."

"Iso's very good at keeping secrets. Too good, in my experience."

"Her own," Eliza said, thinking about her rifled purse. "Not anyone else's. Besides, she might tell him in order to upset him."

"Okay, that was one alternative. The other is to do nothing, and see what happens, which basically puts us at the mercy of Walter and the loose cannon that is Miss LaFortuny."

Eliza grimaced. She disliked the woman and felt guilty about disliking someone ostensibly well intentioned. But there was something creepy about her.

"The final option is to let Walter have some sort of direct contact with you. A call, or a visit. Clearly, a letter didn't satisfy him."

The teakettle sang. It had belonged to Eliza's mother and was an anachronistically silly item, emblematic of the late 1970s, an enamel kettle that was meant to resemble a puffer fish. Inez had decided she hated it soon after buying it. Eliza hated it, too, but she hadn't been in any position to disdain her mother's hand-me-downs when she and Peter started living together the final year of school. Now this fish had traveled with them from Wesleyan to Houston to London and back again to its home state of Maryland, earning Eliza's affection on the basis of its sheer longevity, its staying power. Her kitchen held many of Inez's castoffs—simple things, with no stories, no distinction—and she loved them all. Her mind cataloged them now, all those little relics of the house back in Roaring Springs—a particular mixing bowl, a bottle opener, a long spoon used to stir Sunshines. She had wept—wept—when a ceramic jar, used for holding kitchen utensils, had been misplaced during the move back to the States. Eventually it was found, unharmed, in a mislabeled box, and she had wept again with joy.

"A call," she said. "I can handle a call. But it has to be understood that we will talk during school hours, only."

"And do you think," Peter asked, "that he'll be satisfied, then, that you'll have nothing to worry about?"

She chewed her cookie with unusual care. "Probably not."

"Eliza—do I know everything about what happened?"

"No," she told her husband. "But then—I'm not sure I do, either."

20

"LOOK AT THAT GIRL, the shine on her," Walter said.

Where were they? They were in Manassas, Virginia, on the outskirts, about as far east as they ever seemed to get. Walter's path reminded her of the Spirograph she had owned as a little kid. They were traveling in a fixed circle, rotating according to a pattern that made sense to him, making great loops through western Virginia, western Maryland, and easternmost West Virginia. She wondered if he was circling his own hometown, if he was as homesick for his house and parents as she was. But he could go home anytime, couldn't he? She refused to feel sorry for Walter in his homesickness. It wasn't the same as hers at all. He had freedom of movement. If she ever got away from him, she would make sure to—

"Go talk to her," Walter said.

The girl was at a makeshift stand, filled with homemade jars of something. The sign promised that all proceeds would go to Darlene Fuchs, whoever she was.

"What?"

"Go talk to her. Make friends."

"I don't know how to do that."

"Sure you do."

But she didn't, not anymore, and she wouldn't.

"I'll do it," Walter said angrily, downshifting into a lower gear and turning around. Elizabeth had been watching him drive, trying to figure out if she could ever take the truck, but the stick shift was baffling to her. She had sat in the backseat during Vonnie's driving lessons and thought it looked easy, but both the family cars were automatics. And even Walter sometimes ground the gears on this old truck.

"Excuse me, miss?"

The girl—and Elizabeth could see instantly that she was a girl, not quite her age, although tall and shapely—had more than a shine on her. She was movie-star pretty, with hair worn long and straight, not the most current style, but becoming to her. Her eyes were sea green, a color made more vivid by the pale green oxford shirt she wore, a Ralph Lauren emblazoned with a tiny polo player. Elizabeth thought of that preppie style as played out, but it worked on this girl.

"Yes?" she said. Her voice was southern, although not like Walter's. Different southern. Classy southern.

"I want to buy some clothes for my sister, but I don't know this area very well and I just thought someone as well dressed as you might be able to help us out."

She looked down at her own clothes as if she had forgotten what she was wearing, as if her perfect outfit was a lucky accident. Yet the oxford cloth shirt was paired with plaid Bermudas, which held hints of the same green. The arms of a pink sweater, picking up the other theme in the Bermudas, hugged her neck. She did not look like the sort of girl who sold jams and jellies on the roadside, on a pretty Saturday afternoon. She looked like someone who should be at the football game. A cheerleader. Or if not a cheerleader, someone with a boyfriend, or a gaggle of female friends, laughing in the stands. A long driveway rose behind her, going up and over a hill, no house in sight. A sign affixed to a post read T'N'T FARM. Elizabeth somehow knew it was not a real farm, but someplace very grand, a place that concealed its grandeur behind this silly name, which was just a sneaky way of being pretentious show-offs.

"I'm not sure I bought this around here, but if you go over to the mall—"

"How do we get there?"

"It's not far. You just go up that way and make a left on—"

"But I'm not from here. Those names mean nothing to me. Is it on your way? Could you ride part of the way with us and show us? I'll give you five dollars for your trouble."

She shook her head.

"Five for you and ten for your cause. I bet that's more money than you've raised so far today."

Don't, Elizabeth thought. *Please don't.* But the girl had grabbed her little tin cash box and was climbing into the cab of the truck, into the space that Elizabeth made by jumping out and holding the door open for her. Elizabeth marveled at the way she left her little jars there, trusting that they would be there when she got back. Trusting that she would be back at all.

"Did you make those jellies yourself?" Elizabeth asked.

"Uh-huh. It's green pepper jelly, from an old recipe in my mother's family. My daddy told me that trying to sell green pepper jelly around here was coals to Newcastle, but I thought it was better than a car wash, or a bake sale."

"Who's Darlene Fuchs?"

"A girl in my grade, at Middleburg Middle." So the girl was younger than she was, no more than fourteen. "She has Hodgkin's lymphoma and her family doesn't have any insurance."

Elizabeth could feel the girl assessing her. Not judging her, not mean or catty in her scrutiny, merely taking in the truck, their clothes, Walter's accent. She might raise money for them, if they were in dire straits. She would show them how to get to the mall. But she had already marked Elizabeth as Other, someone not like her. This was why, Elizabeth realized, no one ever noticed them. Walter had tainted her, made her part of his world.

"Aren't you worried," Elizabeth asked her, "that someone will take your jelly?"

"Not around here," the girl said. "We don't even lock our doors most nights."

"What's your name?"

"Holly," she said. Elizabeth waited, but she didn't say: What's yours? The girl was rude in the way that only very polite people can be, so complacent about her excellent manners that she forgot to use them sometimes.

The truck lurched forward, eager and overanxious. There was a strong scorched smell, a hint of sweetness beneath it. Walter had leaned too hard on the clutch, trying to get up the hill. "Holly," he said. "That's a pretty name."

"Thank you."

"A pretty name for a pretty girl. You're a lovely young woman, you really need someone to take care of you. You don't buy into that woman's libbers stuff, I bet, not really. Look at the natural world, how labors are divided. The males hunt and defend and provide, the females nurture their young, feather the nest. If a woman doesn't want to have children, that's one thing. But it's unnatural for the woman to leave the home."

Holly shifted in her seat, looking to Elizabeth, then back to Walter. Elizabeth realized that Walter was using the knowledge gleaned from the book, although expressing it in his own words. Elizabeth had understood that he liked the book. He had stolen that library copy, after all. But she had not realized until now that Walter took the text literally, that he believed it was like the directions on cake mix, simple and foolproof. Say these things, and you'll get a girlfriend. She wanted to tell him: *She's only a middle-schooler.* She wanted to say: *She doesn't understand what you're talking about.* Instead, she looked out the window, at the green-and-gold blur that was Virginia in the first week of autumn.

She found herself thinking about being little, five or six, and longing to order the hundred plastic dolls offered for a dollar in the back pages of some comic, probably *Betty and Veronica.* A hundred dolls for a dollar! It seemed too good to be true. It probably was, her mother counseled her. The dolls would be tiny and cheap. But it was Elizabeth's dollar, she could spend it as she chose. She sent away for the dolls and they arrived, even smaller and cheaper than her mother had prophesied. But her mother did not say, *I told you so,* or, *Let this be a lesson to you.* She said: *Let's make a doll tree.* They tied curling ribbons around the dolls and hung them on the boughs of a potted ficus. That night, when her father came home, he had burst into laughter. *Strange fruit,* he spluttered, *strange fruit.* Then: *Inez, you have clearly found your niche, working with the criminally insane.*

After a brief, baffled moment, her mother had started to laugh, too, then explained the joke to Elizabeth. They had played the song for her on her father's stereo, pulling the record out of a thick five- or six-album set of which her father was inordinately proud, one with a watercolor of a woman with a flower in her hair. They had talked to her about the history of the South and civil rights. They were kind and thorough and respectful. But the thing was: Elizabeth had loved that tree. It was beautiful to her, and it made her sad when her father's reaction transformed it into a morbid joke, a joke that overtook her original joy, squashed it beneath the stories of lynchings and the civil rights movement. Walter was like Elizabeth at age six, seeing what he wanted to see. True, he was a grown man, and he should have known better than to believe a silly book. Still—she felt protective of him, in that moment, sorry for him.

YOU FELT SORRY FOR HIM?

The Virginia prosecutor snapped those words back at her, the way an impatient parent or teacher barked in the face of an obvious lie. That was odd, because this prosecutor, as opposed to the Maryland one, had always been kind and careful with her. The Maryland one had been exasperated with her from the start.

But this was the first time they had gone over the day in such detail. They had been talking for hours, and Elizabeth, now known as Eliza, was tired.

"Not exactly sorry. But I understood what was going on inside his head."

"Then you must have felt even worse for Holly." The young lawyer was nodding, encouraging her. "Because you knew exactly what she was going through."

"Yes," she said, wanting to please him. Then, after a quick glance to her parents, "No."

"You didn't feel bad for Holly." Repeated in a flat tone, as if that would make her aware of how ridiculous she was. "You didn't understand what was happening to her."

"I didn't know what she was thinking. I didn't *know* her."

"But she started to cry. And you knew what you felt when Walter took you."

"Yes, but—"

The prosecutor cut her off. "That's all you have to say. That she was crying, that she seemed upset, that she realized things had taken a bad turn. You see, Elizabeth"—in court, she would still be Elizabeth—"the details that matter are the ones that show Walter kidnapped Holly and took the contents of the cash box. So let's just focus on that. He didn't let her go when she asked, right?"

"Right." Holly was pretty even when she cried. *Mister, mister. Please just let me go, mister. My daddy will pay you, mister.*

"And he took her money?"

"He asked for it and she gave it to him."

"But this was after she had asked to be let go, right? How much time had passed?"

"An hour? Maybe more, maybe less. The clock in the truck was broken. Walter always said the cobbler's children went barefoot and a mechanic's car was never as nice as the ones he worked on."

The prosecutor showed no interest in Walter's insights.

"So he takes Holly's money."

"Yes, to buy us hamburgers."

"Right. Still, it was Holly's money and Walter took it from her. By force."

"Yes, I guess so. I mean, he took the box from her and she didn't want to give it up. He didn't have to fight her or anything, but he did have to kind of peel it out of her arms."

The prosecutor nodded. "Right, he took the money and then—?"

"He gave it to me and sent me into the McDonald's to buy the food because he didn't trust Holly to behave if we went through the drive-through lane."

The silence that filled the room reminded Eliza/Elizabeth of a verse they had sung in middle school chorus, the Robert Frost poem "Stopping by the Woods on a Snowy Evening." This silence, like the one in the poem, was dark and deep. Not lovely, though, definitely not lovely, anything but lovely. She heard, literally heard, her mother swallow. Heard—not saw, but heard—her father take her mother's hand, the tiny intake of breath made by the prosecutor. She could suddenly hear everything. The hum of the fluorescent light, the water cooler gently burping out in the hallway, her own hands moving back and forth along the thighs of her black cotton pants. Brushed cotton twill, pleated, worn with a high-necked shirt fastened with a brooch, an outfit modeled after one she had seen in a movie.

"Could you repeat that, Elizabeth?"

"He gave me the money and sent me into McDonald's to buy the food." She was proud of how consistent she was, how she said it, word for word, almost exactly as she had said it before. That was very important in these things. But the prosecutor did not seem proud of her.

"And you—"

"I ordered three Quarter Pounders. Walter didn't like pickles, so I had to wait for his to be made special. And I had to make sure I knew which were the Diet Cokes and which was the regular Coke. Walter drank regular Coke, but he thought girls should drink Diet Coke because soda can make you fat if you're not careful. We just guessed that Holly would eat the same things we did, because she wouldn't say what she wanted. And I had to make sure to get enough ketchup packages. They never give you enough, only two little measly ones, and they can be grudging if you don't ask right."

"Grudging?"

"That was Walter's word, I guess. I took it back to the car and we drove a little ways until we found a place where we could eat, hoping the fries didn't get cold. Holly didn't want to eat hers, though, so Walter did, picking out the pickles. I don't know why he couldn't do that with his own sandwich to begin with."

"Elizabeth?"

"Yes?"

"When you went into the McDonald's—why didn't you tell someone what was happening?"

"What do you mean?"

"That you were kidnapped, that your kidnapper had another girl in the car?"

No one had asked her this before, but then—no one had gone over this part of the day in such detail. When she was rescued, the questions had been quick, mercifully so. *How was she? What had he done to her? Had he—?* She was the one who told them about Holly, the scream in the night, the campsite in the mountains, the landmarks that she could remember. And for weeks, months, that had been enough. But now they were preparing for Walter's trial and everything—everything—had to be discussed in great detail. She had to tell the story the same way, in her own words. She thought she was doing that.

She had forgotten the Quarter Pounders.

"I couldn't. He said he would hurt me."

"But he was in the car. With Holly."

"Yes, because she couldn't be trusted."

"And you could?"

"When I was good, he was nicer to me." She looked to her parents. Her mother nodded, encouraging her, although she looked slightly stunned. Her father looked angry, but not at her. He was glaring at the prosecutor.

"How did you earn Walter's trust?" the prosecutor asked, and her parents could no longer contain themselves.

"Really—" her mother began. "Why must you—" her father said, trying to use what Eliza recognized was his professional voice, but not quite controlling it as he usually did.

"What do you think Walter Bowman's lawyer is going to do with this information?" The prosecutor's manner was bland, like one of the jocks at Eliza's new school, the kind of boy who lets a girl know she wasn't even worth teasing. "She had a chance to get away, to save both of them. She didn't."

"So don't put her on the stand at all," her father said. "You'll get no argument from us."

"I need her testimony about the cash box, and how Walter refused to let Holly go. I have to establish the kidnapping or another felony to ensure he gets the death penalty, and we can't prove rape."

Eliza pondered that, then realized: He meant Holly. They couldn't prove Walter raped Holly. What he had done to her didn't count.

"Eliza's behavior is consistent with dozens of hostage cases," her mother began.

"Stockholm syndrome, I know." The prosecutor's voice was bitter, belittling. "That worked so well for Patty Hearst."

"No, not Stockholm syndrome, not exactly. She didn't sympathize with her captor. But Elizabeth"—her mother had trouble remembering the new name—"is a young girl and she believed he had the power he claimed he had. He threatened her. He threatened us."

The prosecutor looked to Eliza. She nodded, then realized he would not be satisfied with a nod. "He told me all the time that he would kill me and my family if I tried to get away from him. He said he would kill them while I watched."

He looked down at his notes. "Back at the roadside, where you first met Holly—why did you get out of the truck and let her sit in the middle?"

"Because that's what Walter wanted."

"Did he say that?"

"No, but I understood. He gave me a look, and I realized that he wanted the new girl to sit next to him."

"The new girl?"

"Holly. But she wasn't Holly yet. I didn't learn her name until she was in the truck."

"You were the new girl, once."

Eliza didn't understand his point. "Not really. There wasn't another girl, when he took me."

"You saw him with a shovel, digging a grave."

"Yes, but I didn't know that. I just saw a man digging."

"A grave for Maude Parrish."

"That's who you found there, right?"

The prosecutor didn't always answer her questions. Apparently, he owned the questions. "So you were the new girl, after Maude. And you knew that when Walter switched girls, he got rid of the old one."

"No . . ." It was different, not at all the same.

"Elizabeth, why do you think Walter kept you alive? Why did he kill every girl but you?"

"I think," she said, "it was because I always did what he told me to do."

The prosecutor asked her to leave, so he could speak to her parents privately, but her parents refused. She was sixteen, she was going to testify in court. She should be part of every discussion.

"Okay, I'm going to lay it out for you. The prosecutor in Maryland is scared to go for the death penalty in his county, precisely because he has no evidence that Maude was kidnapped. Walter Bowman refuses to confess to any other homicides, although there are quite a few missing person cases that seem plausible. The murder of Holly Tackett is our only chance to put this guy to death, and I can't afford to give the defense anything to play with."

The Lerners were united in their mystification, staring at this young, pompous man in bewilderment.

"A smart defense attorney is going to go to town with this. Suggest Elizabeth wasn't a victim at this point, but an accomplice. And once you let that idea worm its way into the courtroom, you've got all sorts of reasonable doubt. What if Elizabeth was the one who pushed Holly into the ravine, out of fear, or even jealousy? What if Elizabeth was really Walter's girlfriend?"

"That is offensive beyond belief," Inez said.

"A good attorney isn't going to worry about giving offense. He'll be playing for big stakes. He's playing for Walter's life."

"And you're playing," Manny said, "for his death. That's quite a game you've got going there. Some would call it playing God."

The prosecutor studied Eliza's parents. "You're enlightened types, right? Don't want to see the guy die. Don't want to see anyone die. But then, you've got your daughter. Two other families, probably a lot more, weren't so lucky."

"As a father," Manny said, "I want to strangle him. When I see him, I want to go over to him and pound his face off, knock him to the ground, kick him until he coughs up blood. But I know that's not right, and I shouldn't do it. Nor would I have the state do it for me, by proxy. So, no, I don't believe in the death penalty, if that's what you're asking."

"The Tacketts don't feel the same way. Fact is, that's who the commonwealth of Virginia represents in this case. Not your daughter. Holly Tackett and Virginia. I hope you haven't let your own"—he paused for a minute, seeming not so much to search for a word, as for the spin he wanted to place on it—"altruistic ideas influence your daughter. I hope this story about McDonald's, which I'm hearing for the first time, isn't something you've cooked up to create enough confusion about events that a jury will be reluctant to consider the death penalty."

Inez put a hand on Manny's arm, almost as if she feared he

would try to do to the prosecutor the things he said he wanted to do to Walter. But, of course, he stayed in his chair.

"The only thing we've instructed our daughter to do," Inez said, "is tell the truth. Tell the truth, and not look for reasons this happened to her, because there are no reasons."

"That's a nice thing to tell your daughter and probably very helpful," the prosecutor said, trying to scoot back to their side, reunite the team. *Yea, Eliza! Boo, Walter!* Only he had slipped, revealed his true loyalties, and Eliza knew she could never trust him again. "But jurors will want reasons. I'm trying to anticipate the worst-case scenario. I'm sure things will work out."

Things did, at least as far as the prosecutor was concerned. Walter's defense attorney was far from expert, and he treated Eliza with an almost bizarre politeness, as if she had a condition that should not be referenced directly. No, it was the prosecutor who asked her about the trip to McDonald's, and made her tell, in excruciating detail, what Walter did to her the night after Holly died. It was Jared Garrett, a few months later, who devoted a large section of his book to the theory that Elizabeth Lerner might have been Walter Bowman's girlfriend and coconspirator, whom he decided not to implicate for reasons known only to him, given that he never testified. If Elizabeth had been raped, why was Walter allowed to plead guilty to a lesser charge of kidnapping and assault? Garrett cited no sources for his theories, asserting only that there was a "school of thought" that Elizabeth Lerner may have evolved into something more than a hostage. "School of thought!" Vonnie had snorted. "There's only one student in that school and he's the village idiot."

It didn't matter. By the time Garrett's book was published, the sordid imaginations attracted to his kind of journalism had moved on. A serial killer known as the Night Stalker was terrorizing Los Angeles; two dead girls in the Mid-Atlantic simply couldn't compete. The crimes of Walter Bowman had been eclipsed even in

Virginia, where a high-achieving college student had enlisted her German boyfriend in the murder of her parents. Elizabeth Lerner was Eliza Lerner, enrolled in a new high school in a new county, her hair back to its natural color and curly disorder. Nobody knew her past, nobody cared.

OR WAS IT THE OTHER WAY around: nobody cared, so nobody knew? Sitting at her kitchen table more than two decades later, Eliza found herself taunted by that question. Was it so unthinkable that Walter Bowman might have chosen her over Holly? She knew what her parents would say: Walter was mentally ill, incapable of any genuine feeling. Walter was a sociopath. Walter had not *chosen* anyone.

Yet he had, and only he knew why. Whatever he wanted now—and she had known from the first letter that he would not be satisfied with a one-sided contact, that his very words "I'd know you anywhere" were meant to remind her of a marker on a very old debt—she wanted something from him, too. She needed to ask: "Why me?" Was that wrong? Was it ego-driven, irrational? Did the very question desecrate the memories of the others, and if that was the case—then so what? Wasn't she entitled to ask that question, in private, of the one person who actually could tell her if there was a reason she was alive?

But if she dared to ask Walter that question, she had to be prepared for other answers, less pleasant ones. She had to confront the fact of the girl who walked into McDonald's, focused on nothing but ketchup and pickles. She had to think about what happened later that night. "We have to go," he'd said, and they went, breaking camp in silence. As they drove down the long switchback in the dark, he handed her Holly's metal box, now empty, all those well-intentioned dollars gone, some for food, the rest crammed into Walter's pocket. "Toss it," he said, grunting with disapproval at how ineptly she hurled the box from the truck. "You can't throw for shit." It was rare for him to use profanity, and the word felt like a slap.

The box was found a few days later, helping searchers pinpoint the campsite that Elizabeth had described for them, and then Holly's broken body on the other side of the mountain. Elizabeth was praised for being cagey enough to let this potent clue fall close to the roadside.

But perhaps Walter had it right: She just couldn't throw for shit.

Part II

CARELESS WHISPER

Released 1985

Reached no. 1 on Billboard Hot 100 on February 16, 1985

Spent 22 weeks on Billboard Hot 100

21

THE NEW PHONE SAT in the alcove off the master bedroom on an end table rescued from her parents' basement. Eliza had been shocked at how much resistance the local phone company had given her about adding a second, dedicated line to the house, but perhaps that was because she wanted the most basic package possible, with no extras and a limited number of outgoing calls a month. *Why not get a cell phone?* the helpful young woman at Verizon had queried. *Or just use your call-waiting feature?* Why indeed? She could get a cheap, disposable mobile, toss it when—well, whenever. She knew that what she wanted wasn't exactly logical, but it made sense to her. She wanted to limit Walter's access to her, her home, to one slender wire, one no-frills touch-tone telephone. It was bad enough that *he* was the one who called her, and collect at that. She could at least pick the instrument and set the time frame for when he was allowed to call, ten to two weekdays, when the house was empty.

The children had been curious about the new phone, drawn to it as children are drawn to any novelty, but its lack of features quickly dampened their interest. They had been told that this was an outgoing line for emergencies only. Peter had gilded the lily by claiming Homeland Security recommended Washington-area residents have old-fashioned desk phones, ones that did not require electrical outlets. Unfortunately, this inspired falsehood inflamed Albie's imagination, and there was another round of nightmares. Eliza was exhausted in a way she had not been since Iso was a colicky infant, moving through the days under the fog of a constant headache.

Yet the telephone remained silent. There was, apparently, not a little bureaucracy involved in talking to a man on death row. For every rule that Eliza had invented—the dedicated line, the hours during which Walter was allowed to call—the Department of Corrections had far more. Or so Barbara LaFortuny informed them when she had taken the new number and forwarded it to Walter. It was a week since they had installed the phone, and it had rung exactly once, sending its full-chested sound through the house.

It was an automated service, claiming that her car warranty was about to expire.

Now the phone sat, beige and squat, utterly utilitarian. It was, in fact, almost identical to the phone that the Lerner family had installed in the "phone nook" in the Roaring Springs house, although that phone had seemed terribly sleek and modern at the time. Manny and Inez, permissive in most things, felt the telephone was an incursion on family life, and they insisted on having only two extensions, one in their bedroom and the other in the hall. The girls could speak as much as they wanted, but it would be in the hall, with no chair, only the scratchiest of rugs on which to rest.

Vonnie, undaunted by the public venue, sat cross-legged in front of the hall phone as if it were Buddha or Vishnu. She stalked, she paced, she sometimes even put it on the floor and circled it, almost as if it were a campfire around which she was dancing. Fierce Vonnie, who was happy to march under the flag of feminism, saw no irony or contradiction in boy craziness. She was a passionate person, someone who lived a big life with big emotions and ambitions, and reaped big rewards as a consequence. Germaine Greer—the early Germaine Greer, the feminine eunuch posing in her bikini—was her role model. It was hard for Eliza to say Vonnie had been mistaken in her self-image. Never married, largely by choice, she had enjoyed affairs with an impressive assortment of men. Older, younger, richer, poorer. One or two were famous, most were wildly successful, and even the slackers were interesting, creative types. Vonnie had a big life, something out of the novels that Eliza preferred, the ones that managed to be respectable while still being replete with all the lifestyle details—clothes, food, home furnishings—that were disdained in so-called sex-and-shopping novels.

But Eliza preferred her sideline view of her sister's life. And unlike larger-than-life Vonnie, Eliza had been spared what their mother dubbed the Vikki Carr curse. Part of that was the simple good luck of meeting Peter when she was eighteen and falling into a relationship that, whatever its ups and downs, was pretty much without doubt. But even with her high school boyfriends, she had been . . . diffident. She almost never called them, for example. Vonnie sneered that Eliza was a throwback, that she was betraying all womanhood with her willingness to let men call the shots. Eliza didn't think so. She just didn't have that much to say.

But sometimes she wondered if Walter's self-help book, the

one that had urged women to embrace their "natural" roles, had left more of an imprint than she realized. While traveling with Walter—a euphemism, yet not—they had gotten into the habit of going to yard sales, and he would sometimes let her buy a book, if it was cheap enough. She had picked up a copy of Mario Puzo's *The Godfather,* of which Walter did not approve, so she had to read it during her brief moments alone, in the bath or on the toilet. She would soak in the tub—and tubs were fewer and far between, once Walter got the tent—and read until the water was tepid. She imagined what Don Corleone would do if she were his daughter, or even the daughter of a friend. He wouldn't kill Walter, not on her behalf. That would not be justice, as he explained to the undertaker whose daughter had been raped by the two college boys. But they would do something pretty bad to him, she was sure, especially if she asked them to avenge the girl whose body had been found in Patapsco State Park.

She still had the book with her when the state police picked them up near Point of Rocks. At first the book had reminded her of the time with Walter, and she hadn't wanted to read it. But then her high school boyfriend had said they should watch the film on his family's VCR, and she'd decided to finish the book first. She had plunged back in, following Michael into his Sicilian exile, feeling a bizarre kinship with him—she had been exiled, too—then on to his wedding night, where he had discovered his young bride was a virgin, and a virgin was the very best thing to be, according to Mario Puzo. She had stopped reading there and forgotten about the book until Vonnie had discovered it during summer vacation, while looking for the latest copy of *TV Guide.* (It was an article of faith in the Lerner household that Eliza's bed, the territory beneath it, was a kind of Bermuda Triangle where all sorts of things came to rest.) The book's spine was broken on the page where Eliza had abandoned it, and Vonnie, emerging from beneath the bed with a few dust bunnies clinging to her hair, as unruly as Eliza's but not as red, looked at the pages, then at her sister.

"How would *he* know?" she said. Vonnie was exhausting and infuriating, but also loyal. Eliza, filled with warmth at this memory of her sister, decided to call her for no good reason, although she was almost certain to be dumped straight to voice mail. She began heading downstairs to the den, the coziest spot in the house.

The other phone rang, full-throated, robust. It had no answering machine, no voice mail, another decision on which Verizon had fought with her. It would ring forever if Eliza allowed it. Phones never rang that way anymore. It was one of the interesting things about older movies, where phones might ring six, seven, eight times, or—in that one gangster movie of which Peter was so fond—something like thirty-seven times. Nowadays, phones rang maybe three or four times, then rolled over to voice mail, or got picked up by answering machines, or—

She picked up on the seventh ring, almost hoping it was news about her car warranty or mortgage or credit card. The automated voice gave her a moment of hope. But this time, the voice was asking if she would accept a collect call from Walter Bowman.

She said she would.

"Elizabeth?"

"Yes."

There was an echoing metallic sound that seemed to go on and on. "Excuse me," Walter said, and the noise grew louder, swelled, then fell back, ending with a few faded clangs.

"What was *that*?" She had intended to ask him as few questions as possible, to put the burden of conversation on him, but her curiosity got the better of her.

"Oh, one of the guys went down to Jarratt and got a stay, so we're kicking him back in."

"Kicking—?"

"We kick the doors, in solidarity, when a man gets a postponement. Although I have to tell you, I don't really have much for this particular fellow. He's managed the trick of being both the meanest and dumbest man here."

She was nonplussed. It felt like the polite conversation a salesman makes as he settles in, getting ready to launch into his pitch. She wanted to blurt out: *What do you want? Get to it, stop stalling.* Before she could ask, her cell phone buzzed from her pocket. She glanced down at its screen. Iso's school.

"Walter, can you hold on? There's another call coming in on my cell and . . ."

She did not want to explain why the call could not be ignored, but nor was she happy when Walter said: "Sure, I understand. You've got young kids."

"My husband told me he might need me to pick him up at the airport today," she lied, with a promptness that made her rather proud. The old-fashioned phone could not be muted, so she walked out into the hall, determined that Walter not overhear the conversation with Iso's middle school.

It was the principal. "Can you come in, Mrs. Benedict? We have a . . . situation."

"Is Isobel hurt? Sick?" In her worry, she couldn't help using her daughter's full name.

"No, just something to discuss before it becomes a problem. And we know that Iso's brother is in elementary school, so we thought it would be easier to have you come in now, rather than complicate your life with after-school detention, which means Iso would miss the bus."

"Detention?"

"Only if it were warranted and it's not." A pause. "Yet."

She walked back to the beige phone, tried to think what she could say. "Walter, I'm sorry, but this is urgent—"

"Sure, sure," he said. "We'll catch up later. We have a lot to talk about."

As anxious as she was about Iso and the unspecified *situation,* Eliza couldn't take Walter's invitation to end the call. "Do we? Do we really have that much to discuss?"

"I think so," Walter said. "And although I know you doubt this, it will be mutually beneficial, Elizabeth. Really, you have to believe that I have nothing but your best interest at heart. I'm doing this for you."

She said good-bye, grabbed her purse and her keys, headed out to the garage, and then, almost as an afterthought, dashed back inside and threw up in the powder-room toilet.

22

TRUDY TACKETT WAS IN HER CLOSET, taking careful inventory of her clothes, a biannual ritual in which she banished the warm-weather months and welcomed the cold ones by sorting, folding, and mending, as needed. Also eliminating. As needed. She was ruthless about culling things. She had to be. Trudy had been exactly the same size since her wedding day forty-four years earlier, with the exception of her many pregnancies, and clothing had a way of mounting up. She reversed the process every April, although not with the same sense of satisfaction. She liked the arrival of the shorter, colder days, which seemed to pass more quickly than their summer counterparts. A June day required so much of a person. Enthusiasm, cheer. She didn't doubt that seasonal affective disorder was real, but wasn't it also possible to suffer from a surfeit of sun? Here in her closet, Trudy was glad for the lack of natural light, even if it meant missing the occasional grease spot, or navy masquerading as black.

"This alcove would make a wonderful dressing room," the real estate agent had purred to Trudy almost two decades ago, but it was Terry who had taken those words to heart and hired a company to transform the space. Most women would envy that kind of spousal devotion, and Trudy was grateful for it in an absent, distracted way. She did remember being bemused that the closet designer had included a small bench upholstered in tufted velvet. Trudy liked clothes well enough—obviously, someone had shopped for this wardrobe—but she didn't want to sit in her closet and *commune* with them, for goodness' sakes. And she couldn't imagine why else one would have a bench in a closet, even a clever little one such as this, with storage hidden under its bland beige seat, round and pale as a mushroom, or Miss Muffet's tuffet.

(*What's a tuffet?* Holly had asked when she was five, looking up from an ancient copy of *Mother Goose,* Trudy's own. A hassock. *What's a hassock?* A tuffet. Holly had laughed. Holly had been the only person who glimpsed that side of Trudy, the girly silliness that had never found a place in the hypermasculine, rough-and-tumble Tackett family. Terry and the boys joked the way they played games—fast, rough, loud, on point. Until Holly arrived, Trudy was the straight woman, the dowager. Once Holly left—well, there wasn't much to joke about.)

But now the time had come that Trudy sometimes needed that bench, that hassock, that tuffet, to put on slacks, hose, shoes, all the things she had once slipped on while standing on one leg, nonchalant as a crane. Her balance was no longer reliable, and her lower back was prone to going out over the smallest indignities. *I'm deteriorating,* she told Terry cheerfully. She imagined her body covered with little Post-its, each one marking a specific area of decline—the creaking knee, the popping hip, the stiffening shoulders. She pictured a suit of Post-its, sharp yellow edges riffling in the breeze, at once stiff and pliant. She would like such a suit, an outfit that would announce her edges to the world.

She gathered the pastel clothes of spring and summer, imprisoning them into plastic garment bags, shoving them to the rear of the closet as she brought forward the darker, more somber clothes of fall and winter. She brushed the collar of a moss green suit, which still had the tags attached. She had purchased it at Saks five years ago for one express purpose and would not wear it until that day came.

The suit was for Walter Bowman's execution. This fall. She was going to wear it this fall. November 25. The third time would be the charm.

She had planned the entire day in her mind, down to the smallest detail. Lord knows she had time enough to do it. They would drive down to Jarratt in Terry's car. It was her understanding that they could avoid the press, watch in camera, but she wouldn't mind if it didn't work out that way. She could walk past the protesters with her head held high, speak briefly to the reporters with appropriate solemnity. She would not even wince at the inevitable questions about her feelings. The fact was, she wasn't sure how she was going to feel. Exhausted, primarily, wrung out by the necessity of seeing this through. Granted, very little had been required of her over the past twenty-two years. The prosecutors—Bowman had outlasted three of them—had done their jobs well, persevering through two appeals and a retrial. It had been her choice to attend every day, to make sure that the jurors and judges knew how much Holly was missed, mourned. That was all she had done, sit and wait. Still, Trudy felt like a woman she once knew who spent every plane trip tugging at her armrest, as if to keep the plane aloft. She arrived everywhere with throbbing pain from wrist to elbow, but she arrived, didn't she? Prove she was wrong.

After the execution—Trudy had a plan for that, too. She and Terry were going to drive straight to Richmond and check into the Jefferson Hotel. The next morning, they would visit Holly's grave in—oh, infelicitous name—the Hollywood Cemetery. Terry had generations of family there. It was a beautiful place, almost too beautiful, with tourists forever tromping through to see the graves of presidents, including Jefferson Davis, and the statue of the black dog that stood vigil over one little girl's grave. When Holly was first interred in the family mausoleum there, Trudy had thought it would be unbearable, sharing her annual visits with the disinterested tourists. She had found she didn't notice them at all.

Indeed the cemetery proved to be the one place where her sadness fit, a jewel in the perfect setting. Grief was allowed there. Back in the world—first in Middleburg, now in Alexandria—people kept making the mistake of thinking she might be happy again. Trudy had tried, she really had. She was a polite person, and politeness meant making others feel better even if it made you feel like shit. But it was exhausting, impossible. No, the cemetery was the only place where she was allowed to *be*. Even its distance, a solid two-hour drive on the best of days, proved a blessing, a bubble of time long enough for the transition back to the world where she didn't fit. "You have so much to celebrate," insisted well-meaning friends, referring to her sons and their children, all healthy and happy. That is, her sons were healthy and their children, who had never known Holly, had no problem being happy. Trudy was grateful for those blessings, but they felt like coins tossed in a fountain, wishes that came true only if one believed in the magic of wishes. She wouldn't have minded if the cemetery were another hour or two down the road. It would have given her that much more time to be unapologetically miserable.

Trudy had thought a lot about journeys, how the speed of transportation had transformed essential passages. Her ancestors had arrived in the New World in the eighteenth century, on ships that had required months to make the journey from France to Charleston. Her own parents had taken an ocean liner to their European honeymoon, a trip so leisurely that the clocks had advanced only an hour per day. If you thought about it, shouldn't most newlyweds have a week at sea, in the unreality of a stateroom, to prepare for the all-too-real reality that was marriage? Trudy and Terry Tackett—*How cuuuuuuuuuuuuuute,* her Sweet Briar roommate had caroled when Trudy returned from her very first date, knowing she had met the man she would marry—had only a weekend at the Waldorf-Astoria. He was an army surgeon who had to go straight back to work on Monday.

A weekend, a week, a month, a year at the Waldorf-Astoria would not have been enough to prepare Trudy for the life she was thrust into at twenty, when she dropped out of college to marry Terry. She was part of the last generation to do such things. Vietnam was on the horizon, although it wasn't called Vietnam yet. The next thing she knew, she was in Germany, then at Fort Sam Houston in San Antonio and babies, sons, were arriving with alarming speed. Terrence III, Tommy, Sam. Terry had wanted to call him Travis, after one of the heroes of the Alamo, but Trudy decided that the *T* thing had to come to an end at some point. Too cuuuuuuuuuuuuuuute. They were, as a family, constantly on the verge of being dangerously, enviably cute. She saw it in their Christmas cards, in the macho contentedness of their household, where bones broke and teeth got knocked out and digits were almost severed, yet everyone persevered, thrived even. Her sons were like something from a science fiction novel; nothing could hurt them. She came to believe that a head could get cut off and a new one would grow back in its place.

Then three miscarriages and, finally, Holly, born when Trudy was thirty-three. To say the family doted on Holly was inadequate, to say that they worshipped her would be blasphemous, and Trudy was still a good Catholic then. Holly was one of those golden children who made cranky strangers smile. Outgoing, bubbly, sweet. Her father and brothers had been overly protective, seeing molesters everywhere even when she was a pudgy grade-schooler. But Trudy had always worried that Holly's appeal was larger, transcending sex. She was like a little puppy that everyone wanted to cuddle, hold, possess. A person who had never been tempted to break a single rule might want to steal this child. Trudy, separated from Holly, even for a moment, in a grocery store or shop, would worry that her daughter had been spirited away by someone enchanted by her company. Trudy had been—not glad for the miscarriages, never glad, but resigned to the idea that it wasn't a bad thing, the age gap between the boys and Holly, the fact that she was the only girl. No female, no age peer, should ever have to have been in competition with Holly. Trudy was happy to be her handmaiden, the nurse to her Juliet, but a girl close to her age would have resented her.

Elizabeth Lerner almost certainly had.

Her inspection of her closet done, her bedroom reordered, Trudy trudged off dutifully to her daily walk. It was a glorious fall day, and Old Town Alexandria was its most precious self. Scarlet and gold leaves drifted to the sidewalks, almost as if the town were a theater set and someone was leaning out of the sky with a box of silken fakes, throwing them down at suitable intervals. The day, the neighborhood, shone—shop windows gleaming, delicious smells wafting from the restaurants, people strolling aimlessly, as if they had no greater responsibilities than to acknowledge the loveliness of it all.

God, how she hated it. Had loathed it from the day they had moved here, even though she was the one who had lobbied for the change, and chosen their new location. The boys were gone, disappearing as sons do into their wives' families, and now the holiday gatherings rotated among their households, so Trudy and Terry no longer needed a big house. It was easier for Trudy and Terry to visit each son—up to Boston, out to Kansas City, down to Jacksonville. Besides, the town house was not only small, but completely lacking in . . . resonance. The familiar items were there—pieces of furniture with real history, paintings from Trudy's family, the everyday dishes, the fancy china—but it felt like a set, or one of those re-created rooms in the Smithsonian. She could imagine a tour guide's nasal spiel: *This is where the Tackett family ate* (without appetite), *this is where they slept* (fitfully). It was as much a mausoleum as the one in Hollywood Cemetery.

She checked her watch, noting she had to walk for at least fifteen more minutes to meet her doctor's expectations, and turned down Princess Street toward Founders Park. It had been a shock when Dr. Garry had lectured her about diet and exercise at her last physical. "I weigh two pounds less than I weighed on my wedding day," she told him. But, as Dr. Garry had sussed out, she had remained at that weight largely by eating as little as possible and smoking. She had borderline high blood pressure and frighteningly high cholesterol. That is—it frightened the doctor. Trudy wasn't the least bit perturbed. When she noticed her hair thinning, a possible side effect of the statin he had prescribed, she simply stopped taking it. She wondered how long she was going to get away with that maneuver.

But she was walking, as advised, and doing silly little exercises with soup cans. She was not depressed, despite what her doctor thought, and she was far from apathetic or self-destructive. She happened to *like* smoking, something the nonsmokers of the world could never understand. She had given it up only to avoid being a hypocrite in her children's eyes. During the trials, she had started sneaking one or two a day with one of the assistant prosecutors because it was a good time to chat, assess how things were going. Because she never bought cigarettes, only bummed them, she didn't think of herself as smoking. By the time everything had worked through the legal system, she was a full-fledged smoker again, up to a pack a day. Now she was down to five, and she measured out her days in those slender treats. Number one was puffed in the laundry room, with a cup of tea, shortly after Terry left for work. The second was for early afternoon, after completing the prescribed walk. Number three was at 3 P.M. on the dot, with another cup of tea, but this time in the kitchen, while listening to *Fresh Air* and blowing her unfresh air out the window. Four was postdinner, back in the laundry room, and five was a quickie in the powder room right before bedtime. Terry knew, of course. He wasn't stupid, and he hadn't lost his sense of smell. He knew, and he let it go. She wondered if he would be similarly forgiving should he learn about the Lipitor she had stopped taking, the fact that her cholesterol was above 300, that her blood pressure was 138 over 90 the last time she checked it with the cuff at the local CVS.

She had reached the park. Terry had explained to her once that the marina was in Virginia, but the Potomac, at least here, was considered part of D.C. Who made such determinations? Why did they matter? She thought about the surveyors, moving carefully down the slope, the all-too-apt names on the map: Lost River, Lost City. In the end, they had prevailed, but how she hated Walter Bowman for forcing that exercise on them, for requiring them to prove on which side of the state line he had killed their daughter.

Now, at last, he was going to die. Once that was done, Trudy would decide how much she wanted to live, if she would throw away the cigarettes and reclaim the Lipitor. She had been stashing the pills in a piece of Tupperware, refilling the prescription to avoid discovery. It wasn't that she was vain, but— She reached a hand up to her hair. It was thicker. That wasn't her imagination.

On the way home, she varied her route and passed St. Mary's. She had attended once or twice after they moved here, and people were generically kind. Her preferred brand of kindness, truth to tell. But the rift between her and her church remained irrevocable. Not that her priest back in Middleburg had ever been direct enough to argue against her desire to see Walter Bowman put to death. The Catholic Church may be opposed to the death penalty, but the issue wasn't a deal breaker, like abortion or same-sex marriage. No, Trudy had been the one who had tried to persuade the priest to change his mind. She hadn't been delusional enough to think that she could change the church, but it had seemed vital to her that at least one of its representatives should, if only in private, agree with her, endorse her decision on moral grounds. She had converted for Terry's sake, broken faith with her Huguenot ancestors, borne out the old saying about converts being the best adherents. A little disingenuous affirmation seemed the least the Catholic Church could do for her.

At the time of Holly's death, Father Trahearne was still in the parish, but he had retired before the trial. (Sent away, whispers had it, another problem priest, but Trudy couldn't believe his issues went much beyond drink.) His replacement was younger, dull and earnest. Father Trahearne, at least, would have enjoyed the argument. He might have even had a chance of changing Trudy's mind. No—no, he would not have been able to do that. But he would have understood that she needed to have the conversation, that she was confessing, in a fashion. The new priest squirmed, uncomfortable with a discussion in which he did not have the moral high ground.

Trudy didn't miss the church, although it had been central to her adult life. She missed Father Trahearne. She missed *her* church, the specific space, back in Middleburg. She missed the parish activities, which had filled her days. But she didn't miss The Church, which she felt had denied her empathy. Ah, well, it was composed of a body of single men who had never fathered children, at least not officially. How could they really understand her situation?

When she let herself back into the house, she was startled to see Terry there. Was it Friday? He often ended office hours at noon and played golf on Fridays, but she was pretty sure it wasn't Friday. Besides, he wouldn't come home first. He would go straight to the club.

"Is something wrong?" She could not remember the last time she had asked that question. Everything was wrong, always. Wrong was the status quo. Her life was wrong, with little slivers of okay.

"A development over at Sussex," he said.

He took her hand. Trudy and Terry, Terry and Trudy. How cuuuuuuuuuuuuuute. They had been. They had been beautiful, with strong white teeth and broad-shouldered sons and the most gorgeous little girl anyone had ever seen. They had been invincible. That was why they called their farm T'n'T—nothing in the world was stronger than they were.

"Is he dead?" Even as she asked, she wasn't sure how she would feel if Terry said yes, Walter Bowman had died, found a way to commit suicide, keeled over from a heart attack. But he was only in his forties. His cholesterol was probably below 180.

"Our friend at the prison called me. Bowman's found Elizabeth Lerner, although that's not the name she's using now. She's been added to his approved contact list. At his request, but she agreed."

"Is she going to attend the execution?" Even as she asked it, she realized the question was nonsensical, a non sequitur, but she couldn't think what else to say.

"Our friend at Sussex doesn't know." They had befriended a secretary over the years, earned her confidences by proving themselves discreet. And by giving her gift cards several times a year. "It's her understanding that Bowman wants to talk to Elizabeth, and she agreed. That's all. For now."

"For now."

"But you know Bowman. He's always looking for a way to get a stay. He's always got an angle."

Trudy wanted to say: *So does she.*

Instead, she announced: "I have to take some things to the cedar closet." She walked down the basement steps empty-handed, indifferent to whether Terry heard the snap of the match flint on the box, or smelled the heavenly tobacco that rose up and filled her lungs. She wrapped her arms around her middle, and she could swear they ached, from wrist to elbow. So close to the destination and she was still tugging, still trying to keep this plane aloft all on her own. Prove that she wasn't.

23

THE PRINCIPAL IS YOUR PAL. The old mnemonic device sounded in Eliza's head as she walked down the halls of North Bethesda Middle, her footsteps echoing in the classes-in-session hush. She had always struggled with homonyms, and the dominance of spell-check had not been a boon to her. She had Peter run his eyes over the rare things she wrote, and he almost always found one *hear* for *here*, or a *too* for *two*. There were also certain names she found it hard not to flip. Thomas and Thompson, Murray and Murphy, Eileen and Elaine. *The principal is your pal*. Maybe once, but not these days, where principals were like federal judges, saddled with mandates that allowed them little discretion.

The principal here was Roxanne Stoddard, a stylish, professional type who would not have been out of place in a K Street lobbying firm. And she had an almost rock star aura in the community. When people heard that Iso was in North Bethesda, almost everyone said, "Oh, Roxanne Stoddard. That's wonderful." Or even: "I saw Roxanne Stoddard at Louisiana Kitchen at eight-thirty one night and she was clearly going over work even as she ate crawfish étouffée."

Today, she wore a pea green suit and plum suede heels, making Eliza feel at once short and dowdy. But she was also warm, carrying her authority lightly.

"Iso," she said to the angelic figure who was masquerading as Eliza's daughter, "I'd like to speak to your mother in private. Is that okay?" It was clear Iso had no say in this.

"Of course, Mrs. Stoddard." Iso caught Eliza's eye as she left the office, her face all innocence, as if to say: *I have no idea what this is about. Must be some terrible misunderstanding.*

"How is your family settling in?" Another round of polite preamble, only much more appropriate than Walter's. "It must be a big change."

"More a large assortment of small changes, if that makes sense. But, yes, I think we're settled now. Children adjust so quickly."

Please tell me that Iso is well adjusted. Please let this be an announcement of some prize she has won, or an amazing result on a standardized test.

"Iso is doing well here. She is popular with her classmates and, to my chagrin, a little advanced in some classes, although she has a lot of territory to cover in American history. But her math and English—it makes me wonder at the difference in educational standards. And, of course, she's an amazing athlete."

Eliza beamed, even as she anticipated the huge "but" that she knew was about to drop on her head, like a cartoon anvil.

"I do wonder, back in England—was there much emphasis on bullying?"

For a bewildered moment, Eliza thought the principal was asking if the UK encouraged bullying.

"Oh! I think there were the same general concerns. Mean girls and the like."

"And the problem of subtle bullying?"

"Subtle . . . bullying? Isn't that an oxymoron?"

Roxanne Stoddard frowned, and Eliza glimpsed her power, how awful it must feel to be one of her students or teachers and inspire her disapproval. "Not at all. It's an important distinction. Bullying is hard enough for teachers and administrators to detect, and students are loath to report it. But at least we can see the physical transgressions. Subtle bullying is all about exclusion, making other students feel not welcome."

"Has Iso—?"

"It's unclear at this point. For now, we're willing to chalk it up to cultural differences between her old school and North Bethesda Middle." She had a way of pronouncing the school's name as if it should be written in gold and heralded by angels with little trumpets. North. Bethesda. Middle! It was the only pretentious note in her otherwise down-to-earth demeanor.

"What do you want me to do?"

"I have some materials for you, the same ones our faculty use." The principal passed Eliza a thick manila envelope. "As I said, we're not certain what happened. The girl involved—she swears it's a misunderstanding. But one of the conundrums of this type of bullying is that the victim mistakes it for hazing. The child—and they are children here, no matter how worldly they think they are—believes if she endures it with good grace, she'll be invited into the inner circle."

"The girl—does she have some sort of disability?" Eliza was trying to remember Iso's story, about the girl in her class who was to receive an iTunes gift certificate for her birthday.

"What?"

"Never mind. Just thinking about a classmate that Iso described to me."

"This girl is not disabled. She's not as bright and athletically gifted as Iso, but that's the point. Not everyone is going to be. The strange thing is that Iso, at heart, seems unsure of her own place within the circle of popular girls, seems more threatened, possibly because she's a newcomer. I think that's why she might have told the girl she wasn't allowed to sit with them."

"That's . . . all? She told a classmate that she couldn't sit with them?"

"That's more than enough," Roxanne Stoddard said with stern disappointment, as if Eliza had asked: *"That's all? Just one joint in her locker? That's all? An oral sex party with the boys' wrestling team?"*

"Obviously, I haven't read the material yet." Eliza gave the envelope a friendly pat, as if it were a novel she couldn't wait to be alone with. "But, surely, cafeteria cliques are as old as time, and not something likely to change."

"Mrs. Benedict, we have a zero-tolerance policy on bullying. Because there is some ambiguity here, we"—a royal we? a committee? a tribunal?—"have decided not to invoke the minimum punishment. If Iso had been determined to be in violation, she would have been given after-school detention and prohibited from school activities for a month. That's the minimum penalty. The maximum is suspension."

Eliza was torn. She understood that the policy was humane. She knew firsthand that her daughter was capable of an imperious indifference toward others. She was appalled that Iso was one of those popular girls who derived power by excluding others. But, still—was this grounds for suspension? Children needed a little grit in their lives, environments that fell somewhere between velvet-lined egg crates and *Lord of the Flies*.

"I'm sorry, Mrs. Stoddard. Iso's father and I will make sure she understands the policy, and the consequences of violating it. It is subtle, as you say."

The principal smiled, her pal again. "She is, at heart, a sweet child. And, however quickly children adjust, she has been through a big change. I wouldn't wonder if she's a little homesick for London, her old school. That would go a long way, I think, toward explaining her moods."

"Her moods?" Eliza had thought that cranky Iso was a family phenomenon. She was sunny and generous with her friends, her teammates.

"She seems a little distracted at times. But, as I said, I'm sure it's just the dislocation. She's doing really well in her classes." The principal looked at her watch. "Speaking of which—there are only forty-five minutes left in the day. Why don't you take her home? If I send her back to class, it will disrupt the teacher's lesson."

Eliza left the principal's office, her homework tucked under her arm. She had to stop herself from reaching for her daughter's hand, stroking her hair, fashioned in a perfect ponytail today. "Let's go," she said. And then, once out of the building: "We have time to get ice cream, if you like, before we pick up Albie."

Iso regarded her mother suspiciously. "Ice cream?"

"Sure."

"Why?"

"Why not?"

Iso thought about this. "It wouldn't be fair to Albie."

"Not everyone has to get the same things all the time in order for life to be fair."

Eliza had undermined her own sales pitch, referenced too directly to what was happening at school.

"I have a lot of homework. If we go home now, I could get started and you and Reba could walk up to Albie's school as usual."

"How about we all go to pick up Albie, then make a Rita's run?"

"All the way over to Grandmother's?" It was funny how Iso and Albie unconsciously referred to the house as Inez's, never Manny's, but then—it was Inez's domain. Eliza's father would live anywhere, happily, as long as he was with Inez. He cared nothing for his physical surroundings.

"I'm sure there's one closer. And if not, there's always Gifford's or Baskin-Robbins."

Iso gave a tiny nod, conferring her favors on Eliza. It was a win-win for Iso. She got a treat, but Albie's presence would ensure that Eliza didn't press her. She was a shrewd girl, and Eliza couldn't help admiring that trait, which she had conspicuously lacked at the same age.

Then again, it was Holly—golden, self-assured Holly, not even a year older than Iso was now—who had gotten into Walter Bowman's truck for the promise of fifteen dollars, while Eliza was the one he had to drag in by the wrists. Frankly, Eliza didn't give a shit if Iso had hurt some girl's feelings by denying her a place at a lunch table. Her fear was that this very same confidence could lead Iso into a situation that she wouldn't be able to control.

BUT LATER, AS SHE WATCHED Iso and Albie eat dinner-spoiling double scoops at Baskin-Robbins, she realized that Walter Bowman, held within a cell and his own parentheses, was not the problem. The problem was the other Walters, all the Walters who sprung up from the soil no matter how many times you mashed them flat, like the army of skeletons that grew from dragon's teeth in the story of the Golden Fleece. The commonwealth of Virginia was going to kill her tormentor—Eliza was startled to consider that word, to see for the first time the hidden *mentor* inside the sadist—but she couldn't begin to find and punish all the people who might hurt her children.

And yet, somewhere else in their own town, perhaps at this very moment, there was a mother who was comforting a child who believed Iso was the enemy.

24

IT WAS NEVER REALLY QUIET on Sussex I. It didn't matter how many men were here, whether it was close up to full or spindly as it was now, with fifteen men rattling around a unit built for fifty. It was a loud place. The sound was weird, too, hard to pinpoint, whipping around corners and bouncing off walls, almost like a living thing that was stalking them all. Banging someone in, ingrained tradition that it was, was almost painful for Walter, but he wouldn't deny anyone that honor. After all, he had the distinction of being the only man here who had been welcomed back twice.

Now, lying awake at what he figured to be 1 A.M. or so, he listened to the noises that seemed to prevail at night, roaming the unit like little forest creatures. Pops, whistles, echoes. You would think a person would get used to it, after twenty-plus years, but he still found the night sounds disturbing, and although it was not the noises that wakened him, they made it that much harder to get back to sleep. He thought he might have a condition of sorts, some kind of overly sensitive hearing. His father had hated loud sounds—the television, the radio, all had to be kept at low hums. He said he needed it that way because he spent his days surrounded by clanging and banging. As a young man, Walter had thought his father crotchety. But now that Walter was forty-six, he wondered if it was a change that came with age, if the ears just got plain worn out over time.

Forty-six. His father had been almost that old when Walter was born, his mother a few years younger. He was what they called a change-of-life baby, and he knew the exact moment of his conception: Christmas Eve, or maybe an hour into Christmas Day, after his mother had had some apple brandy. It was, his sister told him once, easy enough to date. It was the only time their parents had sex that year and probably the last time, ever. Of course, his sister could have been teasing. Although she was thirteen years older and should have known better, she had been hard on Walter, jealous of her new sibling. He always thought she resented him for getting the good looks that she could have used. Ugly as a mud fence, as the saying went, and the fact that Walter had never seen a mud fence didn't get between him and understanding that phrase. His mother said his sister was plain, but Belle—unfortunate name—was ugly, aggressively so, with a lazy eye and a big nose and a witchlike chin. She had been lucky to find a man who wanted to marry her. A decent-looking guy at that, who made a good living. Some men just didn't respect themselves.

Belle was his only living relative, and she had cut off all contact with him shortly after his parents died, a one-two punch, within six months of each other. Lung cancer had taken his father, and his mother had died from the stew of complications that went with diabetes. They had both been in their seventies, but Belle blamed it all on him, said they had died from the shame of being his parents. *Why don't you die, then?* Walter had asked. Belle said she was lucky enough to have her own name and live in a different town, that she had escaped being Walter Bowman's sister, otherwise she might be dead, too. To which he said: bullshit. He didn't doubt that his arrest and his trials had been hard on his parents, but—lung cancer, diabetes! The men on Sussex had nothing on God when it came to killing people in painful, prolonged ways. The hardest case here hadn't taken more than a few hours to kill anyone. God took months, years.

Besides, it wasn't as if his parents had dropped dead in the immediate aftermath. They had both hung on for seven, eight years. Belle had just been looking for an excuse to cut him off, and once she buried their mother, she had one. She would be almost sixty now, her own children grown and, almost certainly, the source of some heartache for her. And he would be dead short of fifty, if the commonwealth of Virginia had its way. As of this year, he had spent exactly half his life in prison. Walter supposed some would see a neatness to that, a pleasing symmetry.

Walter begged to differ.

He sighed, practiced some techniques recommended for insomnia—breathing, counting, emptying his mind, meditating with the mantra Barbara had supplied him—but he could tell that this was going to be one of those nights where he was destined to lie awake. Sometimes he wondered if a part of his mind was greedy for a few more hours of consciousness, if it was trying to grab every moment of wakefulness it could. *It's okay, buddy,* he soothed his fretful subconscious. *Don't count me out yet. We might have years ahead of us, still.* Funny, how hard it was to get two parts of his own mind to talk to each other.

November 25, the fretful half roared back. *Less than two months. And you didn't even get to talk to her today!*

It's okay, he said. *It's okay.*

Walter was not the least bit perturbed that Elizabeth had needed to cut their conversation short. He assumed it was something serious—and definitely not a husband requiring a ride from the airport. Funny, how she still couldn't lie for shit. Whatever it was, it was serious, but not scary-serious, not an injured child. He would have heard that in her voice. But something involving one of the children. What did children require that was serious, yet fell short of actual harm? He had no idea.

He had no doubt that Elizabeth was a good mother. But he was still disappointed that this was all Elizabeth's life had amounted to, that this was what she had chosen to do with the great gift he had conferred on her. Ironic, he knew, because he was the one who was always advocating that women return to their natural roles. But he had never meant all women, just those women who took it too far, imagined themselves men. Fact was, he hadn't always thought about Elizabeth as *female,* although he could understand why people were confused on that score.

The boy they banged in today, he had stolen an eighty-seven-year-old woman's purse, then raped and killed her. Disgusting. Walter could never understand someone like that, nor would he ever understand those that thought he should. The outside world saw the men in Sussex I as indistinguishable from one another, a clump of monsters and savages. But the fact that their crimes fell into the same category didn't make the men the same. Walter might not even be here if it weren't for a stupid metal box found on the side of the road. Well, they had the kidnapping charge and the rape charge, but those could have been mitigated by a smart lawyer, not that he had a smart lawyer back then. He had one now, though, in Jefferson D. Blanding, who, he suspected, was actually named Jefferson Davis Blanding, after the president of the Confederacy, and had the bad sense to be ashamed of it. Not that Walter held Jefferson Davis in any esteem, and he would be the first to remind people that West Virginia seceded from Virginia rather than be part of the Confederacy. But no one's responsible for his name.

One's actions—yes. And no. He had done what they said he did. In a different system, he might have owned up to his crimes more readily. There was a part of him that would have liked to tell the whole story, although the catch was that he didn't understand his own crimes until he'd had years to think about them. Here, in Sussex I, amid all the indignities, there was this one freedom, absent in the outside world. A man got to think. A lot. Walter had thought about what he had done, and he saw there was no way he could ever live outside prison. He belonged here. In fact, if he were scientifically inclined, he would want to find a way to extend prisoners' lives so they could serve multiple life sentences. He owed Holly Tackett a life, he owed Maude Parrish a life. And, yes, he owed the other girls, too, but it wasn't his fault that he had never confessed to those crimes. That was the system, refusing to make a deal, refusing to acknowledge that he had any power. Wipe out the death penalty and I'll tell you everything, he had said more than once, but they wouldn't even entertain the notion. Justice for the one—the rich girl, the doctor's daughter—trumped justice for all. That wasn't right.

The other thing that bothered him about his situation, as he chose to think of it, was that he didn't understand what it meant, to be judged by a jury of one's peers. He wasn't fool enough to take it literally, to think that they had to find a dozen Walter Bowmans. Still, what was a *peer*? There had been women on his jury, for example, and with all due respect, he did not think women could really understand what he had decided was a temporary insanity, the bottled-up energy of a young man who knew he had something to offer, something of value, but couldn't find anyone who understood that. Today, with the Internet, he'd have no problem finding a woman. As he understood it, based largely on advertisements he saw for dating services and articles he read in magazines, technology had brought back good old-fashioned wooing. He had been in such a rush, as a young man, anxious and urgent. Could women even understand that? Did they know what it was like to have an erection at the wrong time, or what it would be like not to have one at the right time? His hard-ons had been like a faulty check-engine light, the kind that popped up just because you didn't screw the gas tank tight enough. Like the ladies who came into his father's shop, all fluttery anxiety, he had worried that he would ignore them at his peril.

But even if a woman could understand such things, why did one's peers judge a man? Shouldn't his victims have the final say? Oh, he could imagine a prosecutor's comeback for that. How convenient for a killer to want his victims to judge him. But there was Elizabeth. He hadn't been lying when he said he felt the greatest guilt toward her. What he did to her—*that* was a betrayal. The others, he didn't know them, they weren't real to him. But Elizabeth had been his copilot, his running buddy. Charley to his Steinbeck.

The next time they talked, he resolved he would say "I'm sorry" first thing. No small talk, no edging into the conversation. He would say the words he had never been allowed to say to her, one on one, the words that had burned in his throat and his chest all these years. He had understood, of course, why he had never been allowed to speak to her, why even during her cross-examination he had been instructed to regard her with the blankest of faces, listening with sorrowful eyes that never quite met hers. Still, there had been a part of him that always felt it wasn't such a strange thing to ask, a final good-bye, just the two of them, maybe in a room in the courthouse, an armed guard standing outside. He had known better than to ask, but that didn't mean he knew not to want it. He still wanted it.

No, he had to blurt it out, straight and true: "I'm sorry."

Then maybe she would finally say she was sorry, too.

Part III

IN MY HOUSE

Released 1985
Reached no. 7 on Billboard Hot 100 on June 8, 1985
Spent 22 weeks on Billboard Hot 100

25

"I'M SORRY."

The words came so fast, tumbling out the moment the collect call was approved, that they were almost cut off. Eliza stared at the beige receiver in her hand, wondering if Walter had been speaking into space, if he was reaching the end of a long and breathless recitation.

It had been a week since his last call, although Eliza marked the passage of time as a *week since the school had called*. She hadn't forgotten Walter; the telephone was there every morning, the first thing she saw. But it was Iso who dominated her waking hours. It had been a tiptoey time in their household, she and Peter trying to observe Iso without crowding her, attempting to judge if she was headed toward real trouble. When she made fun of Albie—was that bad, or typical sibling behavior? Should Eliza let that go, in hopes that it would satisfy whatever aggression Iso needed to express, or should she nip it in the bud?

Eliza's parenting had always been natural and easy, largely uninformed by texts and experts. Even her parents, experts in their own right, had encouraged Eliza to find her own way as a mother. For years she had felt that her immersion in children's literature had been better preparation than any parenting guide. There it was, all the fears and emotions and needs of childhood. When other mothers asked where she sought guidance, she often said, "Everything I know about parenting I learned from Ramona Quimby." People thought she was being glib, but she felt those particular books, written from a child's-eye view of the world, were indispensable. Inez once told Eliza she was a good mother because she had never forgotten what it was like to be a child. Like nursing mothers who squirt milk at the sound of any baby's cry, Eliza could be catapulted into childhood by a tantrum or a plaintive whine. She remembered it vividly, perhaps because it was sharply fenced off in her mind. The before time, the Elizabeth time.

So while she could never forget Walter, embodied as he was by this bland, beige instrument—the phone of Damocles, Peter had taken to calling it—Iso was uppermost in her mind, Iso was the present, Iso was a situation that could be improved, changed, monitored. Walter was the past. And not her responsibility.

"Elizabeth?"

"Yes, I'm here."

"I'm sorry. Did you hear me say that? I'm sorry. I wanted to say it first thing, in case we get interrupted again."

Oh lord, Eliza thought. *I hope we don't get interrupted again.* She felt that her life had already reached its drama quotient for the next decade. Any more worries—a call from a neighbor that Reba had gotten out of the yard, even a rumble in the Subaru's motor—might push her over the edge.

"I'm sorry for everything. I'm sorry that I kidnapped you. I'm sorry for the way I treated you, in those early days, when I wanted to make sure you would do whatever I said, when I said all those awful things about what I would do to your family. I am sorry, most of all, for what happened the last night."

"What happened?" She meant only to echo his words, to question the euphemism.

"When I—the sex." He had clearly misread her tone.

"The rape."

"Yes," he said, his voice a somber whisper. "I am sorry that I raped you. In some ways, I am sorrier for that than for anything else I did."

She sat on the edge of her bed, examined the quilt, the sheets, the shams, all new. Peter, who traveled widely, had wanted to fit their bed with expensive sheets, Frette or even Pratesi. Eliza had argued that their bed should continue to be hospitable to children, children who still spilled things and forgot to put the tops on their markers. She had ordered this carefully mismatched set from a catalog, mixing striped sheets with a riotous quilt. There was already a stain on the dust ruffle, if one knew where to look, and some ink on a corner of a sham, but that came from Peter working in bed. No matter how much money Peter made, no matter how mature Iso and Albie became, they were never going to be a Frette kind of family.

"Elizabeth?"

Again, that prompt, bordering on a demand. How dare he? What did he expect? That she would say it was okay? That she would offer forgiveness? This wasn't Albie, using the guest room towels to wipe off Reba's muddy feet, a typically dreamy, well-intentioned mistake on his part. It wasn't even Iso, suspected of the crime of subtle bullying.

"Thank you," she said. "You've never said that."

"I never had a chance to speak to you."

"I mean—in other, um, venues. You never spoke of it."

"Other ven—oh, interviews. So you read them?"

"Sometimes." She had, in fact, avoided them until a month ago, when she had reread everything, trying to figure out how Walter had gotten back into her life.

"I hate to say this, but I was told by my lawyer not to address any of the things where charges weren't brought. Not even in my own defense."

"The other girls," she said, suddenly feeling protective of her little ghosts.

"I've never spoken of the other things I was accused of. Not even to you, not even when I wanted to . . . scare you."

"No, no you didn't. But the things I read made it pretty clear—"

"The things you read about yourself—were those true, Elizabeth?"

He had scored a point there, although she thought it unfair. True, Jared Garrett had speculated, with no seeming facts at his disposal, about Walter's sexual proclivities. He had raised questions of premature ejaculation, necrophilia, pedophilia. It was, after all, impossible to libel a convicted killer.

But the standards for Eliza should have been different. Shouldn't they?

"I can understand that you don't want to talk about the crimes with which you were never charged."

"There was a time," Walter said, "when they wanted to bury me with every unsolved murder from South Carolina to Pennsylvania. They made my father vouch for my work schedule, went through his files."

"Yes, but there are still a lot of missing girls . . . one was from Point of Rocks."

"That was just a place to cross the river, Elizabeth, nothing more. Elizabeth"—she wished he would stop the repeated use of her name, which made him sound like a salesman, or someone who had just read Dale Carnegie—"I don't want to go over all of this, I really don't. I called to tell you that I'm sorry for what I did to you. That's long overdue."

And inadequate, Eliza thought. What had she expected? To her, Walter's attempts to communicate had been a continuation of his long-ago crimes, not a refutation. He held her captive again, violated her again. Despite his letter, she had not really expected an apology, yet he had made one today, clear and unambiguous. What did he expect in return? What did he deserve?

When Iso was small, she had quickly learned to lisp "I sorry," even as she continued to do the very thing for which she was apologizing. Albie, by contrast, was almost too remorseful, brooding over his misdeeds long after he had been forgiven. A decade or so ago, Peter had written a piece about the nature of modern apologies, stringing together a spate of real and not-so-real ones—the official government acknowledgment of the Tuskegee experiment, a baseball player's belabored rationale for spitting at an umpire, the ongoing discussion about reparations for slavery. This would have been, in fact, about the same time that Iso was careering through their little bungalow in Houston, throwing out "I sorry" as if it were confetti, her private little parade of destruction rolling past, leaving Eliza to clean up all of the mess. They had tried hard to teach their children the importance of genuine remorse, what it was to say and *mean* "I'm sorry."

They had spent less time, Eliza realized now, on the nature of forgiveness. She told her children that when someone was sincerely sorry for a misdeed, he or she must be forgiven. And in the context of a family, that was true. Family members must forgive one another. (Although—another stellar example from children's literature—Jo did not need to forgive Amy for burning up her manuscript, and Eliza always thought Amy's near-death experience was a bit heavy-handed on Louisa May Alcott's part.) But then again—if one doesn't forgive someone, doesn't one, in a sense, lose that person forever? And what could be better than to lose Walter in that sense? She was under no obligation to forgive him. Was she?

"I appreciate that. I appreciate that you said it straight out, without any of those weasel words that politicians use."

"Weasel words. I love that. You always did have a great way of talking."

She did? No, Eliza wanted to say, that was Vonnie, the writer and star debater. She had been proficient with words, even tidy with them. But creative? She was not one to fish for compliments, and she would never, under any circumstances, invite Walter to praise her, yet she found herself saying wistfully, "I never saw myself that way."

"Well, you weren't talky. Thank god. But you used words in an interesting way. I wasn't a big reader when I met you, but I've become one here and words are real to me now. They have, like, shapes. And colors. Some of them are so right for what they are. *Dignity,* for example. *Dignity* is like . . . an older cat on a windowsill, his paws folded beneath him."

She wanted to disagree. She didn't want to have any common ground with Walter. But she thought of words in this way, too, and he was onto something.

"That's a good image," she said. "Cats are dignified, whereas dogs—"

She stopped herself. Everything she knew about dogs had been gleaned from Reba, who was not at all typical of her species. Besides, she would no more invoke Reba with Walter than she would speak of her children, or her day-to-day life. It was Elizabeth who spoke to Walter, a grown-up version, but Elizabeth nonetheless.

"I never cared for dogs."

"I remember." All dogs barked at Walter.

"You know another word I like? *Serendipity.* I was thinking about that very word when I saw your photo. The magazine used it to describe what people might find at local farmers' markets. But that doesn't make any sense. There's no serendipity in what the earth produces. There's bad luck, sometimes—droughts and pests. But there's no serendipity to it. Then I turned the page. Me finding you—that was serendipity."

"And what does *serendipity* look like to you?" she asked, keen to change the subject, to move him away from the moment he had found her. She wasn't sure, in fact, if he was referring to this past summer or a summer long ago.

"I . . . well . . . I'm not sure I should tell you."

"That's okay."

"No, I shouldn't have secrets from you. I think of *serendipity* as a woman. A green woman, with stripes."

"Oh."

"I know, I sound nuts. I'm sorry. The thing about dignity—I've thought a lot about that. How to die with dignity."

"Really?"

"We have a choice here. Lethal injection or the electric chair. I almost chose the electric chair. I didn't want to . . . fade away. Although there are those who say even lethal injection might be cruel and unusual. It takes twenty minutes. Did you know that? Twenty minutes from the dose until they pronounce a man dead."

"Hmmmmmm."

"One thing I know for sure—I'm not going to let the media know what my last meal will be. I'm allowed to keep that private, and I will." A pause. "You have some choices, too, you know."

Another noncommittal noise, only this one ended up, to imply a question. "Hmmmmmmm?"

"You can be a witness. In private, they don't have to let the media know."

"I don't think that's of interest to me, Walter."

"Why?"

"I don't feel that's something I have to explain to anyone. It's just not what I want to do."

"Because you're against the death penalty." Fishing, probing.

"It's just not something I choose to do."

"I am going to go with lethal injection, if that makes a difference."

"No thank you, Walter." He did manage to bring out one's good manners. She remembered Holly in the pickup truck. *Please, mister, please.*

"Then how about coming to see me? Alive, I mean, here at Sussex I?"

"I don't think that would be possible."

"Well, it wouldn't be easy. Almost no one gets on the visiting list for a death row inmate, unless it's a lawyer, maybe a journalist. But they would make an exception for you, I'm pretty sure."

"Maybe," she said, meaning to say only that she might be an exception, not that she would consider it seriously. In fact, that might be the best way to go: have Peter approach prison officials and make the request, all wink-wink, nudge-nudge, we'll understand perfectly if you have to say no. Make them the bad guys, instead of her.

She reminded herself that Walter was the bad guy.

"I would really like," he said, "to say I'm sorry in person. I don't think it means as much over the phone. I don't think you believed me."

"You did a fine job," she assured him. "It was a great apology."

"But you didn't forgive me."

"I don't think I'm the person who can forgive you, not really."

"You're the only one I care about." There was a buzz of conversation in the background, a quick exchange, and Walter came back on the line. "That's it for today. I gotta run. I'll call you later."

She hung up the phone and lay back on her bed, staring up at the ceiling. *You're the only one I care about.*

Stop, she prayed to the lighting fixture, one of the old-fashioned touches in the house that had never been updated. Eliza loved it, but Peter had recently held some sort of gauge to it, discovered that it generated heat to some obscene temperature within minutes. He wanted to rewire the overhead lamp, or at least replace its regular bulb with a fluorescent one. But Eliza loved this rose-colored globe of cut glass, couldn't bear to see it replaced or fitted with a bulb that would cast a colder light. *Please stop,* she prayed, remembering a book where a boy thought God had lived in the kitchen light, because his mother was always addressing it, shaking a wooden spoon. Eliza wasn't the kind who would shake a spoon at God or demand anything. She wasn't even sure she believed in God, but she still couldn't resist asking him this favor. *Please make him leave me alone.*

26

BARBARA LAFORTUNY WAS ONE of the wonders of her twice-weekly yoga class, the kind of older woman whose effortless flexibility and strength mocked the girls with more perfect bodies and outfits. She was, in fact, a little smug about her standing as one of the best in the practice, which she realized was antithetical to the experience, but there it was. If you couldn't face the truth about yourself, then you weren't ready for the truth about anything, and Barbara recognized this fact about herself: She was competitive. She liked to win.

Yet, for all her skill at holding difficult poses, she failed at the most basic task of all: stilling her mind. Right now, she was in child's pose, about as relaxed as a person could be, or should be, and her mind was racing, racing, racing, far outside this pleasantly dim studio in a converted mill.

"Be kind to your body," cooed the instructor. "Tune into what it's feeling."

She tried, but all she managed to locate was the caffeinated rumble of her heart. This was a 9 A.M. class, what Barbara thought of as the ladies-of-leisure and college-students class, because who else was free at 9 A.M. every Tuesday and Thursday? Technically, she belonged to the first group, but she didn't see herself that way. Barbara had been up since six, checking her Google alerts, eating a healthy breakfast of homemade whole-grain bread and organic almond butter, reading the *Times* on paper, the local paper, and the *Wall Street Journal* online.

Barbara had never been a patient person, and her near-death experience had not changed that aspect of her personality. She sometimes thought her impatience, her shortness with fools, had contributed to the attack. Not that she was making excuses for the boy, who was one of the rottenest kids she had met in her years of teaching. That boy had been dead inside, with flat, lightless eyes. But he might not have attacked a more good-humored, patient teacher. Barbara had humiliated him in front of his friends. And if he had lashed out then, in an impulsive fit of anger, she almost could have made sense of it. But he had waited for her by her car, in that ill-lit parking lot, springing up, knife in hand. Luckily, he was as inept as an assailant as he was in the classroom, and he had mistaken the blood gushing from her face for a mortal wound and left her there. The attack had led to many profound changes in Barbara's life—a new purpose, an interest in healthful food and pursuits, the amazing gift of prosperity, which only led her to hold the rich in greater disdain. But it had not made her more patient.

Walter, however, had patience to burn. Too much, she sometimes thought. She wondered if prison had perverted his relationship with time, if he didn't understand how little they had.

Bureaucracies moved as nimbly as eighteen-wheelers, as Barbara knew from her years in the public school system. They needed time and space to turn this thing around, and yet Walter could not be more goddamn nonchalant.

She raised her right leg behind her, swung it down into pigeon pose, gloating a little at the openness of her hips. Some of the thinner women in the class looked absolutely constipated.

Or maybe Walter wanted the drama of everything happening at the last minute, which was truly harebrained. She had said as much, the last time they spoke: *No drama, Walter. Then too much attention will be paid, and she will run away. She's a scared little mouse.*

Barbara knew from scared little mouses. Mice. She had been one, behind her cranky facade. She had skittered to her car in the morning, worried it wouldn't start, skittered into the school, tried to teach history to bored seventh and eighth graders, skittered out of the Pimlico neighborhood at day's end, cooked dinner, fretting over calories and fat and cholesterol. Graded papers in front of the television, usually falling asleep there. Rinse, lather, repeat.

Then she had awakened in the hospital, her face bandaged, twelve hours, a half day, lost to her. She had known even before they removed the dressing that the repair—she could not dignify it with the term *surgery*—had been botched. She could sense how lumpy the scar was, how large the stitches. They had not bothered to summon a plastic surgeon to the ER. That might have been another lawsuit, another arrow in her quill, but the hospital had been quick to remedy its work, and the result wasn't bad. Her scar was like a ghost smile, a little happy face off to the side. "For Halloween," she once told Walter, "I might go as both of the Greek masks that represent the theater."

Yet it was in that moment—waking up, disoriented, unsure of the damage done—that Barbara realized she was no longer scared. This was before the settlement left her well fixed, before she even really knew what happened. But she understood this: *She wasn't scared anymore.* She had almost died. She didn't. There must be something she was supposed to do.

The first task she tackled was finding out everything about the boy who had sliced her face, following him through the system. Tuwan Jones was fourteen, a juvenile, and it was harder then to try juveniles as adults. Barbara didn't have a problem with that, although she believed her assailant to be beyond rehabilitation. Someone, a parent or a relative, had killed that boy long ago. He was sent to the Hickey School, where he promptly became an escape artist, leaving at every chance, only to be flummoxed by the surrounding suburbs, so still and quiet. Tuwan could get out of Hickey, but not out of the neighborhood. He never got much farther than Harford Road, the main strip nearest the school. They called Barbara every time he escaped, a courtesy and probably a defensive measure against future lawsuits. Tuwan had no intention of coming after her. He didn't even remember her. He was released from Hickey at the age of sixteen. By eighteen, he had finally managed to kill someone and was sent to Supermax in Baltimore City.

Perhaps another person would have taken this experience and resolved to prevent such tragedies, to help young men before they became assailants. But Barbara had been there already, on the front lines, and she had little confidence that she was the type of person who could change others. Instead, she became fixated on the idea of the death penalty. It was wrong to kill. Someone had tried to take her life from her, and failed. Given a chance to live, she had to become a better person. Not nicer, necessarily, but more confident, vigorous, even a little selfless. Perhaps men on death row could become better people, too, if only they could be spared execution.

And although Maryland had its share of interesting inmates, the best ones, the ones whose cases really deserved to be reconsidered, had all been taken. Barbara wanted an inmate more or less to herself, she wanted to champion someone that no one else thought worthwhile. She wanted to take a perceived monster and persuade the world that he was human.

Which is what led her to Walter, back in the 1990s, when his first execution had been set. She could not believe the bloodlust at the time, how keen people were to see him die. The man she saw in newspaper photographs and courtroom sketches looked gentle to her, resigned. Besides, it wasn't immoral of him to challenge the state of Virginia's right to execute him on jurisdictional grounds. "Loophole," editorials snarled. "Technicality," complained pundits. But Barbara, the former history teacher, knew that state lines were more than arbitrary markers on a map, that the United States were the united *states,* and if Holly Tackett had been killed in West Virginia, then Walter should have been tried there. That was no technicality. It was a cherished tenet of most conservatives, the right for states to make their own laws, the insistence on less interference from the federal government. It was hypocritical for these same conservatives to claim that state lines didn't matter when they wanted to kill someone.

She began writing Walter. He seemed skeptical of her at first. Other women had written him. "Crazy women," he later told her. "They want a boyfriend. I can't be somebody's boyfriend in here. Where were these women when all I wanted was a girlfriend?"

She thought that was funny, even self-aware. Over time, she began to pull out bits and pieces of Walter's life. The late-in-life parents, the coldness of his home, the consistent undermining by all those around him. She sent him an IQ test and he scored above average, although he admitted that he had never done well in school. Eventually, they began to talk about sex. Walter said his first sexual encounter was with a local girl who was sort of a for-barter prostitute; she had sex with men whose services she needed. He would go over to her house and help her with various tasks—putting up curtain rods, for example, or moving heavy furniture. But she was so businesslike about the arrangement that Walter never enjoyed it quite as much as he thought he should, didn't really count it. "In a lot of ways, I was a virgin," he said of the year he ended up on the run. He was, Barbara realized, hopelessly confused about sex and women.

"I'm not that man anymore," he told her. "If I left here—I don't know. But I'm not going to leave here, and I think that's right. But that's the thing that seems weird to me. They locked me up, and I'm a better person for it. Cured, even. I needed to be locked up, no doubt about it. But when they execute me, they're going to kill the wrong Walter. The one they want to punish doesn't exist anymore."

Barbara was the only person who seemed to agree. Virginia was going to kill the wrong Walter, commit murder as surely as he had. The state had spent millions toward this goal, far more than it would have if it had just allowed Walter to be a lifer from the start.

She reclined on her mat. Barbara had caught an infection from using one of the center's mats, or so she believed, and she now brought her own bright fuchsia one. It was the part of class she hated the most, the part where she was supposed to empty her mind. My mind does not empty, she wanted to protest.

Instead she lay on her back, counting the days. November 25. Under Walter's 1-2-3 plan, he wouldn't even broach his request to Eliza until the third time they spoke, and Barbara was unclear whether he was counting that first, truncated conversation. He might enjoy more phone privileges as the execution date came closer, but still—Barbara thought he should just blurt it out, let it stew in her mind.

"I know her better than you do," Walter had said, which was infuriating. He seemed to think he was closer, in some ways, to this woman than he was to Barbara. *You don't know Eliza Benedict,* she wanted to tell him. *You know a girl, one who hasn't existed for years. And you might not even have known her, as it turns out.* Barbara didn't like Eliza Benedict and would give anything if they didn't need her. She had disliked her the first time she saw her, walking down the street with that ugly dog. She had resented her . . . calm. This was a woman who clearly had no problem relaxing. Barbara had wanted to yell at her from the car: "A man's going to die because of *your* testimony. But he's not the same man who committed those crimes. You are killing a ghost, a phantom. How do you sleep at night? How can you live with yourself? You probably want him to die, but no court would give him death for what he did to you."

She muttered *"Namaste"* but didn't bow her head to the teacher. Barbara rolled up her mat and rushed out into the world, her muscles supple and stretched, her mind seething. Forty-seven days. They had forty-seven days to get to the governor and petition for a commutation. Forty-seven days to break down a shoddy little story that had somehow managed to stand, all these years, a child's rickety tree house that should have fallen to ruin long ago. Forty-seven days to pry something out of Elizabeth Lerner that she might not even realize she had. It was like that child in that movie wandering around with stamps worth millions while grown-ups died. What if they had to hire a hypnotist, or some other professional? Barbara needed to go online, she needed another cup of coffee, she needed to see if Jared Garrett had returned her latest e-mail.

27

TRUDY TACKETT HATED THE WORD *privilege.* It was tricky, loaded, another benign word that had been twisted into an insult. It now was some comfortable zone above the fray, life lived at an altitude so rarefied that one didn't even know the fray existed.

But Trudy had always been aware that she was fortunate—in her family, in her family's wealth. She was aware that she and Terry lived in a charmed universe, where there was little worry about money, even when they had to contemplate up to four college tuitions. But they were not extravagant or showy people, especially by the standards of Middleburg. She looked at price tags. Sometimes. And she had never taken their good fortune for granted. That was what galled her. She had been grateful in her prayers, aware of the luck in which her life was steeped. Even when she had the string of miscarriages, she had not railed against God, had not asked *Why me?* In the wake of Holly's death, she had turned to the church for strength, praying for the courage to find some kind of meaning in it all. Father Trahearne had recommended the book of Job. Which, in retrospect, was the beginning of the end of Trudy's life as a true Catholic.

But, no, she had never used money, and never expected special treatment because of it. Trudy had always felt vaguely embarrassed by the perks of money—boarding an airplane first because one was in business class, for example. That seemed a little gauche to her. But then she met a problem that all the money in the world couldn't solve, and her ideas began to change. She and Terry didn't pay for Walter Bowman's prosecution, which meant they also had relatively little say. Oh, everyone was *nice*. It was the dawn—flowering?—of the victims' rights movement, with Mothers Against Drunk Drivers and Parents of Murdered Children chapters. There was no doubt in Trudy's mind that everyone, from the sheriff's deputy who had found Holly's body to the lowliest clerk in the prosecutor's office, cared about Holly almost as much as if they had known her in life. That's how amazing her daughter was. Not even death could vanquish her charisma. It helped that the Tackett family had been early adapters, in terms of video, and had hours of those old clunky VHS tapes of Holly. They had played an edited clip, during the closing arguments, and Walter Bowman's attorney had barely objected. Even he, Trudy believed, understood how extraordinary Holly was. Later, the new attorney, the unfortunately super-capable Jefferson Blanding, had argued the videos were introduced improperly and should have been screened only during sentencing, not at the actual trial. In hindsight, it would have been better if Blanding had been Bowman's attorney all along. The first one's incompetence had caused them all sorts of problems and delays. In a state more lenient than Virginia, it might have resulted in the death penalty being vacated altogether.

So—privilege, money. They were not things of which Trudy had ever availed herself. Until the day that a young clerk at Sussex had called Terry out of the blue and said she was the person who read all of Walter's incoming and outgoing correspondence, to make sure it met the prison's standards.

"Is there something specific we should know?" Terry had asked.

"Oh no," the woman had assured him. "He's careful. He understands the rules and he wouldn't violate them. But the women who write him—they're all over the map. I mean, there's nothing that interesting now. But there might be. You never know."

"Interesting?"

"Who's on his call list, for example. Whether he thinks he has a valid shot at an appeal. I mean, all the lawyer stuff—that's in person or on the phone, strictly confidential. That's a right that can't be tampered with. But when Walter turns around and tells someone else what's going on—that's not protected."

Trudy had picked up the extension at Terry's invitation. It was hard for her not to break in, explain to Terry what was going on. *She's inside, she wants a bribe, she'll tell us what we need to know.* Since Holly's murder, Trudy had learned that Terry, like his daughter, was dangerously trusting. She had to be the vigilant one, the mean one, the cynic.

"If you knew," the woman continued, "how little they pay us to work here. It's really kind of shocking." The voice had a youthful twang, yet Trudy believed it had to be someone older, someone who had put in enough time in state government and was ready to play the angles. Did she make this offer to the victims of every man on death row? Granted, it wasn't a large population, and as

Trudy had learned, most victims were as poor as the perpetrators. But even if this clerk picked up ten, twenty dollars a month from five families, that would be quite the little stipend.

"We would appreciate," Terry said carefully, "any help you could give us."

"Same here," the woman said. "Why don't you write me? I'll give you my PO box."

The first month, Terry had sent twenty-five dollars, in cash, and they had received a rather perfunctory report back. The next month, he sent an American Express gift card of $100, and the report lengthened considerably. Yet, over the years, the information hadn't amounted to much. Walter was not as loose with details about his legal situation as the clerk had led them to believe, although one of his correspondents, Barbara LaFortuny, was more reliably indiscreet. And it was distressing to be told of the women who wrote him what could only be called love letters. What was wrong with people? With women? Trudy couldn't imagine men writing lovelorn letters to female murderers.

It was more distressing still to hear that Walter and Elizabeth had corresponded and that it had somehow slipped through their source's net. "We spot-check," she had defended herself, when called on this oversight. "And her letter might have arrived on a day when I wasn't working. But I can swear to you up and down that he did not send any letters to Elizabeth Lerner from this facility. We would have been on that like white on rice."

"But she's not Elizabeth Lerner," Terry had pointed out to their source, careful not to offend, but also perturbed at what thousands of dollars had failed to buy. "She's Eliza Benedict."

"Right, and how do you know that? Because of me. You also have her phone number, which you can drop into any online reverse directory and get an address. That's more important than any ol' letter she sent."

Trudy did not agree. But now she found herself studying the

ten digits. What would she say, if she dared to dial them. (Trudy was still old enough to think "dial," even if she was modern enough to use a cell phone.) The words *How dare you* came to mind. Those would cover a multitude of sins.

That phrase jolted her and she pulled out her Bible, tried to find the reference, but she had to cheat and use the Internet to narrow it down. Various things covered a multitude of sins, apparently. Love and charity. In Peter, it was written: *Love covers a multitude of sins.* That was not a passage that interested Trudy today, or any day. She kept clicking until she found a Web site whose interpretation worked better for her. From James 5:20. *Remember this: Whoever turns a sinner from the error of his way will save him from death and cover over a multitude of sins.* Love could help a sinner repent, the Web site instructed, but it must not turn a blind eye. That was not justice. Perhaps Trudy had been affiliated with the wrong church all these years, perhaps she should have embraced the hard-core fundamentalists. Her parents, both descended from Charleston's French Huguenots, had been scandalized enough by her conversion to Catholicism upon her marriage to Terry. If Trudy had joined a church where people rolled on the floor and spoke in tongues, they would have been just as mortified by the sheer tackiness of it all. Her parents were alive, distressingly healthy. Distressing because it meant that Trudy was genetically predisposed to live a long time.

How dare you? What are you thinking? What are you up to? She found herself dialing—okay, furiously poking—the ten numbers that she had managed to commit to memory without even trying, this at a time when she could barely remember an errand from room to room. The phone rang and rang and rang and rang. She imagined the house in which it rang, a house with a husband, maybe children. A happy house. *That* was privilege.

How dare she. How dare she.

28

ISO WAS GROUNDED. GIVEN THAT this was a first for her, it was also a first for Eliza and Peter, who were still trying to work out how to define the punishment. They allowed her to play soccer, because they had rationalized that Iso's transgressions should not punish the entire team. (Although her team was quite good, its bench was a little thin, and Iso's nonparticipation could force them into forfeits.) She was permitted to watch television, but only programs that other family members chose. Eliza hoped that this would at least lure Iso out of her bedroom, force her to interact with her family. Finally, they had taken her phone away and limited her computer time, but Iso said she needed to use the Internet for some of her homework, and she appeared to be telling the truth.

Appeared to be was the key phrase. For Iso, while now an exemplary citizen at North Bethesda Middle School, had been caught lying about her after-school activities. She had told Eliza that she and a classmate needed to go to the library on a Saturday to research a project; the other girl's mother would pick them up and bring them home. Eliza had checked with the other mother, not out of suspicion but caution. If Iso had garbled the message in any way, two young girls might be left waiting in front of the library at dusk. Granted, they would be in supersafe Bethesda, almost within walking distance of the Benedicts' house. But Eliza wanted to be sure she wasn't imposing on the other mother.

"The library?" The mother, Carol DeNadio, had a warm, throaty voice and laugh. "I wish Caitlin wanted to spend Saturday afternoon at the library. No, I was going to drop them off at Montgomery Mall."

Eliza, caught off guard, embarrassed and humiliated that Iso had set her up this way, blurted out: "Is that safe?"

"The Montgomery Mall? Safe as anywhere, I suppose. Especially when the girls are together in their gaggle. Iso has lovely manners, by the way. I wouldn't mind if that rubbed off on Caitlin."

"Th-th-th-thank you."

"I suppose that's from living in England? Or maybe you're just a better mother than I am." The latter was said with breezy self-deprecation. "But, seriously, I've been dropping Caitlin off there since she was eleven. I give her three hours and strict instructions. She's not allowed to leave the mall, and there will be hell to pay if she's not at our meeting point. Also, her phone has to be on, and she has to take my calls. Screen me, and she loses the privilege."

It certainly sounded harmless enough. So why had Iso lied about it?

"I didn't think you would give me permission," Iso said, her eyes focused on a spot on her bedroom wall, somewhere between her parents' heads. The wall, by Iso's choice, was a pale, pale lavender.

"We certainly won't now," Peter said. "You know how we feel about lying, Iso."

She sighed. "Yes, it's the one thing we must never do." Parroted back in a tone that bordered on mockery, as if it were ridiculous, this mania for truthfulness.

"Why did you think we would prohibit it?" Eliza was genuinely puzzled.

"Because you're always blah, blah, blah, shopping is evil, the more stuff you buy, the bigger your carbon footprint, blah, blah, blah. And when I want to go to McDonald's, I have to hear the whole *Fast Food Nation* thing, E. coli and worms in my stomach, whatever."

"It's true, shopping for shopping's sake is a bad habit," Peter said. "As for hamburgers, I think if you're going to eat one, you should eat a really good one."

"The really good ones, the ones you like, are at restaurants and cost eight dollars. At McDonald's, I can get a full meal for less than five dollars."

Eliza did find this amusing, father and daughter in a discussion over relative economics, the cost of values. Peter was willing to pay for taste. Iso wanted quantity. It wasn't that far removed from Peter's work at his firm, where they were banking on the idea that people with certain values would be drawn to their investment tools, even if they could get faster, better results through other companies.

"Let's not get derailed by hamburgers," she said. "The fact is that you lied to me, Iso, and we can't have that. You have to be punished. By the way, if you had asked me, I probably would have been okay with you going to the mall. My own parents were very strict about that when I was young. They had a lot of blanket rules about how I was allowed to spend my time, and I resented it. You couldn't pay me to go to a mall now for recreation. But when I was fourteen, it was all I wanted to do."

"Really? Granny I and Grampy M were strict?" Eliza no longer remembered how her parents' initials had become affixed to their names, or why.

"Not about most things. They merely hated the idea of the mall."

"But things were safer when you were young, right? You had a lot more freedom."

Iso's comment wasn't meant to provoke. She was just repeating something she had heard or intuited. *The world used to be so safe.* No, that wasn't a sentiment she was likely to have picked up at home. Eliza found the current culture of paranoia a good cover for her. She could be careful about her children without anyone thinking she was odd or strict.

"Iso, you're grounded," Peter declared. "For two weeks."

"What does that mean?"

Several days in, they were still trying to figure that out. Could Iso walk Reba? That was a tricky one. It was nice to see Iso taking an interest in the dog and volunteering to do an essential task, but also unusual. "If you take Albie," Eliza had decreed. Iso decided she didn't want to walk Reba after all. Could she call a friend about homework? Only if she did it from the kitchen telephone, within earshot. If Albie was watching television and Iso joined him in the family room, could Iso at least mention to him that there was probably a better program? No. Because Albie would give Iso anything she wanted.

It was true, Albie was a completely indiscriminating television watcher. Today was Sunday, a gray, drizzly one that managed to be at once humid and chilly. Peter had gone into the office, and Eliza was trapped in the house with Albie and Iso. That was the problem with having a child under house arrest. One had to stay with her. Early in the afternoon, the three found themselves in the family room, regarding one another warily. A game? They couldn't agree on one. A jigsaw puzzle? Iso couldn't be bothered with anything that uncool. Books? Even Albie seemed to find this appalling. Eliza grabbed the remote and turned it to the only channel she really liked, TCM. If she could design her perfect cable system, it would have only TCM and maybe AMC, although she hated the way the second network edited films and inserted commercials.

Mist-shrouded mountains, clearly a set, rose into view. Gene Kelly, Van Johnson—"Oh, it's *Brigadoon,*" Eliza said. "That's a wonderful movie."

Albie, who probably would have watched a test pattern without complaint, crawled onto the sofa and nestled into Eliza's side, and she tried not to show how overwhelmingly happy this made her. Iso lay on the floor, chanting, "BOR-ing." But eventually Gene Kelly caught her attention.

"I don't get it," Albie said. "How does the town sleep for a hundred years?"

"It's magic," Eliza said.

"But that funny man said they worked out a promise with God. Is God magic?"

Big question. Eliza and Peter had not given their children much of a religious education. Part of her, the reflexively honest part, wanted to say, "Yes, religion and magic are pretty much the same thing." But she imagined Albie carrying that wisdom to school, the hell to pay later. Instead she said, "God is always seen as an all-powerful entity, whatever religion you believe."

"That doesn't really look like Scotland," Iso complained. She spoke on some authority. The family had taken a driving trip through the Highlands the summer before last. "It doesn't look *real.*"

It didn't, and Eliza missed Gene Kelly's usual archness, that slight smirk of ego he brought to most roles. Here, he was just a straight-up romantic, while Van Johnson got to be the dissolute wisecracker. Still the movie was marvelous and so romantic. Except, of course, for the character of Harry Beaton, who had to watch his true love marry someone else, knowing all the while that he must stay in Brigadoon or the village would perish. Brigadoon's bargain with God was fine, if your true love happened to be there already. But what was a Harry Beaton to do? He really had drawn a tough hand.

Eliza's sympathy for Harry vanished when he attacked his true love at her wedding, lashing out: "All I ever did was want you too much."

Of course it ended happily—at least for Gene Kelly and Cyd Charisse. But what of the other Brigadooners—Brigadoonites?—who might not meet their true loves in the small village, or who might not love with a ferocity that awakens a town that otherwise would slumber for a century? What would happen over the years, as the town's residents became more connected by blood?

A phone rang. A single phone, up in her bedroom.

"The security phone!" Albie sang out, thrilled to be here to witness the mysterious instrument in action. Her instinct had been to ignore it, but now she would have to go answer it, refuse Walter's charges, and tell the children that it was just a test, like the test of the Emergency Broadcast System. In the case of a real emergency . . .

And as Eliza headed to the stairs, she was reminded that Iso was not the only liar in their family.

By the time she reached the phone, it had stopped. She glanced at her watch: 2 P.M., on a Sunday. She did not think Walter would have broken the rules, at least not so quickly. Over time, she could imagine him becoming careless, forgetting what he was supposed to do, or no longer caring. But not on this, his third call. A wrong number? How could one know unless the phone was answered? Why hang up?

"I thought it was going to be Homeland Security," Albie said wistfully. "I thought we were going to be told to evacuate. That would be exciting at least."

"I think," Eliza said, "we can come up with something to do that might be almost as exciting." They spent the afternoon making cupcakes, with much emphasis on decoration. Even Iso, denied the television, joined in, and eventually Peter. They ruined their appetites, filling up on cream cheese frosting and miniature cinnamon disks and squiggles of pressurized decorating icing, straight from the can. Their appetites destroyed, they ended up driving over to Five Guys for a late supper of hamburgers and fries, passing the very mall that had cost Iso her freedom. Eliza saw Iso cast it a wary glance, as if the mall itself was the source of her problems. In a sense, wasn't it? Whether it was the apple in Eden, the Roy Rogers on Route 40, or Bonnie Jean, betrothed to another in a village where there was no chance of meeting someone new, and no chance that the love of one's life might ever disappear—in the end, wasn't it *yearning* that led one astray, the pining after something or someone that had been denied?

Iso's punishment was to end the next day, and Eliza found herself wishing that she might commit a new infraction in the remaining hours, resulting in another week of forced companionship with her family. Hadn't she noticed how much fun they'd had? Didn't her sides ache from laughing at her father's antics with the frosting, the froth of family jokes that had carried them through dinner and then to Rita's, as if there had never been all those cupcakes? That night, as she tucked in Albie, he said: "Can we do that every Sunday? Cupcakes and Five Guys and Rita's?" She understood. She felt the same way. But unlike Albie, she knew how hard it was to replicate a perfect day. Wasn't that the story of yet another movie?

Back in her room, she took Iso's phone from the nightstand. Tomorrow, at breakfast, she would have to give it back to her, and the wall would go up again, separating Iso from the family.

The phone rang—but not the phone in her hand, the one that sat by itself, dedicated to one caller and one caller only, a caller who had been told never to call on weekends or evenings. It rang once, twice, then fell silent, like someone poking her in the back and running away.

Part IV

WHO'S ZOOMIN' WHO?

Released 1985

Reached no. 7 on Billboard Hot 100

Spent 23 weeks on R&B/Hip-Hop Charts

29

BARBARA LAFORTUNY SAT OUTSIDE the Baltimore train station, parked in the line reserved for those waiting, staring idly at the enormous man/woman statue with the glowing purple heart. Purple heart made her free-associate—from war, and the honors given for valor, to the old Baltimore thrift store by that name. When she first started teaching, Purple Heart was a terrible taunt used by the children in her class about wearing clothes from there.

But ultimately the statue made her think of her and Walter, the way *they* intersected. They were close enough now that they even squabbled like an old married couple. Certainly, Walter had the capacity to exasperate her like no one else on God's green earth. He was secretive and a control freak to boot, an almost valiant temperament for a man on death row, who controlled nothing in his life. Every time they made a plan—every time—he changed it on her. First he said, *Go slow, don't rush, don't worry. She'll come see me and then I'll bait that hook.* Now he had decided just as arbitrarily to jump ahead several moves, just like that, no explanation.

Yet Barbara had already set Plan B in motion, at Walter's insistence, and there was no calling it back. So here she was, parked outside Penn Station on a sunny October day, waiting for the Amtrak from Philadelphia. She frowned at a driver idling in the drop-off lane, which was clearly marked, ignoring the line of cars backing up behind her, the chain reaction of problems she was causing. She should be in the waiting lane, like Barbara, or parked on the traffic circle. Barbara hated people who didn't follow the rules. She gave her horn a little tap, tried to get the driver's attention, but the woman was clearly an expert at tuning out the world. Barbara got out of her car and walked over, rapped on the woman's window, forcing her to roll it down and acknowledge Barbara's presence.

"You're in the wrong lane," she said to the driver.

"I pulled in by accident and I'm only going to be a minute," the woman said. "People can still get around me."

"Not that easily, and traffic is backing up behind you clear to St. Paul Street. Just pull around the circle and you can get in the correct lane to wait."

"Do you work here?"

Barbara wasn't one to be derailed by irrelevant questions. A person didn't have to work somewhere in order to insist on civility and order. "You really should pull around."

"And you should mind your own business."

Barbara took off her sunglasses, which not only allowed her to make eye contact, but also showcased her scar, that phantom smile. She wasn't deluded enough to think it made her look tough or intimidating. But she believed that it announced that she had lived in this world, that she knew things others did not. "I'm sure you think you're the special case, that you have all these rationalizations for behaving as you do. But you are one person inconveniencing many, and there's ultimately no way to rationalize *that*. Is your presence in this line a matter of life and death? Will someone suffer if you do what everyone else is doing, without a fuss?" Even as Barbara was speaking, cars were pulling around, honking and squealing, the drivers making irked faces. They seemed to lump her in with this woman, think she was part of the problem. But now that they were in a standoff, pride was involved. Pride—someone else's—had almost killed Barbara. Still, she couldn't back down.

"I will take down your tag number," she said. "And make a complaint. Did you know that citizens can do that? Complain to the MVA about other motorists' bad behavior?" She wondered as she said this if her threat might be true. It should be true, and that was good enough.

The woman looked balefully at Barbara, put her car in gear, and lurched forward, almost running over Barbara's foot in the process. You would think that cars that had been stalled behind her might show Barbara a little gratitude for breaking up the bottleneck, but they just drove furiously past, dropping off their passengers with no acknowledgment of Barbara's efforts for them. She dashed across the lane to her own properly parked car, but even before she could open the door, she saw her visitor coming out of the station, a colorless, meek-looking man in a sports jacket and a homburg. She recognized him by his tentativeness, the wary, unsure glance of a person being met by someone he doesn't really know. She flung up an arm, waved him over.

"Ms. LaFortuny?" he asked.

"Mr. Garrett," she said, shaking his hand. "I'm such a fan."

Now *that* was a lie. She was really piling them up today. She and Walter both considered Garrett's book a joke, a travesty. But he might be useful, if deployed correctly, and wouldn't that be a great joke on him?

"How was your trip?" she asked.

"Uneventful," he said. "I guess that's all one can ask for. I can't believe government subsidizes that service."

She knew she shouldn't argue with him, but she hated that kind of knee-jerk critique. "I believe the northeastern routes make money for Amtrak. Besides, this country needs more rail service, not less."

"The covers were torn on half the seats," he said. "And there was no coffee in the café car."

"Do you want a cup of coffee? There's a Starbucks not even three blocks from here—"

"No, I'm fine. I just think that's outrageous on general principle."

So it was going to be that kind of day.

She drove toward the county, taking him on a tour of the Lerners' old neighborhood, driving into the state park, circling back to the now rather worn-looking neighborhood where Maude Parrish had lived. He claimed to have seen these sites before, but Barbara doubted him. Garrett was a lazy man, according to Walter, content to sit in a courtroom and read official records but reluctant to initiate anything on his own. He had never spoken to Walter's sister, for example, never even tried as far as they knew. (Thank God, given her feelings, but still, how hard would it have been?) He hadn't even been particularly dogged about getting to Walter, or his lawyer. But that way, he didn't have to deal with all the messy contradictions. Long before the Internet and blogging, Jared Garrett had the thumb-sucking incuriousness of a person who can't be bothered to muddle his theories with fact. He now kept a blog on cold cases, throwing up his wildly speculative ideas willy-nilly. His grammar was suspect, and as best as Barbara could tell, he couldn't even be bothered to spell-check half the time.

They stopped for a late lunch in Clarksville. They were only a few miles from where the Lerners lived. She wondered if Garrett had even gleaned that much information, which was available via property records.

"Vegan?" he said with dismay, studying the menu.

"You'll never know. I ate here before the switch and found out that most of the entrées I liked were vegan all along."

He ordered the chili, which Barbara knew to be absolutely delicious, but seemed glum about it. He was probably not much older than Barbara, but he had a bowling ball of a gut and a terrible pallor. Why did people treat themselves so horribly? Barbara was well aware that she had the great gift of leisure, that it was easy for her to go to yoga class and shop the farmers' market and choose healthful restaurants, but this man was clearly making no effort to take care of himself. She thought of Walter, struggling to maintain his health in prison. She had sent him books with basic yoga instruction and he had adopted a vegetarian diet despite much protest from prison officials, who wanted to honor dietary needs only for religious or medical reasons. *Fine,* Walter had said, *I'm a Muslim now. Put me on the vegetarian diet that you give them.*

"Ms. LaFortuny—"

"Barbara."

"I don't mean to be rude and I'm sure you mean well, but when you approached me and said you had significant new information to share, I expected more than a tour of places I saw twenty-some years ago."

"Things change. I thought it might be helpful for you to revisit places, see them anew."

"Helpful if I were writing about the Walter Bowman case, but I'm not. I devote my time to cold cases now."

"There are those who think they can link various cold cases to Walter Bowman."

"Yes, and I'm one of them. But unless Walter wants to give an interview before his execution—?"

She took a bite of her roasted corn quesadilla, sipped her tea. "Well, he might. Walter's talking a lot these days."

"To other journalists?"

She forced herself not to smile at Garrett's sense of himself as a journalist. He was an accountant for the state of Pennsylvania, and he hadn't published a book for at least fifteen years. Nothing he had written was even in print.

"No, not other journalists." She lowered her voice. "To *her.* Elizabeth Lerner."

His shock was gratifying. "Why?"

She gave a mystified shrug. "He doesn't tell me everything. I just know he added her to his call list and they've been speaking regularly."

"I always thought—I *said*—that things between them were much more complicated than anyone wanted to admit. People criticized me, but she did have multiple chances to escape."

Barbara almost felt bad. Engaging Jared Garrett's sordid imagination was like teasing an animal or a small child. Too easy to be fair. And she honestly didn't want to cause the woman pain, but she was their only hope. To save a life, to prevent a terrible miscarriage of justice—why, anything was permissible. Elizabeth Lerner had nothing to be ashamed of. Unless she let Walter die, and then she was a killer, more cold-blooded than any death row inmate.

"And you know where she lives, her phone number? Do you think she would talk to me?"

"No," Barbara said, relieved to be back in her usual world of blunt, tactless candor. "I mean, Walter has her phone number, but that doesn't mean I do." Another white lie. "Besides, I don't think she would talk to you now, because she's still keen that no one know her whereabouts, her past. Perhaps if Walter goes, however—"

"If? I didn't think there was much doubt."

"I think it's important to leave the mind open to possibility. Certainly, there's no harm in hoping."

"Elizabeth Lerner." He shook his head as if he had seen a celebrity, albeit one he didn't particularly admire. "Her parents threatened a libel suit against me. They even talked about an injunction."

"They were her parents," Barbara said. "Of course they felt protective of her."

"Do you have kids?"

"No," Barbara said. "I never married, not that I needed a husband to have children. But I don't like children much."

"Weren't you a teacher? I mean, I know you had a horrible run-in with one student, but before that, did you like them?"

"I don't remember, but—no, I don't think so. I liked my subjects, government and history. I thought they were important, and I wanted to share them with others. But I wasn't drawn to teaching because of a blanket love for children. I accepted children as a necessary condition. You?"

"Me? I never was a teacher."

"Do you have children?"

"No. My wife and I—it didn't happen for us, and we accepted that. God's will, and all."

"You didn't want to adopt?"

He lowered his voice, although there was no one in the restaurant to hear them. "No, never. You do what I do, you learn some things."

"What do you mean?"

"About adoption. In crime. Those kids are damaged."

"Oh, that's ridiculous. There's no empirical data to support that. Death row is full of men who were raised by their biological parents. Biological parents who beat them or mistreated them, in most cases. Some of the men I've met would have been better off if they had been adopted."

"You think having bum parents is a reason not to execute someone?"

"Yes, in fact, I do. But then, I don't think there's anything that supports the state's right to murder. Killing is wrong or it isn't. If it's wrong for an individual to take someone's life, it's wrong for the state. The state doesn't steal from thieves—"

"It seizes money. It exacts fines."

"That's not the same thing. The state doesn't sexually assault rapists. Why is it only with homicide, and only a particular type of homicide, that we insist on this kind of justice?"

"Walter Bowman did some pretty horrible things."

"Yes, he did. He'd be the first person to tell you that. And he accepts that a lifetime in prison, with no chance for parole, is fair."

Jared had abandoned the chili and was picking at the corn bread that accompanied it.

"Look, I can't promise anything," Barbara said. "But there's a possibility that Walter will give you an interview. Walter *and* Elizabeth. But you have to be patient."

"How do I know you can deliver either one of them? Why should I believe that you even know where Elizabeth Lerner is?"

"I'll show you after lunch."

30

"SO WHAT HAVE YOU BEEN up to?" Walter asked Eliza. It was a natural question. So natural it seemed even more unnatural.

She found herself tempted to tell him about their perfect Sunday. Of course, she would not. She would not speak of her children to Walter, ever, and, so far, he had the good sense not to inquire about them. Besides, it would have been insensitive to prattle on about her happiness, cruel and taunting. That, of course, was part of the appeal. It would have been a way of saying, indirectly: *I am where I am, I have what I have, because I am a good person at heart. You are where you are because you're bad. Just because I was dragged into your life for almost forty days doesn't make me bad, too.*

But the more pressing need was to have

the conversation with someone, anyone. She had tried to engage Peter on the topic, but satisfactory husband that he was, he was a man and not one inclined to wax poetic about a day of cupcakes and movies. Vonnie had no patience for such conversations, and Eliza's own mother often ended up talking about how difficult Vonnie was when Eliza spoke of her trials with Iso. As for friends—she had yet to make any. People were friendly, but they seemed to think she was reserved. Funny, because Eliza had been considered ebulliently capital *A* American during her London years, and now her countrymen—countrywomen?—seemed to find her cool, detached. Or perhaps she had yet to make friends because most of the parents she met were in Iso's peer group, where Eliza was probably known as the mother of the subtle bully. Maybe, in retrospect, she should have overlooked Iso's lie about the mall if only to form an alliance with that friendly-seeming mother.

And here was Walter, someone who knew her in a way that almost no one did. With the exception of her parents and Vonnie, there was no one left in her life who had ever called her Elizabeth. She remembered being sixteen, filling out the papers for her new school. "Why can't I change my name?" she had asked her parents. "Legally?" her father asked. "I suppose it could be done." "No, I mean, just change it, call myself something else." "Bureaucracies are bureaucracies," her mother said. "Your name has to match the name on your birth certificate or they won't enroll you." "But I could shorten it, say it's something else, or use my middle name." "Of course you can," her mother said.

Her full name was Elizabeth Hortense Lerner, after her maternal grandmother. Elizabeth Hortense Babington had lived on Baltimore's North Side, walking distance from the Quaker meetinghouse she attended. But then—she walked everywhere and didn't even own a car, relying on cabs for journeys that could not be made on foot. If she had been someone else's grandmother, Elizabeth and Vonnie probably would have considered her queer, this thin, black-clad woman with long, woolly hair, out of time and out of place as she marched through the city's streets. Elizabeth had always been proud to carry her name, Vonnie a little bitter that she had been named for their father's mother, Yvonne Estelle. It was awful to cut down her grandmother's elegant name, almost like cutting up a wedding dress for bedding. But it presented so many possibilities: Liz, Lizzie, Beth, Betsy, Bette, Bets . . . Eliza! It retained more of her real name than any other version yet sounded different enough that it was plausible no one would put it together. It was Uh-liz-a-beth Lerner who had been kidnapped a county over. E-Li-Za Lerner was the new girl.

So she had amputated "Beth" and never looked back.

"My life is very ordinary," she told Walter. "It doesn't produce much drama."

"Same here," he said, with a laugh. That was new. She didn't remember Walter being able to laugh at himself. "But I guess, in your case, that's a good thing. You've put together a very nice life for yourself."

"That wasn't what you said in your letter."

"What do you mean?" Puzzled, on the boundary of hurt.

"You said you expected more of me."

"No," Walter countered. "I said it wasn't what I *envisioned* for you."

She couldn't argue the words; she had shredded the letter. But she could contest the meaning. "But that was the implication. That you expected me to achieve in a career setting."

"No, I don't think so," Walter said. "I mean, no offense"—she braced herself for the insult that inevitably followed those words—"but you didn't even like kids. You were always pointing out how grubby this one was, or complaining about the ones who cried."

"I was?" She had been fifteen. She didn't remember thinking about children one way or another, but neither had she been thinking about a career. Her only goal was to be . . . grown-up.

Which she thought meant being some version of Madonna, crashing with a friend in a funky apartment where the phone was covered with pink fuzz and seashells, and where there was enough money for carry-out pizza, if not much else. Later, in college, she was the type of student who truly dreaded the question "What's your major?" not because it was such a cliché, but because she couldn't answer it until junior year, when she began to study children's literature with an eye toward becoming a librarian. Even then, she wasn't choosing a career path. She had been drawn to children's literature because it gave her an excuse to reread fairy tales, and her own young favorites, *The Mixed-Up Files of Mrs. Basil E. Frankweiler, Are You There God? It's Me, Margaret.* But her intellect had been engaged by the work in a way it never had been before—and never was again. Although she started graduate school in Houston, she dropped out when she was pregnant with Iso.

"No one likes children when they are a child," she said now.

"Do you remember going to Luray Caverns?"

"Yes." The answer was actually more complicated. Her time with Walter—it existed in some odd space in her brain, which was neither memory nor not-memory. It was like a story she knew about someone else, a story told in great detail so many times that she could rattle it off. It was The Three Little Pigs, The Boy Who Cried Wolf, Little Red Riding Hood, one of those grim Grimm fairy tales filled with horrible details—collapsing households, devoured animals, Red and Grandmama stepping out of the wolf's sliced-open belly—made tolerable by their happy endings.

"I tried to leave you there that day."

"You did *not*."

"I thought about it. There was a group of schoolchildren, a few years younger than you, and they were loud and rowdy, and I thought, I'll just back away and she'll start talking to those kids and as soon as she's distracted, I'll run to the parking lot and drive away."

She was weeping, as silently as possible, determined that he not know. "I don't believe you."

"That's understandable. I don't doubt it sounds self-serving. You know what I did—taking you—it was so stupid. If I had had a moment to think about it, I would have realized that you didn't know anything, that you couldn't hurt me. I thought, *I have to kill her. She's in the wrong place at the wrong time.* But—look, whatever you think about me, whatever the law says about intent and first-degree, I never *planned* to kill anyone. It happened, yes, but I would be in this, like, other state. I wouldn't even really remember doing it."

"Walter—this is not a conversation I can have with you."

"I'm sorry, I'm just trying to explain why I couldn't hurt you."

"Walter, you more than hurt me. You raped me. Which would have been awful enough, under any circumstances, but I not only had to endure the rape, I had to endure it while assuming that you would kill me afterward, as you did with Maude."

"I never told you what I did."

"I found you at a grave. I understood what had happened. And then there was Holly . . ."

He sighed, the misunderstood man. "I didn't kill Holly. And the thing is, you know that. You've always known that, but people talked you out of it, told you it couldn't be."

"Stop."

"I'm sorry. I don't mean to upset you, Elizabeth. But if we can't speak honestly of what happened that night, to each other . . ."

"I didn't see anything. *I wasn't there.*"

A long pause. "I've clearly upset you, and that's the last thing I want to do. Truly. Where were we? Talking about you, as a mother. As I said, I just didn't think it interested you much. That's all I meant, when I wrote you that time. I wasn't denigrating what you do. I just never thought that was what you wanted."

"You don't know me, Walter."

"Now that's just hurtful, Elizabeth. Yes, I harmed you. There's no doubt in my mind that I victimized you, and I only wish I had been called into account for those things. That I wasn't is not my fault." He had her there. She and her parents had asked that Walter not be prosecuted for rape, and he had accepted a plea bargain on the kidnapping charge, meaningless in the larger scheme of things, years attached to a life sentence that wasn't to have lasted this long. "And I don't know all of you, no, but, then—do you know me? Can you understand that I have changed, that I do understand the importance of making amends to those I've harmed?"

She felt she should apologize. Then she felt furious, being put in the position of thinking, even for a moment, that she owed Walter Bowman an apology.

"Elizabeth—I wish I could say these things face-to-face, let you see how remorseful I really am. Clearly, I can't persuade you over the phone. But if I looked into your eyes, I think you would see I am a different man."

"I don't think so . . ."

"If I could see you—maybe I could apologize for everything."

"You did apologize. You apologized the last time we spoke. You apologized just moments ago."

"No, I mean for *everything*. Maybe, if I saw you, I would talk about those things I never talk about."

"Are you saying—?"

"I'm not going to be more explicit over a phone line. But if you come to see me—you might be surprised by what I would say."

His comment about the phone line, the implication that it was insecure, jogged her memory. "Walter—did you call Sunday?"

"No." Adamant, but not defensive. "You told me during which hours I could call, and I've followed that to the letter." He almost seemed to expect praise.

"Someone did. Called and hung up, at least twice. Have you given this number to anyone else?"

"Well, it's on my sheet. And Barbara knows, but I've told her not to use it, ever. But, no, I haven't *given* it to anyone. I wouldn't want anyone else to have it."

"Oh. Okay."

"You'll visit?"

"No. I mean—I'll talk about it—I mean, I'll think about it." Again, she didn't want to admit to the intimacy of her marriage, how she reviewed all important decisions with Peter.

"Time is running out," he said.

"I realize that."

"And once I'm dead—well, let's just say that some secrets are going to go with me. But maybe that's what you're counting on?"

"What do you mean?"

"Nothing. I don't know. A person gets a little ornery, at times, living as I do. I'm not a saint. And I'm offering you something pretty big, Elizabeth. But it's only for you, no one else."

"Walter—I need to go."

"Right—there's soccer practice on Wednesday."

How do you know that? But she didn't ask. He wanted her to ask, she was sure of that much. Still, he knew he had rattled her. The pause alone gave her away.

"Good-bye, Walter. We'll talk soon."

"In person, I hope. Eventually."

"We'll see." But, again, she had paused, given herself away. He knew she was considering it.

31

THE WOMAN IN THE WINDOW seat looked over Jared Garrett's shoulder at the notes he had arrayed on his tray table. He had hoped she would. He had taken out his index cards because he was bored and restless, his mind churning from the events of the day. It seemed primitive to him that Amtrak didn't provide wireless service on its trains. He would have been better off driving, after all, but he had assumed he could do e-mail en route. Now he was stuck on this wheezy old regional—only a sucker or a fool would pay extra for the Acela, which cut a mere ten minutes off the trip—with another forty minutes before he arrived back in Philadelphia. He could actually write, he supposed, but it felt odd to write without the option of the "publish" button, waiting to reward his efforts. Of course, the Bowman story was bigger than his blog. He must not waste it there, tempting as it was. He remembered when people criticized him as a cut-and-paste writer because he had managed to deliver his manuscript on Bowman within six weeks of his death sentence in the first trial. That pace seemed positively leaden by today's standards.

"Colored index cards," the woman said. "Are you a writer?"

"Yes," he said. If his wife were here, she would roll her eyes or give an exaggerated sigh. She saw his writing as a hobby, one used to escape her in the evenings, when she parked herself in front of the television to watch reality shows. She wasn't entirely wrong.

"What kind of books do you write?"

"Nonfiction," he said. "Usually about crime."

"True crime?"

"Nonfiction," he repeated. "Fact crime is probably the best label. One of my books was nominated, once, for best fact crime." He did not mention the name of the prize because it was not well known, but it was a prize, and he had been nominated for it. And *fact crime* might not be the most elegant construction, but it was better than *true crime.* Of course, *fact crime* was problematic, too, as it sounded almost like a criminal act driven by fact, like a so-called hate crime. But *true crime* had acquired a nasty taint over the years.

"Would I have read any of your books?"

The inevitable question. He wanted to turn it on her, say, "How would I know what you've read or not read? Are you a world-famous reader?"

Instead, he said: "My best-known book was about the Walter Bowman case, but that was over twenty years ago. I haven't published for a while."

"Walter Bowman?" The name clearly didn't resonate with her. But then—Walter Bowman didn't resonate. Jared always felt that Walter's lack of charisma had dampened interest in his book, kept it from becoming the success it might have been. If only he could have written about someone like Charlie Manson or Ted Bundy. He had thought he lucked out, all those years ago, when the big guns didn't come to Virginia. Turned out the big guns knew what they were doing.

But now—now the story had its long-missing climax, and it was going to be all Jared's. Oh, other journalists might write about the execution. But no one would get to talk to Walter. He had Barbara LaFortuny's word.

"A spree killer, back in the eighties," he said. "Probably a serial killer, but that was never proven."

"Is there a difference?"

He began to explain but almost immediately felt the woman's attention drifting away from him. He interrupted himself, pointed to the cards arrayed before him: "I should get back to my work," he said.

"Of course," she said with apparent relief. "I'm going to go to the café car." He couldn't help noticing that she took her computer bag and purse. She would probably stay in the café for the rest of the trip, drinking white wine, sizing up the men. She was on the prowl, Jared decided, a lonely woman on a train. He was grateful for his thirty-year marriage, his solid life with Florence, even if she did roll her eyes at him from time to time. A woman alone—that was a sad thing. Barbara LaFortuny had seemed pathetic to him, although he had tried not to betray this. No one liked to be pitied.

He had Googled her, of course, as soon as she had e-mailed him. She had made a point of telling him that she wasn't some sad sack, pining for Walter, but he thought she was kidding herself. Walter was good-looking, at least in photographs. Less so in person, but she had never seen him in person. She may not admit it, but LaFortuny was motivated by something more than a principled stand against the death penalty.

Still, it seemed clear, after several e-mails, that she really did have something to offer. He had taken a sick day from work, reasoning that his sick days were one of his remaining benefits in a world of shrinking benefits and he shouldn't be penalized just because he was healthy. By not taking his sick days, he was cutting his own pay, in a sense. But the first half of the day, spent driving around sites he had long ago explored on his own, had been a big honking disappointment, and he had begun to feel that he was being taken, especially when she drove out to a large county park.

"Walter Bowman's never been linked to this area," he said, thinking of his own obsessive map, how he had examined every missing person case. The true-crime bloggers who followed the Bowman case fell across a wide range, from total apologists who would deny even the two obvious murders to those who basically put every missing teenage girl, 1980 to 1985, in his column. Jared was one of the more moderate, believing that Walter could be linked to at least four unsolved murders and four missing person cases in the Mid-Atlantic region. Jared had his own formula based on distance, opportunity, and victim. Distance: Walter Bowman had never been more than three hundred miles from home in his entire life and, per Elizabeth Lerner's testimony, he seemed to rotate around a fixed point in his mind, staying in Virginia, Maryland, and West Virginia. Opportunity: He had nonconsecutive days off and, before he killed Maude Parrish, had never spent a single night away from home. Finally, victims: Both were young, under sixteen, and not the least bit streetwise, so throwing in every random hooker killing was really missing the mark. Hookers didn't fit Walter Bowman's pattern.

But then—neither did Elizabeth Lerner, not in the looks department.

At any rate, he had known, when Barbara turned into this suburban park, that it had no connection at all to Bowman and he was beginning to get a little angry at being suckered this way. He was on a six-thirty train, and that was by Barbara LaFortuny's instruction. She said she had tickets to a play, or something. That had been over lunch, at a vegan place called Roots, which hadn't exactly thrilled Jared.

"Sounds like you have a nice life," he said, just to make conversation, hoping to conceal his dismay at the menu offerings.

"I do," she said. "Being attacked was one of the best things that ever happened to me. Not because it freed me from working, but because it showed me that my life was empty, purposeless, and that was through no one's fault but my own."

He pulled out his microcassette recorder, more to be polite than anything else, and let her drone on and on about her life. Perhaps this was all she had to offer, he thought. Perhaps she thought it was a great gift, the Walter Bowman story, as strained through the eyes of his greatest supporter. The thing is, she hadn't told him a single thing about Walter that he didn't know, and her insistence that Walter had changed—he couldn't buy it. Barbara LaFortuny had a near-death experience through no fault of her own. She should be able to see that Walter wouldn't be able to experience that kind of awakening until they strapped him to the gurney. And even then, even if some miracle happened and he didn't die, he probably wouldn't change.

She had let one tantalizing detail drift across the lunch table. "You know about the autopsies, right? What wasn't there?"

"What wasn't . . . oh, yes. I wrote about that. I thought you had read my book?"

"I did. I just wanted to remind you."

"It doesn't matter, not in the case of Holly Tackett."

"No, it doesn't. If one believes the testimony of Elizabeth Lerner. And you seem to be the one person willing to be skeptical of her."

"I merely raised some questions. Killers have patterns. Elizabeth Lerner breaks the pattern in almost every way. She finds him, he doesn't find her. He takes her and—if you believe her—doesn't attempt sex with her for weeks, and then only once. She's not a tall, shapely blonde. If she's not actively helping him, why does he keep her around? I mean, I know the prevailing theory was that she was a witness and Walter always killed while in some sort of near-psychotic state, brought on by the other victims' sexual rejection of him. And maybe all she did differently was submit, not fight him. Still, no, I think there's always been something off about her testimony."

The check came and Barbara LaFortuny picked it up, although she seemed surprised that he didn't offer. But he had come down here on his own dime and he sure hadn't chosen to eat vegan. What did she expect? And now she had brought him to some park. What could she possibly have for him here?

"Athletic field number nine," she said, stopping the car.

"What about it?"

"It's at the top of this hill. I have to stay here, because she knows my car, my face. It's not a face people easily forget." She laughed at her own lopsided visage, as if it were a delightful joke. "But you can probably walk up and get close enough to see her."

"Her?"

"Elizabeth Lerner. Although, of course, that's not the name she uses now. But go on, take a gander."

"What name does she use now? How did you find her?"

She smiled. "We'll save that for another day. I just wanted you to know how much we can give you, if you're patient."

"We?"

"Walter and I."

"How can Walter have any influence over her?"

"As I said, they're talking."

"Will I be able to recognize her?"

"Look for the redhead, with the redheaded son and a rather

ugly dog. Her daughter is number seventeen, I believe. Doesn't look a thing like her. If anything—well, you'll see."

He felt ridiculous, trudging up the long drive in his loafers and work clothes. If he were one of these parents, he'd make him for a pedophile. Yet the parents, almost all mothers at this time of day, paid him no mind. The drive was on an incline and he was puffing and sweating by the time he arrived at field nine. A quick sweep—no one. Wait, there was the redheaded boy and dog, romping along the sidelines.

And there she was. He would not have recognized her in a crowd, or without the expectation of seeing her. She was curvy, whereas the teenage Elizabeth had been straight up and down, with no shape. (He had speculated, too, that Walter might have confused sexual leanings. Walter hadn't liked that, but it was fair, given what Elizabeth looked like and how he had made her dress. And it was consistent with the other evidence.) But there was something else that was different about her, something that took him a moment to diagnose.

She looked happy. Wind ruffling her hair on this pleasant October afternoon, eyes trained on—which one? Oh, the little beauty, long-legged and lean, not at all like her mother, at least not like any version Jared ever saw. The daughter—the daughter looked more like Holly Tackett than she did like her mother. Not in the coloring, but in her grace, her long-limbed body, her ease with herself. Out of her soccer uniform, in street clothes, she would appear much older than she was.

Elizabeth wasn't one of the more vocal mothers, but she was clearly proud of her daughter. And when her son came running up with the dog, his small grubby hand thrust forward to show her something, she inspected his offering with grave interest.

Jared watched her for a little while longer, hoping that her husband might arrive, or that the game might end and he could, discreetly, follow her to her car. With a license plate, he wouldn't be dependent on Barbara LaFortuny. He could get a name, an address, a phone number. Perhaps he could ask some other parent about the team, figure out where it was based, how to get the roster. But, no, that would invite attention. If he had his camera, he could pretend to be a photographer, but photographers did not dress like auditors, as he did, being an auditor. No, better to keep his distance. For now.

He remembered the one photograph he had managed to take of Elizabeth, back in the courthouse hallway, camera held hip level. "Hey, Elizabeth," he had called, and she had looked back, for only a split second, which was all he needed to grab the shot. It wasn't great, but it was better than the damn school photo, which had been used on her missing posters. She looked startled, wide-eyed, even a little guilty. They had used it on the cover, with Walter's mug shot and a heartbreaking photo of Holly Tackett between them.

His train slowed for the approach to Philadelphia. He couldn't wait to get home, to get on the Internet. He must not write about this yet. But it would be fun tonight to sit in his study and read the other bloggers, to imagine their envy and astonishment when he broke this story. How had Walter found her again? Perhaps she had found him.

32

"OCTOBER GIVETH AND OCTOBER TAKETH away," Peter intoned the next morning. Golden autumn had been replaced by a dark, lashing storm, almost monsoonlike. Eliza felt she had no choice but to drive Albie to school. She struggled with this, on principle. Was she being overprotective? Hadn't she walked to school in driving rainstorms? And Albie was used to the wet because of England. But this was the kind of downpour in which visibility dwindled to nothing, and she could not bear to think of dreamy Albie walking along the streets in his slicker, which was nowhere near bright enough. If she had her way, Albie would wear a bright yellow coat and hat like the little girl on the Morton salt box, but even Albie had enough fashion sense to choose dark navy. Besides, it was touching how much Albie cherished the novelty of the ride to school, especially when Reba automatically piled in. Apparently Reba understood that the walk to school was not about her. It had a purpose, a mission, and if she was in on the nice days, she should go along on the dreary ones, too.

Yet the moment they dropped Albie off, the rain stopped, the sky cleared, and the day felt freshly scrubbed, an enticing invitation to do something, anything, outdoors. Eliza, who had no shortage of tasks at home, believed she was heading there when she pulled out of the school's driveway. Somehow, she found the Subaru nosing east and north, toward Baltimore. She did not take the highways, preferring the secondary roads, the very ones on which she had learned to drive, skirting close to her parents' home and even detouring past her old high school—although it wasn't *her* school, the windowless octagon that she remembered more or less fondly. That hopelessly small structure had been demolished back in the 1990s and replaced with a handsome brick-and-glass rectangle that allowed light to pour in from every angle. She continued along Route 40, little changed to her eyes, although the Roy Rogers had been replaced by a Church's Fried Chicken. The road dipped, as it always had, and all the trappings of the suburbs fell away as she descended into the section that was bordered by the state park. The leaves were just beginning to turn, and they glistened in the sun. She parked in the lot and let Reba out. She didn't have a leash, but she knew the dog would stay close to her, even in a novel environment, full of new smells.

They walked, following the spindly waterway that was the Sucker Branch, even after hours of heavy rain. She told herself she couldn't be sure where she was, not really. There were no landmarks, and she hadn't been here since August 1985. It would be impossible to pinpoint the exact place where she had seen Walter, tamping down the earth with his shovel.

That is, it would have been impossible if it weren't for the plastic spray of flowers tucked at the foot of an old oak tree.

A coincidence, she told herself, then Reba. "It's a coincidence." Reba looked as if she were considering this information. The bouquet was bedraggled; it had been out in the elements for quite some time. It might be trash, for all Eliza knew, something tossed here, not left in memorial. Who would have trudged into these woods to leave a plastic nosegay at a site where Maude had spent barely a day? Eliza tried to remember what she knew about Maude's life. She had attended Mount Hebron High School. She had been on her way to work at an ice-cream parlor on Route 40 and gotten a ride with Walter. She was tall and thin, one of two children whose divorced mother was just scraping by. This was all from information that filtered out during the trials. Walter never spoke of what he had done, except in the most general way.

"He must have said something," the prosecutor had insisted. Baltimore County was known for the ferocity with which its state's attorney sought the death penalty in all applicable cases, and the Howard County attorney had happily ceded the case to him, saying it was almost certain that Walter had killed Maude here, just over the county line, not where she was taken. But they couldn't prove it was a capital crime if Maude had gotten into Walter's car willingly, and he said she had. And there was no evidence of rape. The assumption was that Walter used a condom, unusual but not unheard of, although this did not explain the lack of trauma to Maude's body. There were a lot of gaps in the case, and they leaned on Elizabeth to fill them in.

He must have said something about Maude, the prosecutor said.

No, Elizabeth told the prosecutor, Walter had offered varying stories about the girl whose grave he had dug—she fell out of the car, she fell in the park and hit her head. But he spoke vaguely about other crimes he might have committed, and that was only in order to scare Elizabeth to do whatever he asked her to do.

" 'I've done some terrible things,' he would say. 'I didn't want to do them. I was left with no choice. But I will do what I have to do.' "

In the end, Walter was convicted of murder in the first degree and given a life sentence. He had already received the death penalty in Virginia, so it didn't really matter. The Maryland prosecutor had spun the whole experience as a saving to taxpayers. Maryland would be spared the cost of Walter's appeals, and the cost of his maintenance over the years, yet justice had been done. The prosecutor said.

Eliza and Reba kept walking, inhaling the dense, wet smells of the woods in autumn. The leaves would have been thicker, in summer, it would have been harder to see as far as she could today. If she had been able to spot Walter from a distance—no, she wasn't supposed to think that way.

Eventually the path led back into the old neighborhood, her mother's Brigadoon. It was unchanged, almost as if it had slumbered through the past two decades. Although they probably had cable now, Eliza thought, noting a small satellite attached to one roof. She walked among the stone houses, assigning each one its past, astonished at how much she remembered. The Sleazaks had lived there, old man Traber there. (She had been stunned to learn from his obit, which her mother clipped for her a few years ago, that this stereotypical crank, the original get-off-my-lawn guy, was actually a well-regarded society painter.) The Billinghams' door was still scarlet, a scandalous choice back in the 1980s, when the community board debated if the color might prevent the neighborhood from being included in the National Register of Historic Places, a status it had long coveted.

The primary difference, Eliza deduced from the cars, was that the neighborhood's residents were more prosperous now, or more inclined to flaunt their wealth. Her mother wouldn't have cared for that. And she wouldn't have liked the fact that a woman in a BMW slowed when she saw Eliza and Reba, regarding them with frank suspicion. She drove past them, turned around, and came past again, rolling down her window as she pulled abreast of them.

"Can I help you?" she asked Eliza. "Are you looking for someone?"

"Just taking a stroll down memory lane. I lived here, as a child."

Eliza pointed to the house where she had grown up, the house she had never fully appreciated until her family decided to leave it. Could they have stayed? Were they wrong to cut themselves off from their pre-Walter life? Hers was not such an unusual name. Media exposure was not as intense then. She wasn't Patricia Hearst. If she told this woman her maiden name—that quaint term, yet also literal in her case—the woman would probably evince no recognition. Who remembers names, anyway? The runaway bride, the girl killed in Aruba, the girl killed in Italy—they made headlines, yet Eliza couldn't name one of them to save her life.

"Well, it's almost impossible to buy here now," the woman said. "Houses are sold before they even go on the market."

"Even since the mortgage crisis?"

"Houses here *never* lose their value," the woman said. Eliza felt like a blasphemer for suggesting that Roaring Springs could be touched by anything as commonplace as the world economy.

"What do they go for these days?"

Judging by the look on the BMW driver's face, Eliza had progressed from blasphemer to merely classless. The woman lowered her voice:

"I heard that the Mitchells got almost $500,000."

The number was at once laughably low, relative to what Peter had paid for their house in Bethesda, and shockingly high. Eliza's parents had paid no more than $40,000 for the house in the 1970s and felt like robber barons when they sold it for $175,000 in 1986. *We could have lived here,* Eliza thought. The commute would have worked out. Iso and Albie would have attended her old schools, walked down Frederick Road to the Catonsville branch library, eaten gyros at the old Greek diner, although Maryland's gyros were thin pleasures when compared to the falafels they had known in London.

They could have walked along the Sucker Branch, too, wandered into the park. Did parents still allow children to do such things? No, probably not. But that detail did not derail Eliza's fantasy. She had never blamed the location, the park. No, the problem with this spasm of nostalgia was that she was longing for her children to reclaim the territory she had ceded, Elizabethland, the realm of her pre-fifteen-year-old self. And if they wandered back into her past, she would have to tell them everything about the girl that she used to be. As far as they knew, there was no home between the Lerners' early years in Baltimore City and the house they owned now. An entire chapter of the family's life was missing, and Eliza's own children had never noticed.

"That much," she said to the woman in the BMW, widening her eyes in what she hoped would appear to be wistful awe. In some ways, it was. She and Reba turned around and headed out of the neighborhood. She had a feeling that the woman watched her go. That was okay. It was good to be vigilant. She wouldn't deny anyone that right.

Passing Maude's temporary grave again, she stopped and examined the bouquet. So sad, but then—what did the parents of the missing do? What territory did they mark, what did they visit? *I'll tell you things,* Walter had promised. *Things I've never told.* But was it her obligation to listen?

Part V

HOLIDAY

Released 1983

Reached no. 16 on Billboard Hot 100

Spent 20 weeks on Billboard Hot 100

33

"A PRISON IS A CORPORATION, a world unto itself," said Jefferson D. Blanding, Walter's lawyer. "Entrenched, committed to its own rules and policies. They don't like to make exceptions for *anyone*."

"So I learned," Peter said, "when I called. That's why we're here, in hopes that a two-prong approach might help."

"Here" was Blanding's office in Charlottesville, Virginia, near the bricked-in Main Street mall. It was a Friday, and the children had an in-service day, which meant that teachers reported but students did not. Eliza remembered these from her Maryland youth, but she certainly didn't remember so many of them on the calendar. At any rate, the three-day holiday had given them a chance to drive here on the pretext of a visit to Monticello, a trip so drearily self-improving that Iso didn't smell a rat. Albie was game, if a little vague, about who Thomas Jefferson was. All the more reason to visit Monticello.

"You assume that I'm in favor of this," Blanding said. "I'm not sure I am."

"It's what Walter wants," Eliza put in. She didn't mind letting Peter be the more aggressive one in this conversation, but she liked to keep her hand in, not allow Blanding to think she was some sort of throwback who let her husband call the shots. Peter just had more experience in arguing with people.

"I serve my clients' best interests. That doesn't mean I blindly do their bidding. Walter has not always been the best steward of what is good for Walter."

Eliza nodded. "He wanted to take the stand in his first trial," she told Peter. "He had a different lawyer then and—well, he probably wouldn't have helped himself, insisting that everything that happened was an accident. But that was a very long time ago. In our conversations, he does appear to have changed. He's more thoughtful, more measured."

"Agreed," Blanding said. "Still, I'm skeptical."

What could Eliza say to that? Walter's current lawyer had good instincts. Of course, they hadn't told him what Walter had promised in return for Eliza's visit. Peter saw their decision as strategy, nothing more, but Eliza was also protecting herself against the perception that she was being played by Walter, that he was toying with her. She would not be surprised if Walter was luring her to the prison with a promise he had no intention of keeping. Oh, he would tell her *something,* reveal some nugget of information that fell short of full disclosure, then argue the technicality, claim she had misunderstood. Walter was like a ten-year-old boy that way. Eliza's mother had long believed that Walter had experienced something particularly wounding in his youth and that he reverted to the boy-self when threatened or upset. There had been times, all those years ago, when Eliza had felt older than Walter, or at least more knowledgeable in the ways of the world. She remembered watching him grab a handful of the pastel mints in a bowl by the cash register at a diner, then telling him later, as gently as possible, that he should have used the plastic spoon. He had been humiliated, offended, and gone on the attack. "I'm clean," he said. "I wash my hands after everything, which is more 'n you can say."

He was right about that. Sometimes when Eliza found herself exhorting Albie to wash up, she remembered Walter's criticism of her young hygiene.

Peter asked Blanding: "Does the fact that he's been given an execution date give us more or less leverage?"

"A little more," Blanding said, looking pained. He was sad that Walter was going to die, Eliza realized. Was it a personal sadness, a professional one, or a combination? "But not if there's publicity. If you want to come in there with a reporter, or if you give interviews before or after the fact—they won't want to have anything to do with you."

"Mr. Blanding, I've spent my entire life avoiding this topic. I wouldn't want anyone to know that I've visited Walter."

"Oh, people will know," the lawyer said. "It's a state agency, but it's also just another office, where people gossip about anything out of the ordinary. And it's extremely unusual for a death row inmate to receive a visitor, especially from one of his—" He paused, groping for a word.

"*Victims*," Eliza supplied. "But then, I guess that's the paradox of death row. They don't tend to have many living victims."

The lawyer was not particularly handsome, but he had pale blue eyes, made more vivid by his shirt, and a touching earnestness. "Mrs. Benedict, I understand that you are Walter Bowman's victim. I never forget that. I also don't allow myself to forget that he killed Holly Tackett and Maude Parrish."

Maybe more.

"That makes two of us," she said, and even Peter looked startled at the brittle glibness of her voice, not at all like her, although it was a tone she found herself using more and more with Iso.

"I've represented a lot of men on death row," Blanding said. "They're not monsters, not a one of them. It would be easier, in some ways, if we could say that of them. They have done monstrous things and most don't deny that. Some are mentally ill, although they don't meet the standard that would allow them to plead insanity. Others have IQs so low that it's hard to imagine how they functioned at all in the world. But they all are capable of remorse, and that's what most feel. Especially Walter."

She wanted to believe him. Yet—if Walter had changed, could he answer her other questions? Would he remember the man he was and why he had treated her differently from the others? Assuming there was a new Walter, could he explain the old one?

"Let's cut to the chase," Peter asked. "How does she get in to see him?"

Blanding played with a pen and pencil set on his desk, the kind of item that a child gives as a present, thinking it grand. And his coffee mug was a lumpy, garish green thing, made by loving if not terribly skilled hands. "It wouldn't hurt if you knew someone with some clout in Virginia. Connections are powerful."

Peter stiffened. "I was a journalist before I went into finance. I don't have those kinds of relationships and I'm still not comfortable with them. I don't like trading favors."

"But your bosses, their friends—"

"They don't know about me," Eliza said. "About Walter and me."

"Mrs. Benedict—"

"Eliza, please."

"My two cents? As the execution approaches, your ability to remain anonymous recedes. I'm not saying you're wrong to want to live a life that isn't defined by what happened to you as a teenager. And if you were still in London, or even on the other side of the country, maybe you could do that. Maybe. But the execution is going to shake memories loose, excite interest. People will almost certainly try to track you down through your parents and sister, who *haven't* changed their names."

"You make it sound like I went into hiding," Eliza said, bristling. She had never denied her past. She simply had chosen not to let it be the single thing that defined her.

"Didn't you?" Blanding asked, his manner as mild as his name.

"No. I shortened my name in high school to avoid . . . complications. Then I met Peter, and we decided to marry, and, well, do you know your Jane Austen? Can you imagine what it's like to be wonderfully close to Elizabeth Bennet, if only on legal documents? It's pretty much every Janeite's fantasy."

"It seems to me," Blanding said, "that a woman who loved Austen would be more excited by the prospect of being Elizabeth Darcy."

This was the moment, small and charged, in which Eliza could tell they were deciding if they were going to be allies or adversaries. She laughed, choosing to be an ally. It was an astute comment, funny and informed. She wished Blanding were *her* lawyer.

"I'm sorry," Blanding said. "I didn't mean to suggest you were hiding. I suppose it's more correct to say that you don't wish to be found. Yet sitting in Sussex I, Walter did find you. What makes you think that the *Washington Post* can't?"

"I'm not worried about saying no to the *Washington Post*. I am worried about finding the right way—and time—to talk to my children about this. Our son is already prone to nightmares, and Iso went through this terrible obsession with mortality when she was five or so. There never seems to be a right time to tell them about me."

"And what will you tell them about the death penalty? Will you say that you agree with the commonwealth of Virginia's decision to execute people for certain crimes? Will you inform them that most civilized countries don't put their own citizens to death?"

"How we parent," Peter put in, "is a private decision. Do you have children, Mr. Blanding?" He, unlike Eliza, had missed the clues: the pen and pencil set, the coffee mug.

"Two, an eight-year-old and a three-year-old," he said.

"Well, then you understand that some things are off-limits, not for others to comment upon."

Blanding started to say something, checked himself. "I'll do what I can do because I know it's what Walter wants and I can't see how it will harm him." Again, Eliza felt guilty, wondered if the guilt read on her face. She didn't like deceiving this man. "I don't expect you to understand this, but I've really come to like him. He has such an interesting mind. I like the way he turns over words and phrases. He sees more than most people."

But what, exactly, does he see? What did he see in me?

Peter and Eliza walked back to the hotel, hand in hand. "I could live in Charlottesville," he said, but it was the only time either of them spoke during the walk, and he was just making conversation. Eliza didn't think she could live here, although she didn't blame Virginia for the memories she had of it. Still, it had been odd, skirting Middleburg on the way here. She could tell she and Peter were both weighed down by the secret they had withheld from Blanding. If Walter did confess to her, Blanding would not think her well intentioned. He might, in fact, believe her to be completely disingenuous, a glory hog who had considered only herself in this enterprise. But she could not allow herself to be affected by what Blanding, or anyone, thought of her. She was doing the right thing for the right reason. Almost.

The children wanted to spend the rest of the afternoon at

the indoor pool, delighted as only children can be by the steamy, almost fetid room, with its fogged windows and chlorine smells. Eliza had never really liked swimming. She could do a passable bastard stroke, somewhere between breast and fly, and she was strong enough to swim in the currents of the Atlantic. It had been nice, when Iso was small, to go to the flat, friendly beaches of South Texas, where the steady stream of cars posed far more risk than the lazy wavelets that lapped the shore. But she didn't really care for water. Whereas Peter was in his element, joining the children in the pool. She admired his body, still trim and athletic despite the fact that he had less time to exercise. She wondered if he still admired hers and decided to decide that he did.

"Mommy. Mommy? Mommy, Mommy, Mommy, Mommy?"

"What, Albie?"

"Aren't you going to come in?"

"I didn't bring a suit."

"Then I'll come out."

"That's okay, darling, I'm having fun watching you."

Albie swam-walked back to his father and spent the next half hour squealing happily as Peter flung him away with great force. Peter would move toward the children like a lumbering gorilla, grunting the song about the man on the flying trapeze. Even Iso, presumably too big for such nonsense, begged for a turn, shrieking with laughter. They did this over and over again, never tiring.

Change the sound track and the setting, and it might look terrifying, Eliza thought. But did that work the other way around? Were there terrible things that could appear lovely if framed differently? She remembered a moment in a Piggly Wiggly, when she had been difficult and obdurate, arguing for a snack that Walter had arbitrarily decided was off-limits. This was toward the end, perhaps a day or so before they happened upon Holly on the road. Walter put his hand on the back of her neck, viselike.

"How nice," the checker had said, "to see a brother and sister who are affectionate with one another."

Three days later, he took her to dinner in a nice restaurant, one with linen tablecloths and silver, and told her she could have anything on the menu. Again, the waitress complimented Walter on his solicitous manner toward his little sister.

An hour later, he raped her.

Eliza watched as Albie, then Iso, flew through the air with the greatest of ease, screaming with laughter.

34

TRUDY DID NOT CONSIDER HERSELF a Luddite. She *liked* technology. But she also believed machines required several generations before they became attractive. Televisions, for example, and all their accessories—it had taken years before someone had figured out how to design a system that wasn't a welter of cords and extensions, snaky as Medusa's hair. Computers, too, were hideous when they first came along, and while laptops were smaller, they were still ugly to her way of thinking. Even those clamshells, especially those clamshells, which one was supposed to carry like a purse. As if Trudy would ever own such a purse. And no matter what computer one used, e-mail itself was ugly, begging the eye to skim, flee. She wanted no part of it.

She prided herself on keeping a stock of rich, creamy monogrammed paper, writing notes as necessary. Or picking up a phone—a phone, not a cell—when she had something to say to someone. Her sons had pleaded with her to get an e-mail account, dangling visions of daily photos of the grandsons, more frequent communication. But e-mail, in Trudy's view, wasn't communication. It was a one-sided conversation, zipping back and forth, barely connecting. Terry had an account and she checked it a few times a week, but she never hit the "reply to" button. And, yes, sometimes, there were photos of grandchildren, but they existed only on the screen, she had to sit there if she wanted to look at them, as she didn't have a proper printer for photos. "We could send them to your phone," her sons said, but her cell phone was just a phone, with no other capacity, and it spent most of its life in its little cradle of a charger.

But since Terry's conversation with their Sussex friend, Trudy's mind had returned again and again to a tantalizing detail: *I got you the number. You can put it in a reverse look-up.* She hadn't understood what the woman meant at the time and hadn't wanted to ask, revealing her presence on the line. But Trudy was an old hand at puzzling through things, and she put it together eventually. All she had to do was plug Elizabeth Lerner's number into the computer and there it was, her street and zip. She could even call up photographs. *O brave new world,* she thought.

Trudy had dialed Elizabeth Lerner's number several times since she obtained it, at first hanging on only to hear it ring over and over, then hanging up on the first or second ring. No voice mail, how odd. And why was no one ever home to answer it? She always called on weekends or around supper, the most likely time to find people at home. Did they ignore the calls, thinking she was a telemarketer? Did they have caller ID, which would out her as T Tackett? Idly she picked up her phone, even as she continued to stare at the photograph of the Benedicts' white, nothing-special house. She thought longingly of T'n'T, their farm in Virginia, which had managed to be gracious and comfortable, no small feat when someone has three rowdy sons. The name—she didn't regret it, refused to find belated menace in its pun. The Tacketts hadn't even chosen it, although they had laughed when a friend had made the joke at a party, then later gave them the painted sign they put at the foot of their long drive. She had considered it arch acknowledgment of their good fortune. Trudy always had known that life could blow up at any moment. But perhaps *that* was hindsight.

She listened to the phone ring. She knew the photograph was not live—the trees were green and leafy—but she couldn't help feeling that she was watching the house, that she might see a curtain twitch or a light come on, even hear her own call ringing inside. Answer me. Talk to me.

Not even an hour later, she was standing in front of it. Funny, because the Maryland side of the Beltway always seemed miles, galaxies away, a place she seldom ventured. But the highways had been almost eerily empty. Oh, it was Saturday, she remembered. Terry had gotten up to go play golf, not go into work. She zipped around 495 and across River Road, telling herself that she was bound for Tysons Corner, then the Saks on Wisconsin Avenue.

But she was on Poplar Street. She parked her car and walked around the house. No sign of life. Brazen, uncaring, she let herself in the backyard—the low gate had a latch that she could easily slide open—peered into windows. Children lived here, their detritus was all around. (Really, was it that hard to pick up after children, or get them to clean up after themselves? Trudy had never allowed this kind of disorder.) Elizabeth Lerner had children and, presumably, a husband. This was not the house of a single mother, although that would explain the mess. A dog's bed, a big one—so they had a dog, too. She found herself trying the door handle, testing it to see if Elizabeth Benedict dared to live in an unlocked house, as the Tacketts once had. They had never locked the doors at T'n'T, not when they were in town, and what if they had? Holly had been taken at the foot of their driveway.

The door was locked.

"Are you looking for the Benedicts?"

She almost jumped a foot into the air, more at the sound of the name than the surprise of the voice. Her interlocutor was a man, in his sixties, neatly dressed for a Saturday morning in suburbia, in a short-sleeved shirt and slacks, real slacks, not khakis.

"Yes," she said. "I just happened to be passing through and I'm an old friend, someone they haven't seen for years. I took a chance that they would be here."

"They went away for the weekend, but they expect to be back Sunday night. They asked me to take in the paper. Shame that you missed them."

"That's what I get for not calling first. I'll leave them a note."

She had no intention of leaving a note, but she figured that lie might keep him from describing the incident when the family returned. She even went so far as to walk to her car, take a piece of paper from the pad she kept in the glove compartment, and pretend-scrawl a note. Only somewhere along the way, it ceased to be pretending and became real. After struggling over how to begin—she could not bring herself to use the word *dear*—she wrote:

Elizabeth,

Please call me at your convenience.

Trudy Tackett

After a moment's thought, she included her cell, not the house number.

She stood at the front door, the piece of paper in hand. Once through the slot, it couldn't be taken back. But what could be taken back in this world? Nothing, really. Apologies, trials, even executions, didn't change that. The past could not be undone. Bones healed. Everything else stayed broken forever. *She has suffered, too,* Terry would say during the trial, glancing at Inez Lerner, but Trudy wasn't convinced that the lines etched into her face were anything but evidence of a woman who didn't take care of herself and, by extension, didn't take care of her daughter, who had failed to take care of Trudy's daughter. Trudy hated Inez Lerner on sight. The hippieish clothes, the graying hair, the two bangles she wore on her wrist, which once, just once, clacked together in the courtroom, loud as a gunshot, making everyone jump. *Why are all your children alive?* she wanted to scream. *What makes you so special?* Inez Lerner had not loved her children more, or watched them with more care. Holly had been at the foot of the driveway, not in a park. Holly had been raising money to buy a wig for that unfortunate girl who had lost her hair during chemo, not wandering around aimlessly, just looking for trouble. Even today, she felt the childish complaint rising in her throat, the hot tears of frustration: *It isn't fair.*

Trudy missed Holly every day. Every day. And now she was looking at a shabbier version of the life her daughter might have had. House, husband, children, dog.

She put the letter in the slot, feeling as if she had launched a message in a bottle, something that had no chance of reaching civilization, much less the person who needed to read it. Logically, she knew it was there, waiting for Elizabeth Lerner to come home, that it would strike her as cruel—a bucket of water propped on a door's upper ledge, a rug over a hole in the floor. Yet to Trudy, her note felt insubstantial and flimsy, capable of disappearing without a trace.

That's because what she really wanted to do was strike a match and burn the place to the ground.

35

NORMALLY, WALTER LIKED TO TALK to his lawyer. Blanding was kind and intelligent. He raised Walter's game. He also made Walter feel like he was part of a larger world. He wasn't all-business, far from it. They talked about current events and discussed, within ethical limits, the other men that Jeff represented here. Today, for example, Walter told Blanding again how happy he was that the kid, the grandma killer, had gotten a stay. It wasn't a lie. He was happy for the lawyer. He was happy, in principle, even if he didn't care about the individual involved.

Still, even with that conversational tidbit, Walter had found it trying, talking to Jeff, because he had something to hide. *Are you sure this is a good idea? Is there something you're not telling me?* Walter had come to be a little conceited about his own intellect over the years, especially after repeated intelligence tests showed he was above average. Not genius, or anything extraordinary, but definitely above average, and that had given him confidence that he could hold his own in any conversation, maybe even control them. But it was one thing to control what he said when he communicated with Elizabeth, another to lie to Jeff, with whom he had always been scrupulously honest. Jeff trusted him. He had never asked why Walter had written Elizabeth and arranged to have her on his phone list, or even questioned Walter's story about seeing her in the magazine. (Lawyers didn't even have to know who was on their clients' phone lists, but Walter had told Jeff so it wouldn't look like he was hiding anything.) Still, Walter had never lied to his lawyer before and he felt bad, misleading him now. But if he told him everything—no, he would never allow Elizabeth to come see him.

"I mean, I think it's wonderful that you want to apologize to her in person," Jeff said. "But how it ends up making you feel—well, it depends on what you expect, going in."

I expect she's going to keep me from going to the death chamber, buddy. "What do you mean?"

"Well, she might withhold the, I don't know, emotional experience you expect. I mean, if you want forgiveness or absolution—I don't think you're going to get that. She's nice enough—"

"She always was a nice girl."

"But she's pretty firm in her insistence that people not forget that she was a victim, too."

"She was," Walter said. "She's entitled to feel that way."

"Okay, that's easy for us to discuss in the abstract. But I want you to think about what it will be like, to be face-to-face with her, through the glass, and to hear her say that she won't forgive you, that she can't forgive you. That might make things a lot harder."

Things. That was Jeff's way of saying this was real, that Walter was going to die this time. Twenty-plus years, a literal record on

Virginia's death row, if not in other states. Twenty-plus years, and he wasn't even fifty yet. Who wouldn't do what he was doing, in his situation? Who wouldn't fight for his life?

The girls—the girls had fought, struggled to breathe. He had felt terrible, doing what he did to them. But if they lived, they would have told, and that seemed so unfair. It wasn't his fault. It had taken him a long time to get to a place where he realized that it was possible to feel remorse without accepting the labels that society put on things. He was sorry that he had to kill those girls, *but it wasn't his fault*. He wasn't stupid enough to say that out loud, even to Barbara, although he had confided in her a few details no one knew. To Jeff, he talked only about the remorse, his belated understanding that no one should take another person's life.

But if he had come to that realization all on his own, why couldn't the commonwealth of Virginia have the same epiphany? That was the true unfairness of things. He agreed: It had been wrong to kill those girls because it was wrong to kill, always. *Always.*

He decided to put Jeff on the defensive, make him be explicit: "So this is it, huh? No chance this time of anything stopping it."

"There's always a chance, and you know we'll cover it from every angle. Appeal to the Supreme Court, ask the governor for a commutation."

"Be straight with me."

A pause. "It's hard to see any other outcome at this point."

If only you knew! It was hard not to brag to this earnest young man, a top-flight thinker, about the plan Walter had concocted. It was hard not to tell him that his discovery of Elizabeth's picture, while a coincidence, had happened after months and months of Barbara trying to get a lead on her. (At one point, she had even called her mother and sister, claimed to be an old friend, but they had been appropriately skeptical. He liked Barbara, surely he did, but that voice! You just couldn't imagine a girl like Elizabeth being friends with someone who had that voice.) He knew that Jeff wouldn't approve of his tactics, but he would be pleased with the result, downright proud of him. Jeff put him in the mind of Earl, the mechanic back at his father's place, the one person who seemed to realize that Walter had something to offer. He wondered what had happened to Earl, if he had gotten out of the Marines alive, if he had ever opened up his fix-it business. Did he know of Walter? He hated to think of Earl, reading about him in the paper all those years ago, believing he was a monster, lower than low.

"I understand," he assured Jeff.

"It's just—it would be awful if this meeting didn't bring you the peace you expected."

"I can deal with that, Jeff. It's not about me. It's about her." A beat. "How did she strike you?"

A pause on Jeff's end. "Nice."

"You said that already. That's one of those say-nothing words." Nice was *ice* with an *n* butting in front of it, making it even colder and more colorless. *Nice* was nothing.

"Okay, kind of placid, then. Her husband has the big personality, and she seems to be used to letting him run things."

"You mean, he's bossy? Domineering?"

"No, just very much in charge, the fighter in the family. She doesn't seem to have much appetite for conflict."

Oh, I know that. I'm counting on that.

He didn't press Jeff further on the subject of Elizabeth, feeling that was too risky, might tip his hand. Now, lying on his bunk and staring at the ceiling, the sounds of Sussex I sharp and harsh around him, he allowed himself to remember the affection he had felt for her, almost in spite of himself. Was it love? He wasn't sure it could be called love. But they had something, all those years ago. There was a bond. He could make her do anything. Wasn't that proof of something between them? He had granted her life. If you thought about it, he was kind of a god. And it was time to call that marker in.

36

"WHO'S TRUDY TACKETT?" ISO ASKED.

"How do you know that name?"

They had just crossed the threshold in a cranky heap, tired and worn-out from the trip, in which they had been stuck in a terrible backup on I-66. The precipitating accident was apparently quite bad, according to WTOP, which Peter had switched off after hearing that two people had been killed in the collision. By the time their car inched past the accident site, the ambulances and helicopters had long departed, leaving behind two cars so mangled that it was impossible to imagine anyone surviving the crash. If they had left Monticello earlier, as Iso had urged repeatedly, they might have been here when it happened, their car could be another one in the pileup.

Eliza couldn't help saying that out loud, without the Iso part, hoping her daughter would make that connection. "If we had left earlier, we might have been in this very spot when it happened."

"At least that would have been interesting," Iso said. "Unlike the rest of the day."

Monticello had been a bit of a bust. Iso had attempted to wear her iPod headphones the entire time, and when Peter remonstrated, she had stalked through the tour with a boredom so palpable it felt like a weapon, aimed at them all. Albie, sensitive to his sister's moods, had found it hard to take in the old house, and his confusion about Thomas Jefferson hadn't helped. (Midway through the tour, it became obvious that he thought they were going through George Washington's house. Eliza and Peter really needed to help him with his American history. He could rattle off the Tudor monarchs but couldn't even name the first three presidents.) At any rate, Eliza's nerves were already raw when Iso casually tossed out a name that always made her flinch.

"Trudy Tackett," Iso repeated. "She signed this note that was with the mail, although it's not in an envelope. See? Says she wants you to call her."

Eliza glanced at Peter, knowing the name would not necessarily resonate with him, but hoping he would step up and say something, which she could not imagine doing just now. She felt as if a piece of clay was lodged around her larynx, slowly hardening. Trudy Tackett. As Jefferson Blanding had told her a mere two days ago, she wasn't that hard to find.

"She went to school with your mom," Peter said. "At least, I think that's how you know her. Right, Eliza?"

She nodded, then managed to croak: "Her daughter. It was her daughter I knew."

"Why would she leave you a note?"

"She was probably in the neighborhood." Again, it was Peter who spoke.

Iso had expended about as much curiosity as she could on her mother's behalf. She went into the family room and turned on the television, and Albie joined her at the opposite end of the sofa. He would spend the next hour stealthily closing the distance between them, patiently taking territory one inch at a time. Eventually, he would get too close and Iso would scold: "Get away from me. You smell" or "You breathe too loudly. You make funny noises." Albie would retreat, then start over again. He loved her so much. Why couldn't Iso see that, glory in it? Eliza had felt the same way about Vonnie when they were young, and she bet that Vonnie missed it, regretted the way she had squandered that affection. No one in the world loved you quite the way a younger sibling did.

She and Peter rushed upstairs, as if unpacking their small overnight bag was an urgent, complicated matter, requiring them both. And it felt good, Eliza discovered, to have something to do with her hands, to sort the dirty clothes into piles, to get a wash going.

"I have to admit," Peter said, "I didn't remember who Trudy Tackett was. She's one of the relatives, right."

"Holly," Eliza said. "Holly's mother."

"Oh." Peter knew Holly's significance. Or thought he did. "It could be a coincidence. She doesn't necessarily know that Walter has been in touch with you."

"What did Blanding say? It's an office, like any other. People gossip. Someone at the prison could have told her."

"About the calls. Not about the visit, because it hasn't been arranged."

"For all we know, they listen in on his phone calls."

Bereft of chores, she sat on the bed.

"I would think she wouldn't care, one way or another. Her daughter's murder at least ended in a trial, with a death sentence. What more can she want?"

Eliza shrugged, as if in agreement. But she was thinking: *So much more. She wants so much more. She wants me to be dead, and her daughter to be alive.*

They had spoken only once. It was the second day of Eliza's testimony, and she had eaten something that disagreed with her. It wasn't nerves; her father was felled by the same waves of nausea, this odd feeling of wanting to throw up but not producing anything. About midway through the afternoon, they broke for a recess and Eliza had rushed to the nearest bathroom. She still couldn't get anything to come up, no matter how much she retched.

When she came out of the stall, Trudy Tackett was standing there. She was a pretty woman. Of course, she seemed ancient to Eliza at the time. Funny, because Mrs. Tackett was younger than Inez. But her suit was unusually formal, even for court, and she wore very thick, unbecoming makeup.

"I'm Holly's mother," she said.

Eliza nodded. She was under strict instructions not to speak to any of the spectators, and she assumed that Holly's mother knew the rules. She didn't want to be rude, but she didn't want to do anything wrong. That could lead to a mistrial, the last thing she wanted.

"She was younger than you," her mother said. "A month away from her fourteenth birthday, in fact. We were going to have a lovely party."

Eliza widened her eyes to signify that she thought this a nice idea, a lovely party. She wanted to leave, but Mrs. Tackett stood squarely in her path, and Eliza couldn't see how to go around her without being rude.

"I mean, I know Holly looked like she was sixteen or eighteen. Don't you think we knew that? Her father and her brothers spent most of their lives with their fists balled up, ready to hit men just for looking at her. But she was playing with dolls as recently as two years ago. She wasn't in a hurry to grow up, like some girls. She certainly didn't worship Madonna."

That was one of those stray details that had become something so much larger than it was—the hair ribbon, the gloves and boots Eliza was wearing when she was kidnapped. Now she was defined by those things, and she could barely remember them.

"I didn't worship her," she said, feeling misunderstood. "I . . . liked her. I liked her style."

Her current role models were Molly Ringwald and Ally Sheedy, high-necked blouses and big skirts, brooches and pearls.

"You should have taken care of her," Mrs. Tackett said. "You were older. You knew what was going on."

"I couldn't . . . I didn't . . ."

"You should—"

Another woman pushed her way into the bathroom just then, and Eliza escaped. She never spoke to Mrs. Tackett again, although she felt her eyes on her, the day of closing arguments. (She had not wanted to attend, but the prosecutor had said it would look bad if she wasn't there.)

She always felt that Mrs. Tackett had been interrupted just as she was about to say the words that Eliza feared the most: *You should be dead. Everyone knows that you're the one who should be dead and Holly should be alive. You let her die so you might live.*

Part VI

CRAZY FOR YOU

Released 1985
Reached no. 1 on Billboard Hot 100
Spent 25 weeks on Billboard Hot 100

37

LIKE THE LOVELORN TEENAGER she never was, Trudy kept returning to Elizabeth Lerner's neighborhood—the scene of the crime—over and over again. She would get in her car, intent on nothing more than buying a carton of milk or dropping off Terry's dry cleaning and, next thing she knew, she was crossing the Potomac in a trancelike state. And once a river was crossed . . . well, everyone knew that saying. She did this one, two, three times, and ended up stuck in horrible traffic jams one, two, three times. On her fourth trip, she surfaced from a long blank spell just in time to apply her brakes and avoid rear-ending the car in front of her.

Then she discovered that she could walk to the local Metro stop and take the train all the way up to Bethesda, changing only once, in downtown D.C. It was a long journey, but the D.C. Metro was reliably neat and orderly, and it wasn't dangerous to zone out on the subway; all she risked was missing her stop. But she never missed her stop. In sensible walking shoes, ones purchased for a London trip taken in dutiful honor of their thirtieth anniversary, Trudy made her way to Elizabeth Lerner's house, hoping—for what? A glimpse of her? A confrontation? Could she really walk up to the woman and ask to know why she had not called Trudy? It had been only a week, give or take. But Trudy believed that Elizabeth would have called within the first twenty-four hours if she had intended to respond at all. Why was she ignoring her?

She had not told Terry about these trips. He wouldn't forbid her to make them, but he wouldn't approve, and she found that she still cared about his approval, more or less. She had gone back to hiding her cigarette smoking, for example, and continued to pretend she was taking her Lipitor. When would those subterfuges catch up with her, if ever? If Terry confronted her—difficult to imagine, but it had happened a few times during their marriage—she would say she was trying to even the actuarial odds, given their genders and the age difference. She was tired of outliving people. She felt as if she were going to outlive everyone—her husband, her sons, her grandchildren.

Everyone except Walter Bowman.

The prosecutor said there was no way he could get a stay this time. There may be some pro forma filings at the last minute, an assertion that lethal injection was cruel and unusual, but those would be token protests, lawyers earning their money. Still, it had been disturbing when that one man had been given a stay just last month and the Supreme Court had agreed to hear his petition. Third time's the charm, Terry said grimly.

Unless Elizabeth Lerner had something up her sleeve. Why else would she be talking to Walter? Perhaps she was going to make some big show of forgiveness, issue a public statement about her opposition to the death penalty, make Terry and Trudy the bad guys.

Setting a brisk pace, Trudy began her walk around the neighborhood. She drew absolutely no attention. It had been a long time since Trudy had attracted attention, and she liked to think she had been gracious about that transition. Married young, the first three pregnancies coming so swiftly, she felt she had been on a shelf since her twenties. Interestingly, around the time that Holly entered adolescence—Trudy was in her late thirties, then—she had a second flowering. And although Holly had started drawing increasingly sexualized attention about the same time, Trudy had not felt competitive with her daughter. Quite the opposite. Like a good tennis partner, Holly elevated Trudy's game, inspired her to take more care with her appearance. Her marriage picked up a little charge, especially as Holly began to attend sleepovers and they had the house to themselves for the first time since, well, the first nine months of their marriage, before the arrival of Terry III. Although she was, reflexively, a Democrat, Trudy had felt secure in Reagan's America, secure in Middleburg. It had been a prosperous time, and the bad news—Lebanon, famine, the Unabomber, the Mexico City earthquake, Leon Klinghoffer—seemed so very far away. Or, in the case of AIDS, based on other people's decisions. Terry's gaze was the only one she craved.

In the wake of Holly's death, Trudy became almost too visible, recognized—and therefore pitied—everywhere she went. In Alexandria, she settled into anonymity and was grateful for it. Granted, she couldn't really take anyone new into her life because that would involve telling the story, which was unbearable. Better to have a child who was, in fact, the Unabomber's victim, because that one word was all the shorthand required. Walter Bowman and his crimes fell into some muddy nether region. He wasn't nickname famous, as Terry once observed, not like some serial killers. People in Virginia tended to remember him, but not by name. Once, after the move to Alexandria, Trudy had tried to speak of her life with a neighbor, only to have the woman blurt out: "Oh my God, you were the mother of that beautiful little blond girl." Terry said she should take solace in Holly being remembered that way, but that wasn't being remembered. "Beautiful little blond girl" could be one of many. In that moment, Trudy understood the world at large had lost track of her daughter. It was the *crime* that people remembered, not the victim. Walter's execution would be the last chance to remind the world of a singular life lost.

Lives, Trudy reminded herself. There was the other girl, Maude, possibly more. When she was at her lowest, Terry tried to cheer her up by saying that there were women who didn't know what had happened to their daughters, who had endured even more than she had. Was it wrong that Trudy didn't really give a shit?

She usually allowed herself to walk past the house four times, on a loop of her design. She felt that was credible, that someone might walk that way for exercise. She walked more quickly here than she did in Alexandria, feeling much more purposeful. But she never managed to see anyone coming and going from the house. Perhaps her note had scared them away, sent them into hiding? But, no, the house looked lived in. *Over* lived in.

Today, on her third pass, she decided to do something she had not yet dared. She walked right up to the door and knocked. There was a television on somewhere in the house, clearly someone was home, but it seemed an eternity before footsteps creaked toward the door. She was being inspected through the fish-eye.

"I hear you in there," she said. "I know you're there. Now open up and talk to me, Elizabeth Lerner."

The door opened, but just a crack, and the eyes that met Trudy's were considerably lower than she had expected, far beneath hers. Hazel eyes, in a tanned face. A girl's face.

"I'm not sure you have the right house. My mom's maiden name is Lerner, but she always goes by Eliza."

Oh no, not always.

"Of course," Trudy said. "But someone's old teacher tends to be formal."

"You were my mom's teacher?"

"Yes, at"—amazing, the things that the mind could grab under pressure, the details about Elizabeth Lerner that were always there—"at Catonsville Middle School. She was one of my best students."

The girl frowned, seemingly sullen at being told of her mother's achievements.

"That is, she scored quite well on tests. She wasn't always the most meticulous on her written work, or in keeping deadlines."

"Are you sure you don't mean my Aunt Vonnie? She's the smart one. My mom says she just got by."

Oh, didn't she. "Your mother was always modest. Is she home? May I come in?"

"She's—" The girl was struggling. Her mother wasn't home, but she wasn't supposed to reveal that information. She probably wasn't supposed to answer the door to strangers. "She had to go to my school, but she'll be right back. Right back," she added.

A dog poked its nose through the door opening and gave a tentative growl. Trudy offered her closed fist, allowed the dog to sniff it.

"Shush, Reba."

"Is that your dog?"

"Not really. I would have chosen a better one."

"May I come in and wait for your mother? I don't get up here very often and I'd hate to miss her."

"I don't know . . ."

"You can call her if you like, tell her my name. Tell her Mrs. Tackett has stopped by."

"Oh, Mrs. Tackett. The one who left the note. I thought Mom said she went to school with your daughter."

That hurt, but Trudy didn't care, for the door was now open wide to her.

38

STRANGELY, OUT OF ALL the things that should have bothered her, it was the *logistics* of the call from school that had floored Eliza, at least in the initial moments of trying to take in the information. *Iso had been caught stealing and was suspended from school, effective immediately.* This meant Eliza had to come to school to pick her up, then return for a meeting at two, but that would make her late to pick up Albie for their walk home, so she had to arrange a playdate for Albie, a situation made more difficult by the fact that she didn't really know the mothers of Albie's friends. Desperate, she had done something she had never dreamed she would do—withdrew Albie early and taken him to the Barnes & Noble on Rockville Pike, then parked him in the children's section with strict instructions to sit there, read a book, and speak to no one. If asked where his mother was, he was to insist she was in the store. She gave him Iso's cell phone just in case. Lord knows, it would be a long time before Iso was allowed to use her phone, if ever.

Then it was back to North Bethesda Middle, where she had to sit through the humiliating recital of Iso's transgressions. Stealing, lying—

"About the lying," she put in, wishing Peter could have gotten away for this meeting, but it had been impossible. ("Even if I could get away from work today, I'd never get there in time," he had told Eliza.) "It's my understanding that she lied when asked if she had stolen something."

"Yes, but that hardly mitigates her behavior," said Roxanne Stoddard, magnificent today in a bouclé purple suit.

"No, but—she lied to cover her ass." She flushed for speaking so crudely in front of the exemplary principal. "Sorry. It's just that I understand why she lied, although I don't condone it. We've always told our children that lying is the least acceptable offense." In her disordered, rattled state, she went so far as to think—*And she didn't lie to me, her mother. She lied to you!* As if that mattered. "Still, it's harder for me to understand why she's stealing something she already owns—an iPhone. She has one. Well, not an iPhone, but a perfectly good cell phone."

"Mrs. Benedict—based on what teachers have told me, Iso is a very angry, unhappy girl."

"Well, she's moody. She's an adolescent."

"Yes," the principal said dryly. "I have some experience with adolescents."

Eliza blushed, although she didn't believe that the principal's life among hundreds of young teens gave her any moral authority in this discussion. She may have more quantitative experience, but no one could know more about her children than Eliza did.

"I want to show you an assignment that Iso wrote for English class recently. The teacher asked students to recast a real-life experience as the plot of a well-known television show."

Eliza decided this was probably not the best time to roll her eyes, but really? A television show? Peter would be apoplectic when she told him, probably start talking about private school again.

"This is Iso's story."

The principal passed three sheafs of paper across her desk to Eliza. On the first page, in Iso's almost too-neat handwriting, was the title: *Everyone Loves Albie.*

> *Iso: Let's get a dog.*
>
> *Iso's mother: No, they are dirty and have fleas and Albie might be allergic.*
>
> *Iso's father: I don't have time to walk a dog.*
>
> *Iso: I'll walk the dog.*
>
> *Iso's parents: NO!*
>
> *Albie: I would like to get a dog.*
>
> *Iso's parents: OKAY!*

She skimmed down the page, to the next and the next. "It wasn't anything like this," she said. "It's true, we didn't choose the dog that Iso wanted, but Reba was so forlorn, so needy. But it was Peter's idea—"

"No one assumes it's a factually accurate portrayal of your home life, Mrs. Benedict. I don't think even Iso would maintain that. She was clearly going for humor—in fact, you'll see she got an A, because she fulfilled the main objective, which was working within an existing form."

Great. North Bethesda Middle is training my daughter, thief and liar, to be a sitcom writer. I feel so much better now.

"By the end of the semester, they'll be writing sestinas," the principal said, as if privy to Eliza's thoughts. "Mr. Klemm knows what he's doing. Which is why, given all the other things going on with Iso, he knew to share her written work with me. This is an angry child."

"I honestly don't know what Iso has to be angry about. If she thinks we favor her brother—that's all in her head." The principal kept her gaze steadily on Eliza's face, and she found she couldn't stop talking. "But it is a vicious circle, in some ways. Albie is a sweetheart, very kind and compassionate, he's like a little love sponge, soaking it up, giving it back. Iso has always been cooler, much more self-contained."

"Has she ever told you how distraught she was to leave England?"

"Distraught? Far from it. She treated it as an opportunity, a chance to fashion a new identity for herself."

"Just because she treated it as an opportunity doesn't mean she really feels it is one. She lived in London for six years, Mrs. Benedict, almost her entire school life. She's homesick."

"This is home."

"To you."

Not really, I have fewer friends than Iso.

"Well, she's never said a word to us."

"No, I imagine not. And if it weren't for this, I'm not sure I would understand how desperately she misses it."

The principal passed the contraband iPhone toward Eliza, its screen showing the latest log of dialed calls. The numbers all began with the 011-44 prefix for England.

"But . . . we would have let her call from home. Peter even has Skype on his computer. She could have used that. We encouraged her to stay in touch with her friends."

"Yes, but then she would have had to tell you who she was calling."

"And that would have been so difficult?"

"The texts are rather explicit. Not what people call sexting—I think that's overblown—but a little provocative. And the boy is seventeen," the principal said. "Iso thinks you wouldn't approve."

"Seventeen? *I don't approve.*" She realized her voice was too loud, but she couldn't help herself. Her mind was racing, trying to figure out who the boy was, when the connection had been made. Iso must have been sly about it, because Albie would have spilled whatever he knew, no matter how keenly he yearned for Iso's approval. What had Eliza told Peter, not so long ago? Iso was good at keeping her secrets, no one else's.

"They've been communicating via Facebook, on the school's computer," the principal said. "Iso was sophisticated enough to know how to get around the school's block—you just add an *s* to the http address—but didn't realize that she was still leaving a trail despite cleaning out the cache. She was lectured on this earlier in the semester and she begged the media center director not to turn her in. At the time, the messages and postings were pretty innocuous, so we let it go."

"I actually asked Iso if she wanted to set up a Facebook account when we moved. She said Facebook was queer."

"Clever of her, you have to admit. Because then it never occurred to you to look for her there."

"It never occurred to me to look for *anyone* there. I'm not much for social networking."

The principal's smile was sympathetic. "Look, we had to suspend Iso. We have a zero-tolerance policy on theft. But I think the things happening at school are just a sideshow to the anger she's bottled up. Iso's having a very good time playing Romeo and Juliet, in her mind. My hunch is that this boy didn't become a big thing to her until there was an ocean between them. Iso's not interested in sex. Like most of my girl students, she's fascinated by love. If a flesh-and-blood boy—if this boy—showed up on her doorstep, she wouldn't have a clue what to do. Who were the teen idols of your youth?"

"I listened to Madonna."

"No, I mean who were the safe boys, the ones you felt free to fantasize about when you were Iso's age?"

"Seriously?" Eliza was laughing even before she could get the answer out. "George Michael, in his Wham! incarnation. Can't get much safer than that."

"Yes, and I liked Tito Jackson. All very safe, like these *Twilight* books. In my experience, most girls, smart girls like Iso, are pretty savvy about their limits. They find a way to explore sex and love without putting themselves in harm's way. I'm just sorry that Iso has taken it to this level."

"Me, too," Eliza said.

"Not to pry—but do you talk to your daughter about such things?"

"Sex, you mean?"

"No, sex, the birds-and-bees part, is easy. I was thinking about love."

"Love? Romantic love? I don't know. I suppose it came up sometimes when we read fairy tales together. I actually did my undergrad and some grad work in children's literature. I didn't want Iso to be overly invested in prince charmings. In fact, we read a lot of the Oz books together because the heroines are strong and completely indifferent to romance. But then Albie came along, and I couldn't help noticing how hapless the boys were. The one good boy character turned out to be a fairy princess in disguise. The other one is Button-Bright, and all he does is get lost. . . ."

Her voice trailed off as her words reached her own consciousness. The principal was nodding, not unkindly. Eliza added on a feeble note: "Iso had moved beyond bedtime stories by then, anyway."

"I don't doubt it. And I don't think there's anything the least bit unusual about Iso. It's natural for girls her age to be secretive and sly. Healthy, even. But she crossed a boundary when she stole this phone, and it was important to intervene now. After all, it's not only the phone, but the cost of these calls, which were outside the family's plan. Unfortunately, the girl who owned the phone thought she had lost it and was scared to tell her parents, so this has been going on for two weeks."

"Well, Iso will make restitution. That's easy."

"Yes, but it's not enough. My suggestion and it's just a suggestion? Take her out of the soccer league for the rest of the fall."

"She'll die. She'll hate me."

"She won't die. But, yes, she will hate you for a while. Still, she needs to understand how serious this was."

ELIZA TRIED TO CALL PETER on the way home, but his assistant said he was in the kind of meeting that could be interrupted only in a life-or-death emergency. Eliza was tempted to say, "Well, this is it," but thought better of it. She would have liked to speak to Peter before she confronted Iso back home, but Albie was in the car, and that little pitcher really did have enormous ears. It would be unfair to Iso to discuss her situation in front of her brother. Eliza would go home, invoke the sitcom line, "Wait until your father gets home." (It was quite the day for sitcoms. Eliza felt a laugh track should have been bubbling beneath the scene in the principal's office.) She wouldn't use the phrase ominously, simply make it clear to Iso that this was such a serious matter that it required two parents, united.

"Iso?" she said, coming in through the garage.

"I'm in here, Mom." Her voice showed not a hint of apprehension, which was maddening. She should be a little afraid to face Eliza after a meeting at school.

"Here?" she echoed.

"In the dining room, with your old teacher. We made tea."

Oh, so that's why you're calm. You have a witness. You know I can't bitch you out. Then: *Old teacher?*

She and Albie entered the formal dining room, which the family seldom used. The table had been set for a small but proper tea, the fish-shaped teakettle sitting on a trivet, cookies spread fanlike on a plate. They were Eliza's secret cookies. More stealing? Was Iso trying to impress her mother, or the visitor, an incongruously well-dressed woman who was instantly, tantalizingly familiar to Eliza, her name just on the tip of her tongue, but the context made no sense. Teacher? She didn't remember ever having such an elegant teacher.

"Trudy Tackett," the woman said, standing up and holding out her hand. "I've been enjoying getting to know your daughter. She reminds me so much of my daughter at the same age."

39

WALTER WAS OUTSIDE FOR HIS hour of recreation for the first time in almost a week. Legally, the men on Sussex I were supposed to get an hour a day outside, but something was always coming up. They claimed they found a weapon, put the whole place in lockdown, then they said there was a piece of fence that needed repair, although they could have just not used that particular dog run, as Walter thought of the individual recreation yards the men used. Today, for example, there was no one on either side of him, no way to talk, or play a hand of cards. That was okay. He wasn't feeling very sociable today. He was happy to be with his own thoughts, feel a little light on his face. He always had looked better with a tan, bad as it might have been for his skin, according to Barbara.

Back in the day, when Walter realized what his future was—what his *lack* of future was—and found that he could accept it, his first thought was: *I'll probably learn to play chess.* He wasn't sure where this idea came from. Like most people, he knew what he knew about prison from the movies, but this was before *The Shawshank Redemption,* before *The Silence of the Lambs,* although he now knew about both films from talking to men who had arrived here later. The one prison movie that Walter could have described in detail was actually about a juvenile facility, and no one there was playing chess, that was for sure. *Bad Boys,* with Sean Penn. He had never met another person who had seen the film, not since he was inside. Say *Bad Boys* and people immediately assumed you were talking about those other movies, which came way later.

Elizabeth had seen *Bad Boys,* though. She shouldn't have—it was R-rated and she was only thirteen when it was released. He told her as much, but let the lecture drop because he was keen to know what she thought of it.

"I don't know," she said. "I like Sean Penn, but I wish he would do more movies like *Fast Times at Ridgemont High*. This one was so depressing."

"That movie where the girl took her top off?"

"Yeah. He was funny in that."

"He was stoned."

"His character was." Oh so prim and proper, as if he didn't understand the difference.

"I just don't think that's funny, being high," he said, and they had dropped the subject. They never agreed on movies or music. Still, he wished they could have talked more. He wanted to ask her if she thought the movie was right, about how much rape there was in prison, or if that was only in the juvenile places. Even then, in the back of his mind, he knew it was going to be prison or death for him, and he was actually more scared of the first. He could imagine death. He had seen death. He couldn't imagine life in a cell.

But over the weeks, months, it took the system to sort out his crimes and decide how to punish him, Walter had come to understand and accept the contours of his life. *Contours*—a lovely word, exactly what it sounded like, a big round vase. He wasn't going to be found innocent, not in the case of Holly or Maude, and that was all because of Elizabeth, the state's star witness. Without her, they wouldn't have had anything. She had found him at Maude's grave, she had been there the night Holly died. It was lucky that he hadn't given her specifics of the other things he had done. Oh, he had made vague references, especially in the beginning, when he had to get her to obey him. "If you knew the things I'd done . . . I've snapped a girl's neck before and I'll do it again." But he had been cagey enough to withhold the specifics, and she couldn't tell folks anything more than what she had seen. If only he had killed *her*—but he hadn't, and that was that. Certainly he had known what would happen if they were caught, and he had realized, after Holly died, that such an outcome was more likely. Holly wasn't the kind of girl whose disappearance and death went unavenged. This time, he had stolen a princess, and the kingdom was going to rise up, outraged. Sure enough, he was in custody less than forty-eight hours later, and that began the second half of his life, the part spent behind bars.

Still, in the early years, his days had some variety. There were the trials and, in the case of Holly, appeals and retrials. The first retrial had been filed before the twenty-one days expired, and no one could complain about that. Stupid woman juror had talked about the penalty phase, said she knew for a fact that he wouldn't get death in Maryland, so they had to give it to him in Virginia. And the bitch would have lied, too, perjured her way through the investigation if she could have, but there were other jurors who were honest enough to admit the conversation had taken place. Then he had petitioned on the grounds of incompetent counsel, which hadn't gotten him a new trial but had gotten him Jefferson, who was quite the busy little beaver. He was the one who had started poring over maps and begun to question whether Walter was in Virginia or West Virginia when Holly died. Yes, he knew folks were outraged when they got the order to send the surveyors out, that they talked about technicalities, how it was just a line on a map. But, hell, who wouldn't want to be on the right side of a line that was literally the difference between life and death? If that campsite was on the West Virginia side, then he should have been tried in West Virginia, and West Virginia had no death penalty. Who could blame a guy for trying?

Eventually, life had settled into a slow gray haze. He did some of the things he set out to do. He read a great deal, especially military history. He practiced yoga. He corresponded with people who wrote to him, although no one had the staying power of Barbara LaFortuny. It seemed that the people, the women, who contacted him wanted something he simply couldn't give. He thought about a religious conversion, but he found he believed less and less as time went on and he respected faith too much to fake it. If there was a God, then the world would make more sense. That much seemed clear to him.

But chess? No. He tried it, especially during that period when that nice army retiree was next to him in the yard. That guy, Hollis, said it was possible to hold a chessboard in your head and talk the moves. Over time, Walter learned to do that, but it was all he could do. The strategy of chess—the necessity of sacrifice, the impossibility of keeping every piece safe—bothered him. He hated sending those little pawns out into the world. And the games were long. He liked things that moved faster.

This, his dance with Elizabeth—it had gone at just the right pace. True, he had played it a little close to the edge, as Barbara kept saying. Elizabeth was due at the prison next Saturday, and he was to be transferred Monday morning to Jarratt, his third trip to the Death House. In fact, no matter what Elizabeth decided, he would still probably have to make that trip, but he didn't mind. At least it was a variation in routine and it would end up making him the stuff of legend. Walter Bowman, the only man to come back from the Death House three times. He would be seen as invincible.

And if she didn't cooperate, as Barbara kept fretting? They would still have enough time to sic the reporter on her, to let her see how quickly *her* world could be broken. But he hoped it didn't come to that. It would be much nicer if she would just see that there was a right thing to do and she had to do it. He had no desire to antagonize Elizabeth, nor hurt her. But he was trying to stay alive and all was fair, etc., etc.

He had really come to enjoy their conversations these past few weeks and wondered if she felt the same. He wasn't ignorant. He knew the pain he had caused her and didn't expect her to understand that there had been pain for him, too. When they first began to speak, he was intent on his plan, his agenda, and couldn't loosen up much. But as he got into the swing of things, figured out the rhythm of their talk, just how hard he could push, he had risked a few digressions. He had told her about his reading and how he had finally read *Travels with Charley,* which hadn't been at all as she had described it. He had teased her about Madonna, her big idol, and asked if she went to her last concert in rubber bracelets and lace leggings. Her present life was clearly off-limits, and she shut him down if he probed too much, or dropped hints about what he knew. But they did, in fact, have a shared past.

Once, only once, had he invoked Holly. "You didn't like her much," he said, and she had become heated, told him she didn't want to discuss Holly. But he knew he was right. Elizabeth *hadn't* liked Holly. She was fearful of being displaced by her and—she was right to be. Holly was the one he wanted. Elizabeth was the one he got. Further proof that life wasn't fair. And proof that he was long overdue for a lucky break. Not just overdue, but utterly deserving.

40

ELIZA EASED HER BODY INTO BED, joints aching as if she had completed a marathon. She had, in a sense, run a marathon of mothering today. A biathlon, if one threw Trudy Tackett into the mix, only what would you call the second event?

Without saying a word, Peter reached for her shoulders and began to knead them. She was grateful he didn't want to talk further about the afternoon, that he knew to leave her in peace.

"You didn't call," Trudy had said, almost accusingly. It seemed to be Eliza's day to face down older women who were disappointed in her, in her manners, in her parenting. "I waited, but when I didn't hear from you within the first few days, I knew you weren't going to call."

"I didn't have anything to say."

"To me. It's my understanding that you've been speaking quite a bit to another old acquaintance of ours."

Eliza was almost grateful then for the humiliation of the trip to North Bethesda Middle School. It gave her a reason to speak to Iso, if not Albie, in the controlled measured tone she needed. "Iso, go to your room. I don't think you'll be surprised to find out that you're grounded again. We'll talk more about this later. Albie, Reba's been cooped up for a while, as have you. Why don't you take her into the backyard?"

Both children did as they were told, although Iso seemed puzzled, as if her mother's reactions were hard to fathom. Eliza waited for the whine of the back door, the slam of Iso's bedroom door. But the latter was actually closed with quiet decorum. It was so quiet that Eliza went halfway up the stairs to make sure the door was shut, then came back and closed off the dining room.

"What did you tell her?"

"*She* told me. I'm the mother of a childhood friend—according to you. She has lovely manners. Is that the English education? She talked a great deal about London."

"Yes, she misses it." *Or so I just learned,* Eliza thought. Did Iso confide in everyone but her mother? Could Trudy tell her about this seventeen-year-old Simon with whom Iso had been exchanging texts and calls on her pilfered phone? "What did you tell her? What do you want, Mrs. Tackett?"

"I want to make sure that you're not up to anything."

"Up to anything?"

"I know you're speaking to him. Don't deny that."

"I didn't deny it. Not that I'm accountable to you."

Trudy Tackett's composure was hard fought, which became apparent as it cracked. "You most certainly are. My daughter would be alive if it weren't for you."

"No," Eliza said. "No." She cocked her head. Was that a door opening in the hall? Had Albie and Reba returned to the house? She lowered her voice. "I couldn't save Holly. I'm sorry if it seems that way to you, but it's true."

"Save her? You were an accomplice. You lured her into his truck. If it weren't for you, she never would have spoken to him. She knew better than to engage with some strange man. You made everything possible."

"Mrs. Tackett—it's not my fault that I was there. It's not my fault that I had gotten used to doing what he told me to do. I was fifteen, not much older than your daughter."

"Holly was young for her age. She was a child, no matter what she looked like, and you offered her up to that monster."

Eliza held Iso's cooling mug of tea in her hands. The worst thing about this conversation was—she understood. She knew what Trudy Tackett felt, and she couldn't fault her for it. If Iso had been harmed under the same circumstances, Eliza would be inconsolable, desperate to find reasons, someone to blame. Where would her anger and rage go? It would cut a path to the sea.

"I'm sorry. You have to believe that. But you also have to believe that I was as much Walter's victim as anyone else."

"Then why are you talking to him? And considering a visit, last I heard."

She must know someone inside the prison. Certainly, neither Jefferson Blanding nor Barbara LaFortuny would confide in Trudy Tackett. "It's what he wants."

"Why do you care about what Walter wants? You were his victim, as you said. What hold does he have on you?"

She was tempted, of course, to tell Mrs. Tackett what Walter had promised, to let her know that she was on the side of the angels, beyond reproach. She hadn't killed Holly, but she hadn't saved her, either. Was that the same thing? She had resolved to live. Was her decision to live the same as willing Holly to die? It was a question beyond psychology, beyond philosophy, beyond theology. She had chosen to live, which she believed meant doing whatever Walter said. Holly was the one who had fought and run.

"I don't, not really. I have my reasons to see him, but they're my reasons."

"He's not to be trusted."

"With all due respect, I don't need you to tell me that, Mrs. Tackett."

"You're not to be trusted."

That was unfair. At least, she thought it was unfair. She felt feverish, then all-over chills. The flu season had started early this year. Great, all she needed was the flu, when the visit to Walter was so near. Would a prison stop her from entering if it was determined that she was contagious?

"Mrs. Tackett, I don't know what you want, and I'm not sure I could provide it even if I did. I can't make Holly alive. I can't. Don't you think I've revisited, time and again, what I did. What I *didn't* do? But I was a victim, too. I was."

Even to her own ears, she sounded unpersuasive.

"Your children—they don't know, do they?"

"No."

"Is that because you're ashamed?"

"It's because I want them to feel safe."

"No one is safe in this world, ever. I proved that to you today, didn't I? Your daughter let me into your home, simply because my name was familiar to her. I could have been anyone. I could have done anything. I could have hurt your child."

A sudden memory. The Lerners were in a beach town where parking was at a premium and the street was crowded. Eliza couldn't have been more than seven. Her father started to back out of his parking place just as a little boy burst away from his mother and ran behind the Lerners' car. Her father stopped in time, but the mother turned on him, screaming. Later, as they crossed the main boulevard, the same woman leaned out of her car and yelled: "I ought to run over your kids, see how you feel about it."

"Your husband was an army surgeon, wasn't he? Assigned to hospitals where he treated casualties from Vietnam, as I recall. Was it only when your own daughter was killed that you figured out the world wasn't safe? Or was that simply when you began to care?"

"You think you care. You think you know. Believe me, you don't."

"That's probably true."

Mrs. Tackett bit her lip, apparently more offended by Eliza's concession than anything else she had said. She gathered her purse and stood to leave. "The book—the book said you might have been his girlfriend."

"The book is wrong. He raped me."

"But Holly and the other girl"—the other girl. Couldn't she hear herself? Was it asking too much that she know Maude's name? "They never found any proof of sexual assault."

"He wore a condom. At least he did with me. I can't speak for the others."

"A rapist who wore a condom. But we only have your say-so for that."

"My say-so? Do you think I'm a liar, Mrs. Tackett?" She felt the color rising in her cheeks, a pulse pounding in her temples, her neck.

"I didn't trust you then, and I don't trust you now. I've waited a long time for justice, and it just seems terribly coincidental that you're talking to Walter now, when he's scheduled for execution."

"What would be justice in your eyes?"

She steeled herself to hear: *For you to die and for my daughter to come back to life.* But Trudy Tackett was not that cruel.

"This. The execution. This is what Terry and I get. It's not enough, but it's all we get. Please don't interfere."

"I assure you—"

"Your assurances don't carry much weight with me. I'm sorry if that sounds rude, but it's true. You've never been completely truthful about what happened. No one's ever called you on that. But now I have."

"And do you feel better?"

Trudy Tackett had to think about this. "Never."

LYING IN BED WITH PETER, who had fallen asleep even as his hands worked her shoulders and stroked her hair, Eliza wondered if Mrs. Tackett—she could never call her Trudy, nor had she been asked to, she realized—was replaying the conversation in her head, in her bed. Was Dr. Tackett with her? Was he still alive? Yes, she had spoken of him in the present tense. Did he know what his wife had done today, what she had been doing? She had been to their house at least once before, delivering the note that Eliza had mistakenly ignored, and Eliza supposed she was the source of the off-hour calls on the Walter phone, as she thought of it.

The thing was, Mrs. Tackett wasn't wrong. Eliza had never told everything. The part about McDonald's—Eliza had been forced to testify about that in open court, the prosecutor reasoning that it would seem far more damaging if the defense introduced it. Not that Walter's overmatched attorney knew what to do with the information. His only objective seemed to be to get Eliza off the stand as quickly as possible. But the fact was, after she had seen the prosecutor's reaction, not to mention her own parents' momentary dismay, Eliza had stopped being completely forthright about what had happened during her last forty-eight hours with Walter. She didn't lie. Even she knew she was no good at it. But, like the daughter she would one day have, she was exceptional at keeping secrets, and that was the path she had chosen.

Certain things would remain unsaid. No one was ever going to look at her that way again.

After their McDonald's supper, their unhappy meals, they had driven up a switchback in the mountains, near the national park, but not a part of it. Walter hadn't wanted to pay to enter the park, much less interact with the ranger at the gate. It was dark, and they had to move slowly, the headlights catching deer, who looked malevolent to Eliza. Holly was weeping openly, constantly by then. Eliza yearned to comfort her but didn't know how. She tried, at one point, to pat her shoulder, only to have Holly recoil as if Eliza intended harm.

Once he found a place to camp, Walter set up the tent he had bought at a Sunny's Surplus and unzipped one of the sleeping bags, telling the two girls to lie on it. The night was chilly, but Eliza understood that Holly wanted no contact with her. "I'd give you both sleeping bags," Walter said, "but I need something to pad the bed of the truck, if I'm going to sleep there and give you your privacy." Eliza curled up into a ball, shocked by the cold, wondering how much longer they could sleep outside at this rate. The tent was another one of Walter's big ideas. It had been expensive, but he had argued it would pay for itself quickly. Only, it hadn't, not by a long shot. He hadn't realized, when he bought the tent, that most camping sites, the ones with showers and restrooms, had charges, too. It had been days since he had landed any work. Holly's money was the first real cash they had known in a while. She wondered how much there was, if they might check into a motor court the next night—

"Elizabeth?" Walter had entered the tent and was standing over them.

"Yes?"

"Go sit in the truck for a bit. I want to talk to our new friend here."

She did. She always did whatever Walter told her to do. She went and sat in the truck. Not in the bed, as Walter had probably intended, but in the cab, in her usual seat, the windows tightly rolled up. Still, she couldn't help hearing what happened next. Screams, sobs, a terrible bellow, like a lion's roar, then a streak of white, which must have been Holly's hair flying behind her as she ran, Walter not far behind her. She studied the keys in the ignition, which hung from a chunk of turquoise. Even if she could figure out the clutch, she could never drive back down that switchback. Still, she reached for it, flicked it, hoping to turn on the heater. No, you had to press the clutch in to turn the engine on, and Walter would be mad if she used just battery power. She slid behind the wheel, managed to turn it over after a few tries, then returned to her seat. Warm air filled the car, along with the sounds of a country song, "Have I Got a Deal for You." She and Walter had worked out a compromise on the radio. He controlled it for forty-five minutes and then she got fifteen. He said that was fair because he was older and it was his truck. He said he really didn't have to let her listen to those pop stations at all, that he was a good guy. He told her they were bad girls, Madonna and Whitney Houston and the Mary Jane Girls and Annie Lennox, and even Aimee Mann, although all she did was let the world know that her boyfriend was hitting her. He didn't like any of the songs that Eliza liked except for one, "Everybody Wants to Rule the World." When that one came on, he would nod in agreement, say it was very true. He also liked—

"Why'd you turn the engine on?" Walter asked. His face was scratched, and he was breathing hard. "You know better than that. You're wasting gas."

"I was cold."

"Then why are you still shivering?"

She hadn't even noticed. But she was shivering, and her teeth were chattering so loudly it was amazing she could hear the music at all.

Part VII

EVERYBODY WANTS TO RULE THE WORLD

Released 1985
Reached no. 1 on Billboard Hot 100 on June 8, 1985
Spent 24 weeks on Billboard Hot 100

41

"DO YOU WANT TO STOP?" Vonnie asked. "There are a bunch of places at the next exit, and we're making good time."

"I'm not hungry."

"There's a Dairy Queen." She drew out the syllables, knowing what tempted Eliza. "And a Cracker Barrel."

"That's okay."

"Who knows? Maybe we'll find a Stuckey's."

Eliza began to laugh, almost in spite of herself. "The infamous peanut log, which you insisted on having—"

"We both wanted it."

"And it was awful and Daddy copped one of those attitudes he had every now and then, said we had to eat it, because we had been adamant about wanting it, that it would be our treat every day of the vacation until it was gone—"

Vonnie put on their mother's voice. "Oh, Manny, I'm sure the girls have learned their lesson." She switched to a lower octave. "They must learn proportion in some things, to stop being so wasteful. Children are starving."

"So, on the second night at the—what was it called?"

"The Martha Washington Inn. In Abingdon." Vonnie's memory always amazed Eliza, but maybe it was just another facet of Vonnie's certainty about everything. She believed she was right, and no one called her on it. "They took us there because it had a good theater and they were going through one of those phases where they thought we were philistines."

"Not you, never you."

"Yes, me too. Daddy thought I had atrocious taste in my recreational reading, and you didn't read at all when you were young. So they took us to Abingdon to see *Of Mice and Men*. Which was pretty good, but what we all remember is what happened when you and I tried to flush that Stuckey's peanut log down the toilet in the Martha Washington Inn's quaint antique bathroom. If only we had used the ceramic bedpan that was provided for purely decorative reasons!"

Of course. That was why Eliza had started reading Steinbeck a few years later. Because the play had moved her, all of eleven years old at the time. It was 1981, the first year of the Reagan administration, and their parents felt like exiles in their own country, out of step with the times and the mores. Their father was prone to moods like this, a situational depression generated by the culture around him. It was as if he saw his children being borne away on a stream of cheap toys and stupid sentiment. As a parent, Eliza understood better now. She often felt the same way about the things that Iso and Albie coveted, their susceptibility to trends and advertising. But she was less inclined to counter as aggressively as her father had, to insist on trips to Gettysburg and Antietam and the Franklin Institute in Philadelphia. The trip to Monticello notwithstanding, as that had been more of a cover for the need to go to Charlottesville.

If Eliza and Peter had been inclined, they could have married *this* trip to a visit to Williamsburg and Busch Gardens. Instead, they had claimed that Peter and Eliza were going on a getaway to Richmond, which had been written up in the *New York Times* as an ideal weekend retreat. They assumed the children could stay with their grandparents, but it turned out that Manny and Inez had their own plans for the weekend, a trip to the Greenbrier in West Virginia, and Eliza could not bear to disturb their genuine getaway for her fake one. Instead, she called Vonnie, who declared she would be happy to stay with her niece and nephew. But Peter countered that it might be better for the two women to hit the road together. "No knock on your sister," he said, "but I would be distracted beyond all reason, wondering if she would remember to pick Albie up at school on time. Besides, Iso's still grounded, and she'll find a way to get around Vonnie. Your sister may be able to go toe-to-toe with most secretaries of state and the chairman of the Fed, but she'd be outwitted by a thirteen-year-old intent on making contact with some pimply boy in North London."

Eliza was pretty sure that this *was* a knock on her sister, but she decided not to fight about it. The two hadn't been alone for a long time, perhaps not since Eliza's children were born. They had seen more of Vonnie in London than they had since they had moved back to the States because Vonnie's work brought her there more often than it did to Washington. Even then, their visits tended to be dinners at London restaurants where people were constantly swanning up to Vonnie and kissing both her cheeks. Vonnie always chose the restaurants, so presumably she preferred that kind of atmosphere. She found multiple excuses not to come out to Barnet for dinner—so very far, and the Underground didn't run that late, never mind that she could have spent the night in their spare bedroom, but she always had early meetings the next day. No, she met Eliza and Peter in the trendy restaurant of her choice, then sent them home weighed down with expensive, but not-quite-right, gifts for the children.

It was 9 A.M. and they had been on the road since seven, anticipating a fearful journey past the famous Capital Beltway knot called the Mixing Bowl. Although Eliza knew it only by its reputation, as delineated in the "on the eights" traffic reports on WTOP, she feared it. The Mixing Bowl was like the soulless killer in one of those serial horror films. It rested at times, but it never died. Eliza decided they should leave as early as possible in order to avoid rush hour. To her amazement, traffic in D.C. was quite heavy at seven, but they were going against the flow and sailed through the dreaded Mixing Bowl with such ease that she almost felt a twinge of disappointment. They would reach Richmond well before lunchtime, hours before they could check into their room. They could have left Saturday morning, but visiting hours were relatively early. Eliza, advised by Barbara LaFortuny, had decided it was better to arrive a day early, then make the short trip from Richmond, past a town amusingly known as Disputana and into Waverly, home to Sussex.

Not that Barbara had ever been allowed to visit Walter, she told Eliza. But she knew other men at Sussex I and II, and she was familiar with the procedure. Her voice had sounded wistful, actually, when she spoke of Eliza's trip. "I've never met him. Can you imagine? All these years and I've never seen him, face-to-face. Yet I know him as well as I know anyone."

It had been hard not to ask: "And just how well do you know anyone, Barbara?"

"Did we ever come to Richmond when we were young?" Eliza asked Vonnie now. The city that was coming into view seemed vaguely familiar.

"I don't think so. We drove through, on one of my college trips, when I went to check out Duke."

"I'd forgotten about your college trips, how the whole family went along."

"That was because both Mother and Father wanted to go, and they couldn't leave you at home alone."

"Really? I didn't remember that part. I thought you insisted they both go, said you needed their input."

Vonnie laughed. "Does that sound like me? I didn't even want to go on college trips. I knew Northwestern was the right place for me, but they said I had to apply to at least five schools and visit each one. I picked the other four knowing I wouldn't like them as much as Northwestern—UNC, Duke, Bennington, and NYU. A big state school, an idiosyncratic almost-Ivy, a private school on a par with Northwestern, and a big-city school. It made me look open-minded. But I wanted a strong journalism program and a strong theater department, and only Northwestern had both."

"So you went through that whole charade and put them through all those trips, your mind made up the entire time?" It was all too easy to imagine Iso doing something similar.

"Why not?"

"Wouldn't it have been simpler to tell them how you felt?"

"No, it would have been simpler for *you*. I broke them in, Elizabeth." Vonnie was prone to use the old name when discussing their childhood. "All the privileges that you took for granted—I won them for you. I bet you weren't told that you had to apply to at least five colleges and visit all of them."

"No, but I didn't have your grades, your opportunities. I had to have a safety school. A safety-safety, even. I still don't know how I got into Wesleyan."

Vonnie coughed-laughed.

"What?"

"Oh, seriously, Eliza. You can't be that naive."

"I don't know what you're talking about."

"Your essay. I helped you punch it up, remember? You all but told them what happened to you."

"I did *not*."

"Yes you did."

"My essay was about Anne Frank."

"And your personal connection to her. It was subtle—especially after I helped you revise it—but there could have been no doubt in the minds of the admissions officers that you had first-hand knowledge of what it was to be held captive. That you were a victim of a brutal crime, with that hard-earned knowledge that people are not basically good."

"That's just not true."

Vonnie shrugged, fiddled with the radio, probably looking for the local NPR affiliate or even, God help them, C-SPAN. The prime minister's "question time" was one of the highlights of Vonnie's week, although Eliza knew that was usually broadcast on Sundays. "I'm not criticizing you," she said. "You're entitled to use your experience."

"I've never *used* it."

"You've never really had to. It's always there, like . . . like . . . some huge dog, sitting at your side. A big dog, that never barks or growls or shows its fangs, but it's so huge, who would dare? You've effectively been spared from criticism for twenty years now. You're untouchable. Like—to use a reference from your world—Beth in *Little Women*. So good, so sweet and with that horrible destiny hanging over her head."

"Spared by whom? Only you, our parents, and Peter know about me. And our grandparents, but they're gone. No one else can see this dog. If you want to talk about how you feel, have at it. But don't put it on me."

"Okay, fine. I'll own my feelings." Vonnie paused. She was

going to say something difficult, Eliza realized, the kind of thing that could never be unsaid. "From the day you were taken, I've always felt that our parents became less interested in me, and my achievements. They almost lost you, so you're more precious to them. They can't help it. They try, because they're smart and compassionate people, but nothing I do can compare to what you give them simply by existing. And, no offense, Eliza, but existing is pretty much all you do."

It was the last bit that stung. Until then, she had been okay.

"I'm a mother and a wife. You probably couldn't survive a day in my life. In fact, the reason we're making this trip is because Peter didn't think you could handle a day in my life." That was cruel and would only damage the already tenuous bond between her sister and her husband, but Eliza was too angry to fight fair.

"Don't twist this into some mommy-war argument. You know I'm not that simplistic. You . . . float through life. You let life happen to you. I think you're a great mother, and I know you put a lot of energy into what you do. But you live the most reactive life of anyone I know, Eliza. Jesus, if there's one thing I would have learned from your experience, I think it would be to never let anyone else take control of my life. Instead, you've handed yours over. To Peter, to the children. And now you're giving it back to Walter Bowman."

"I'm going there because he's agreed to tell me what he's never told anyone else. How many girls he killed, where they are."

Vonnie was silent for a few minutes, and Eliza focused on the car's GPS, which was narrating their way to the B and B, not having an alternate location to offer. She hated the GPS voice. It always sounded a little smug to her. She rather enjoyed it when construction or some other unanticipated problem put the GPS in the wrong, not that the voice ever admitted that she had screwed up.

"And then what?" Vonnie asked.

"What do you mean?"

"He confesses to you. So what? Has it occurred to you that it won't be considered valid if his lawyer isn't present? That it might not settle anything, just stir things up? It's occurred to Peter, I can tell you that much."

So Peter and Vonnie had discussed this, outside her hearing.

"When did you and Peter hash this out?"

"Last night. He was up late, working. As was I. I went downstairs to scare up a glass of wine. You know, someone should tell Peter that just because wine is expensive and French, doesn't mean it's good."

Oddly, that offhanded criticism softened Eliza's anger. It, at least, was classic Vonnie, careless and thoughtless.

"Back when we were teenagers, you once said that everything would be about me from now on. Isn't it possible that your own perceptions became reality? That you see what you look for?"

"Yes," Vonnie said. "But isn't it also possible that I'm right? That I've lived my entire life in my sister's shadow?"

"Not in the world at large."

"Fuck the world at large. It's the family I care about."

That was news. "Are you worried that what I'm doing will become public? That all the old stuff will be dredged up again?"

"No. I know that's not what you want."

"So why are we talking about this?"

"I don't know. Maybe we're talking about it because it's always there and yet we never have. Maybe it's not a big dog but just the old clichéd elephant in the room. I've always understood that what happened to you happened to you. But it happened to the rest of us, too. To Mom and Dad. To me. We were there. Not Peter. Yet it's Peter whom you trust, more than any of us. It's Peter who shapes your life. You follow him wherever his job leads him, make the sacrifices necessary to make his career possible, even as you give up on your own."

"Vonnie, this may be the hardest thing for you to understand, but I never considered dropping out of graduate school a sacrifice. If I hadn't withdrawn, I'd probably still be there, trying to write a thesis on the children's literature of the 1970s, and bored to tears. I learned a long time ago that I just didn't have that much to say about Judy Blume's *Forever* and why a boy would name his penis Ralph, given its associations to vomiting. Talk about semiotics."

Vonnie laughed, and the air cleared. They continued to laugh throughout the day, old stories bubbling up to the surface. The Stuckey's log (again) and their attempt to feign innocence as peanut-fouled water overflowed their bathroom at the charmingly quaint Martha Washington Inn. More memories followed throughout the day in Richmond, as they strolled through the fan district, ate dinner at the *New York Times*–anointed charcuterie restaurant. Vonnie remembered the terrible woman who had threatened to run them down at the beach, but also how Mr. Sleazak, their society painter neighbor back in Roaring Springs, had asked Inez to pose nude for a portrait, saying it would be "Just for me." It was a most satisfactory day and one that had done the impossible—taken Eliza's mind off tomorrow. She wouldn't be surprised if the fight itself had been Vonnie's attempt to distract her. She was a good sister, in her way, and her way was all she had.

But that evening, as Eliza tried to fall asleep in a strange bed, away from Peter, Iso, and Albie, she found herself reviewing the day's events. Of all the funny stories she and Vonnie had shared, almost every one came from *before*. Was that because Vonnie had left for school? Or because the Lerner family lost its ability to be silly after Eliza came home? Strange, but she had never considered until now the totality of what Walter had taken, from all of them. From the day she came home, the Lerners had lived with a sense of remission, grateful yet skittish. They were well today, but that could end tomorrow. Of course that was true of every happy family. The difference was that the Lerners *knew*. Having been unlucky once, they could be unlucky again. There was no protection, no quota system when it came to luck. It was like that moment in math when a child learns that the odds of heads or tails is always one-in-two, no matter how many times one has flipped the coin and gotten heads. Every flip, the odds are the same. Every day, you could be unlucky all over again.

42

"BACK AGAIN, MISS LAFORTUNY?" asked the young woman at the Hampton Inn's front desk.

"You know me. I like to check on my boys."

The clerk, a sweet-faced girl who should have taken better care of herself—everything about her appearance screamed poor nutrition and lack of exercise—smiled noncommittally. Like most people that Barbara met, she seemed torn between admiring her advocacy work and being horrified by it, with horror having a slight edge.

"How many you got now?"

"Just three, and they never let me see the one on death row. But I have the two others, and I am allowed to visit them from time to time. If they're good. And I'm good."

"I'm sure you're always good, Miss Barbara," the girl said. Not even two hundred miles from Baltimore and yet the manners were markedly different here.

"Oh, you'd be surprised. I can be a rabble-rouser."

"I bet you can," the girl said agreeably, going through those mysterious computer clicks that seem required of every transaction these days. Barbara wondered if teaching, too, now required moving through computer screens. Grading was probably done electronically, come to think of it. In her day, she had pressed hard, in ink, so her judgment would pass through multiple sheaves of paper. Cs. She had mainly given Cs, which had been slightly better than most of her students deserved. She'd never make it in today's more lenient environment.

Barbara had started writing her two "boys" at Sussex after she began her relationship with Walter. She had sought them out specifically for their location, keen to have a reason to drive down here, although she realized that she would never be given visiting privileges with Walter. Still, it made her feel closer to him, just passing through the gates of Sussex. And the two men she had chosen did need her. Both were African-American, and there was no doubt in her mind that their sentences were harsher because of that. Bobby Ray, the one she would visit tomorrow, had been a drug addict who ended up killing two women in a robbery attempt that could only be described as pathetic. The women were addicts, too, and also African-American. If they had been white, he almost certainly would be on death row with Walter. But that was small consolation to Bobby Ray, who yearned to take his sober self into the world, to find out what it might have been like to live clear-headed. He didn't go so far as to say it was unfair for his sober self to be locked up for what his drugged-up alter ego had done, but Barbara could tell it pulled at him. She believed he deserved a second chance, but she also had a hunch he would blow it, should that day ever come. Sobriety may have been forced on him in prison, but responsibility had not, not in any real way. Bobby

Ray was not equipped for the real world, not that she would tell the parole board that, if the day ever came. She would file a brief in his favor and do everything she could to help him succeed.

She unpacked her small bag, although she would be in the room no more than fourteen hours, checking out on her way to the prison. She wondered if Eliza Benedict was in this very motel, or if she had opted to drive down tomorrow. Perhaps she would see her at the breakfast buffet in the morning. She called the front desk, asked to be connected to Eliza Benedict's room. "No one by that name has checked in, Miss Barbara," the desk clerk said. Lerner, then? "No, ma'am, and no one with a reservation under either name."

All for the best. Barbara's presence would unnerve Eliza, perhaps even make her suspicious. She probably shouldn't have come down at all, but her trip was legitimate, and Bobby Ray looked forward to their visits. Why should he suffer? Besides, it was good karma, for Walter. She was putting her energy into the air, trying to create an aura.

She removed the bedspread—a friend who had attempted to organize Baltimore motel maids into a union had told her that motel bedspreads crawled with bacteria—and lay on the sheets, flipping through the channels to CNN, watching the crawl across the bottom of the screen. On Tuesday, one way or another, Walter's name would be there. Actually, his name probably wouldn't be used. He would be reduced to DEATH ROW INMATE or VIRGINIA SERIAL KILLER. The latter bothered her for several reasons. It wasn't correct, for one thing. Was two even a serial? By temperament, Walter was more of a spree killer; the odious Jared Garrett had that much right. Based on what Walter had told her, she believed he had a psychological defect that had been triggered by something the two girls had said or done. A woman in Texas had claimed she went temporarily insane when her lover's wife shushed her, and next thing she knew, the woman was lying on the floor of her garage, hacked to death by her own ax. That woman had been acquitted. But Barbara had never tried to draw Walter out on the killings. Such a discussion seemed prurient, distasteful to her. Besides, that Walter no longer existed. Like Bobby Ray, he was a different man in prison than he had been before.

Unlike Bobby Ray, he had no chance of testing that new persona in the world at large, yet he would probably be more successful. Walter had skills. Walter had really thought about what he had done.

But it was Barbara who, in her letters, had pointed out to him the glaring inconsistency of Elizabeth Lerner's testimony, the hole that a more competent attorney could have driven the proverbial truck through. Why had no one else seen it, for all these years? Because no one wanted to see it, no one wanted to lean too hard on that brave young girl who had managed to survive the terrible rapist/killer. Even Walter had failed to notice.

She called for a mushroom-and-onion pizza from a nearby delivery place, made a pot of tea in the carafe, but only after washing it carefully. Her friend who had warned her about the bedspreads also had told her of seeing a hotel maid use a toilet brush to clean out a coffeemaker. Think about that. Think about all the little crimes against humanity, all the rudeness and unkindness, that go unchecked, day in and day out, things done by people who thought of themselves as good, the same people who cheered and posted nasty Internet comments when a man like Walter was killed. They used words like *animal* and *monster,* openly yearned for more painful, sadistic executions. They were killers, too, cowardly ones who contracted their bloodlust over to the state, telling themselves that their murders were in the service of justice.

43

WALTER WOKE UP THINKING about ketchup. Why was he thinking about ketchup? Oh, because he was remembering that *advertisement* for ketchup, the one that showed it quivering on the edge, with all the ceremony of a first kiss, and the song coming up under it. An-ti-ci-pa-a-a-a-shun. He had read recently that the song had, in fact, been written about a date, although he had a hunch that *date* meant *sex* in this particular case. In Walter's experience, too much anticipation could wreck things, set you up to expect more and better than you got, then psych you out. He didn't want to feel an-ti-ci-pa-a-a-shun, didn't want to be dependent on gravity, or some other force of nature, to make things drop, unfold, happen. He wanted to be the one who made things happen. Again. Finally.

He reached for himself, but not because he was thinking of her. He didn't feel that way about her, plain and simple. He had always wanted to apologize for that, but how, exactly? Talk about adding insult to injury. Even with her, he hadn't been thinking about her. Maybe that had been the trick all along. Love the one you're with, think about someone else.

But he liked her. He was looking forward to seeing her, talking to her face-to-face. Plus, word would get around that a woman had come to see him, and that would give him some real cachet, especially if people heard she was attractive. Not that she would show up in that green dress, hair slicked up and back, but she would probably look okay. He just hoped he got to stick around and enjoy the burnishing of his rep. Then again, if he did stick around, he would be famous for a lot more than getting a visit from a redheaded woman.

Barbara had wanted him to write a script, had even suggested they practice on one of their phone calls. Role play, she called it. A script! Role play! Barbara trying to be Elizabeth! That would never work. He needed to be loose, spontaneous. But he also had to be mindful of the clock. Time could and would run out on this game.

Just as he found his release, an all-too-familiar sound reverberated through Sussex I, the loudest, most dreaded sound in a place full of loud, dreaded sounds. *No. No. Please, God, no. Don't do this to me.*

44

ELIZA AND VONNIE APPROACHED the prison gate with the kind of nervousness endemic to those who have seldom been in trouble, aware that they were entering a world where power was distributed quite differently from the one on the other side of the fence. They would have to do as they were told, go only where they were allowed, speak as permitted. It was a lot of freedom to relinquish, even for an hour, even in the name of a good cause. Eliza's palms were sweating, and Vonnie looked tense.

So when the guard said, "Sorry, ma'am, no visiting hours today," the instinct was not to fight or argue but plead confusion.

"This is a rather extraordinary circumstance," Eliza said. "If you check the list, I'm sure you'll see my name."

"Oh, I have your name. I have everybody's name," said the guard, not unkindly. "But no one's going in today. They found something in Sussex II last night, and the whole prison went into lockdown. You'll have to come back for the next scheduled visiting day, which should be in two weeks."

"The man she's visiting will be dead next week," Vonnie put in, leaning across her.

"That a fact?" Bland, unmoved. "Well, there's nothing I can do about anything. Nobody's going into there today, I can tell you that much. And no one's any happier about it than you are."

"There has to be a way," Vonnie continued. "There's always a solution if—"

"Naw," the guard said. "There doesn't and there isn't. No visiting hours today. Y'all can come back in two weeks."

Eliza wanted to put her head on the steering wheel and weep. The only thing that stopped her was that she wasn't sure if she would be crying for the families she had hoped to comfort, or for being thwarted in her own selfish desires. But she couldn't help thinking that it was her own disingenuousness that had undone her, that this would never have happened if she had been completely honest about what she hoped to achieve. With Peter, with Vonnie. With herself.

"Buck up," Vonnie hissed, and Eliza realized a tear was trickling down her cheek. "This is a roadblock, nothing more. Trust me, I will get you in to see him."

VONNIE PROVED TO BE RIGHT, although she would never have the satisfaction of going back and flinging that knowledge into the face of the imperturbable guard. And Eliza knew she wanted to do just that. Her sister had never been a gracious winner.

But she was a shrewd strategist, with sound instincts. Her first decision was to extend their stay in Richmond, where she furiously worked her iPhone and MacBook all day Saturday and into Sunday, often simultaneously. Walter was to be moved to Jarratt, home of the so-called Death House, Sunday evening. Visits there were rare, even for lawyers, Jefferson Blanding warned them, and sure enough, Eliza's request was turned down by every official at the Department of Corrections. A part of her was almost relieved. She wasn't going to face Walter after all, but it wasn't her fault. She had tried to do the right thing. Why not go home, content with that knowledge? She said as much to Vonnie, who had turned their B and B into her command center, cursing its unreliable Internet connection as she searched for numbers and e-mailed journalist friends who knew how to find people on the weekends.

"Is that what you want?" Vonnie asked. "I'm doing this for you."

"I don't know. I didn't want to see him, but—if there are other girls, don't their parents and relatives deserve to know?"

"*Deserving* is a tough word. Yes, it would probably be better for them to know. And better for others to stop pinning their hopes, as it were, on Walter Bowman. But it's not your responsibility, E. Don't shoulder this burden if you can't."

"I can, however. I can do this, and I should."

"Then I'll keep calling."

Vonnie, now turning her attention to politicians, was cagey. She didn't tell anyone what Eliza might accomplish in her visit until she made it to the top of the food chain, the governor's chief of staff. Instead, she kept telling everyone that these were special circumstances. Eliza wasn't even sure to whom she was speaking when she finally said, "Look, there's something else you should know." It might have been the governor himself. All Eliza knew was that Vonnie said "Uh-huh, uh-huh" many times over, scribbled a few notes, and spent lengthy intervals on hold before saying good-bye in her terse way.

"You're in. But there are a few ground rules. Security in the facility itself is different, which is why this is such a big deal. You won't be speaking to him through glass, but bars. They're going to have the deputy put masking tape on the floor, and you cannot cross that line. Get me? You cannot come within arm's reach of him, or the deputy will physically drag you away and it will be over."

"So not an issue. Anything else?"

Vonnie paused. "They also want us to record the conversation."

Us. Eliza liked the sound of that first person plural, actually. "Is that legal?"

"If it isn't, that's their problem. I could take notes anyway. I have a pretty competent shorthand. The final thing is, they want us there first thing Monday, as soon as he's had breakfast. That gives them a full day to deal with whatever Walter tells you."

"Deal?"

"The way I understand it, let's say he confesses to you about, I don't know, even as few as four murders. In each case, they want to be able to go to the families, tell them what's happened, then have the families agree that they're comfortable with the fact that there won't be actual court cases, even though Walter's confessions aren't legally binding. Feel me?"

"Vonnie, you sound ridiculous when you use that ghetto argot."

"Thanks. The point is, they can't have a glory-hog prosecutor coming forward and declaring that he wants to try the case. Which may, in fact, be Walter's real agenda, Eliza. He probably thinks that these twenty-third-hour confessions start the clock over. And this is a complicated issue for the governor. He's anti–

death penalty, personally, and has fought the expansion of the death penalty while in office. But he's a lame duck, and he doesn't like to interject himself into these cases. Yet if some grandstanding prosecutor from outside Virginia insists on a trial, he'll have no leverage over that person. He's already reaching out to governors he thinks might become involved."

"As you said, Walter could be counting on this. But what if he's lying simply for the hell of it? What if he confesses to things he didn't do and then he's executed? Is that fair to the families involved?"

Vonnie sat on the soft, fluffy, inevitably overdecorated bed. The room was even more quaint than their famed one in the Martha Washington Inn. Used to five-star hotels, Vonnie had been sneering at every item in the room—the pillows, the crockery, the embroidered samplers on the wall—since their arrival. But now she put her arm around Eliza, something she hadn't done—well, ever.

"Presumably, he's cagey enough not to overreach. In total, according to the governor's people, there are eight missing person cases, from 1980 to 1985, that he conceivably could be linked to, based on geography and opportunity. If he claims anything off that list, then they're going to decide he's disingenuous and let this whole thing drop, very quietly. Eliza—you have to sign a confidentiality agreement with the state in order to have this meeting. Frankly, it pisses me off. They have no right to do this. But given that you've never wanted to speak about any of this, I didn't think I was wrong to give that up."

Uh-huh, uh-huh, uh-huh. So that's what it was all about. Vonnie wasn't wrong, but Eliza felt a strange surge of anger. She had *chosen* to be silent all these years, but that was her prerogative. How dare someone else impose that condition on her? She felt as she had when she was fifteen, going on sixteen, and all the various adults—

prosecutors, judges, even her parents—kept insisting her story was hers to tell, yet instructed her in how and when to tell it.

"Okay, so I sign a confidentiality agreement. If that's what it takes, that's what it takes. At least I'll be telling the truth when I say I can't speak of it."

"One more thing—"

Vonnie's voice sounded dire, but Eliza couldn't imagine what else she had to impart.

"They wanted to know if you want to be a witness."

"God, no."

"That's what I thought, but I didn't answer for you on that score. Said okay, conditionally. Look, let's go to that Caribbean place for dinner if it's open on Sunday. Go out for dinner and see a girly movie, something you'd never see with Peter or the kids."

They managed the dinner, but the multiplexes of Richmond were short of the kind of female-bonding experience they desired. They settled for a Batman movie, in what Eliza still thought of as a dollar house, although it cost five. She found it appalling—not because it was loud and violent, and not because it was hard to see, or imagine seeing, the pain in the young actor who had died before the movie's release, but because in Batman's world everyone was a vigilante or an amoral opportunist. Each person thought he was *right*. But wasn't that true of the less-stylized world in which Eliza now lived? Even Walter, for all his talk of change and redemption, probably had rationalizations for what he had done. But that was the one thing he had spared her. He had never spoken of anything he had done, not even the undeniable fact of Maude's death, or Holly's. Why was that?

Because, Eliza admitted to herself, he planned to leave her alive. That was his advantage over her, as much as his strength and brutality. He had decided that he wouldn't kill her. What might she have done with that knowledge? Could she have saved Holly, after all? Did she have power then that she couldn't glimpse or fathom? Did she have any now? Less than twenty-four hours ago, only a few people knew what Walter had promised her—or so she believed. Had she walked into a trap? Was she once again making her way up the Sucker Branch, about to stumble on something that she would be better off not seeing, not knowing, wandering too far from the path?

At any rate, it was too late to turn back.

Part VIII

VOICES CARRY

Released 1985

Reached no. 8 on Billboard Hot 100 on July 13, 1985

Spent 21 weeks on Billboard Hot 100

45

SECURITY AT THE GREENVILLE FACILITY was even stricter than at Sussex, with checkpoint after checkpoint, search after search. That was to be expected, Eliza supposed, when someone was visiting a place known as the Death House.

But the building itself was a stark contrast to the grimly named facility, a small jailhouse, with a deputy at a desk and just one cell.

"It's like the old *Andy Griffith Show,*" Eliza said, standing at her taped mark, her eyes fixed on it, not ready to look at the man in the cell. "Where they locked up Otis, the town drunk."

"If Otis was going to die," Walter said, his voice pleasant. "If you look to the side, you can see the death chamber."

She looked to the side. Then—and only then—she looked directly at Walter. Although still quite trim, he was larger than Eliza had expected. Larger and younger. A slight man, he had been obsessed with his height, insisting that he was five nine, when it seemed apparent to five-four Elizabeth that he couldn't possibly be more than two inches taller than she. Once, Eliza remembered, he had spent a long time studying a catalog photograph of shoes with Cuban heels and asked her what she thought of them. By then, she had spent enough time in his company to know how to disagree with him without seeming to. She told him the shoes were great (they were hideous) but *too* stylish, so trendy that they would go out of fashion long before he got much wear out of them. Men's shoes were well made, she told him, parroting something she had heard her father say, choking a little bit at the memory. A man had to buy shoes that *endured*. Walter and Elizabeth had similar conversations about a cologne he thought would make him irresistible, and whether he should wear a T-shirt and white blazer like Don Johnson on *Miami Vice*. "Not after Labor Day," she had advised, wondering if she would be with him when Memorial Day arrived and he once again petitioned for permission to wear linen pants and loafers without socks. He had been a small man and now he seemed to loom above her, despite the chunky heels on her boots. Did adults grow? Had he learned to stand straighter? Or was she drooping in his presence, burrowing into herself?

As for his face—lack of sunlight had its advantages. Walter was pale and remarkably unlined, his green eyes vivid. He had also always insisted, to the point of being boring on the subject, that he was a good-looking man. He wasn't wrong. Yet he wasn't right, either. He *should* have been good-looking. But there was something that caught at the corner of the eye, even when she was fifteen. *Not like me,* her mind had registered. *Not someone I would know.*

But then—Holly had made the same judgment about her.

"Hello, Walter," she said, although she had said it once already, upon entering. "This is my sister."

Vonnie nodded at him, staring hard, almost rudely. She had never seen him, Eliza realized, not in the flesh. Their parents had, in court, but Vonnie had been away at school.

"Hello, Yvonne," Walter said, and Eliza was comforted to realize that much of what Walter knew about her came from official documents and newspaper reports and courthouse testimony, where nicknames were seldom used. She had not let Vonnie's name pass her lips during the thirty-nine days they had spent together. Right now, if he dropped her children's names to unnerve her, he would probably call them *Isobel* and *Albert*. "This is my deputy, who's also named Walter, although I think you'll be able to tell us apart. Helpful hint: He's the one with the gun."

Walter's newfound sense of humor. The deputy also was a broad-shouldered African-American and insanely tall, at least a foot taller than Elizabeth.

"We've met," Deputy Walter said, his voice a honeyed drawl that also would have been at home in Andy Griffith's Mayberry, if Andy Griffith's Mayberry had been the kind of place that employed towering African-American deputies.

"Would you like a chair?" Walter, the original Walter, asked.

"No, that's okay."

"This may take a while."

"You're standing."

"That's because I can't pull a chair up to the bars. If I could, I would. But there's no reason for us both to be uncomfortable."

There's not a chair in the world that could make me comfortable right now.

"I'm fine." She watched Vonnie snake her hand into the deep pockets of her jacket, a laughably fashionable wrap that only heightened the dowdiness of Eliza's suburban mother garb of slacks and sweater. But the pockets were a boon. Vonnie was starting the microcassette recorder.

"You look wonderful, Elizabeth." Her full name hurt in Walter's mouth. "But then—I saw your photo, I knew how you'd look. How do I look?"

"Well," she said. He wanted more. "Fit."

"I'm only forty-six. It's hard for us to get exercise, but you'd be surprised what you can do in a cell, with no equipment but your own body. Barbara got me into yoga. I'm not much on flexibility, but my strength—I'll show you." To Eliza's surprise—and apparently to the deputy's consternation, as the man seemed to tense all over—Walter put his palms on the floor and then leaned forward until his knees rested against his elbows, his feet up in the air, his entire weight balanced on his arms.

"The crow," he said, holding the position nonchalantly. "Hey, do you root for the Ravens or the Redskins?"

"What?"

"I mean, I know you grew up in Baltimore and its environs"—*environs*—"but now you live in the D.C. area, so it just popped into my head, which football team do you choose?"

"Walter, I don't think this is an occasion for small talk."

"Oh, so it's going to be like that?" Standing up, dusting off his palms, but not particularly offended as far as she could tell. Relieved, almost playful. "Okay, but before we cut to the chase, as people say, there is something else we have to talk about first. The night that Holly died. And what happened after."

She looked at the deputy, who had the good grace to try and pretend that none of this was happening, that he was watching them because it was his duty, yet unengaged. "I—" She looked at Vonnie, who understood her distress but had no solution.

"Hey, Walter?" That was Walter behind bars, talking to Walter at the desk.

"Yes, Walter?"

"Do you need to hear what we're going to talk about?"

"I need to watch. You know that. I have to watch."

"Watching's okay. Do you have to *hear*?"

The deputy thought for a moment, nodded, took an MP3 player from his desk drawer, and plugged in the earbuds. Eliza couldn't identify the music, but she could tell it was loud, loud enough so she could hear a tinny buzz. But he kept his eyes fastened on them, and she was not sorry for that.

"Tit for tat," Walter said, inclining his head toward Vonnie.

"But—?"

"Just us. That's nonnegotiable. She can go back to wherever they want to hold her, but she can't stay here."

The two sisters exchanged glances, but it was hopeless. Vonnie had secreted the microcassette player in her pocket precisely so her purse could be examined by the deputy as Walter looked on. They had made a great show of having their bags examined when they entered. They would have to forgo the taping. Vonnie knocked on the door, and another deputy came to escort her away.

"Hush, hush," Walter said. When she looked at him, stony-faced, he added: "It was a joke, Elizabeth. Remember how much you liked that song?"

"I did. I liked a lot of songs that summer. I don't like them now."

"I ruined them, I guess."

She selected her words with care. "When you hear a song, it's natural to remember where you were when it was popular."

"I ruined the songs." He looked genuinely contrite. "I hadn't thought about that. I may have ruined the songs, but I didn't ruin you. Look at you, Elizabeth."

She considered this. Her life had not been destroyed by Walter, far from it. She had an unusually good life, especially for these uncertain times. She had Peter, she had Albie and Iso. She had her parents—hale and hearty into their seventies. And, as the past forty-eight hours had reminded her, she could even rely on Vonnie, impossible, exasperating Vonnie. What did she lack, what had been denied her?

The world at large. No truly close friends, just Peter's friends and some acquaintances. And this wasn't a function of the multiple relocations or the temperaments of the women she had met in Houston and London and now Bethesda. It wasn't, as she had always rationalized, because she was too eastern in Texas, too American in London, too Baltimore for Washington-centric Montgomery County. She couldn't even blame her lack of friends on being the mother of the girl who might be renowned as the subtle bully and sneak thief of North Bethesda Middle. Eliza didn't have friends because friendship led to trust and confidences. The thick black line drawn through her life, demarcating where Elizabeth ended and Eliza began, had always made that impossible, at least in her mind.

"No, you didn't ruin me. But the fact that you didn't destroy me doesn't mitigate what you did."

"I'll say it: I raped you." Walter's voice was low, as if to ensure these words would be heard by her, and her alone. Out of consideration or shame? "I did. I would never deny your experience. You were raped, and I did it. But can you see that it felt like love to me, Elizabeth? Just a little."

She shook her head. "This is not what we're supposed to be discussing. There is no point in talking about this."

"Actually, there is. Because before I can tell you anything, you need to understand this—that night with you was the first and only time in my life that I had sex."

"No—" She wanted to turn her back on him, hide her face as she sorted through her emotions. It was a lie, it couldn't be, why was he doing this to her? "You've said . . . I read . . ."

"I lied. I lied because I was ashamed. That's how screwed up I was. I was more ashamed of my lack of sexual experience than I was about the things I'd done. I made up this whole story about how I'd done it back home and everyone assumed I'd done it to the other girls. The true first time—the only time—was with you. Remember? That hotel near the Blue Ridge Mountains?"

IT WAS THE NIGHT after Holly had died. Walter had barely spoken throughout the day. He was dazed, semicatatonic, and Eliza had to prompt him to do the smallest things. Moving forward when lights turned green, speaking up when the waitress asked his order at dinner that night.

The hotel was a nice one, an actual hotel, with a restaurant, the kind of place that had linen tablecloths and an elaborate mural that showed people in old-fashioned clothes picnicking. Had there been that much money in Holly's little tin box? A credit card? Walter urged Elizabeth to order whatever she wanted, but her stomach was sour, and she knew he would be angry if she wasted this food, expensive as it was. Yet Walter wasn't eating at all. He cut his steak into ever smaller pieces, mashed his baked potato as if it were something he wanted to kill.

"Your dad eats even less than you," remarked the waitress.

"I'm not her dad," Walter said, and something in his voice made the waitress flinch. He softened his tone. "I'm her brother. She was a change-of-life baby, and now our parents are dead and all we have is each other."

"That's . . . nice. Real nice."

They went upstairs. Eliza reveled in the shower, the nicest she'd had in weeks, although she had to put back on her dirty old clothes. The bedspread was wonderful, too, an old-fashioned white one with a raised design. It had been almost a week since she had been in a real bed, and she fell asleep quickly, the television humming in the background. She wasn't sure what time it was when she awoke to find Walter standing over her.

"Turn over," he said.

She did, even as she said, "Please don't, Walter. Please?"

"I'm sorry," he said. "I have to. But I'll put some music on." He picked up the remote, flicking through the channels until he found MTV. Madonna singing "Lucky Star." "You like this one, right?" He turned her so she could face it, but she shut her eyes tight, not wanting to see anything, remember anything.

He was behind her. She had read a book one time, one of the best dirty books ever, where a woman's boyfriend was always turning her over, and it was revealed that he really liked boys. But she didn't think that was what was going on with Walter. He was having trouble. He was having a lot of trouble. "Dammit," he said a time or two, arranging and rearranging her limbs, talking to her body the way he sometimes berated his tools during one of his handyman jobs. Eventually, he found his way. It hurt so much that she could not imagine that it ever wouldn't, that anyone would do this voluntarily. His mouth was next to her ear, her neck, but he didn't kiss her, and his arms were braced on either side of her, as if he were doing push-ups. He seemed to be holding his breath. Finally, he gave a little yelp, more surprised than anything else. Madonna was still singing, rolling across the floor, sending up thanks for her lucky star.

"I'm sorry," he said for the second time. She was crying, her face pressed into what had been the most wonderful bed in the world and was now the worst.

The next day, he was absentminded again, but she stopped helping him, retreating into her own trancelike state. They stopped at a grocery store and ended up having a fight over a box of cookies. He relented and let her have them, but not before pushing her hard enough that she stumbled and went down to her knees. Shortly after they crossed the Potomac into Maryland, he was pulled over for driving too slowly, and if he thought he had anything to fear from the state police, he sure didn't act that way.

"Who's the young lady?" the officer asked.

"Elizabeth Lerner," Walter said. "I'm taking her home. She's been missing, a runaway, but I've convinced her to go home."

Did he expect the trooper to wave him through? He didn't seem the least bit perturbed as the trooper walked back to his car, made a call on his radio. Before Elizabeth knew what was happening, Walter was on the ground, his hands above his head, and the state trooper was shouting at him not to move, even as he assured Elizabeth that she was going to be all right, that she was safe now.

And she started to cry. Because she was safe. Or, perhaps, because she realized she would never be safe again.

"THAT'S NOT POSSIBLE," she told Walter now. "You raped Maude. You tried to rape Holly." Walter was gripping the bars. She wished she had something to grip. She wished she hadn't refused the offer of a chair, but it would be weak to ask for it now. Besides, she didn't want to engage the deputy. It was strange enough that he was watching them.

"I couldn't. With the others. I tried, but it never worked. The first one—she laughed at me, and after that, I never could. Except with you."

This was her opening. "Maude wasn't the first one." Tentative, yet determined.

"No."

"Who was?"

He held up a hand. "Before I tell you what I promised to tell you, Elizabeth, I want you to think about the penultimate night." He was obviously pleased with himself, if only for the use of *penultimate*.

"I'd really prefer not to."

"It's important."

"I don't see how."

"Important to me, then. You went to sit in the truck."

"You *told* me to go sit in the truck."

"I gave you the keys. You locked yourself in. The doors were still locked when I came back to the truck. I knocked on the window, and you let me in. You sat there the entire time."

"What else could I have done? I couldn't drive, and I couldn't climb down that mountain in the dark."

"You told the prosecutors that you saw Holly running, me following."

"Yes. First I heard her—she screamed. Then you shouted, like you were in pain. I always assumed she had done something to you."

"Clawed at my eyes. Someone taught her that. Some women, they go for the—" It was almost comical, how he gestured at his crotch, failing to find a word he considered proper or impressive enough. "It's better to go for the eyes. Tell your daughter that."

"Do not talk about my daughter."

"Okay, okay. Just trying to be helpful." He held up his hands to signal his supplication. "Yes, I probably did scream, although I don't remember that. Here's what I do remember, that's a lot more important: I didn't go after Holly."

"You did. I saw you."

"No you didn't. Not if you were locked in that truck. The truck was parked on the far side of the tent, Elizabeth, away from the flap. Holly didn't run toward it—probably because she didn't trust you to help her—"

"That's not fair, Walter."

"We're way beyond fair now. She ran toward the trees, toward the darkness. You couldn't have seen her. And you didn't see me chase her, because I *didn't*. I was trying to find her, to help her—"

"You called her name. I heard that. And then she screamed. I heard that, too."

"But you didn't see me chase her, because I didn't. All these years, that never occurred to me. I didn't think about where the truck was. And you were so adamant in your testimony, so unwavering."

And so determined to say what the adults wanted to hear. This was true. She had resolved not to disappoint anyone again, not to let anyone know how cowardly she had been. Yet there was the image in her mind's eye, an image that had tortured her for years, that flash of white, Holly's streaming hair. Walter had been right behind her, almost close enough to grab that banner of hair. Hadn't he?

"She fell off that mountain, just like I said. All these years, I didn't see how I could get anyone to believe me, because there you were, telling people I chased her, that you saw it. But then Barbara came along, began looking at things, reconstructing things. She was the one who realized it couldn't be the way you said. She was the one who said I had to find you, get you to tell the truth. You probably didn't even know you weren't telling the truth. They brainwashed you."

"If anyone brainwashed me, it was you," she said. "You intimidated me to the point that you could trust me to do anything. I was scared all the time. Scared enough that I went and sat in the truck because you told me to. So scared that I didn't try to get away from you, no matter how many chances I had."

"Well, if you could be brainwashed by me, you could be convinced by other people, too, right? You always were susceptible, Elizabeth. You wanted to do what other people wanted you to do. First me, then the lawyers. There's no shame in that."

Then why did it feel as if he wanted her to feel exactly that, as if he was trying to find a way to push those buttons. "The prosecutors didn't threaten to kill my parents and my sister if I didn't cooperate with them. The prosecutors didn't hit me, early on, when I didn't do their bidding, or tie me up. The prosecutors didn't rape me."

"Didn't they? They got you to tell a lie. That's perjury, Elizabeth, and perjury is a felony. Same as rape."

"Not quite. Not at all."

"Still, it's wrong to lie in court. I don't think you lied consciously, but you were wrong. She really did fall, Elizabeth. I didn't push her. Even if you did see me chase her—and you couldn't because I didn't—you couldn't see what happened, how far I was from her when she fell."

She shook her head. "I don't believe you."

For a moment, he looked angry, and Eliza could feel the deputy tightening, coiling, ready to leap in, although she was still on her mark, several inches behind it, in fact. Walter had planned out a version of this conversation in his head, and it wasn't going his way, any more than any of his conversations with grown women had ever gone his way. She wasn't a girl anymore, and she was thwarting him. It felt good.

His voice tried for a cajoling tone. "That's your right, isn't it? To believe me or not believe me, based on the facts. That was my right, too. To have a jury hear the *facts*. To have them decide, based on the facts, if I did what I was accused of doing. My rights were denied me, because of your testimony. My lawyer wouldn't put me on the stand, wouldn't let me contradict the star witness, because you were so convincing."

"Walter—I told the truth."

"You thought you did, but it couldn't be." He lined up his left forearm on the bars. "There's the truck, see? With the headlights where my fingers are." He wiggled his fingers. "The tent was behind it. Holly ran in the other direction. Barbara drove to the campsite, and it's the same, after all these years. She even went at the right time of year, last fall, almost to the day, so everything lined up. You couldn't have seen what you said you saw."

"Last year—you've been looking for me all this time, haven't you? It wasn't an accident. You didn't just find me in the pages of *Washingtonian*. It wasn't destiny, or serendipity."

"Well, yes and no. I mean, yes, we were looking. But it was an accident, how I found you, and that's a *kind* of serendipity. That's how I knew you were supposed to help me. I turned the page, and there you were." He paused. "You got so pretty, Elizabeth. I always knew you would. You weren't my type, when you were young. I liked those tall blondes. Can you blame me? That's what a young man likes. But it's right, about beauty being skin deep. You're beautiful inside, and it finally got to the outside. And you're too good inside to let the lie stand. Not when it could cost me my life."

"The governor doesn't want to issue you a stay under any circumstances."

Walter raised his eyebrows. "Funny that you should know that. I mean, I know that. Barbara and Jeff know that. This governor would prefer not to be dragged into this at all. But how do *you* know that, Elizabeth?"

She looked at the floor, at the masking tape, reminding herself that she was safe. She would not cross the creek again. He could not grab her wrists, force her into a truck. So why were her knees shaking?

"Just common sense," she said. "He almost never does."

"You still can't lie. That's why I'm not mad at you."

He wasn't mad at her? That was rich.

"I know you believe what you testified to. At any rate, you're right. He's not going to commute my sentence unless something really big happens. Like, the star witness against me recanting her testimony. I wouldn't get a new trial, under Virginia law. But if you told him that you had come to realize you were mistaken, or that the prosecutor put words in your mouth—he would have to listen, give me a stay."

"Why would I do that?"

"I can think of three reasons. One, it's the right thing to do. Can't believe I need to give you more, but here goes." He had been holding up his index finger, and now he added the middle one. "Two, I don't see why I should share any information with you unless you prove you're a trustworthy person. Truth for truth, Elizabeth. If I owe those other families the truth, then you owe me the same."

"I have always been truthful."

"Okay, then three. I still have time to give Jared Garrett an exclusive. I've written pages and pages and pages, which are in Barbara's possession. He always thought things were different with us. Maybe he was right. Maybe that's a truth that needs to go out there in the world, that we were boyfriend and girlfriend and you got jealous when I fell for Holly."

There it was, the thing she feared most. She would be outed. Her past would become present, truth and lie would mingle, and she would spend the rest of her life explaining herself. She would have to explain to her children what happened to her, yet persuade them that they could still feel safe in this world, that their parents could protect them. Albie's nightmares, Iso's secrecy—this wasn't going to help. And if Jared Garrett published Walter's version of their relationship, how would she convince Iso that her clandestine flirtation with a seventeen-year-old was out of bounds? It was everything Eliza had feared—and, she realized, she could handle it.

Still—she was disappointed in Walter. She really had wanted to believe that he had changed. And she didn't feel naive or stupid for the hope he had stirred up in her, the ruses he had used to lure her here. This was the way she wanted to be, the way she would continue to be. Like her college-essay role model, Anne Frank, she believed that people were basically good. Most people, at least.

"You're not going to tell me about the others, are you?"

"I will if you call the governor and my sentence is commuted to life. Then I'll tell you everything."

"No you won't. Because even if you failed to rape them, you tried, and that would mean the death penalty in those cases, too."

"Let me worry about that. Isn't living with my crimes, as an aware and remorseful person, more of a real punishment than killing me? Every day I'm alive, I have to think about what I did."

"But do you?"

"What?"

"Do you? I mean, yes, every day is an opportunity for you to think about your victims, that doesn't mean it happens. I have a feeling, Walter, that the only person you've ever really thought about is yourself."

He lowered his voice, and she almost crossed the invisible barrier despite herself.

"I think about you. Every day. The time we spent together—that's about as happy as I ever was."

"Then I'm sorry for you. Because that was not a happy time, Walter."

"You're the only woman I ever made love to."

"I was the fifteen-year-old girl you forced yourself on sexually. It's not the same thing."

"I cared about you. I still care about you. This is as much for you as for me, Elizabeth. I know you. You always did the right thing. You couldn't tell a lie to save your life. They tricked you into believing their lies."

"Walter, I believe you killed Holly."

"But do you believe that I deserve to die for that? You and your family, that's not your way."

"It wasn't our choice. The prosecutor asked the Tacketts what they wanted. He asked twelve citizens of Virginia if they thought it was fair. They said yes, and there's nothing I can do about it."

"But there is." His voice scaling up, strangled. "All you have to do is pick up a phone, say you've realized, talking to me all these weeks, what you got wrong. I'm not asking to go free, Elizabeth. I'm asking not to die. You can save me. Only you can save me."

"No, I can't, and I never could. I'm sorry, Walter, I really am. But you're asking me to lie."

"Quite the opposite."

Worse, he was asking her to do the most unnatural thing in the world, to comb over her memories of that night. What if she had unwittingly perjured herself? What if, in her refusal to relive that night, she had gotten it wrong? What if—and then it came to her. She saw herself on the country road with Iso and Albie, her heart in her throat as she wrested the car back into the correct lane, the ghostly deer disappearing *behind* them, the white tail triggering the image she was always trying to bury. She had slid across the seat to turn the key, so she could have heat and music, then she had looked up as she returned to her own seat—

She almost wept from relief.

"Walter, I could see you. I saw you in the rearview mirror."

"That's a nice story to tell yourself, isn't it? Maybe you can lie, after all."

"I'm not lying. I looked up, I saw you both. Did I see you push her? No, but I never said I did. I saw you chase her. You were right behind her, almost on her heels. If she had run off that mountain as you claim, you would have been right on top of her."

Walter's eyes slid sideways. It was his eyes, that was the tell, what was off in his otherwise handsome face. Narrow and small, they were never looking where they should be. They eeled away when a direct gaze was required, fastened on another's eyes when it was inappropriate, got caught studying cleavage and legs.

"But it's plausible, what I'm saying. Worthy of reconsideration."

"I won't lie for you."

"You'd do it for your kids, for your husband. You'd lie for them."

"I suppose I might, if it came to that. But that's different. Even you have to realize it's different."

He extended his hand through the bars, and the deputy was on his feet, just that fast, shoulder to shoulder with Eliza. He needn't have worried. She had no intention of moving closer to Walter, although it was hard not to collapse against Deputy Walter, use his bulk.

"I love you," Walter said, and even the earbudded deputy had to be able to hear that, or read his lips. The deputy shook his head in disgust.

"Walter, you're lying or you think that's true. Either way, it's sad."

She walked away, gathered her things from the deputy's desk, turned back. "The others," she said. "It would be a comfort to their loved ones, if you could make a clean breast of things. I wish you would."

"Well, that was up to you." Petulant as Iso.

"No, it was always up to you. I admit it. I wanted to be the hero. I wanted to come out of here with all the names and details. I thought if I could set the record straight about the other girls, I might finally forgive myself about Holly."

"You did have a chance to save her." Green eyes glinting. What happens when beauty doesn't free the beast, doesn't release him from his curse, knows him but still cannot love him?

"I couldn't see that at the time. I wish I had, but I didn't. But I couldn't save her that night, Walter. What I saw might be contestable, but what I heard wasn't. You pushed her off the side of that mountain. Pushed her because she fought back."

"That's right," he said, triumphant. "You're alive because you were weak. Because you weren't worth killing. After I had sex with you, all I wanted to do was take you home, because it wasn't good, wasn't good at all. How do you like knowing that? You're alive because there's nothing special about you, because *I didn't want you*. You're the one I got stuck with, not one of the ones I chose. How do you feel, knowing that?"

Eliza assumed he didn't want an answer, but she took his question seriously all the same. "Well, I'm truly glad I'm alive, so I guess I'm glad for the reason, whatever it was."

She nodded to the deputy, ready to leave. Steps from the threshold, she dropped her purse, all but flung it to the floor, and its contents, a remarkable collection of items that screamed mom—messy, disorganized mom at that—went skittering across the floor. Phone, Kleenex, wallet, change, checkbook, lipstick, comb. Deputy Walter fell to his knees, gathering it all up. She had known she could count on his automatic courtesy.

And in that instance, she stepped back toward the bars, passed her taped mark on the floor, kept going until she was inches from Walter's face. They were almost eye to eye, he had not grown at all. She brought her arm up and saw Walter flinch, enjoying the look of unease on his face, the fact that he didn't know what she was going to do. But she didn't hit him. She placed her hand on his shoulder and said: "I know you're scared, Walter. You have every right to be. There's no shame in being scared to die. But I couldn't save Holly, and I can't save you."

He was sobbing as she left. Partly out of frustration, she would guess. He had poured his energy into finding her, taking care to seduce her this time, and he had come so close to getting what he wanted. But he might be crying from fear, too, the overwhelming realization that he had no options, no out. She understood how he felt, was inside his head, experiencing the cold slap of fear and frustration. She knew him as well as she had ever known anyone, including her husband and children. Walter was all the gaps within her, the connective tissue that joined the two halves of her life. He was the neighborhood where she could never live again. He was the missing syllable, dropped from her name, yet forever a part of her, with her always, no matter what she called herself.

God help her, she would know him anywhere.

Part IX

EVERY DAY

Released in 1985 by James Taylor
Never charted on Billboard Hot 100
Album peaked at no. 34 and remained in the top 200 for 54 weeks

JARRATT, VA [AP]—Walter Michael Bowman was put to death by lethal injection Tuesday night at the Greenville Correctional Facility here, his death witnessed by the parents of his final victim, a thirteen-year-old girl that he kidnapped, robbed, and attempted to rape in 1985.

"We waited a long time for this day and we feel that justice has been done at last," Dr. Terrence Tackett Jr., the father of Holly Tackett, said in a brief appearance before reporters, his wife, Trudy, at his side.

Bowman, who had been on Virginia's death row longer than any inmate in the prison's modern history, declined to make a statement and asked that the details of his final meal be kept private. However, in the hours before his execution, he authorized a friend to release a posthumous statement to the media. . . .

46

TWO WEEKS BEFORE CHRISTMAS, Eliza was walking Reba in the evening, marveling at the freakishly warm weather. Perhaps a more serious person—Vonnie, or even Peter—would fret about sixty-degree days in mid-December, but she couldn't help enjoying them, especially on a clear night such as this, the stars vivid despite the haze of lights from central Bethesda.

The night was so lovely that she walked much longer than she had planned, trying to think of clever insights for the neighborhood book club she had joined. It was an odd group, made up of older men and women, many of them government retirees, with only one other mother. Eliza had found them through her single neighbor, the one who was kind enough to take in their newspaper when they went away. The group read *classics,* the neighbor had said, almost warningly, and while wine was consumed, they tried to stay on point during their discussions. No gossip, no chit-chat, no competitive hors d'oeuvres. Eliza did not consider this a deterrent. The January book was *The Mill on the Floss,* and Eliza wanted to be thought intelligent, prove herself worthy. Hadn't Vonnie read a lot of Eliot? Perhaps she should call her—

She was lost enough in her thoughts that she did not notice Barbara LaFortuny's humpbacked car creeping up behind her. However, Reba did, planted herself and issued one muted, but undeniable bark as the car idled to a stop.

"It's okay, girl."

Barbara rolled down her window. She was hard to see in the darkness of the car's interior, while Eliza was under a streetlamp, exposed. Still, she could make out the various shapes of Barbara's remarkable hairstyle. All that time, all that effort . . . did she really think it was attractive? Architecturally impressive, yes, undoubtedly. But attractive? Just because you worked hard on something didn't make it worth doing.

"Hello, Barbara."

"I hope you're proud of yourself."

Eliza considered this. "In some ways, I am. But I'm more proud of Walter."

"You have no right to be proud of him. He didn't do it for you."

She believed this was true. "Still, he did the right thing, in the end, releasing that statement. Two families now know what happened to their daughters. I just feel sorry for the others."

"What others? Walter had no other victims, and he never would have been given the death penalty for the two murders to which he did confess, if only because—" Barbara, ever the advocate, ever wound up, always wielding her talking points like a squadron of flying monkeys. If only she could hear anything that others said in the rare spaces she left between her words. *Holly, Maude, Dillon, Kelly.* Eliza's ghosts all had names and faces now. She wondered if that meant they might stop visiting her.

"I feel sorry for all the families who pinned their hopes on Walter Bowman, thinking he was the answer to the questions that torment them. As a serial killer, he proved to be something of an underachiever, didn't he?"

She had hoped she could make a small joke, but all she did was set Barbara off again.

"He *wasn't* a serial killer in the classic sense. I really do believe he suffered from a kind of temporary insanity—"

A less kindhearted person might have laughed at Barbara then. Eliza didn't laugh, but she also couldn't bear to let her keep talking. "I'm sorry, Barbara."

"For not doing the right thing?"

"No, I'm sorry you lost someone you love."

"It wasn't like that with us." The more Barbara automatically denied any romantic attachment to Walter, the more Eliza believed it was so. But, as her own parents might have said, Barbara got to be the expert on Barbara.

"I didn't mean it that way. You cared about him. I think it's nice that you cared about him."

"You certainly didn't. You let him die. You let him die because he knew the truth about you—that you were cowardly, that you are a liar—and now that he's dead, no one will ever know. That's why you let him die. To bury your own shame."

Eliza was angry now and her instinct, upon anger, had always been to flee. Instead she took a second to gather her thoughts. *Life isn't a timed event,* as Vonnie said. *The clock's not on you. Take your time.* Barbara had no power over her. It turned out no one cared about Elizabeth Lerner after all these years, not really. She and

Peter had told Iso about Walter, and they would tell Albie when he was older. Interestingly, the secret had made Iso feel important, in a good way, although she didn't see any parallels between her secret life and her mother's, could never be convinced that her string of covert PG-13 text messages was like a bread-crumb trail along the banks of the Sucker Branch, another girl wandering off the path and into something she couldn't control. Iso was merely proud that her parents acknowledged she was more of a grown-up than Albie.

"Well, Barbara, if you feel that way, you can always call Jared Garrett, send him the other letter that Walter dictated to you, release it to the world at large. Why haven't you?"

"It's not what Walter wanted." Said stiffly, grudgingly. "But I might, one day. I do what I think is right, not what's easy or expedient."

"That's a nice way to be," Eliza said, meaning it.

She began walking again. A few seconds later, Barbara's car drove past, as round-shouldered and dejected as a car could be. Eliza wondered why principled Barbara, whose license plate exhorted others to save the bay, hadn't chosen a hybrid. *Everybody wants to rule the world*—but only according to his or her own ideas about what mattered. There wasn't a principled position that couldn't be followed to an extreme where it then clashed with someone else's equally fervent beliefs. Eliza studied the stars above her, wished she knew the constellations, as Peter did, that she could identify more than the Big Dipper and the North Star. To her, the stars were simply random points of light. Some bright, some dim. Some far, some relatively near. Some lucky, some unlucky.

She let herself and Reba in through the kitchen door, listened to the cheerful beep-beep-beep of the security system, which signaled that a door had opened. They used the system religiously, but it wouldn't be enough if anyone was determined to do them serious harm. There would never be enough alarms and walls and dogs and gates and spyware to protect one's self and one's family. Beep-beep-beep. It was like being guarded by the Road Runner.

But then—the Road Runner was pretty resilient.

"You know what I would like to do tonight?" she asked Peter, who had barely glanced up at the door's chime, so intent was he on his laptop, the work he had brought home.

"Find a Rita's that serves this late in the season?"

"No." She laughed, thinking of Rita's scarlet neon promise. ICE * CUSTARD * HAPPINESS. Could happiness really be that simple? Maybe it could be, if she only would let it. Certainly, if unhappiness came for her family again—*when* it did, because no one got a lifelong pass, no one, even Trudy Tackett would discover now that all life's banal tragedies were waiting for her—there would be little solace in having been on guard all along, wary and pessimistic. She would just feel stupid for having missed so many custards.

"No, I'm not hungry. Plus, I have my secret stash of biscuits if I need a treat."

"I thought Iso found them. Again."

"She did. And I hid them. Again."

"What, then?" Peter pulled her into his lap. "Name your heart's desire and I'll give it to you."

She did not feel the need to tell him she could do this for herself. And, in fact, she might need his assistance, given what paint and humidity could do to a house over the years. Did they have a straight razor? A paint scraper to use as a pry? Her mind inventoried the contents of various drawers, then spread to every corner of the house. Iso would be in her room, doing lord knows what, Reba at her feet, enthralled by Iso's contempt for her. In the next room, Albie should be in bed, radio on, night-light off. Indifferent to baseball throughout the summer months, he had decided suddenly and arbitrarily that he was a fan of the Arizona Diamondbacks. He now listened to something called "hot stove baseball" as he fell asleep, then came to the breakfast table with breathless tales of pitchers and free-agent signings. From T. rex to A-Rod in the blink of an eye. Here was Peter, warm beneath her, capable of holding her weight without complaint. But she could hold his, too, if it came to that.

"Tonight—tonight, I'd like to sleep with the windows open."

AUTHOR'S NOTE

THIS BOOK, LIKE MANY I'VE written, was inspired by a true crime. But this time I'm not going to mention it. For one thing, the real case is unrecognizable, even to those who know it well, in this particular incarnation. And it involved the sexual abuse of a minor. There are many other key differences, but to enumerate them would be to make this a guessing game, which is not my intention. The bottom line is that there once was a man who raped and killed his victims, with one exception, and that man was put to death for his crimes. One day I got to thinking about the exception, the sole living victim. That's all you need to know about the book's origins.

As always, many generous people helped me in my research. My old friend Kathryn Kase opened doors for me among defense attorneys who represent prisoners on death row. Virginia attorney Jon Sheldon, who saw two clients put to death in the final months of 2009, was incredibly helpful and generous with his time, providing me with details about the sights, sounds, and daily life at places I would never be allowed to visit—Sussex I, Virginia's Death House and execution chamber. (The Mayberry comparison belongs to him.) He also helped me puzzle out how I could credibly keep a man on Virginia's death row for two decades, as Virginia moves more swiftly than almost any other state in putting people to death. The commonwealth of Virginia has excellent online resources about its correctional facilities, with details about everything from corresponding to inmates to visiting hours. I have my own definite ideas about the death penalty, but this is a novel, not a polemic, and I did my best to make sure that every point of the triangle—for, against, confused—was represented by a character who is recognizably human.

Thanks, always, to Vicky Bijur, Carrie Feron, and everyone at Morrow, including but not limited to Tessa Woodward, Liate Stehlik, Sharyn Rosenblum, and Nicole Chismar. Thanks to Alison Chaplin. Ethan Simon was an invaluable informant about public schools and their current policies. However, the version of North Bethesda Middle School used here is completely fictitious, although its rules and procedures are consistent with guidelines on the Montgomery County school's website. And while I've stolen many, many friends' anecdotes over the years, I feel that Lisa Groves deserves a special shout-out for the way I pilfered that Stuckey's peanut log from her childhood.

This book is unusual for me in that most of the geography is fudged, although there is a Sucker Branch in Patapsco State Park. Roaring Springs will probably be mistaken for Oella, but it's really another version of my beloved Dickeyville. The action is set in 2008 and is consistent with the calendar, although not necessarily the weather. But, mainly, I sat in front of my computer and made stuff up. That's what novelists do. And I watched a lot of music videos, circa 1985, at MTV.com, which I believed at the time to be vital to the process. But maybe I'm just another person who likes to rationalize what I do.

Baltimore, Maryland
January 2010

FROM

LAURA LIPPMAN

AND

WILLIAM MORROW

Questions for Discussion

1. Describe Eliza as an adult and as a teenager. How has she changed? What of her personality is the same? How did the trauma of her kidnapping impact her relationship with her parents, her sister, her husband, her children?

2. What did Eliza have in common with Walter's other victims? How was she different? Why didn't Walter kill her too?

3. When she visits the parents of Walter's last victim, Eliza can't help but think of their daughter and her role—or lack of it—in her death. "She hadn't killed Holly, but she hadn't saved her, either. Was that the same thing? She had resolved to live. Was her decision to live the same as willing Holly to die? She had chosen to live, which she believed meant doing whatever Walter said. Holly was the one who had fought and run." Discuss the questions Eliza raises about her own culpability. Does Eliza share any blame for Holly's death?

4. How would you characterize the relationship between Walter and the teenage Elizabeth? What about his relationship with the adult Eliza?

5. How did knowing Walter as intimately as she did save Eliza's life? Which person knew the other better? Did she owe Walter his life—or anything at all—since, ultimately, he spared hers? Did he know her as well as he thought? Was he surprised by the outcome when she finally visited? Were you?

6. What does Walter want from Eliza? Why does she agree to see him? What does she want from him?

7. Walter mused about the trial that convicted him. "Shouldn't his victims have the final say? But there was Elizabeth. He hadn't been lying when he said he felt the greatest guilt toward her. What he did to her—that was a betrayal. The others, he didn't know them, they weren't real to him. But Elizabeth had been his copilot, his running buddy. His Charley to his Steinbeck." Why did Walter feel guilty about Elizabeth? How did he betray her?

8. Eliza had felt protected by the invisibility with which she cloaked herself, taking her husband's name, moving abroad for several years. Can we ever truly hide from those who want to find us? What is the emotional cost if we try? What was the cost for Eliza?

9. Eliza wished her son could stay young and innocent for years. "But she knew there was no spell, no magic, that could keep a child a child, or shield a child from the world at large. In fact, that was where the trouble almost always began, with a parent trying to out-think fate. Stay on the path. Don't touch the spindle. Don't speak to strangers. Don't pick the rose." Why does Eliza think this way? What does she mean by "that was where the trouble almost always began"? Do you agree with her assessment? Are we overprotective of our children? How can we gird them for the perils the world offers?

10. When she was asked if Walter deserved to die, Eliza responds, "It doesn't matter what I think. He was sentenced for the murder of Holly Tackett, and her parents made it clear that they approved of the death penalty. I wasn't con-

sulted." Do you think Walter deserved to die? Why is it so difficult for Eliza to offer her opinion? Do you think she feels guilty for surviving?

11. Eliza's sister Vonnie accuses her of "existing. . . . You let life happen to you. You live the most reactive life of anyone I know. If there's one thing I would have learned from your experience, I think it would be to never let anyone else take control of my life." Is Vonnie correct in her assessment? Has Eliza learned this lesson?

Here is a preview of Laura Lippman's next brilliant and suspenseful novel, available in hardcover from William Morrow in September 2011.

1

They throw him out when he falls off the bar stool. Although it wasn't a fall, exactly, he just slipped a bit and lurched against the bar, but they said he had to leave because he was drunk. He finds that funny. He's too drunk to be in a bar. He makes a joke about a fall from grace. At least, he thinks he does. Maybe the joke was one of those things that stays in his head, for his personal amusement. For a long time, for fucking forever, Gordon's mind has been divided by a thick dark line, a line that divides and defines his life as well. What stays in, what is allowed out. But when he drinks, that line gets a little fuzzy.

Which might be why he drinks. Drank. Drinks. No, drank. He's done. Again. One night, one little slip. Tomorrow is a new day.

"You driving?" the bartender asks, piloting him to the door, his arm firm yet kind around Gordon's waist.

"No, I live nearby," he says. One lie, one truth. He does live in the area, but not so near that he hasn't driven here in his father's Buick. He doesn't want the bartender to let go of him. The contact feels good. Shit, did he say *that* out loud? He's not a faggot. "I'm not a faggot," he says. It's just been so long since his wife slipped her hand into the crook of his elbow, so long since his daughters put their sticky little hands around his neck and whispered their sticky little words into his ears, the list of the things they wanted that Mommy wouldn't let them have, but maybe Daddy would see it differently? The bartender's embrace ends abruptly, now that Gordon is out the door. "I love you, man!" he says, for a joke.

Only maybe he didn't. Or maybe it isn't funny. At any rate, no one's laughing and Gordon "Go-Go" Halloran always leaves 'em laughing. That's his gift. That's his curse.

He sits on the curb. He really did intend to go to a meeting tonight. It all came down to one turn. If he had gone left—but instead he went straight. Ha! He went straight and look where that had gotten him.

It isn't his fault. He wants to be sober. He had strung together two years this time, chastened by the incident at his younger daughter's first birthday party. And he managed to stay sober even after Lori kicked him out last month. But the fact is, he has been faking it for months, stalling out where he always stalls out on the twelve steps, undermined by all that poking, poking, poking, that insistence on truth, on coming clean. Making *amends*. Sobriety, real sobriety, as opposed to the string of sober days Gordon sometimes manages to put together, wants to breach that line in his head and Gordon needs that division, thin and fragile as it may be. Take it away and he'll fall apart, sausage with no casing, crumbling into the frying pan.

Sausage. He'd like some sausage. Is the IHOP still up on Route 40?

Saturday morning. Sausage and pancakes, his mother never sitting down as she kept flipping and frying, frying and flipping, loving how they all ate, Gordon and his brothers and his father, stoking them like machines. Come Saturday morning, I'm going away. Hey, hey, hey, it's Fat Albert! When he moved back home four weeks ago, he asked his mother to make him some pancakes and she said, "Bisquick's in the cabinet." She thought he had already started drinking again, assumed that was why Lori had thrown him out. It was easier to let her think that. Then it turned out it was easier to *be* that.

When it came down to it, drunk and sober were just two sides of the same coin and no matter how you flipped it, you were still your fucked-up own self. It sure didn't help that his current AA group meets in his old parish, now a Korean Baptist church. That's just too weird, sitting on the metal chairs in an old classroom. Drink and the line gets fuzzy. Get sober and the line comes back into sharp relief, but then everyone starts attacking the line, says he has to let it go, break it down. *Take down the line, Mr. Gorbachev.* Boy, he is all over the place tonight, tripping down memory lane. How old had he been when that had happened? A freshman in high school and already a fuckup. To hear everyone tell it, he had always been a fuckup, had come into the world a fuckup, is destined to leave as a fuckup. But whoever followed Sean was going to be a disappointment. Sean the perfect. You would think that with three brothers, the two imperfect ones would find a bond, gang up on that prissy middle fuck. But Tim has always taken Sean's side. Everyone gangs up against Go-Go, the name Gordon can't quite shake even at age forty. *Go, Go-Go. Go, Go-Go. Go, Go-Go.* That's what the others had chanted when he did his dance, a wild, spastic thing, steel guitar twanging. *Go, Go-Go. Go, Go-Go. Go, Go-Go.*

Give Sean that: He's the one person who consistently uses his full name, Gordon, not even Gordy. Unfortunately, he uses it with a sigh of disappointment. As in: "Jesus, Gordon, how many times can you move back home?" Or: "Jesus, Gordon, Lori is the best thing that ever happened to you and you've got kids now." Jesus, Gordon. Jesus, Gordon. Maybe he should have been Gee-Go instead of Go-Go.

He sits on the curb. He isn't really that drunk. The beer and the shot hit him fast, after almost two years of sobriety. He was doing so good. He thought he had figured out a way to be in AA while respecting the line. They don't need to know *everything*, he had rationalized. There would be a way to tell the story that would allow him to make it through all twelve steps, finally, without breaching any loyalties, without breaking that long-ago promise. Why does he even care? He bets everyone else has broken it by now, no matter what anyone says. No one keeps secrets. No one.

He gets up, walks down the once-familiar street. As kids, they had been forbidden to ride their bikes along Forest Park Avenue, which should have made it impossible to find their way to this little business district, tempting to them because of its pizza parlor and the bakery. And there was a craft store with an unlikely name, a place owned by the family whose daughters had disappeared. He was little then, not even five, but he remembered a chill had gone through the neighborhood for a while, that all the parents had become strict and supervigilant.

Then they stopped. It was too hard, it turned out, being in their kids' shit all the time, and the children slipped back into their free, unfettered ways. Nowadays . . . he doesn't even have the energy to finish the cliché in his head. He thinks of Lori, standing guard at the kitchen window of their "starter" home, a townhouse that had cost $350,000 and to which he was now barred entry. Is that fair? Is anything fair? Sean is still perfect and even Tim does a good imitation of goodness, Mr. State's Attorney, with his three beautiful daughters and his plumpish wife, who was never that hot to begin with, yet Gordy can tell they still like each other. Tim and Sean, still married to their first wives, still such good boys. They can take the sacraments if they like, while Go-Go is barred from the church. Well, fuck the church!

Where was he? Where is he? On Gwynn's Falls Avenue, thinking about how Sean, of all people, had figured out that if they crossed Forest Park Avenue on Pickwick, then rolled their bikes across the bridge to Purnell Lane, they could technically obey the rule never to ride their bikes on Forest Park Avenue and still manage to get here, to Woodlawn. Or was it Mickey who had figured it out? Mickey had lived above Purnell Lane, after all. It would be in her interest to choose a route that led them so close to her home. Even when they were kids, Mickey had been smart that way. She should have become the lawyer, not Tim.

He walks for ten, twenty, thirty minutes, willing his head to clear. He walks down to the stream, where there had been swans and ducks, then to the public park, once the site of an amusement park that closed before Go-Go was old enough to go there. It survived integration, his father always said, but it couldn't beat back Hurricane Agnes. Still the roller coaster remained standing for years, long enough for him to feel thwarted, denied. Sean and Tim claimed to have gone many, many times, but they weren't that much older. Sean would have been seven or eight when the park closed. Maybe they had lied? It makes Gordon feel better, catching perfect Sean in a potential lie. Soon enough, the hypothetical becomes real to him and he has worked up a nice fury. He gets out his cell phone and punches his brother's contact button, ready to fight with him. But his hands aren't steady and he fumbles the phone as Sean's voice comes on, cool and reserved, he juggles it helplessly, then drops it to the ground, where it's hard to find in the dark. As he crawls around on his hands and knees, he hears Sean's voice, disgust evident. "Gordon? Gordon? Jesus, Gordon . . ."

I shoulda been Gee-Go. Does he say that out loud? His hand closes over the cell phone, but Sean has hung up. Okay, it isn't exactly the first time he drunk-dialed his brother. But he's had a good run of sobriety, so Sean shouldn't have been all pissy and judgmental. Sean had no way of knowing he had taken a drink unless Sean *expected* him to fail. That's unfair. And what kind of brother is that, anyway, expecting—rooting—for his younger sibling to fail? But that's Sean's dirty little secret. His perfection is relative, dependent upon the fuckups of Go-Go and Tim. In another family, he wouldn't even be all that. In another family, Sean might be the problem child, the loser. Especially if he had been treated like a loser from jump, the way Gordon was. They set him up. Of course he did whatever he was asked. He was just a little boy. Any little boy would have done what he did. Right?

His head clearer, he walks to the convenience store, buys a cup of scorched coffee and drinks it in his car. He is less than two miles from home. He has to make exactly four turns—two lefts, two rights. There are—he counts—one, two, three lights? The first one is there, in front of him, complicated because there are actually five points at this intersection, but he makes it through. Up the hill. I think I can I think I can I think I can. Past the cemeteries, through the second light. Almost home. Almost home.

At Forest Park, he turns right instead of left. *Go, Go-Go. Go, Go-Go. Go, Go-Go.* Climbs the entrance ramp behind the Strawberry Hill apartments. I found my thrill, his father sang whenever he drove past, on Strawberry Hill. Mickey's family had moved here and Mickey's mother was hot. Sean and Tommy swore they saw her sunbathing topless once, but they probably lied about that, too. Roller coasters, topless girls—they lied about everything.

Gordon heads west, then makes a U-turn before the Beltway cloverleaf, aiming his car back home along the infamous highway that ends, just stops. As teenagers, they had treated this two-mile stretch as their own little drag strip, but now the secret is out and others race here. He wonders how fast his father's old Buick can go. 90, 100, 110 . . . *Go, Go-Go. Go, Go-Go. Go-Go.* The steel guitar twangs in his ears, in his memory, sharp and awful. Guy could not play for shit, much as he loved that damn, stupid guitar. *Go, Go-Go. Go, Go-Go. Go, Go-Go.* He is dancing, wild and free, his little arms moving so quickly it's almost like he's lashing himself, self-flagellation, and everyone loves him and everyone is laughing and everyone loves him and everyone is laughing and he is splashing through the stream, heedless of the poisonous water, no matter what Gwen's father says about tetanus and lockjaw, desperate to get away, to escape what he's done. *Go, Go-Go. Go, Go-Go.*

By the time he hits the Jersey wall, even the needle on the old Buick's speedometer has given up on him.

2

The Robison homestead is wildly impractical for almost anyone, but especially so for an eighty-three-year-old man living alone, even if he happens to be the one who designed it. Forty years ago, when he began making the drawings for his dream house, Clement Robison could not imagine being eighty-three. Who can? Eighty-three is hard to imagine at eighty-two. His youngest daughter, now forty-four, summoned home—or so she's telling everyone—by her father's accident, doesn't really believe she'll ever be as old as he is. Oh, she expects, hopes, to enjoy his longevity. But the number itself, eighty-three, is like some monstrous old coat discovered in the hall closet, scratchy and smelling of mothballs. *Who left this here? Is this yours? Not mine! I've never seen it before.*

The Robison house was modern once and people still describe it that way now, although its appliances and fixtures are frozen like the clocks in a fairy tale, set to 1985. A mix of milled stone, lumber, and glass, it is set into the side of the hill on a stone base, a door leading into the above-ground basement, but the habit was to use that door only in the most inclement weather. Otherwise, they mount the long stone staircase, which creates the illusion that one is climbing a natural path up the hillside. The steps are charming, but there is something off about them. Too low or too high, they fool the foot, and over the years almost everyone in the family has taken a tumble or near-tumble down. Gwen's turn came when she was thirteen, rushing outside and neglecting to consider that the sheen on the steps might be ice, not mere moisture. She traveled the entire flight on her butt, boom, boom, boom. At thirteen, the end result was a bruised coccyx and ego, nothing more.

Her father, coming outside to get the paper on a cool but dry March morning, missed a step and broke a hip.

"Do you know how many people die within a year of breaking a hip?" Gwen asks her father, still in University Hospital.

"Gwen, I taught geriatric medicine for years. I think I'm up on the facts. *Most* people don't die."

"But a lot do. Almost a third."

"Still, most don't. And I'm in good health otherwise. I just have to be disciplined about recovery and therapy."

"Murph and Fee want you to sell the house, move into assisted living."

"And you?"

"I'm holding them off. For now. I told them I would assess your situation."

They smile at each other, coconspirators. Gwen is his favorite. This is denied, of course, when her much older siblings, Murphy and Fiona, bring up the contentious matter. "I was just more available when Gwen was little," their father says. "Less career obsessed." "Daddy doesn't have favorites," Gwen says. But everyone knows the seven-year gap between Fiona and Gwen is not enough to explain their father's clear preference for her. There is her remarkable resemblance to their mother, dead for almost twenty years. And there is the bond of the house and the neighborhood, Dickeyville, which Gwen and her father loved more fiercely than anyone else in the family. Murph and Fee, living thousands of miles away, have been trying to get their father out of the house for years, decades, ever since their mother's death. Gwen, who remains in Baltimore, has done whatever she can to allow her father to stay in the family home. Should the day come that he really can't live there, it has always been their unspoken understanding that Gwen will take over the house.

Unfortunately, her husband opposes this plan.

"How are things at home?" her father asks.

It's an open question, applicable to the physical status of her home and the up-in-the-air nature of her marriage. Gwen chooses to address the physical.

"Not great. The county came out and pushed the ruins of the retaining wall back on our property, but says it's our job to rebuild it. And even when we do, it won't necessarily address our foundation issues."

"Why—never mind."

"Why did we buy out there when our inspector warned us of this very problem? I ask myself that every day. For me, I think it was because Relay reminded me of Dickeyville. Isolated, yet not. A little slice of country so close to the city, the idiosyncratic houses. And for Karl, it was all about convenience—the commuter train station within walking distance, BWI and Amtrak ten minutes away. Go figure—for once, my dreamy nostalgia and his pragmatism aligned and the result is utter disaster. There's probably a lesson to be learned there."

"The lesson," her father says, "is that you have a six-year-old daughter."

"Don't worry," Gwen says, pretending not to understand. "We've figured out how to make it work once you come home. I'm going to get up at six a.m. and drive over there, do the breakfast and getting-her-off-to-school thing. And I'll reverse it at day's end, be there for dinner and bedtime. But I'm going to spend the nights at your house."

"Gwen—"

"Just for a few weeks. Anyone can tolerate anything for a few weeks." Months, years, her mind amends. It is amazing what one can tolerate, what she has tolerated. "Also, it's not the worst thing in the world, making Kurt curtail his travel, to learn that he's part of a household, not a guest star who jets in and out as it suits him."

"He is who he is, Gwen. You went into this with eyes wide open. I told you all about heart surgeons. And Kurt was already a star. It's not like this sneaked up on you. Not like the chicken."

"What?"

"The chicken. That's why I fell. There was a chicken on the steps, trying to peck at my ankles and all I wanted to do was avoid stepping on it. I twisted my ankle and went over."

Now Gwen is truly worried about her father's mental state. *A chicken?* There haven't been chickens in their neighborhood, ever. Except for—but those birds were far away and far in the past. No, that couldn't be. Her father must have imagined the chicken. But if her father was imagining chickens, what else was breaking down inside his mind? She would almost prefer there was a chicken. Maybe there was. The past few years have seen a flurry of stories about animals showing up in places where they shouldn't be—wild cats in Western suburbs, a deer crashing through the window of a private detective's office and, come to think of it, a chicken in one of the New York boroughs. And

Dickeyville is the kind of place that has always attracted crunchy granola types. It is easy to imagine some earnest, incompetent locavore trying to raise chickens and letting them escape. Gwen will ask around when she goes over there this afternoon, to begin preparing the house for her father's return.

The Robison house is isolated, even by Dickeyville's standards, which in turn feels cut off from much of Baltimore. It is officially the last house on Wetheredsville Road, only a few feet from where the Jersey wall now blocks the street, marking the start of a "nature trail" that one can follow all the way to downtown. The blocked street means Gwen can't use the old shortcut, through what is properly called a park, but which she and her childhood friends always referred to as the woods, and their term was more true to the place. Leakin Park is a forest, vast and dense, difficult to navigate. Gwen guesses that she and her friends covered more of it than almost anyone and even they missed large swaths.

Traffic is surprisingly heavy, the journey longer than anticipated, giving the lie to her blithe words about dashing back and forth between here and the house in Relay. Still, the chance to move to Dickeyville, even temporarily, is providential. Maryland law requires a separation of at least one year to file for an uncontested divorce. She learned this during her first divorce, a sad bit of knowledge she had never planned to use again. Does anyone plan to divorce twice? Then again, after that first failed marriage, the fact is always there, incontrovertible. You're not going to go the distance with one person, your chance at perfection is lost.

But even if she could manage to extend her time in her father's house for up to a year, it wouldn't be enough. It was the spouse who *stayed* who could file after one year, on the grounds of being abandoned. As the spouse who was leaving, Gwen would have to wait two years if Kurt didn't agree and he has made it clear that he won't. Clearly, she can't spend that much time away from Annabelle, but nor can she afford her own place in their current school district. They weren't upside down in their mortgage, but they had virtually no equity and home equity loans were hard to get now, anyway. Kurt has lots of money, but, again, he isn't going to use it to let her leave him. And if she spends even a single night back in the Relay house, the clock resets on the separation. Maybe Annabelle will move into the Dickeyville house and they can keep this information from the school?

But the Dickeyville house will be chaotic, once her father returns. For a "modern" house, it is wildly impractical. There is the first level, the stonewalled basement, with the laundry room and various systems. Then the large glass-and-timber first floor, built to take advantage of the site, but with only a powder room. Yet the top two floors, which have full baths, have narrow halls and tight corners. Their father, appalled at the costs and delays, skimped on his dream house's bedrooms. She will have to set him up in the "great room," where he will have nice views and an unfettered trip to the bathroom. But then her father will dominate the first floor and privacy will be found only in the cramped, dark bedrooms. And how will he bathe? Besides Annabelle would be lonely, as Gwen once was, and she won't even have the freedom to roam the woods. What was safe in Gwen's childhood is unthinkable for Annabelle's.

Her head hurts. It's all too complicated. *Dial it back*, as she tells her writers when they are in over their heads on a story. Concentrate on one thing, one task. Go to the house, make sure it's clean, do laundry, call a nursing service, let the nursing service figure out the best place for her father to convalesce.

Once at the house, she finds three papers in yellow wrappers, several catalogs, but almost no real mail. Her father doesn't recycle—on principle, he believes it's a ruse, an empty, feel-good gesture—so she tosses everything, leaving only the bills on the kitchen counter. The kitchen is small, another victim of the house's cost overruns, but her mother made it a marvel of efficiency. The light at this time of the day, year, is breathtaking, gold and rose. Even with the old appliances, the Formica counters, and old metal cabinets, it is a warm, welcoming room.

Gwen goes upstairs. Everything is in order, there is no evidence of a man in decline. Widowed at fifty-five, her father quickly learned to take excellent care of himself. His closet and drawers are neater than Gwen's, there is an admirable lack of clutter. A single page from the *Times*, dated the day before his fall, is on his nightstand—the crossword puzzle, filled out in ink, without a single error. The puzzle, the tidy house back up his version of events, indicate he's of sound mind. So why does she keep thinking of it that way, as a *version*? The thing about the chicken remains troubling. Glancing out the narrow casement window toward the street, she sees a black-haired man walking two dogs as black as his hair. She knows him instantly by the part in his hair, impossibly straight and perfect.

"Sean," Gwen calls out, running heedlessly down the stone steps that undid her father.

"Gwennie," he says. Then: "I'm sorry. Old habits. *Gwen*."

"What are you doing here?"

"Well, my brother, of course."

"Tim? Or Go-Go?"

"Gordon," he says. Perhaps Sean has sworn off nicknames. Funny, Gwen liked hearing Gwennie, even if it always carries the reminder that she was once fat. Gwennie the Whale. She was only fat until age thirteen. They say people are forever fat inside, but Gwen's not. Inside, she's the sylph she became. If anything, she has trouble remembering that she's growing older, that she's no longer one of the prettiest girls in the room.

"What's the incorrigible Go-Go—Gordon—done now?"

Sean looks offended, then confused. "I'm sorry, I just assumed you knew."

"My father fell three days ago, broke his hip. I don't know much of anything."

"Three days ago?"

"In the morning. Coming down the steps to fetch his paper."

"Three days ago—that's when Go-Go . . ." His voice catches. Sean is the middle brother, the handsomest, the smartest, the best all around. Gwen's mother used to say that Tim was for practice, Sean was the platonic ideal, and Go-Go was a bridge too far. Gwen's mother could be cutting, but her voice was so delicate, her manner so light, that no one took offense.

"What, Sean?"

"He crashed his car into the concrete barrier where the highway ends. Probably going 80, 90 miles per hour. We think the accelerator got stuck, or he miscalculated where it ended. I mean, we've all played with our speedometers up there."

Yes, when they were teenagers, learning to drive. But Go-Go was—she calculates, subtracting two, no three years from her age—forty, much too old to be testing his car's power.

"He's—"

"Dead, Gwen. At the scene, instantly."

"I'm so sorry, Sean." Go-Go, dead. Although she has seen him periodically over the years, he remained forever nine or ten in her mind, wild and uninhibited. The risk-taker in the group, although they had also wondered if Go-Go simply didn't understand the concept of danger, didn't know he was taking risks. She flashes back to an image of him on this very street, dashing across the road in pursuit of a ball, indifferent to the large truck bearing down on him, the others screaming for him to stop.

"Thank you."

"How are your parents holding up?"

"Not well. I came home for the funeral—I live in St. Petersburg now."

"Russia?"

A tight smile. "Florida."

Gwen tries not to make a face. Not because of Florida, but because the Sean she remembers would have been in Russia, a dashing foreign correspondent or diplomat. He's still pretty dashing. Close up, she can see a few flecks of white in his hair, but the very dignity that sometimes seemed silly in a teenage boy suits him now. He has finally grown into his gravitas.

"I feel awful that I didn't know. When is the funeral?"

"Tomorrow. Visitation is tonight."

Gwen calculates, even as she knows she must find a way to attend both. She will have to ask for another half-day at work, make arrangements. There is already so much to be done. But this is Go-Go—and Sean, her first boyfriend, even if she seldom thinks of him in that context. Gwen is not the kind of woman who thinks longingly of her past, who tracks down old boyfriends on the Internet. The Hallorans, along with Mickey Wickham, are more like the old foundations and footings they sometimes found in the woods, abandoned and overgrown, impossible to reclaim. They had been a tight-knit group of five for a summer or two, but it couldn't be sustained. Funny, it has never occurred to Gwen that she and Mickey could disengage thoroughly from the group, but the Halloran brothers had to remain a set, mismatched as they were. Crass Tim, Serious Sean, Wild Go-Go.

"I'll be there." She considers placing a hand on Sean's forearm, but worries it will seem flirtatious. Instead, she strokes the dogs, who are old, with grizzled jowls and labored breathing, so ancient and tired that they don't object to this long interlude in the middle of their walk. Yet old as they obviously are, they can't be more than, what? Fifteen? Sixteen? Which is still older than her marriage to Kurt.

"My parents will appreciate that," Sean says and heads back up the hill. She knows the route, knows the house at which he will arrive after going up Wetheredsville, then turning left on "New" Pickwick, a street of what once seemed like modern houses, small and symmetrical relative to the shambling antiquities for which Dickeyville was known. The Halloran house always smelled of strong foods—onions, cabbage, hamburger—and it was always a mess. Sometimes the chaos could be comforting; no child need to worry about disturbing or breaking anything in such a household. It could be terrifying, too, though, a place where the adults yelled terrible things at one another and Mrs. Halloran was often heard sobbing, off in the distance. The boys never seemed to notice and even Mickey was nonchalant about it. But the Halloran house had always scared Gwen, and she had made sure their activities centered on her house, the woods beyond.

Go-Go, dead. The only surprise was that she was surprised at all.

Most thought he was called Go-Go because it was a bastardization of Gordon, but it really derived from his manic nature, evident from toddlerhood, his insistence to follow his brothers wherever they went. "I go-go," he would say, as if the second syllable, the repetition, would win the argument. "I go-go." And he did. He ran into walls, splashed into the polluted waters of the stream, jumped from branches and balconies. Once, Go-Go spent much of an afternoon running head-on into an old mattress they had found in the woods, laughing all the while.

Now he has run head-on into the barrier at the end of the highway. Gwen can't help wondering if he was drunk. Although she hasn't seen the Halloran boys for years, she knows, the way that everyone knows things in Dickeyville, that Go-Go has a problem. It is implied, if never stated outright, in the lost jobs, the broken marriage, the fact that he returns to the roost for open-ended stays.

Then again, who is she to judge Go-Go? Isn't she pulling the same trick, running home, a two-time loser in matrimony, taking comfort in a parent's unconditional love? Mr. Halloran may be hard as nails, but Mrs. Halloran loved her baby boy. And while most people will assume she is simply a devoted daughter, some will see through her. Her brother and sister, certainly. And Kurt.

That is, Kurt would see through her if it ever occurred to him to look, really look at her. But if Kurt looked at her that way, she wouldn't need to leave him.

BOOKS BY LAURA LIPPMAN

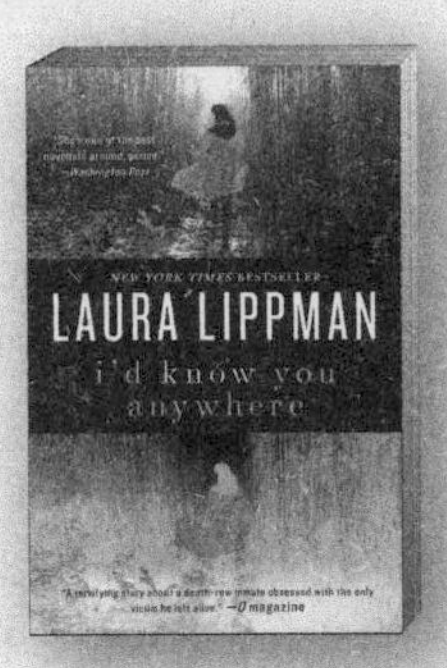

I'D KNOW YOU ANYWHERE
A Novel

ISBN 978-0-06-207075-3 (paperback)

"Lippman's taut, mesmerizing, and exceptionally smart drama of predator and prey is at once unusually sensitive and utterly compelling."
—*Booklist* (starred review)

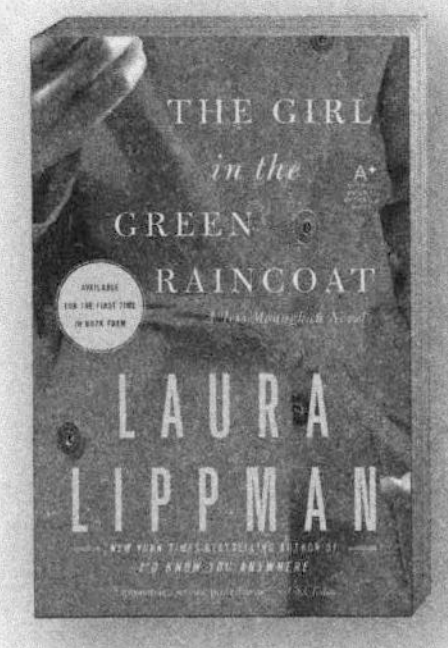

THE GIRL IN THE GREEN RAINCOAT
A Tess Monaghan Novel

ISBN 978-0-06-193836-8 (paperback)

Tess Monaghan, Baltimore P.I., suspects foul play when a girl in her neighborhood goes missing.

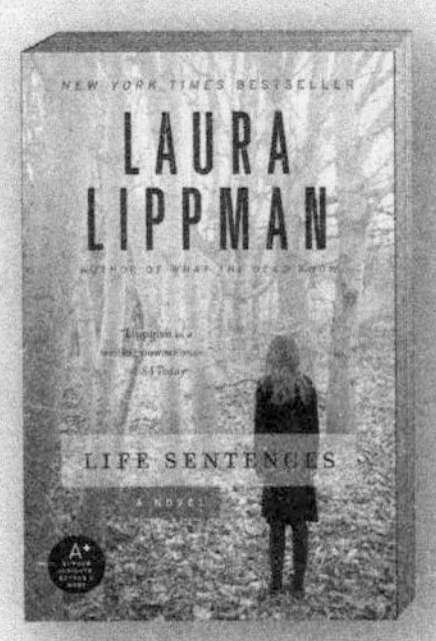

LIFE SENTENCES
A Novel

ISBN 978-0-06-194488-8 (paperback)

"A mystery so taut the reader is nearly afraid to keep going—and simultaneously powerless to stop."
—*People*

HARDLY KNEW HER
Stories

ISBN 978-0-06-149096-5 (paperback)

"Lippman is a writing powerhouse." —*USA Today*

WHAT THE DEAD KNOW
A Novel

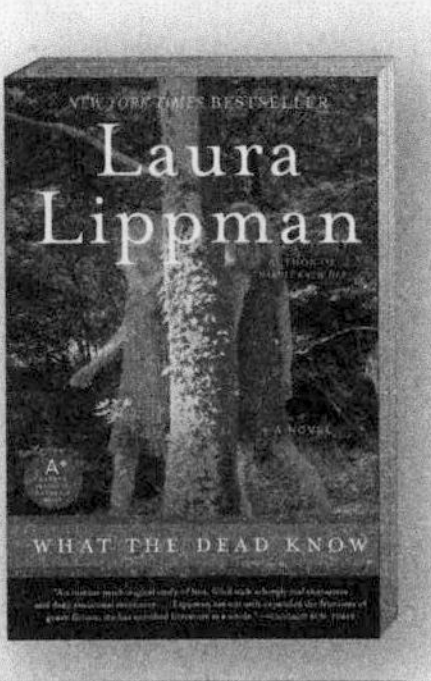

ISBN 978-0-06-177135-4 (paperback)

"Hypnotic . . . gripping . . . a writer at the peak of her powers."
—*Washington Post*